TOURNAMENT

SHELBY FOOTE

TOURNAMENT

SUMMA PUBLICATIONS
Birmingham, Alabama
1987

Copyright, 1949, by Shelby Foote

First edition, Dial Press, 1949

Second edition, Summa Publications, 1987
ISBN 0-917786-56-4

Printed in the United States of America

Cover photograph by William C. Carter

CONTENTS

FOREWORD

Asa Bart's Way

Tournament was Shelby Foote's first novel. Originally written in 1939 and 1940, when he was in his early twenties, it was the book on which he first learned his craft. It was his first assertion of suzerainty over what would henceforth be his fictional demesne, the history and the society of the Mississippi Delta and adjoining areas. It was composed (as what novel of any young man's in that particular time and place could not have been?) in the shadow of William Faulkner, and despite *Tournament*'s having been rewritten from start to finish before publication in 1949, traces of the presence of the High Sheriff of Yoknapatawpha remain throughout. It was very much a "young man's book," lavish in its expenditure of literary capital that could have made up the consist of three or four novels.

It is to Shelby Foote's later fiction as, say, the Symphony No. 1 in C Major of Beethoven is to the Third, Fifth, and Seventh Symphonies. That is, while architecturally it is not as intricately constructed as its successors, and while it is much more sketchy in characterization, it is complete in and of itself, and no mere omen of things to come. Moreover, it is in *C Major*. I may as well say that in certain respects I prefer *Tournament* to much of the later fiction; I emphasize "in certain respects," for surely it is neither as psychologically complex nor as dramatically realized as what followed. What it does offer, however, is a kind of lyrical, even autobiographical access to its subject matter. There is a communicated delight in the writer's sheer ability to reproduce and recreate places, relationships, and meanings drawn from personal experience and from received family history and legend.

The logic for inclusion is not always based either upon the needs of the plot or the dramatic requirements of characterization. Was there, after all, from the standpoint of strict story line any real need for Foote to tell the story of Abe Wisten's business troubles, other than that he was drawing upon memories of his own Vienna-born grandfather, whose career bore no real-life relationship whatever to the acquisition of Mount Holly Plantation by Huger Foote, likewise the author's grandfather and the model for Hugh G. Bart in *Tournament*? Still, in the imaginative dynamics of Foote's fictional world, Abe Wisten certainly *belongs*. And because so much of what makes the novel appealing is its recreation of a time and place, the Mississippi Delta of the late nineteenth and early twentieth centuries, it would scarcely occur to anyone to wonder just what the life of Abe Wisten has to do with the central thrust of Hugh Bart's life. Yet, other than the episode's contributing to Hugh Bart's ultimate attitude toward money and material possessions, which it does only in a thematic way, there is no real dramatic tie-in.

In his subsequent five works of fiction, Foote's method of telling a story would be mainly through the dramatic and psychological exploration of the interaction of his characters within a known historical context, and this is doubtless what has permitted him to continue to grow and develop as a writer. All the same, *Tournament*, to repeat, is no mere literary rehearsal, and it is satisfying to have it back in print again after so long a time.

Those who have written about Foote's first novel have noted that the story of Hugh Bart constitutes something of a search for a meaning to his life that he proves unable to discover in anything he has done, whether in politics, money-making, planting, hunting, trapshooting, poker-playing, or as husband and parent. All his engagements ultimately disappoint him, so that at the end there seems to be no explanation left other than that, to quote the words that his grandson Asa hears him speak on his deathbed, " 'The four walls are gone from around me, the roof from over my head. I'm in the dark, alone.' " Helen White and Redding S. Sugg, Jr., in their book on Foote, note that the figure of Asa Bart suggests a "portrait of the artist," though Asa is present only in the prologue, briefly at the end of Hugh Bart's story, and in the epilogue. They assert quite properly that subsuming all else "there is the grand theme which Asa announces and which recurs throughout Foote's work: the loneliness of the human condition and the inherent difficulty of building any kind of satisfactory life at all." Yet it might also be remarked that something goes on in Foote's first novel that functions as a potential qualification of that bleak theme.

Foote has always insisted that one of the most potent influences on his own fiction has been the work of Marcel Proust. When he revised the novel for its initial publication in 1949, he comments in his introduction to the present edition, he was careful to remove "nearly all the Joyce, most of the Wolfe, and some of the Faulkner; what Proust I encountered I either left in or enlarged on." Somewhat strangely, few commentators on Foote's work appear to have paid much attention to his citing of Proust's role. But in the years that have followed publication of *Tournament*, Foote's acknowledged admiration for Proust's great book has in no way abated. It seems to me worthwhile, therefore, to look at certain aspects of his first novel with the example of *Remembrance of Things Past* in mind.

There is a point, close to the end, not long before Hugh Bart's death and after his fortune has declined almost to nothing, when he comes home late at night after playing poker, and lies in his bed beside his sleeping wife. That day, while talking with a peddler, he had been moved to attempt to recount his personal history. Now he thinks: " 'So there was no one: No one I can tell it to . . .' " He thinks to himself that "his attempt to present the story of his life was like trying to describe a man's appearance by displaying his skeleton. The truth lay in implications, not facts. Facts were only individual beads; the hidden string was what made them into a necklace." Then he adds: "But what kind of thinking was this, in which one minute the skeleton was not enough and the next the string in a row of beads was everything? The abstract was a trap: his brain was not meant for such work."

No reader familiar with Proust can mistake what is happening here. The implications—more than that, the overtly voiced assumptions—of the French novelist's great work are that human existence in time must of its very nature prove unsatisfactory, since it is only a succession of material experiences lacking permanence and devoid of any meaning beyond that of ephemeral sensation. It is only through art—time regained—that the relationships between our otherwise perishable moments of existence in time can be recognized and joined together into a reality that may endure free of chronology. The writer, Proust says,

> may list in an interminable description the objects that figured in the place described, but truth will begin only when the writer takes two different objects, establishes their relationship—analogous in the world of art to the sole relationship in the world of science, the law of cause and effect—and encloses them in the necessary rings of a beautiful style, or even when, like life itself, comparing similar qualities in two sensations, he makes their essential nature stand out clearly by joining them in a metaphor, in order to remove them from the contingencies of time, and links them together with the indescribable bond of an alliance of words.[1]

Nothing in Hugh Bart's experience, or within the community in which he has lived out his life, has taught or encouraged him to look for what is real and meaningful in anything other than material possessions and physical experience. But these had, inevitably as Foote sees it, failed to satisfy him, and now that he has used up most of his days, he is left with no coherent explanation for the way he has lived. It is Time that *was* the reality, but how could he ever know it for what it was, imprisoned as he was within its succession of moments? Thus, like all those characters in Proust who have sought their identity in what one of Proust's characters, the novelist Bergotte, referred to as the "inexhaustible torrent of fair forms," he is left at the close without anything to keep for his own.

How could Hugh Bart find a meaning for his experience, he wonders, since "to tell it properly would require as much time as had

---

[1] The translation here cited is that of C. K. Scott Moncrieff and Frederick A. Blossom, in the two-volume Random House edition of *Remembrance of Things Past* in 1932. Moncrieff translated all but the seventh book, *The Past Recaptured*, which is Blossom's work and in which the quotation above appears.

been required to live it. There was no end to what it would have to contain. All the lives that had touched his own, some of them only slightly, had a share in the telling . . . these and so many others, how could he tell all that? Every one omitted, however, would be a space left blank on a canvas larger than life."

Of course Hugh Bart cannot "tell it." He has been in succession farmer, sheriff, planter, hunter, parent, trapshooter, gambler; these must inevitably remain no more than successive disguises, each separate from the other in his memory, so long as he cannot discover in them what Proust calls their "essential nature" and succeed in "joining them in a metaphor, in order to remove them from the contingencies of time. . . ." And there is not time left to him to do that.

But it does not end there. For soon, we are told, "unexpectedly, he found a link." He had until then been so preoccupied with his own doings that he paid little attention to the presence of his grandson Asa. A few weeks before Christmas, however, he notices the boy at the top of the steps. "What are you watching?" he asks. "Asa looked up. His eyes were gray-green, the same as his grandfather's." Hugh Bart "leaned down, caught the child beneath the arms, and lifted him so that they looked directly into each other's face. And he held him, looking into eyes that were so much like his own."

What Hugh Bart sees in his grandson is analogous to what, near the end of *Remembrance of Things Past*, Marcel Proust's narrator sees when he beholds the daughter of his childhood friend Gilberte and his now-dead companion Robert de Saint-Loup, who in her features bears the impress of her ancestry—not only of her parents but of her grandfather Charles Swann, her grandmother Odette de Crécy, and of the Guermantes family heritage as well. She is thus the living fusion of certain persons who have played so immense a part in the narrator's own history, the union of what to the young Marcel had seemed the impossibly discrete and separate "ways" of the middle-class Swanns and Verdurins and the aristocratic Guermantes. To the narrator she is "very beautiful, still full of promise. Laughing, fashioned of the very years I had lost, she seemed to me like my own youth"; she is "a measure of the long lapse of years I had endeavoured to ignore. Time, colorless and impalpable, had, in order that I might, as it were, see and touch it, physically embodied itself in her and had moulded her like a work of art . . .''

Having identified in his grandson not merely the product but the validation of his having been alive in Time, it is no wonder that when Hugh Bart leaves his house, he "walked with that curious flat-footed stride, guarding his dignity. The gold head of his cane was a dancing gleam of sunlight, flashing on and off and on and off until he passed from sight." When Hugh Bart dies a few weeks afterward it is from a fall from a ladder as he reaches up to place a star at the peak of a Christmas tree he is trimming for his grandson: "Bart lay against the base of the tree, partly covered by the wreckage of cedar limbs, candles still in their sockets, and shards of colored grass. The tinsel star lay by his face."

In the same way, at the close of Proust's novel the narrator declares of an old friend that he "had wavered as he made his way along the difficult summit of his eighty-three years, as if men were perched on giant stilts sometimes taller than church spires, constantly growing and finally rendering their progress so difficult and perilous that they suddenly fall."

It seems clear that it will be Hugh Bart's grandson Asa who will redeem him from oblivion, much as the art of Marcel Proust's narrator will preserve Charles Swann from nothingness. Asa Bart, one surmises, will not himself make the mistake of confusing the "inexhaustible torrent of fair forms" for the reality of time regained, but will write a book *about* his grandfather's having done so, thus confuting the remorseless passage of time through reuniting past and present within the confines of a metaphor—entitled *Tournament*.

Stated thus baldly, it seems a somewhat pat solution to the complexities of human beings in time, place, and history, and in the way that *Tournament* is told, it does appear to be implanted upon the novel, as it were, rather than organically infused throughout the narration. I suspect that this, or something like it, is what Foote means when he describes it as a "young man's novel." It is not that *Tournament* doesn't "work" as a novel; on the contrary, as fiction it works, I believe, very nicely indeed. It holds together well, tells a good tale about an interesting man, and for all the Proust and Faulkner echoes audible throughout its telling, is essentially an original act of the literary imagination. But if we view the direction of Foote's subsequent work, it has not proceeded toward any more such direct portraiture of the artist as a young Mississipian. Rather, the development has been toward more dramatic, "objective" fiction, in which the experience, instead of being drawn relatively straightforwardly out of "real life" (however combined and reapportioned), has been transformed into characters and situations that furnish their own dynamics and set up their own relationships.

Indeed, one might even say of the young Shelby Foote that artistically there were for him two "ways" of discovery, Proust's and Faulkner's, and that what he decided was that for him the route toward realization of his own literary fulfillment lay by way of the latter approach. If so, he would appear to have chosen wisely. All the same, I am not so sure that the option tentatively contemplated in his first novel is meant to be closed out. "Permanently dead? Very possible." And possibly not, too. In any event, not having read a word of it myself, I predict that when the book that he is now engaged in writing, and which is suggestively entitled *Two Gates to the City*, reaches completion, it will be found to contain elements within it that will send the reader back to the "Asa" sections of his first novel, in much the same way that a reader of *Remembrance of Things Past* can look back at an earlier Proustian opus such as *Contre Sainte-Beuve* and see where certain things began.

Moreover, we might keep in mind, too, that just as readers of Proust's great work found that there were really not two separate and mutually exclusive ways to choose from when setting out on a journey, but only one way that encompasses both paths, so a similar discovery may lie in store for Shelby Foote's readers. For the nature of the relationship between Hugh Bart and his grandson Asa in *Tournament* is by no means appropriate to the experience of the author of that book alone. After all, with certain relatively unimportant modifications it was also implicit in the family heritage of the great-grandson of Colonel William Clark Falkner, C.S.A.

Louis D. Rubin, Jr.
University of North Carolina
at Chapel Hill

PREFACE

The first draft of this first novel was written while waiting for a world war to start, and then for us to get in it. That was the one called the Second to distinguish it from the First, known in its day as "The War to End All Wars," along with the Third, which will have to be christened in advance, since there will be no one left to name or even number it once the first few shots are fired and the first few newfangled booms hoist their atomic pillars skyward, mushroom-crowned and lit from within by manmade lightning flashes. "The War to End All" is I think sufficiently apt, and the young men and women writing novels on its eve will be putting words on paper that will soon go up in flames and come down as ashes, if in fact there will be ashes or indeed any residue at all.

Something like that—though the flames could not be nuclear for nearly another half dozen years—came close to happening to this one. I had left Chapel Hill at the end of my sophomore year, not because I didnt like it (I did, a lot: especially those nine stories of stacks at the back of the library, where I prowled in disguise as a precocious graduate student) but because my first extended absence from my homeland made me want to know it better, year-round, and I doubted that it would be long before someone or other, over there across the water, would finally get up the nerve or backbone to stand up to Hitler, in which case I might well get my head blown off before I'd had any real chance to get ready to use it. The wait turned out longer than I'd thought: a full two years. In that time I worked at various jobs, including one as a carpenter's helper in the construction of the Greenville Bridge, which required me to carry lumber from piling to piling along catwalks ninety feet above the chocolate surface of the Mississippi; the pay, I remember, was just over thirty cents an hour, six days a week. I had written stories for the *Carolina Magazine*, seldom missing a monthly issue, and I continued writing through this day-labor period as well, only this time it wasnt stories. It was a novel I called *Tournament*.

Before I wound it up the war was on; Hitler went into Poland and I retaliated by going into the Mississippi National Guard. That seemed to give him pause—the Sitzkrieg "phony war" ensued—but not for long. Presently he "turned loose with both hands," as they used to say of western gunmen on a rampage; France crumpled and England shuddered under day and night bombardments. I kept working, at home on the book and elsewhere at such places as the bridge and U.S. Gypsum, where I pushed wallboard through a micrometer, eating salt pills by the handful and drinking about a quart of water an hour to make up for the sweat I lost retrieving the boards loaded on steel-wheeled dollies in a 140-degree humidifier. I rather enjoyed it: enjoyed finding that I could actually do it, I mean, just as I enjoyed finding that I could actually finish a novel, which I did about that time. I sent it off to Alfred A. Knopf in faraway New York, in part because my fellow townsman William Alexander Percy's *Lanterns on the Levee* was in the works there, but mainly I think because Knopf turned out the best-looking books in America. I always liked well-printed well-bound books, and I wanted mine to have all the advantages I felt sure that it deserved.

After about two weeks—surely the longest two in my lifetime up to then—the typescript came back, along with a note from one of the brightest of Mr Knopf's young editors. His name was Straus and he seemed to know his business. He and some of the others in the office there had read and liked the novel, he said, but their considered joint opinion was that it would not sell. They or some other house could publish it, at perhaps not too great a loss, and I would have the fleeting satisfaction of seeing myself in print, but at the cost of being identified by the nation's bookshops as a nonselling writer—a curse that might well follow me all the rest of my writing life, like the chap in *Li'l Abner* who walked around with his own private and perpetual little raincloud hung directly over his head. Thus Mr Straus. And though it seemed to me that he grievously underestimated the burning in my bosom for just that satisfaction he dismissed as fleeting, I could see clearly enough that he was altogether right in his professional estimate of the situation otherwise, and I decided then and there to take his further advice that I put the novel away somewhere—in cold storage, as it were—while I wrote my second, which he and the others were convinced would profit greatly from my having got my hand in on the first. Moreover I would always be free to come back to that one, he pointed out, and this had something to do with my rejection of an initial urge to commit the typescript to those nonatomic flames I mentioned earlier. I was afraid that if I knew it existed somewhere, even in cold storage, I would have it constantly, distractively on my mind while trying to think up and write the next one. Besides, it seemed to me there was quite literally nothing left on earth to write about.

I need not have worried on any of those counts. By then it was November 1940; the Luftwaffe shifted from day to nighttime bombing in the Battle of Britain, and my national guard division—the 31st "Dixie" Division; we were always called to attention when one of our bands cut loose with the first rollicking bars of that anthem—was mobilized into federal service. In the five years that intervened before I came back home to stay, I had a good many more things to fret about than that rejected typescript gathering dust on a high shelf in my mother's linen closet.

Settling down to civilian life, which afforded the unfamiliar triple luxury of sleeping, eating, and defecating, all under a single roof, I decided I'd had enough of catwalks and humidifiers and instead took a job, under the G.I. bill, writing spot commercials for the local radio station, WJPR; "We Just Play Records," jokers promptly dubbed it, ignoring my contributions to the unremittent stream of sound which, like Tennyson's brook, went on forever. Eventually, out of boredom and desperation, I reached up onto the top shelf of that hall closet and took down the typescript I had put there more than six years ago, back in that other world that had existed before the war that now was over had begun. I read it through, rather cursorily for the most part, and some of it still looked pretty good to me and some of it didnt; Mr Straus had given me sound advice, and I had been right to take it. But that was then. I decided now that the time had come not to take it any longer, at least not wholly. Parts of it seemed to me able to stand on their own. One such, about midway, was an account of the death of a

Confederate veteran on his plantation during the great flood of 1903, which left the problem of what to do with his body until the water receded. Accordingly, I detached this segment, cut and stretched and patted it into the shape of a 22-page story, gave it the title "Flood Burial," and took it to Ben Wasson to dispose of. Retired now, Ben had been a literary agent before the war, and something more. Just under twenty years ago, in New York, he had squeezed his friend William Faulkner's *Flags in the Dust* into publishable shape as *Sartoris*, and he still had connections up the country. One of these was Stuart Rose, fiction editor of *The Saturday Evening Post*, and he sent the story to him.

Within a week the word came back. Rose liked the story very much; a check for $750 would arrive in the next mail. My only remnant of caution was to wait until it got there. Then it did and I went downtown, severed my relations with the radio station, and made three rapid-order over-the-counter purchases: a desk light, a leather jacket, and a 16-gauge Remington automatic shotgun. I still have them, all three, and use them in season—season for the desk light being year-round, so that virtually every word I have written since that day (including these) has been done under its flourescent glare, which makes the words come up nice and black on the white paper.

I was launched; this was the big time; fame and fortune lay before me. All I had to do was keep writing and the checks would keep coming. Accordingly, with the added notion of doubling the size of my next check by doubling the length of my next submission, I wrote a 44-page story that later became the "Ride Out" section of *Jordan County*. Within a week we heard again from Mr Rose. They werent sure, up there, whether this was a long short-story or a short novelette, he said, and they didnt care; their check for $1500 would arrive in the next mail. I was pleased but not surprised. Indeed, I knew too little about the inner goings-on of the publishing business to have any grounds for being surprised at anything they did or didnt do. All I knew was that I was onto a good thing and I kept riding it, convinced that I would soon be rich like both my planter grandfathers, though it's true they both went broke, in the regular Delta style, around the time they died. I invented and wrote a third story, three times as long as the first, sent off the resultant 66-page typescript—"Miss Amanda," it was called; it was later the Barcroft parts of *Love in a Dry Season*—and sat back to wait for Mr Rose's acceptance letter and the tripled check that would follow in its wake. This time the wait was longer, about two weeks, and what came rebounding in the mail was the typescript, together with a note informing Ben and me that the *Post* did not publish stories containing implications of incest.

So quickly do bright things come to nothing. I had scarcely set out on the money trail my grandfathers blazed than I was unceremoniously unhorsed, thus reversing their schedule by going broke near the start of the journey instead of near its end. Presently, however, when my head began to clear from the shock, I saw virtues in the mishap. I had had misgivings from the outset, repressed but recurrent, that if a rigorous apprenticeship was advisable for acquiring the fundamentals of my profession—which I strongly suspected was the case, not only for learning how to write but also for learning how to be a writer—then things had not been going the way they should. Besides, if I was not going to be a well-heeled writer for magazines, it was much better to discover that at the outset rather than well along the road, which would require a long trip back to the starting point. This way, there was no need for starting over; I was just starting anyhow. Then too, I had most of that recent $1500 salted away for a grub stake, and though our relationship now ended for all time—I said goodbye to magazines, much as I had done to catwalks, humidifiers, and radio commercials—I had the *Post* to thank for that. I hope I dont sound ungrateful or overgloating if I point out that it died before I did.

Freed of the need for moving on to an 88-page concoction, I returned to my desk and wrote *Shiloh*, which ran something over twice that length. By the time I finished it, both *Post* stories had appeared and I had heard from a number of literary agents working the New York scene. I chose one and sent him the typescript. After a while he informed me that Dial Press was interested; could I come up and talk? I could. Travel in those days, at least for people in my financial bracket, was mainly by train—out of Memphis by daycoach, a night and a day, then a move up to Pullman in Washington for a good night's sleep before pulling into New York early next morning. I walked the streets for a while, ate a doughnut for breakfast, then went to the agent's office. He took me to lunch, complete with drinks and wine, and then to Dial. Dial in those days was Bert Hoffman and George Joel, both in their middle forties, less than half a foot over five feet tall, in tailored suits and bright bow ties; Bert was the money, George the brains. They liked *Shiloh* very much indeed, they said, but the main thing they liked about it, since they were convinced it would not sell, was the promise it showed. Did I have some particular future work in mind?

Here was the ghost of Mr Straus, or anyhow an echo of his letter of rejection, come back to haunt me from those faroff days before the war. But this time, despite a faint surrounding alcoholic haze given rise to by the lunchtime wine and martinis, I was better prepared for an answer. Yes, I said, I did have another novel in mind—and I gave them, in capsule form, a barebones outline of *Tournament*. They seemed pleased with what they heard: so much so, in fact, that they offered me a $1500 advance to live on while I wrote it. How long did I think it would take? they asked. About six months, I told them, and they said fine.

It took three. July through September of the long hot Mississippi summer of 1948, I rewrote in longhand the by-now dogeared typescript I had resisted burning eight years back. I revised as I went along, removing nearly all the Joyce, most of the Wolfe, and some of the Faulkner; what Proust I encountered I either left in or enlarged on. Then I retyped it and sent it off. The Lord moves in mysterious ways—especially the lords of literature; my first-written novel was to be my first-published after all. It came out one year later, by which time I had finished the second, *Follow Me Down*, and was blocking out the third, *Dry Season*. They came out one a year, and *Shiloh*—my second-written, now the fourth—appeared in the spring of '52, the ninetieth anniversary of the battle, followed by *Jordan County*. By this time, with five novels written in five years, I had moved to Memphis, the true capital of the Delta though it lies outside its borders, and begun my twenty-year-long three-volume Civil War narrative, which was followed in turn by the sixth novel, *September September*, in early spring of 1978. Since then, I have been engaged—

rather shakily, alas—on my seventh, to be called *Two Gates to the City*. They all go back to *Tournament*, even *Shiloh*: even *The Civil War a Narrative*, for that matter.

First novels are like first girls. They never really leave you, in your mind at any rate, no matter how many years and miles or other girls and novels follow that one on your journey through this vale of tears and laughter. I remember the circumstances surrounding this one's appearance, including the fact that it sold 750 copies in my home town alone—which I'm sorry to say amounted to about one third of the national total; Mr Straus was right about sales, you see, despite my fine-tooth revision of what he'd read. In part this hinterland bonanza came because Greenville, in its vaunted role as the Athens of the Delta, prided itself on supporting all the arts. Curiosity also played a part, however, for the rumor got abroad that the main character was modeled on my father's father. There was some truth in this, but only a vestige; he died nearly two years before I was born, and all I borrowed from his ghost was certain dates and happenings to serve as pegs and mileposts; otherwise, Hugh Bart was nothing like him. What's more I was sustained in this disclaimer, one day at this time, while getting a haircut. There was a beauty parlor in back of the barber shop, separated from it by a curtained doorway and with its own private rear entrance. The women back there, of all ages from fifteen to eighty, had to shout at each other to be heard, for their heads were encased in driers that resembled oldtime deep-sea-diver helmets, and I heard one of them—one of the older clients, by her tone—exclaim in a positive, forthright manner that did not welcome contradiction: "They say it's about his grandfather. But I knew his grandfather, and he was a *nice* man."

The compliment was double-edged at best, but I rose from the chair and risked impropriety by putting my head through the doorway curtain and into that female sanctum to thank her; I thank her still, though she has long since gone to her reward. It's true, I had wanted to understand my grandfathers—both of them, for the maternal one is in there too, also in disguise—along with the other men of their time, born on the eve of the Civil War and come of age during Reconstruction, so that it was no wonder they turned out grasping and improvident or that their three almost exclusive forms of relaxation, with golf and bowling not yet on the scene and no war to distract them except the comic-opera one in Cuba, which came too late for most of them, were cards and whiskey and the ritualistic killing of dove and quail and ducks and deer and bear, in numbers not only incredible but downright impossible in the years to follow, such was their skill with the double-barrel shotguns of their day and the skill and stamina of the dogs they raised to detect and run those creatures down. I put none of them into the book as he was in life, grandfathers unexcepted, for the simple reason that a real-life person transported unaltered into a work of fiction would have little of reality about him; his main quality would be flatness. It takes two or three men, rolled into one, to produce one rounded character in a novel, quite as if he needed two or three sets of lungs if he was to breathe at all in that close atmosphere, let alone stand up and cast a shadow. Now it seemed to me that that backroom beauty-parlor *grande dame* understood this, whether she knew it or not, and that was why I thanked her.

My bedrock intention, or hope, was to understand my homeland by studying these composite individuals who had lived in it before me. I knew even then, away back in the dark ages of the Thirties, that there were things that were dreadfully wrong about that land, just as I knew there were things that were good and could be enjoyed, and I tried my best to examine it from all the angles I could imagine. Looking back on the attempt, with the perspective of the years—some two million hardbound words later—I can see now that what I did was right, not only for my purposes at the time, but also for those of the future; I was laying the groundwork for things I would turn my hand to, later on, even though I did not know then what they'd be. I was quite consciously trying to cover and comprehend this patch of earth called Jordan County, which I discovered and developed by basing it on Washington County, Mississippi, where I was born and raised. Basically microcosmic, it has an industrial north, an agrarian south, a capital—Bristol—on the river, and all the various stratums of society on both sides of the line that then divided black and white. Down the years I have tried to look into most of the nooks and crannies, geographical and social, and all the search has been conducted on terrain I first laid out in *Tournament*.

Not that I was all that conscious of what I was doing at the outset: I just did it. Mostly I was thrashing around in the wilds of the English language, as you can plainly see, and much of the time I was as happy as a colt in clover, and I hope you can see that too. Since then, I have looked on the result as a sort of motherload from which I felt free to take anything I wanted; I cannibalized it for all kinds of uses in the books that followed, and I continue to do so through the one I am writing now. I had not intended to reprint it, partly because no amount of revision, including the start-to-finish one that preceded its original publication, can remove its many "windy suspirations of forc'd breath." But it was and is a young man's novel, and that no doubt is how they should be, if anything good is to come from them later. I am glad, after all, to see it reappear, since it was in these pages, all those word-crowded years ago, that I defined my ground and set my sights.

Shelby Foote

Memphis, 1986

ASA

SHORTENING, THE November days had drawn in, sear at first, then gusty with frequent rain. Leaves fell, speckling the lawn, obliterating the paths: they were sodden and viscid underfoot, each a small death. Deadened by the rain, the plantation bell sounded as if from far off; smoke stayed near the ground and the lake was shrouded. Inside the house, the walls sweating drops like tears, sheets of plaster tore from the ceiling and crashed down without warning, filling the rooms with reverberation. At such a time on such a morning, the sun cold and pale like a wet coin, I was born.

Bart was away at a trapshoot in Kentucky. They had a card from him the day before: *These easy pickings. 98-100, 100-100, 100-100. Can't figure how I muffed those two birds* and squeezed beneath: *Got me a grandson?* On the reverse was a lithograph of mountain scenery, grayed, machine-stamped, with the legend: LUCAS BLUFF, FORMED 1783. They showed it to Kate, and she said: "What does that mean, formed? Wasnt it a real bluff? Who was Lucas?" She was distracted: twice that morning she thought the birth had come. Between times she held Hugh's hand. "I'm glad he's shooting well. Just to miss two, thats well, isnt it?" She plucked vaguely at something invisible on the counterpane. "Now maybe he'll come home."

I was born early next day, but Bart did not come home. He did not come home for two more months. Then he came and never left again to go farther than Bristol, thirty miles away, where the family moved: Bart, Mrs Bart, Hugh, Florence, Clive, Kate, I

(Asa the grandson, named after a shooting acquaintance in Kentucky; they had wanted to name me Hugh but Bart said laughing, "No: two is enough. Name him Asa for a fine man, a friend I made last month at the National"; so I was named Asa), three of the Negroes and Billy Boy: into a rented mansion just off the main street of the town, a growing town in 1912, with two hotels, two banks—though one had just gone under—three saloons, four blocks of stores, and a flickering cinema palace which boasted rare traveling companies showing *Ben Hur* and the like and once such high art as *Phèdre*, the classic French pronounced demotically by a woman who sat in a jewel-studded highback chair, aping Bernhardt, croaking the long nasals of words none of the audience comprehended except the French baker and an occasional New Orleans house servant perched in the remote fetid darkness of the balcony called Nigger Heaven.

Residences, post-Victorian adaptations of the old plantation houses, with gingerbread trim tacked to eaves and mansard windows, surrounded the stores and cotton offices. The two hotels were patronized mainly by drummers, mild, glib men who sat in sidewalk chairs or in the lobby, talking women and politics; by steamboat men, expansive and sedate, talking of the river, knowing but not admitting that the railroads already had them beat; and by an infrequent professional gambler, gaunt hold-over from an era that was dead, wearing a shiny hat and full broadcloth, a black mustache and sideburns, wearing too an aura of the royal retinue of the kings and queens of pasteboard nobility. Weekend nights were filled with music, wailing horns and throbbing drum, muted by the sliding feet of dancers at the Elks and Elysian clubs, their murmurous talk and laughter. Later they would fill the streets and the all-night café, noisy, shallow, a bit perverse and heady with youth, while from their beds the townspeople and transients would hear the music and voices, the shrill empty laughter, and would toss and curse or lie quiet and regret.

Bristol was a river town, bounded on the west by the levee with a landing where sternwheelers put in, and on north and east and south by broad flat ash-gray fields of cotton broken occasionally but not much by random cuts of corn and hay. Here Bart and his family moved and lived the last two years of his life. He had sold Solitaire and all his other holdings, lock stock and barrel; he had rented the intown mansion, and now began the intown life.

It was ten years later, visiting down at Lake Jordan on a place adjoining a portion of what used to be Solitaire, that I learned of these final two years from an old man Bart had named Billy Boy. He had a tangled beard and he lived alone in a cabin. Except for the two years in Bristol he had lived there since a morning in 1887 when he first saw Bart. Bart had just dismounted; he stood before the rear steps of the house, wearing riding clothes, boots, and a wide sand-colored hat: a young man, then, maintaining a practiced dignity without the ease he was later to approach. He looked around and saw a man of about forty—though he could not be sure of this within a dozen years, since the man was of that ageless clan who all their lives strove not only with poverty but also with nothingness, glazed with anonymity like disease, so that they did not move toward death by gradual marches over a level plain, as others seem to do, but fell upon it suddenly as if by stepping over a cliff, as though all ravages but one passed over their heads with no more effect than the brush of a wing, though when that one came it was irresistible, overwhelming, clean victorious, and who wore their years not as other men did, upon their flesh and hair, but somewhere within until the burden passed the breaking point and the vessel burst—in disreputable clothes, the trousers tatters from thighs down and supported by a single-strap suspender knotted into the waistband, tow hair looking as if the scalp were in explosion.

"Whats your name?" Bart asked him.

"William," the stranger said. His voice was nasal, depthless, weary.

"Well, Billy my boy, I reckon you need feeding."

So it became Billy Boy, the old man told me thirty-five years later, sitting on the cabin stoop in the noonday sunlight and telling me how all his life he would hear Bart's voice using his name in the time-worn, challenging jest: "Can she bake a cherry pie, charming Billy?"—only Billy Boy, not schooled in even the store-front talk, let alone the folksongs, never knew the answer about her being a dear thing too young to leave her mother; he would just stand there, grinning and biding his time until Bart passed on to something he could understand. But now, the sun streaming golden down the April afternoon, myself seated below him in front of the cabin while he talked in a very old man's voice, now he did not tell about the Solitaire years. Now—calling me Mr Bart too, just as he had called the other one ten and twenty and thirty years ago—he told about the Bristol years, speaking of them as if they had been the final two years of his life too, as if the past eight years had been posthumous, as if when Bart died Billy Boy died too.

"Yes Sir," he said. "It would be about four-thirty when we'd reach the house, just beginning to show some light at the top of the upstairs windows and high in the trees. He would be limp and I would have to guide him up the steps and into the house and up the staircase too. And when we got to the landing, there Miz Bart would be—"

"Mammy's been dead two years," I said.

"Yes Sir," the voice hardly pausing in midstride, like a phonograph when the needle is jarred back a groove—as if it were telling something memorized and feared to break the continuity: "And there Miz Bart would be, dressed for sleep, in a quilt robe and a nightcap, with a candle helt in her hand to throw her shadow back on the wall while she stood there watching us: me holding Mr Bart up against me and him with his head hung down so his chin was on his shirt-front. But she wouldnt say nothing; no Sir. She would just stand there while I waited a minute and then went on, toted him into the room and put him on the bed and undressed him. His head would roll some while I was taking his clothes off and his eyes would come open a mite, glinting a little. Maybe his mustache would be mussed from the shirt coming off, but he still had that proud tall dignity like always. And then I would have the nightshirt on him and the covers tucked up, and he would open one eye

xxviii

a mite wider and say down deep in his throat, 'Looks like you made it again, Billy.' And I would say, 'Sho now. Sho. We always make it.' "

He paused. "I see," I said. But all this time I was thinking: He's not talking to me. He's not talking to anybody. He's telling it to the air. He tells it to the air every day, to keep it alive in his mind.

Then it resumed, the face lifted into the sunlight, the voice oracular, continuing after the silence. "The sad time was the spring we moved away, left Solitaire and the horses and land to go to the buildings and sidewalks and people. That was a weeping spring, the trees plumb up with sap and the honeysuckle drizzling under the arbor. Mr Bart was back from Kentucky and restless (maybe you done it; you was a evermore crying baby, Mr Bart), riding that smoke-colored horse, sitting straight and sharp-eyed and the horse braced up proud too, going through the yard with his hoofs flicking back little chunks of dirt. . . ."

Wait, I thought; wait. This is going too fast. What did he leave out?

"What year was that, the year you came?"

"1887," he said without having to think.

"And when you came you were. . ."

Now there was a pause before he said, "Forty. I was forty, then."

"Is that how old you are?" I said, counting it out on the tips of my fingers.

"Yes Sir."

"Seventy-four. Thats old."

"Yes Sir," the voice said, gathering momentum as it approached the groove I had jarred it back from. "The day I got here he set me down and made me tell about it, about how I left home, left Tennessee. My wife had left me for a trom bone player, but I didnt tell him that, not yet. I reckon I was shamed to."

Flowing on, the pitch invariable, the voice told it all, the decline and fall. And over the telling, like a firm-bodied ghost only faintly vague in outline, bemused but not especially interested, what Billy Boy called the proud tall figure cast his shadow, immense and knightly and biblical in the rich, unreal glare of hero-worship. That was the beginning.

TOURNAMENT

It was in later years, talking to others who knew Bart while he came and strove and went, that I learned the full story, the explanations for the mnemonic monolog. And as the legend, the information grew—was formed as mudflats are formed on the river, layer by layer brought grain by grain by the shifting current, the tricky boils and eddies—I grew to know: first, how a boy of eighteen came across the state, a late-reconstruction Mississippi overrun by north-spawned profiteers and the backwash of her own wild-eyed Negroes, to lodge with a kinsman on lower Lake Jordan and to work there learning Delta farming, the temper and whims of cotton: how at twenty-two he became sheriff of Issawamba County, elected because of his ability at turkey shoots and hunting forays and because of some inner hang for making the small farmers and tradesmen admire the way he sat a horse and picked a crop; how on stepping out of office he went to Jordan County to assume ownership of Solitaire plantation, five square miles of the finest cotton land in the world, paying off the mortgage and establishing himself, no longer an outlander, among the planters; how in 1890 he married Florence Jameson (late-born daughter of General Clive Jameson, the Delta's beau sabreur, inheritor of Solitaire and builder of the mansion where Bart had lived alone) who within the year bore him a son and two years later a daughter and six years later a son again; how he left the lake and spent two years running hard toward destruction and death: and second, how these stages along Bart's road were punctuated by experiences which made him what he was and were explained by his trying to be what he was never meant to be: and third, how when all the facts were marshaled and all the opinions counted, I emerged with the complete figure, yet found myself with no more than when I began hearing it on the cabin stoop that sunny April afternoon—a man cast in the heroic mold, whom facts shook and condition altered, and the thought, the conviction which rose out of the roiling cauldron, that each man, even when pressed closest by other men in their scramble for the things they offer one another with so little grace, is profoundly alone.

XXX

CHAPTER ONE

RISE

OTHER CANDIDATES—there were three others, an older man who had held the office two terms ago and would have held it last term too except that a sheriff could not succeed himself, a young lawyer who had entered the race because his practice brought no liveli-hood, and another farmer—posted campaign placards about the county, littering trees and fenceposts with bold-faced promises of honesty and efficiency. Hugh Bart, the newcomer, the outlander, posted no placards, made no public speeches. "I'm no orator," he said. He was beginning to learn a life-way very different from that of the region where he had been born.

He had not thought he could win until a day two months before election he was called in off the street by one of the other candi-dates, the elderly ex-sheriff, who offered him, in private, the chief deputy job in exchange for his support. It was while this man was speaking ("By God, son, I ah Ive been in the game too long not to know how it's coming out in the end") that Bart realized he prob-ably would be elected. He listened quietly, courteously, while the other man—he was called Judge not only because he rented a law office but also because he dressed the part, long box-back coat, wide black hat, white hair that grew thick above his ears and came to a ducktail at the back, string tie bunched loosely at his throat beneath a mobile, tobacco-stained mouth—spoke his offer, giving it, he said, out of friendship and respect for Bart's qualifications.

"Because I know youre the man for the job," he said, leaning far back in his chair to ease his hemorrhoids, his feet on a half opened drawer of the desk. They were alone; the office was a cubicle partitioned off in one corner of a feed-and-grain store. "Yes. You can do it: I cant." He made a deprecatory gesture with one hand, smiling. "That aint what the people, the voters say, of course. They say I'm the man for the job, seeing Ive held it twice before to their satisfaction. And you, the qualified one, you cant win because—semper eadem—they dont know it."

"How do you know it, Judge?"

"I know men," Judge said promptly. It was a statement he used often. Bart watched him. "Yes," Judge said, speaking carefully. "You all come with me, you and your people. Come with me and we'll swing her."

They were silent a moment, Judge looking at Bart and maintaining an expression of indifference. Then Bart said, "Which one are you worried about?"

"None of them. Not a one of them, son. The fewer votes I get, the fewer ah obligations I'll have afterwards. I can count you my electors by name. Regnat populus: it's in the bag. I just thought I'd tell you." He leaned forward, groaning at the exertion, scraped with his nails at flecks of dried mud on his trouser cuffs, evidently waiting for Bart to speak, then reared back in the chair again. "To tell you the truth, I wish youd keep it quiet."

"Stay in the race?"

"Well—yes."

"Stay in and accept your offer afterwards, after my defeat?"

"After my election, yes," Judge said, watching Bart, who was looking at the desk-top and who then said what Judge had known he would say:

"No, Judge. I couldnt do that."

"Then come with me quietly. Drop out without any fuss, if you have scruples against the other."

As soon as he had spoken the words Judge knew he had said them too quickly. Oh-oh, he thought, I overplayed it. And when he looked at Bart's face he knew he should never have said them at all.

2

"No, Judge," Bart said, "I dont think so." He rose. It was the first time he had moved since Judge had called him in off the street. "I think I'll stay in the race."

"God damn it," Judge said quietly, sitting alone in the office when Bart had gone. His feet still propped on the drawer of the desk, he leaned forward and spat across the cubicle into a bucket in one corner, and with one square palm, the fingers snub and curved as if fashioned for handshakes, slapped his broadcloth thigh. From beneath his hand a thin cloud of dust rose in the sunlight. "I wonder what kind of job I'll be getting out of him."

Judge received no job at all when two months later, the votes counted, Bart the newcomer and outlander went in with a narrow majority. Judge was close behind him. "How about that deputy job?" he said.

"Thank you, Judge, but I wont need one," Bart said, pausing in his laughter. And indeed the whole town was laughing: laughing at the young man who had entered the race because his law practice did not develop. The morning after the votes were counted (he polled four) he came to town wearing a pistol on each hip, walking cautiously down the middle of the street, looking waggishly and with mock trepidation to each side and behind. "What you toting them guns for?" someone asked him. "Aint you read the returns?"

"I read them," he said. He looked carefully over each shoulder. "I read them, and I know any man who's got as few friends as I have *ought* to go round fully armed."

BART'S FOUR-YEAR term marked the beginning of his rise, the incubation period of the legend which was to collect around him. For the first time in his life he could go bird hunting almost as often as he wished. Thus the talk began about his shooting powers. Men hunted with him once and came back pronouncing Bart's the best bird eye in the world. "It aint human," one said. "There would be a flash of a flutter, one of the dogs frozen while the other inched forward, and I'd put my gun up, yelling the dogs to stand, and before I could get half set here came that thunder of their wings, drumming, and whom! whom! his double would go, and he would already be calling the dogs to fetch. There aint any sighting to it: the gun just goes up and shoots without stopping, swings around in a little arc and whom! another bird."

All his life he was to remember experiences gained during his term as head of law and order in Issawamba County: a manhunt, a fugitive barricaded in a cabin, the political spongers: "If I wasnt *for* you I wouldn't be telling you this"; the wildcatters: "I swear, sheriff, there's *thou*sands in it. Thousands. If I had a little cash . . ."; the down-and-outers and whiskey-heads; the gamblers talking out of the sides of their mouths; and a thousand others he met at close quarters for the first time.

The manhunt showed him one facet of the character of the people he was elected to protect. In one sense, he saw, it was like being hired to protect a buzz saw from men who insisted on putting their hands against it. One Negro killed another in a gambling fracas, was caught and jailed, and then broke out. Bloodhounds were brought by their owner, a small sandy-haired man with pale blue eyes and inflamed eyelids. There were three dogs, all on leash, towing the owner across the jail yard as soon as they were unloaded from the wagon. They bayed beneath the violated window of the cell. "Hold them, Chet," Bart told him.

"You hold them, then, goddammit!" the little man cried, bent backward straining at the leash. "You hold them, then," he continued to say, while the hounds towed him, sliding like something in a tableau (for crystallized, halted, the scene would have appeared serene, decorous: it was the cursing, the jeering, the dogs' moiling urgency that made the intensity) across the yard, while behind each of his heels and behind the miniature dust-puffs which exploded there, twin prolonged indentures curved in the August dust like sunken rails. "All they waiting for is your signal, like air another living thing in Issawamba County."

Bart was quiet a moment but not for long; he dropped his glance, speculative with one grave flick, no more. He said, "All right: turn them loose. Let them go."

4

"Hy ah!" Chet cried and began bounding after the dogs, leaping into the air and being jerked incredible distances. They ran with their noses close to the ground, ears pendant beside their tearful bloodshot eyes. From their throats the baying continued deeper than bells, louder, and strangely like them, bass and booming. All this time the sandy-haired little man called Chet, his eyelids red and his eyes blear blue, as if they had been washed in too-strong soap and the color had not held, continued to follow the hounds in a series of strange jerked leaps, screaming "Hy ah! Hy ah!" as if he were hungry and looked forward to eating the fugitive. Bart and the others mounted horses and rode in the direction of the baying.

They had not been out long when they came upon what they were seeking. The dogs circled a tree, their heads up, their thick bald tails held straight and stiff like flagpoles, while the baying continued undiminished, going steady and full like a ship in distress. Above them, among dusty foliage, white teeth grimacing, the Negro crouched. Chet was missing.

"Come on down, boy," Bart called.

"Yassuh, captains; I'm caught for fair. But, captains, please yawl call off them hellhounds."

This none of them could do. So they sat resting after the chase, the fugitive in the tree and the horsemen below, smoking and talking pleasantly but a little loud above the belling, their legs thrown over saddle horns or squatting on the ground, while the bloodhound baying continued unabated, resonant, gonglike, victorious.

They did not have long to wait. Soon Chet ran into the clearing, his clothing ripped, his face and body scratched and filthy from being dragged through briers and marsh until the leash broke. Waving the severed length of leash, his voice as victorious as the baying but shrill and tremulous, he called to them: "Hy ah! Aint that a set of dogs for you? Aint that a set now?" he repeated, waving the frazzled rope, and his face shone through the cuts and mud. This face, the face of the Negro in the tree, the strident crescendo baying of the bloodhounds, Bart was never to forget.

5

Nor this: which occurred in October of the year before his term expired. A young man who recently had taken over management of his father's plantation got into an altercation with one of his white tenants. It had to do with money, a commissary debt. In the argument this young man lost his temper, struck the tenant, and ordered him off the place. The tenant had a wife, a mother-in-law, and five children; he had been on the plantation almost twenty years, having come there after Appomattox. A mild-mannered man, a veteran, he had little to do with his neighbors (white tenants were rare on the lake) but worked hard all year round, farming on shares with the young man's father, who had been his regimental commander, and for the past season with the young man. He took the blow without apparent rebellion, stepping back with his teeth bloody, then left, going toward the cabin to pack his goods. Soon the young man followed; "To see if what he packs is really his," he told someone at the time.

What happened inside the cabin was never made clear. There were loud voices, two sudden silences on both sides of a shot, the second silence broken by a woman's scream cut short by a palm clapped over her mouth, and soon the five children, each about a year older than the one behind him, were herded off the cabin porch into the yard by the two women, one quite old and hysterical running with her hands thrown palm-forward over her head, the other just short of middle age, stern-lipped, walking the two miles into town and into the sheriff's office.

Bart sat at his desk in hunting clothes; he had just come in from the field and was cleaning his short-barreled shotgun. He looked up and saw the woman come in, the crowd pressing their faces against the window. "Shef," she said in a voice that was a bit loud from excitement though there was no nervousness yet; "Shef, Luth says you aint go run him like you run that nigger. He says if you want him come get him." Then her voice shook. "He's kilt Mr Preston's boy."

"Here, now," Bart said.

"But you wont!" she cried, her eyes going wild, rolling with fear and despair. She made flailing motions with both hands.

"Wait," Bart said sharply. "Hold up, here."

Whereupon she grew quite calm again and said in a voice as cold as ice, as empty as husks: "But you best not go, nor none of your men. He's got a gun and a crate of cottridges and he wont be took living. He said come and get him, but mind you he wont be took living."

Carrying the light cylinder-bore bird gun across the saddle, Bart rode the two miles to the cabin where the man had barricaded himself. It was a warm clear day. The doors and windows of houses were open and there were no fires built, though stacks of logs had been hauled from the woods for winter. Just outside town he began to hear the shooting. Soon afterwards he came in sight of the cabin.

A hundred and fifty yards to one side the railroad had been ramped about three feet above the flat land. Men crouched behind this, their guns laid on the rail above, shooting steadily. Smoke drifted before them toward the cabin. At first Bart thought there was no shooting coming from that direction: then he saw dirty white puffs coming at intervals out of the chimney. The tenant had backed into the fireplace and from that point, protected at rear and flanks by brick, was firing toward the railroad. It was the only direction from which he could be shot at, and it was the only direction in which he could fire himself. He was shooting an early Federal repeating rifle, a Burnside, using bullets he had brought home from the war. About every third cartridge would explode and presently the men behind the ramp would see a puff of smoke belly out of the chimney.

Bart stopped the men behind the embankment, but the man in the cabin continued to fire. The shots sounded dull and flat against the silence. One of the men had been hit in the shoulder, the wound bandaged crudely with a strip of his shirt. They wanted to take him to town for treatment, but he would not go; "I'll stay and see you get him," he said. Another man looked at Bart sardonically:

"You kind of come dressed for the job."

"I'll tend to that," Bart said.

"Reckon youll have to," the man said. "It looks like we cant hit him."

What Bart was about to do (before tear gas and the riot gun; they did not use dynamite then, nor even burn them out) had been done by many former sheriffs. "Sorry we didnt get him for you," a man said, but Bart did not answer; he had never killed a man before. How do I know? he was thinking. How do I know?—the thought refusing to continue.

He looked at the cabin for a while, then stepped onto the ramp and went down the opposite slope with short, sliding steps. Walking erect in brown hunting clothes, the double-barreled bird gun in the crook of his arm, he crossed the field toward the front of the cabin, out of the line of fire. As a light, dull explosion sounded and as the men watching Bart ducked behind the ramp, a ball whined over the tracks and a small pearly gob of smoke belched out of the chimney. Then there was silence, the air pregnant, anticipant. Bart thought: I wonder what he's thinking in there, about the silence, the not-firing—and again the half-formed thought reaching its impasse: But how do I know? How do I know?

"Come on, Luther," Bart called. Silence struck again. He stood just off the cabin porch, in front of the closed door. "Come on out, Luther."

"Get on from there," the tenant shouted. His voice sounded hollow, coming from within the fireplace.

"It's no go, Luther. Come out or—"

There was a ripping sound and a clean vertical streak appeared on the door. The deformed lead passed high in the air, screaming thinly. Bart stepped onto the porch, halted before the scarred door. He paused, then raised his boot, kicked forward.

To the men on the ramp (they stood up now, forgetting the whining balls that had lately sped their way) the motion was faint, slow, almost deliberate, miniature across even that short distance. They saw the door fling inward, heard the two shots—one behind another, the first dull and flat, the second louder than anything they had heard since '65—saw the cabin fill with powder smoke, and already were running across the field, many of them leaving their guns. Some were yelling as they ran.

As Bart fell forward he brought the shotgun to his shoulder, thinking: Lord God, I dont even know if I loaded it. The tenant crouched on the hearth, the gun muzzle a black o beneath the hot rushing eye suddenly blotted out by a lick of flame. Continuing his inward fall and seeing down the matted rib the white face screaming with wild hair around its upper half like a nimbus, Bart pulled both triggers. There was a single huge explosion (he said afterwards he did not hear it) as both barrels discharged, blowing the barricaded tenant's head clear off.

When the men from the ramp reached the cabin, entering by the windows as well as the door, they saw Bart on his hands and knees before the body, in an attitude of speculation and urgency, as if he were talking to himself. He was: his mind had crossed the impasse; he was thinking clearly without pause, hearing two voices inside himself: But how do I know mine was right? *You dont. You just know you had a job to do and did it.* But how do I know I was right? *You dont. You just did it, as any man does a job he has to do*—and the question still returning: But how do I know I was right?—and the answer, once and for all: *You dont know. And never will know. Never.*

He never forgot this other voice inside himself, nor the men behind the railroad embankment eager for a death, the unequal, fore-decided contest, the haloed maniacal face grimacing as the old repeating rifle, pointed directly at him, clicked time after time on dud after dud until a round finally fired and missed, the double-barreled explosion blotting the whole scene, and then the rushing roar of all past time and injustice and insolent might of law and order coming through the air to set the two voices going inside his head: When? *Never.*

As SHERIFF Bart came to know many people in Issawamba County. It was considered a rural section (even in Mississippi, even in the

'80s) whose one settlement was Eddypool, the county seat, a one-street trade and law center with a handful of law offices, a court-house, a blacksmith shop, a saloon, two general stores. Bart was the symbol of government, the one officer to whom all others, judge, prosecuting attorney, and the rare special deputy, were adjunct, supplementary. He knew them all, storekeepers, lawyers, small farmers, planters (though there were only a few of these in Issawamba, whose northern boundary included barely the south-ern tip of the lake along whose shores the planters built; the opulent ones were in Jordan County to the north), Negroes, and passing strangers. These men were quite different from any he had ever known before.

One of them was a tradesman, operator of one of the general stores, selling flour and molasses and lengths of cloth. A bachelor, he slept in the rear of the store, and spent his days sitting on the counter talking to whoever was white and would listen. His abuse of Negroes was punctuated only by occasions of waiting on them. Often the abuse would not falter even then, even while he was slicing the cheese or dipping into the cracker barrel, handing a can of snuff down off the shelf or measuring two yards of calico. It would be interrupted only by the abrupt nod of dismissal—"Thatll be a dime" or "Thatll be five cents"—and resumed with the dropping of the coin into the till and the retaking of his seat on the counter, the invective continuing steady, profuse, profane. Into and out of it, the Negro customers walked wooden-faced and deaf, slack-mouthed, the coin palm-sweated while the knife moved through the cheese or the scissors snicked. They knew the weights were never low nor the cloth-lengths false, for they knew that it was part of his creed that a Negro was too low to cheat or bargain with, and they trusted and even respected his honesty.

Many were veterans who had fought with Barksdale or Forrest, Jameson or Van Dorn. Men of all ages, some of them still young twenty years after the finish, others incredibly old, they sat in the sun and talked. Except for the drummer boys and the extremely long lived, they would all be dead within another thirty years, their names preserved in the badly printed books read only by scholars, the frontispiece photographs showing them bearded and stern-lipped in the hour of their prime, wearing firegilt buttons and sabers and sashes, like foreigners who never knew this land or like visitors who came and went and left after themselves only a memory of their passing, a fading legend, a few faint scars on the grass set aside as Federal domain. But to Bart, who sat and listened to their talk, they were very real. It was mostly of running Yankees and surprise surrenders, but occasionally it had something of the fury of the fight, glare of shells, rattle of minies, while the crowd sat solemn around the speaker, their faces drained of blood as the back-yearning voice went on, shouting or level, telling of the shot-torn time, the hunger, the cold, the privation.

Judge frequently visited Bart at the courthouse, where the sheriff's office was. He often remarked that this period of public service was the beginning of a future. "When youre functus officio youll realize just how much it has done for you," he said, reared back in the chair across the desk from Bart. "It's what Ive ah come to talk about. Youve got about eight months of office left, son, and tempus fidgets, as the fellow says. You must think about what youre going to do when you come out. Or have you thought already?"

"I'm going back with my uncle, I guess."

"Farming?"

"Yes."

"Well, listen." Judge hunched forward, his big blue-veined hands lying pale against the desk top. "Youve heard of Union Prudential . . ." Bart shook his head and Judge threw up both hands in bland horror. "Son, you got to start asking round. Else how will you ever get ahead in the world?" Then he told about the Jameson place, Solitaire plantation. "It's up for the having: they want a capable man. I just this morning answered their letter. I told them you were a capable man." Judge smiled. "And you are, aint you? You beat me in an Issawamba election."

Solitaire was the name of the house as well as of the five square miles of land that flanked it. The house had been built in 1855 and '56 by Clive Jameson, son of old Isaac Jameson who had been the region's first settler and who at one time had owned nearly all the land on the eastern shore of Lake Jordan. Built by slave labor, the house had walls more than two feet thick and its ceilings were eighteen feet above its floors. Bricks were manufactured from a clay deposit on one corner of the place; in Indian days, before Dancing Rabbit drove the Choctaws north, it had been a pottery center. There were forty rooms in its three stories, two wings flanking a low porch with squat columns. Into this mansion, furnished with carpets and drapes shipped back from Europe during their wedding tour, Clive Jameson and his bride moved.

Five years later he rode off at the head of a cavalry troop he had organized among the planter families. In four years of war he made his name familiar throughout the South; they called him the Star-Born Brigadier because he had been born in 1833, the year the stars fell. This, however, did not prevent his finding his house gutted by marauders—Yankee and Rebel, bushwhackers as well as soldiers— all the outbuildings burned, gin, barn, and storehouse, the land laid waste like the fulfillment of a page out of Jeremiah. During the fall and winter of 1865 his former slaves drifted toward his back door, unhappy in their new and hungry freedom. He made them share-croppers, in an arrangement little different from that under slavery except that now, in these hard times, neither party profited; they still called him marster.

Defeat brought a mortgage, necessary to start work, which remained totally unpaid in 1882 when the general died and it was foreclosed. His family moved to Bristol to live with a son who ran a lumber company. There were four of them: the wife, the two other sons, and the daughter who was still a child, born late in her parent's life. Their story was familiar; Bart had heard it before.

As Judge told him, the Union Prudential Insurance Company, unhappy holder of many such, held the mortgage on the thirty-two hundred acres. They wanted to sell. "Thirty dollars an acre, all property thereon included, to be paid over a period of ten years," the representative said.

"With how much down payment?" Bart asked him.

"Whatever you have, or nothing." The words were clipped and clear, in a Northern accent. He sat across the desk from Bart, his hat on the floor, crown up, and his briefcase in his lap.

"$96,000," Bart said.

"Yes. In ten years, subject to renewal." The representative sat with his button shoes planted parallel, knees close together, like a woman in fear of assault. He wanted to go home, North; he seemed to be listening for shots. "We are following Mr Wiltner's recommendation" (this was Judge: "Because I know men," Judge had said) "because we believe he knows ability."

"Well, all right, sir," Bart said.

Now the representative moved quickly. Almost before Bart had finished speaking, the briefcase straps flew back with reports like two little whip-cracks and the papers were spread on the desk, the gray print bristling with law phrases, law latin, empty dotted lines, and at the head of the sheets the words: original, duplicate, triplicate. "We'll require witnesses," the representative said. Bart called in two men, one of them a storekeeper, the other Judge, who had been standing just outside the door. All signed.

Straightening up after affixing the sprawling signature that ran in loops and whorls across the page, Judge grinned and extended his hand. "Congratulations. Lets step across the street and crown this glory, this dies faustus." On the way to the saloon he continued to talk. "You can well afford it now, as owner of the once finest plantation in Jordan County."

The bartender leaned forward, a large pale man whose hair was combed in a damp parabola across his forehead, as if it had been painted on with one curved sweep of the brush. Judge said, "Double bourbon."

"Likewise," the other witness said happily.

"A glass of cool water," the representative said. "And please, when is the next train out?"

"Bourbon, John," Bart said.

He was twenty-six that month, May, young enough for almost

any prideful folly. When he left the saloon, however, it was too
near sunset to ride the five miles from Eddypool to Solitair; no
matter how young and enthusiastic he was. But he was there next
morning early. He turned into the driveway just as the sun, a
blood-colored disk, cleared the land line. Its dusty brick rain-
streaked, its pillars scarred by rocks thrown at it by prowlers, the
house had been vacant for two years now; the land had not even
been planted this season. With a febrile advocacy for a time that
was gone, possessing grain for grain the dregs of nothing more
than hope, it surmounted a slope which rose from the lake to the
road and a hundred yards beyond. Bart pulled up directly in front
of the porch and took off his hat, holding it over the pommel.
Leather creaking, he stood in the stirrups and breathed deep. He
had not realized how quiet, how dead the house was until he heard
the saddle creak and the sound of his breath.

The sun rose swiftly; it cleared the roof. It was no longer red;
it was fiery now: he felt it on his face. He spoke, almost shouting;
"Mine!" he cried. The mare turned her long face, back-rolling her
eyes, and Bart shortened rein, dug both heels into her flanks. He
alternately ran and walked her as his exuberance rose and rose. He
still had the hat in his hand, using it as a crop, and he still stood in
the stirrups, the mare driving with a heavy rolling gait, her sides
heaving, when within a mile of Eddypool he pulled her to a walk
and collected his dignity.

As soon as he was back in town he began to make arrangements.

WHEN BART stood in the stirrups and addressed the house as Mine,
he spoke ten years too soon. It was ten years and six months before
he could say Mine in clear truth, ten years of labor.

In back of the house, spared or overlooked by Yankee firebrands,
the old slave quarters squatted in grim remise, their whitewashed
walls blistered and scaling as if by disease or perhaps just longevity
like the cheeks of dowagers. Fifty men and women convicts,
Negroes, were herded into these during chopping and picking

season. Bart rented them from three surrounding counties at twenty cents a head a day, plus food. During the summer they were marched out at 4:30 every morning, excluding Sundays, and at 8:30 every evening were brought back in, having eaten three meals of peas and cornbread—a slab of fatback each on Sundays—cooked in big iron washpots in the field. He paid no mind to the super- stition that said bad luck followed convict labor. It was cheap and it was rugged and obedient. Guards carried shotguns and straps which they could use with the unfailing accuracy of mule skinners. His crops were beautifully weed-free through spring and summer, and in the fall his gin was always the first to hush its high shrill whine. As the year progressed from green-leafed June through purple-bloomed August to white-bolled October, other planters and cotton men came from nearby counties to see the Solitaire crop.

Except for the truck garden he required each family to work on a plot beside its cabin, he planted almost nothing but cotton. At the end of the first year—this was 1887, when long staple cotton brought an average of ten cents a pound on the New Orleans market—the land having lain fallow during the past season, Bart ginned twelve hundred bales and sold them for $60,000. Of this, $25,000 went for furnish, $20,000 for the tenants, $1500 for convict labor, and $2000 for salaries to the blacksmith, the commissary man, and repairs. He finished the year with $11,500 clear to his name in the bank, and of this he paid $10,000 on the purchase price. Now he could look at the house, the five square miles of land, and say Mine and be at least partly right. At this rate he would be a long time getting free, he told himself. But this was only the beginning, the groundwork for the really successful years that followed, when the price and the yield got better.

It was in March of this first year that the man Bart named Billy Boy came and found Bart living in the house. He lived in one room, bare of all save a bed and a table with a washstand and a candle and a box of sulphur matches which he needed getting up before dawn every morning. And it was nine months later, in early December, that Bart left Solitaire, going out by the back door and straight across the fields until he reached the railroad. He sat on a stump until the train came into sight around the bend, then flagged and boarded it. He came back a week later, riding a young bay stallion alongside a borrowed wagon loaded with crates.

"They looked heavy," Billy Boy said later. "We never knowed how heavy, though, till we begun unloading them outn the wagon. Once we got the heft of them, we wondered how them mules had made it from the Ithaca station."

Going slow through December mud, the mules strained in the shafts as the whip cracked over their hips. Bart had been to Memphis, where he had spent the remaining $1500 on furnishings for the one room. Billy Boy and the fieldhands, helping him uncrate the things, thought he had bought them on a spree, not only because of the extravagance but also because of the incipient beard; he had not shaved since he left the house to flag the train. It was dark, thick, short, incult, and it made his eyes look hollow. He was twenty-seven, young for a beard. His hair, which was clipped short and took no part, grew stiff, smoothly piled, like a skullcap surmounting the beard-shadowed oval of face: a face strong even in this country, the short, pointed nose with flared nostrils, the mouth with rather thick lips held close against the teeth, the brows that met above the nose, and beneath them eyes as delicate and limpid as a deer's.

"Bait him," he told Billy Boy, dismounting and slapping the stallion's rump. But when the strange hand went out for the bridle, the horse nickered and shied. Over the small thunder of the hoofs (they looked more dangerous than hatchets) Bart was saying, "Steady, steady now, steady," stroking the satin shoulder till the horse quieted and stood just trembling a little, wall-eyed, and Bart said, "This is Billy Boy. You go with him." Then the stallion was quieter, almost gentle by comparison, following Billy Boy to the barn.

When he got back from feeding and combing the horse Billy Boy found Bart in the yard, opening the crates with an ax. Two of the field hands were scrubbing the room with lye soap and hot water; another was high on a ladder, wiping the ceiling. Billy Boy watched them a while, then went back to the yard and watched Bart open the crates. One held a Persian-looking rug, linen bed-clothes, a tufted spread, and two sets of wine-colored velvet cur-tains. The others held furniture, among which Billy Boy finally identified two chairs upholstered in rep and a four-poster with a high, valanced head and adjustable candle sockets at the foot.

In a smaller crate, heaviest of the lot, was a polished stone bathtub shaped like a shoe and carved about the rim with a design of over-lapping rose leaves. Billy Boy imagined it was a vessel for preparing or serving some special outlandish dish. What will he have them cook in that? he wondered. Whatever it is, we'll be a long time eating it if they fix up enough to fill that thing. Maybe we'll just need to cook one day a month and spend the other twenty-nine or thirty sitting around it spooning toward the bottom. But when will we find time to farm? . . . He imagined he could see them sitting hip to hip in a close circle about the tub, ladling with long-handled implements into the pink and oversweet angel food he believed likely to grace such a container—thinking, wondering: And maybe he'll give a prize to the first one that scrapes bottom.

Before dusk the furnishing had been completed. Windows wore their velvet; the bed was polished and made, its valanced headboard glinting in the light of candles high in their sockets. In one corner, behind a sandlewood screen upon which Japanese maidens and warriors with spears pursued each other across a golden meadow, squatted the tub. Billy Boy still had not identified it, though he believed now it was not for food; It's to piss in, he thought. In one-room splendor the silken cell lay grand as Europe, isolated. On one side, beyond the two windows, were bleak December fields, while on the other three sides, in dusty squalor, were the other thirty-nine rooms, still vacant.

"Heat me a boiler of water," Bart told two of the field hands. Billy Boy stood in a far corner, awaiting the solving of the riddle. Bart walked around the room, feeling the curtains and jouncing the bedsprings. Finally the water was brought, steaming. "Pour it in there," Bart said, pointing. He's going to boil something in it, Billy Boy thought. But aint it mighty late in the day for cooking? "Now get me a boiler of cold," Bart told the Negroes, beginning to undress. He dont want to get his clothes spattered, Billy Boy thought.

When the cold water was poured, Bart tested it with his hand. "Ah," he said, standing naked beside the tub. The Negroes' faces were dark blank; they had passed wondering; now there was only their boundless biding patience with whitefolks' vagaries. It must be something mighty delicate if thats all the hot he wants it, Billy Boy thought, though there was steam still coming off the water. Then he thought in sudden wild amazement: Why, himself! He's going to cook himself! as Bart stepped into the tub, water rising about his chest and armpits. "Ah," he said. Billy Boy hurried forward. "Thats it, Billy," Bart said, pointing toward a small oblong package wrapped in colored paper. "Hand me the soap." Then as Bart wallowed in the water and covered himself with lather, Billy Boy thought: Ah, then this is it. This is what they meant when they said bathing. Ah.

THUS BART began to approach that grand life which he conceived of as composed not so much of the large actions and possessions but rather of the small, undiscussed and apparently birth-acquired habits and gestures, such as bathing, deferential inclination of the head in polite conversation, a manner of holding the arms and shoulders so as to display to best effect the cut and hang of a fifty-dollar jacket. He watched, and as he watched he began to acquire; from this man he took one thing, from that another. The result was a stodginess, an aloof mien which began to resemble misanthropy, except that he was saved by one of the strongest tendencies in his make-up, albeit this was the one he battled hardest against, believing it to be part of a grosser heritage—sheer camaraderie.

Wrapped (he believed annealed) in his practiced garment of restraint, which he wore as a corporal wears new rank, he would find his hand going up to the shoulder of the man beside him, or he would be pushing his hat off his forehead and standing with his feet too far apart, leaning back a little on his heels and talking a little too loud over his exposed vest. The minute he found himself thus, coat spread open, belly shoved forward, he would know that he had dropped what he believed was his air of gentility, and he would snap shut like a turtle jerking back into its carapace. Later he learned to slide back into the other at such times like a good dancer recovering from a misstep.

Men liked him, and he knew this and was proud of it. But he was wrong in his pride. He thought they liked him because of the garment, while actually it was because of the glimpses of what the garment was meant to cover; they thought that individually they had discovered these qualities beneath the surface. From this Bart was to discover, later, that men are no different as classes, storekeeper or planter, but only as individuals. That, however, was late in the downhill years. Now he was young in it, just beginning to watch them, the genteel, the idle inhibited, just beginning to see what he was to strive to become.

Billy Boy resented none of the transformation; his worship went beyond the present, was projected to include not only what was, not only what was to be, but even what was wished to be. Besides, it was too subtly slow to be observed by him. When Bart acquired a mannerism, Billy Boy, when he saw it at all, thought it must have been there all along and that by living with Bart he had developed to the point of being able to remark it. Bart was to him the inexhaustible source whence all good things proceeded; the proud tall figure of a man merely became prouder and taller.

As Billy Boy understood them, proud meant dignified and tall meant handsome. In point of fact, tall was no word for Bart: he was barely of average height, a hair under five feet nine. Proud, however, was a word that would fit. Pride had led him to empty

19

his purse for the sake of furnishing the one room in style. Pride had made him buy the bay stallion. Pride also had prompted the beard. In beginning to grow it he was emulating another remembered custom: in the Black Prairie region where he had been born and raised, a hundred and fifty miles across the state, the patriarch was always bearded. This meant that already, when Bart had no more than begun his rise, he saw himself as the founder of a family, one among those others on the lake. The beard was a failure, though: he shaved it before it was two weeks old. By that time he was moving among the planters.

It began casually, among the men—Allard, Sadlier, Cowan, Ertle, Lane, Dubose, McClain, Kent, Tarfeller, Durfee—and it began, of course, with hunting. There was little else to do through the winter months after selling the cotton and breaking the land. This was a bleak unlovely country from late November through February. Cotton stalks stood rotting in the rain, water in long silver threads filling the bottom-rows, and fog blew in off Lake Jordan. The only motion was from the train that charged through twice a day, shouldering a bank of dirty smoke. But Christmas, which came spang in the middle of all this dreariness, was the exception: Christmas was the gayest time of the year, a season all to itself. All of Christmas Week was exciting, a period set aside for visiting and eating and drinking.

Christmas Day, 1888, Bart moved into the presence of the lake families as one of them. He had known the men from hunting with them; passing their houses on the stallion, he had raised his hat to the ladies on the porches. But it was on this day that he first became one of themselves.

Three men, Clyde Allard, Murphy Lane, and Peter Durfee, came by Solitaire in the middle of the morning. They turned into the driveway in a buggy and pulled up at the steps, sitting with cigars in their teeth and watching the door as Bart came out to welcome them. A fine drizzle of rain was falling. As they got out to enter the house, Durfee reached under the seat for the demijohn. He was a spare, talkative man.

"Leave your bottle, gentlemen," Bart said. He stood aside as they entered. They stood in the gloomy unfurnished front parlor while the Negro, more fieldhand than servant, brought whiskey and water. "Mr Allard, Mr Lane, Mr Durfee: a merry Christmas," Bart said, and they drank.

"The host," Durfee said, and they drank.

There was a pause after the glasses were filled for the third time. Then Lane proposed a toast: "To the coming year, to things that come out of the ground: to cotton and corn and alfalfa, after a merry Christmas." They drank. He was a large man, still young, with a full shovel beard that grew up onto his cheekbones and long brown hair that rained dandruff onto his shoulders whenever he wagged his head. He had served a term in the legislature.

Bart had been spending Christmas morning in his room; when he saw the buggy turn in, he had Billy Boy lay a fire in the parlor. Now they stood looking into the grate, the three visitors ebullient from rapid drinking, their faces flushed in the firelight. "It just comes once a year," Durfee said. "We ought to be able to do it right if it's just a once-a-year affair." Bart stood back from the fire, holding his empty glass. Morning light, pearly because of the rain, streamed through the uncurtained windows.

Allard said, "Once around and lets get on."

"Doll Baby," Bart said.

The houseboy filled the glasses. The bottle was almost empty now; there was barely enough for another round. Allard said, "We'll drink another to Christmas. It just comes once a year." They drank, then leaned forward together, hunching their shoulders and shuddering a bit. They turned toward the door, all three at once, as if by signal.

"Youd better get a heavy coat," Durfee said. "No telling what this crazy weather will do."

"Well. . . ."

"Come on, man," Allard said. "How do you think I took up with this pair? Whats more, weve got a couple others to get before we reach the eggnog."

"Christmas: it's beautiful," Durfee said. He sighed.

"Beautiful once a year," Allard said, sighing too. "You should have done something about that, Murphy, when you were legislating. That would make a good plank in anybody's platform: two, three, maybe four Christmases a year."

"Dont bring up my youth," Lane said laughing.

When they reached the Allard house there were six of them and it was noon. The rain had stopped; the sun came through, shining on the puddles; the air was balmy. It was like October, scented with wood smoke, except for the mind saying Christmas. Negroes in shirt-sleeves sat on their porches, waiting for dinner and talking with that downhill idleness fieldhands acquire during the off months. After the meal they came back onto the porches and sat until they began to shiver. The wind blew lightly; soon it turned quite cold. They went indoors and ate again and danced and finally slept. Toward morning, in the chill gray hour before sunup, snow began falling with a tiny sibilant tinkle against the windowpanes, large flakes that melted as soon as they struck the ground, though on roofs and posts and rails they collected some. The wind had died.

By the time Bart woke up, it was collecting on the dried grass, and as he lay watching it through the bedside window it collected more, building up until a thin white crust had been sifted over yard and barn lot. Only the horse trough, just beneath the window, received the downsift with impervious stasis; in it the water lay like perfectly joined black marble. The precipitation struck its surface without sound or effect, each flake dropping silently to death. Bart watched it. As he lay watching he thought about what now was yesterday, and he believed he knew now what he wanted. He wanted to duplicate. He remembered that Christmas ("Youre not eating, Mr Bart." "To a once-a-year merry Christmas." "That off horse, I got him in Alabama." "Murphy will take you home, Mr Bart. Are the horses hitched?" "Thank you, maam, if the . . ." "To a once-a-year merry . . .") and as the scraps of talk, the kindnesses, blew back in memory like gusts, he knew perfectly what it was he wanted to duplicate.

It took him another year and a half. Then, having made three cotton crops and lifted himself within sight of being clear of debt and doubt (there were more furnishings in the house by then; he had made another two trips up to Memphis) he married.

HER NAME was Florence Jameson; she was eighteen when Bart met her. The day after her nineteenth birthday and the day before his thirtieth, May 1890, they were married at her mother's rented house in Bristol with her three brothers looking on. Mrs Jameson stood stiff and straight at the wedding, like a general at a surrender, while Bart and the girl stood together, Bart watching her out of the tails of his eyes, hearing the minister drone: "Dearly beloved: charge you both now confess it, comfort her honor *I will*, keep thee only shall live *I will*, us do my troth, the Holy Ghost abide in thy peace and the power glory peace together, put asunder have life everlasting: amen." There was a short, deep silence before the outburst of sighs.

The mother and brothers were about the bride, leaving Bart to one side looking older and alone. He thought: Bride, I have a bride; but the word meant nothing, brought no image until he changed it and thought: Wife, I have a wife; and the image rose perfect, actual—of a woman like those others he had seen in homes on the lake, each with a ring of keys at her belt and efficiency at hand like a mule skinner's whip. But when he said bride and even wife, he was translating: what he meant was chatelaine.

They were still gathered in the parlor—a small square room crowded with furniture she had salvaged from Solitaire after the General died and she came to Bristol—when Mrs Jameson finally collapsed and was carried back to her bedroom by two of her sons. She was a stern woman, fifty-eight years old and worn. Into this later life she had been dropped like a fish moved from its accustomed pond into another containing a quite different liquid. In fact, however, she was returning to the life she had left on her wedding day, when she was nineteen too, one of six daughters of a Bristol lawyer. There had been a great deal of surprise and even some outrage when she married Clive Jameson, considering all he had had to choose among, but this had died and disappeared, the more quickly since she never saw her family after the wedding except to nod from her carriage as they waved from porch or boardwalk. After her return from the grand-tour honeymoon, having moved into the completed Solitaire, she never saw them at all.

She bore three sons in rapid succession. They were growing boys when the war came. She saw her husband between campaigns; at other times she heard of him only as everyone was doing, as the South and the North were hearing of him, as the French peasants heard of Bayard or the Hebrews the Angel of Death. When he did come home — and he returned infrequently, apparently to gather corn; he would drop back two hundred miles with his brigade to harvest his crops—it was like eating and breathing and couching with an avatar or a thunderbolt. At table he wore an aura of battle-fury and shell-glare, as bakers at home disseminate an atmosphere of flour and baking bread.

Then the war was over and she returned to Solitaire with her three sons from the resort where she had spent the last two years while marauders tore up the plantation. The sons were a trial by then; they had been spoiled by guests and visitors at the resort: "What, these the gallant Jameson's heirs? Stand up, boys, let us look at you!" Reconstruction (so-called) was under way; she watched adversity grow while the General moved toward the breakdown that finally killed him. In 1871, midway in the struggle, it was with a kind of furious despair that, nearing forty and apparently fitted for marching toward death as vehicles later were streamlined, she discovered that she was three months with child.

To her husband it was less, or nothing. They were sitting at table when she told him, the napkins lying rumpled where the boys had tossed them, trooping out. "I am going to have a baby, Mr Jameson." There was silence, so she said it again: "A baby, General."

"So?" He was looking down at the tablecloth.

"Yes. In May, I believe." She watched him while she spoke, but there was no change in his face. His knees were apart and his hands dangled outside the chair arms. He had begun to get fat on peace and despair; his face, above an old man's paunch let sag by forgotten muscles, was quite different from the one the photographs in the history books would show. He was sitting there when she left the table to walk in the garden an hour before dark, and he was sitting there two hours later when she went upstairs to bed.

Florence was eleven when her father — ex-planter, ex-beau sabreur, ex-everything — died and was buried at Solitaire just before the mortgage men came for the last time and the widow and her two sons and daughter moved to Bristol to live in what she called rented poverty with the third son, the firstborn who had left the lake in something kin to disgrace, like the youth in the parable, to manage a sawmill (he called it the lumber business; that had a better sound) and who now took his burden, not only the widowed mother and maiden sister but also the two grown brothers, with the blind acceptance of an ox taking capstan work. One of the brothers became a poolroom tout, earning occasional fees at jury service; the other secured a deputy post and collected information on local crime history. Mrs Jameson rode it as a feather rides a gale, unresistingly invulnerable.

The daughter, remembering no grandeur, harking back to no era of lightsome beautiful suspension when there was a platoon of house slaves to fetch and carry, should have been better off. She might even have been expected to prosper, as others were doing in Bristol, but she did not. She bore her life as she had borne her childhood diseases, taking what came with neither resentment nor concern. A plain, unremarkable child, plain of face and drab in the economic chaos of her family, Florence lived from eleven to nineteen in the small river town, going to Sunday school and the convent. Her mother hardly noticed her; all the tenderness she knew came from the Negro cook, Aunt Ann, who had been a Jameson slave and had nursed her through childhood.

When Aunt Ann told of high old times before the war, Florence listened rapt but without comment. It was like the other stories she told, of fairies and piles of gold and an invisible person named Dobby Hicks, who was the guardian angel of Negro character: he would stand on your toes, Aunt Ann said, a short little black man not four feet tall, and shake his finger in your face when you were about to do wrong. Dobby Hicks was more real than Clive Jameson, whom Florence already remembered only vaguely, though he had been dead only a short time, as part of that other life back on the lake. She passed from childhood to girlhood to womanhood by such gradual stages that the changes were never remarked, and through them all she maintained her plainness.

When Mrs Jameson heard from one of her sons — it was the deputy; he already had acquired the hard sardonic expression all holders of Southern picayune offices seem to wear — that Bart had arranged with the mortgagee to take over Solitaire, the house her husband had built for her and she had furnished, she sat forward in her chair and pressed her chest against the table edge. "Bart?" she said. "Bart? I never heard of anyone by that name." They were at supper, the five of them cadaverous by gaslight.

"He's sheriff down in Issawamba," the deputy said.

"Ah yes," the second brother said. "Bart. He's a good man in office, I heard. And he should be: he beat that old crook Judge Wiltner to go in."

"Who is he?" the first brother asked, the one who ran the sawmill. "Where is he from and whats he done that sets him up for having a plantation handed him?"

"East Mississippi," the deputy said. "Nobody knows, really. It's no secret: it's just that nobody knows."

"Then how did he get Solitaire?"

"By having Union Prudential . . . I'm sorry, Mother. By having them think he is capable."

"Oh: capable," the first said, going back to his food.

26

"Yes. But it dont matter. Two years from now theyll be hunting for somebody else they think is capable. Or what they call capable, anyhow. Cotton is gone to pot here; we all know that." He rose, chewing, and the leather holster creaked with its pistol burden. Still chewing, he paused at the door and took his pale wide-brimmed hat from the rack, smoothed and creased it with his small hairy hands, then swallowed; "Good night, you all," and left.

Mrs Jameson was looking at her plate, the meager, store-bought food like scraps. "An outlander at Solitaire," the eldest son said. "Things have come a long way."

"Florence," Mrs Jameson said.

"Yessum?"

"When you go by Mr Cleary's tomorrow, tell him I said the bacon was very poor. Tell him I wont put up with this kind of thing much longer."

"Yes, Mother," Florence said.

"I tole um dat bacon want no count," Aunt Ann said, removing the dishes.

"How often must I remind you not to interrupt while we are dining?" Mrs Jameson said.

THE DEPUTY son met Bart soon, on official business between the two sheriffs shortly before Bart went out of office, but it was three years before the mother and daughter saw him. They met at church in January, 1890; he had come with friends from the lake. It was a year since the morning he lay in bed and watched the snow come down. They were introduced on the steps outside. Townspeople and visitors stood in groups, milling a little in the bright winter sunlight, waiting for the bell to sound. "Mrs Jameson, Florence: Mr Bart," someone said, and the bell began to clang, musical and serene. They entered the church.

Bart saw her far to the front. She knelt, her head on her hands on the pew ahead. The church had no kneeling stools; she looked quite small beside her mother, who knelt on a velvet cushion which the sexton kept and put in place for her every Sunday morning. *Dearly beloved brethren, the Scripture moveth us, in sundry places, to acknowledge and confess our manifold sins and wickednesses.* It was the name, Bart thought, seeing in the name of the dispossessed a vision of gone splendor. They were speaking around him, voices rising and murmuring: *We have erred, and strayed from thy ways like lost sheep. We have followed too much the devices and desires of our own hearts. We have offended against thy holy laws. We have left undone those things which we ought to have done; and we have done those things which we ought not to have done; and there is no health in us.* The murmur rose, became compact again above the heads of the kneelers, going rapidly at the close and jerking to a halt: *Amen.*

While the minister spoke aloud and the congregation repeated the Lord's Prayer, Bart looked at the prayer book in his hands. He had not followed the service, though when his neighbor leaned across and pointed to the place he nodded thanks. Book, he thought. A book. I never read a whole book in my life. Then the name flew back against his mind: Jameson. I am where he was and he is where I will be, someday. *Praise ye the Lord. The Lord's name be praised.* The sun beat golden on a stained glass window to his left. It showed an angel standing barefoot in a field of bright green grass, one hand on the head of a fuzzy, blue-eyed lamb. The lamb carried a cross, one of its forefeet hooked around the upright. The bright red of the angel's lips had been misplaced in processing and lay outside the border of the mouth, across the upper lip, like a scarlet kiss of shame. Studying the window, Bart was left sitting when everyone rose. He stood up hurriedly and almost dropped the prayer book.

Harden not your hearts as in the provocation, and as in the days of temptation in the wilderness; When your fathers tempted me, proved me, and saw my works. Forty years long was I grieved with this generation, and said, It is a people that do err in their hearts, for they have not known my ways; Unto whom I sware

28

my wrath, that they should not enter my rest. There followed a long period during which Bart heard nothing, and then as he lurched into consciousness he was aware of rising with the rest. After another hiatus — but very short, for now he was fighting the sleep — he heard them rapidly murmuring the Creed.

Florence, far to the front, moved mechanically through the service, muttering the responses. Mrs Jameson, kneeling on her cushion, prayed fervently, puckering her lips; she did not need the prayer book. *The grace of our Lord Jesus Christ, and the love of God, and the fellowship of the Holy Ghost, be with us all evermore. Amen.* There were sighs as everyone rose and stood watching the procession file past, bowing their heads at the passage of the Cross. Then they smiled and looked about, as if they had just realized that there were others in the building. When the singing died they moved down the aisles, blinking like people emerging from long confinement in a cave. The procession halted on the porch, vestry and rector in brilliant sunshine, the boys looking anxious to leave, uncomfortable in their surplices. Mr Clinkscales, the minister, greeted the members of the congregation as they came past; sunlight was in his hair and glinted on the fillings in his teeth as he smiled and nodded above the shaking hands.

Stepping into the Durfee carriage, Bart looked over his shoulder and saw Mrs Jameson and her daughter coming out; they spoke little to those around them, he noticed. Lake families would drive the thirty miles back to their homes that same day: they had been doing this one Sunday a month for the past five years, ever since the church near Ithaca burned. Bart was quieter than usual during the return trip. When he got down at Solitaire under a high moon (they had stopped halfway for a basket lunch) he thanked the Durfees and hardly heard their goodbyes. He went to his room, undressed, and lay in bed watching the moon. Already he was fooling himself about the desire he felt; he did not speak the name again (Jameson, the original golden Solitaire name); he just thought: What I want is *romance.*

It was no whirlwind courtship but it was short. She was almost nineteen; he was almost thirty. He saw her twice before he spoke of marriage, though his intention had been clear from the first day he went up the steps and knocked. "Youll have to speak to Mother," Florence said.

"If you will call tomorow I'll give you my answer," Mrs Jameson told him. "I must speak to my sons." And when he came back next morning (he had spent the night in town, at the hotel) Mrs Jameson rose from her chair, clasping her hands at her bosom—Like a squirrel, Bart thought—and nodding her head in time with the words, said solemnly: "You have my daughter's hand, Sir."

That was in early April: he was planting. So that evening he kissed Florence clumsily and rode the stallion through the night back to the lake. He arrived well before dawn, in time to get the hands into the field. The wedding was in middle May; they rode the train to New Orleans, stayed two days (he had planned a week) and returned to Solitaire.

CHAPTER TWO

SOLITAIRE

ITHACA, ON the east shore of Lake Jordan, was settled in the early 1820's by migrants who followed Isaac Jameson, father of the General and founder of Solitaire. He came up from Natchez in the spring of 1818, a tall thin man no longer young—he had been born on the Trace in '76 while his father, a Carolina merchant, was moving westward to escape the Revolution on the seaboard, so he was past forty: well into middle age, as it was reckoned then —who rode a claybank mare, breaking trail for the Conestoga loaded with the ten Negroes he had taken as his birthright when he told his father and brothers goodbye for good. "If you want to play prodigal, it's all right with me," his father had said. "But mind you: when youre swilling with swine and chomping at the husks, dont cut your eyes around in my direction. There wont be any lamp in the window for you, or fatted calf either. This is all."

They were glad to see him go, for he had been a problem to them and at times a reproach. He had left home early and his name had turned up in varied connections: with the Burr conspiracy and with Jean Lafitte and Dominique You, with the Mississippi Militia fighting Creeks at Burnt Corn and with Andrew Jackson fighting British regulars at New Orleans. He came home from New Orleans with a leg wound, and as soon as it healed he struck out again, into the northern wilderness with two trappers. Two years later he was back for the last time, in buckskins and moccasins, his hair shoulder length. Next day he was gone for good, having claimed as legacy ten Negroes in a wagon and four

31

thousand dollars in gold, taking this now instead of his share in the Jameson estate when the old man should die. The brothers were willing. The father considered it a downright bargain: he would have sacrificed twice that for Isaac's guarantee to stay away from Natchez with his escapades and his damage to the name.

So he rode north into the wilderness he had just come out of, breaking trail on the claybank mare. For eight days, while the Negroes clutched at seats and stanchions in a din of creaking wood and clattering pots and pans, the Conestoga lurched through thickets of scrub oak and willow, over fallen trunks and rotted stumps: it had a pitching roll, like a ship in a heavy swell, which actually did cause the Negroes to be seasick three hundred miles from the sea. On the eighth day they struck the south end of a lake, veered right, then left, and continued along its eastern shore. An hour later Isaac drew rein, and when the wagon came abreast he signaled for the driver to stop. A wind had risen, ruffling the lake; through the screen of cypresses the waves were bright like little hatchets in the hot June sunlight. "All right," Isaac said. "You can get the gear unloaded. We are home."

Thus he began the fulfillment of a dream that had come to him the previous month. It was May then, the oaks tasseling. He and the two trappers had reached the lake at the close of day. While the sun sank big and red across the water, they made camp on a grassy strip between the lake and the forest. Isaac lay rolled in his blanket, and all that night, surrounded by lake country beauty—overhead the far spangled reaches of sky, eastward the forest murmurs, the whispering leaves and groaning limbs, the hoarse night-noises of animals, and westward, close at hand, the slow lapping of water—he dreamed.

He dreamed of an army of blacks marching upon the jungle, not halting to chop, but walking steadily forward, swinging axes against the retreating green wall. Behind them, level fields lay stumpless and serene in watery sunlight, motionless until in the distance clanking trace-chains and clacking singletrees announced the coming of the plowmen. Lop-eared mules drew plows across the green; the long brown rows of earth unrolled like threads off spools. What had been jungle became cultivated fields, and now the fields began to be striped with pale green lines of plants, burdened with squares, then purple- and white-dotted, then red with bloom, then shimmering white. In a long irregular line—they resembled skirmishers, and sacks trailed from their shoulders like windless flags—the pickers passed over the fields, leaving them brown and desolate in the rain; the stalks dissolved, went down into bottomless mud. Then in the dream there was quiet autumnal death until spring returned and the plowmen, and the dream began again. This was repeated three times, with a mystical clarity.

"Wake up. Wake up, Ike."

"Dont," he said, drawing the blanket over his face.

"Wake up. It's time to roll." In the faint dawn light the lake and forest had the same unreal clearness as in the dream. He was not even sure he was awake until one of the trappers nudged him in the ribs and spoke again: "Ike! You want to sleep your life away?"

For a while he did not answer. He lay half wrapped in the blanket, looking at the lake, the forest. Then he sat up. "You two go on," he said. "This is where I stop."

He stayed three days, alone. A mile back from the lake he found a deserted Choctaw village. The Indians had burned their shacks. There was nothing left but a few shards of pottery in the ashes; grass was reclaiming the paths their feet had worn. During the past month, ever since the treaty of Doaks Stand—Mississippi had entered the Union in December—he had seen them, or others like them, traveling single-file, the braves in filthy blankets carrying nothing, the squaws with children and household utensils strapped to their backs, going north to land not yet ceded by the Chiefs. Isaac rode south to Natchez. Within three weeks of the night he dreamed his dream by the lake he was back again, with the Negroes and mules, clearing ground and bounding his claim.

That was the beginning. During the ten years that followed, he was joined by others drawn from south and east to new land available at ninety cents an acre. Near the south end of the lake one of the migrants set up a general store, which soon was flanked by a blacksmith shop and a tavern called the Ithaca Inn by its owner, a man who claimed to have been professor of Greek at an Eastern university but who never mentioned the circumstances that had prompted his change of career. He did not stay long. Soon no one remembered him, though the village already had adopted the name of his tavern. When Jordan County was formed, in 1827, Ithaca was the leading settlement in the southern district, but Bristol, thirty miles upriver, had outgrown the earlier hamlet and was made the county seat.

Isaac, though he had named his plantation Solitaire to express his bachelor intentions, got married the year before the county was formed. His bride was the daughter of the man who had bought the Ithaca Inn from the wayward professor. Isaac saw her tending bar one warm spring evening when he rode down for a drink: he particularly admired her arms, which were bared to the elbows, and her thick yellow hair. Next day he came back to the tavern and spoke for her. "I'm willing if Effy is," the tavern keeper told him. Along with the plump arms and the tawny hair, she brought into Isaac's house a bustling, cheerful efficiency. That was the union which produced Clive Jameson, the General, who married the daughter of a Bristol lawyer, and that in turn was the union which produced Florence Jameson, whom Hugh Bart married.

When the bride and groom returned to Solitaire after the New Orleans honeymoon, Bart could already see his way toward clear ownership of the five square miles of Delta earth, the equipment to farm it, and bank credit large enough to allow for a disastrous year. Farming was something more than rising before dawn every morning, something more than being able to get a maximum of work out of fieldhands. Now it meant balancing money against labor and risk; it meant sitting at his desk to make decisions. He would sit there, planning and arranging purchases and receiving callers who, alternately voluble and hesitant, discussed the market and uttered sums with reverent voices signifying their worship. As he sat there, the four walls closing in like the walls of a torture chamber, restlessness and resentment would fill him to the bursting point, and he would rise, shouting for Billy Boy to saddle the stallion. He would stomp into his boots and jerk on his hunting coat, take his gun underarm, whistle the dogs, and ride fast across the fields to the creek a mile back of the house. Here he would hunt through dinner-time and half the afternoon, getting pleasure out of the hard recoil of the gun, the acrid smell of powder blown back across his face, the feathery explosion of birds in midair, the sound of brush breaking as the dogs went bounding for quail.

Mrs Bart came into her new life, into the house her mother had managed before her, with the ease her husband expected. From helping Mrs Jameson and Aunt Ann keep a small urban house where no more supplies were needed than for the coming meal, since the store was not two blocks away and any loitering Negro could be commandeered to go there and fetch whatever was wanted, she passed to managing alone a forty-room mansion on the lake. It was one of a dozen more or less like it, located at one- and two-mile intervals down the eastern shore, each a world apart, castle-size and baronial, kept by women who made it their one concern.

Taken as they had just emerged from girlhood (the average bride was eighteen) they called their husbands Mister all their lives. They lived in a lambency of inexperience but were able in times of crisis, war or sickness or death, to choose and decide for the good of the family by drawing upon some antediluvian feminine reserve, like the mother spider or spawning salmon which strives constantly and apparently with all its strength, yet when faced by an unexpected condition, draws upon a hidden well of undefeat to produce the action which surmounts the obstacle and allows continuance of the bland unruffled striving. They bowed their heads to their husbands' slightest whim—allowing the male, brute blunt instrument for providing, to be the intelligence in all decisions which, apparently world-shaking, were of small import in fact—but asserted themselves and handed down irrevocable decisions in matters which were basic and therefore vital. They did this without alarming their husbands or even putting them on the defensive, for the decision was always given in such a manner, spoken in the male-mate language, that it appeared to the husbands as echoes of their own thought, like a stone that had been polished or dipped in gold. They wore clothes which gave inch for inch as much covering as medieval armor and yet were able, laced and stayed as they were, not only to be willowy and tender but also to bear large numbers of children and to raise those who lived (many were stillborn; many died in infancy: every plantation burying ground had its cluster of small anonymous headboards) in the strict formula whereby life was simple because conflicting thought did not cloud it and no battle raged between conception and execution.

Mrs Bart came into the house where she was born and raised, and her return was like the recapture of a perfect childhood. She was competent, exact, open, kind. Her outward calm was never disturbed. She knew her servants well and, though firm, she would say "Do this, please" or "Will you do this, please" (with no question in her voice, though the words supplied the courtesy) and they were content and worked hard for her. Bart watched with amazement her transformation from frightened bride-girl into keeper of a mansion the size of a courthouse, where servants were regimented with the military discipline necessary because of the informality of the plans of the master; there might be two or twenty at dinner.

For now his camaraderie had blossomed. It was as if the marriage license, printed certificate of legality like a thousand others in the region, was the seal set on his invasion of the planter kingdom. Now in truth he could afford the beaming face above the exposed vest, the rocking back on wide-set heels, because now he displayed them among friends, people more or less like himself, grouped about the tideless cypress-screened shores of Lake Jordan with a singleness of purpose like priests whose cult was cotton.

ONE OF the happiest days of Bart's life, a dusty hot day in August, 1890, came very near being his last. He was lying in bed, a .44 caliber bullet somewhere in his midriff, when Mrs Bart told him she was going to have a child. Three men, two at the shoulders and one at the feet, had brought him into the house. The doctor, a small nervous man whose work was more with mules than men—he had garnered his medical knowledge from a handful of pamphlets on animal husbandry and from a working intimacy with the mules' interiors, red gut and white bone—followed them up the stairs, carrying his satchel. He had two satchels: this was the one he called Human. It held a scalpel, a box of calomel, a roll of gauze, and a whiskey-pint of castor oil.

The frightened doctor, probing, never found the bullet. They were downstairs in the office at the time. Bart lay on the couch, hissing and sputtering, his shirt tucked up around his chest, his trousers jerked down around his thighs. "All right, all right," the doctor murmured, probing. "Just a minute. . . . Just a minute, now. . . ." The probing continued without conviction; Bart could feel the instrument tremble in the doctor's hand.

"Let me up from here," he said at last. He rolled sideways so that the doctor had to remove the probe. "If he's killed me, I'd sooner go without you googing in me scared to death. Fix my clothes."

"Let me paint it first, Mr Bart."

"All right: paint it. Paint it."

It was swabbed with iodine out of the medicine chest. "There," the doctor said, standing back to admire his work as if he had painted a picture.

"All right. Fix my clothes." The doctor bandaged the wound. "Fix my clothes." The bandaging done, the doctor pulled Bart's shirt down and hitched up his trousers. Both were bloody. "Fine," Bart said. "As you go out, doctor, please tell Billy to step in here."

Billy Boy had been standing just outside the door. "Sho," he said, stepping into the room.

"Get me a clean shirt, Billy."

"Yes sir," Billy Boy said. "But you best come on upstairs whilst these gentlemen here to tote you."

37

Bart seemed to consider this. Then he turned to two of the men, Murphy Lane and John Cowan. "Youll be kind to do that. And you too," he said to the third man, a nondescript in denim, coatless, who had stood in the street through all the shooting and when it was over had come forward to where Bart lay pitched face down, bloody, with the pistol beneath him. He was a stranger, passing through Ithaca.

"Yair," he said quietly. "Anything you say. That was some good shooting."

Bart looked at him, the gregarious face of the American crowd which gathers for any event. For a moment he seemed to consider this, perhaps wondering whether to thank the man for the compliment. Then he said, "All right, Billy. Gentlemen, lets go up."

"I dont know if you ought to be moved, Mr Bart," the doctor said uneasily.

"It's all right, doctor," Bart said. "If you dont know, I guess we can take the chance."

So the three men gathered around him as before, two at the head and one at the feet, lifted him, carried him up the staircase and into his room, and laid him on the bed. "Thank you. Thank you, doctor." As they were leaving, Bart told Billy Boy: "Get me some paper and ink and a pen." He's going to write his will, John Cowan thought.

When Billy Boy brought the things, Bart turned sideways with a quick intake of breath, hissing, and wrote the letter.

August 13, 1890 Solitaire Plantation

> *Madam—*
>
> *My Regret exceeds all bounds for this evenings Tragedy. Mr. Tarfeller was a gentleman of Honor & Integrety, & my Friend. We never knew a Nobler man. If another could be laid in his place it would be well but Providence decreed other wise. If in any occasion, I can be of Service, be so kind Madam, to inform*
>
>

Yr Humble & Obt Servant

>
> *Mrstress Cass Tarfeller   Hugh Bart*
> *Briartree Plantation.*

38

"Deliver that," he told Billy Boy. Then, hissing again, he rolled onto his back and went to sleep.

Cassendale Tarfeller was the last male of a line that included some of the original settlers of the Lake Jordan country. Recognizing his incompetence, since neither the concentration nor the labor required by farming was possible for a person with his temperament, he had little to do with the work which absorbed other men who shared his heritage. He hired two managers to tend his plantation. He neither rode horseback to the hunting forays nor joined in the poker marathons; apparently he had no interest in any particular thing. In fine weather he would sit on his porch to watch the sun go down, and in the hour of twilight, while lightning bugs wheeled and glimmered down the depth of lawn and honeysuckle pervaded the dusk with its lush oversweet surge, he would fall asleep, toddy in hand, until his wife sent one of the servants to waken him for supper. Poor, he might have lapsed into the role of village ne'er-do-well, but rich as he was—his clothes neat and carefully fitted as only the New Orleans tailors knew how to make them, his manners perfect because they achieved at the outset the ultimate aim of good behavior by never making him obtrusive—he was a part of the society formed by lake planters, and his rare absences were felt at any gathering except those convened for sport or business.

Through his parents' action he had married young. His wife was four years older than he, and she made as good a nurse and companion as his mother had done. To no one's amazement, for she was a competent, determined woman, but obviously (it was said) in moments of character reversal on his part, she conceived and bore him two children, both daughters. He was forty now, though his appearance told this no more than would that of the ne'er-do-well his money kept him from being. The older daughter had married eight months before and moved north with her husband, a young Carolina lawyer who won her while visiting a classmate on the lake. The younger daughter, whose name was Bertha, received all Tarfeller's affection. She was eighteen, a romantic, violent girl.

39

No one came to Tarfeller with the story that was being told and retold over dry goods counters and backyard fences in Ithaca. It came in an unsigned letter addressed to his wife. The closing words were: *If you doubt this, ask your daughter. Ask her, Who is Downs Macready?*

Mrs Tarfeller read it, then sent for Bertha, a headstrong girl left lonely in the big house after the marriage and departure of her sister, idolized by a father who exuded affection in a manner that made her actually ill; she would tremble with something kin to nausea when he put his hand on her head, as he often did, and spoke to her in a droning voice, calling her darling every other word. He's not a man, she would tell herself. "He's not anything," she would say aloud, alone in the bedroom she and her sister had shared through girlhood.

She had begun making phrases descriptive of what she called her plight. Once when she saw her grandfather's pistol hanging in its holster in the library (this was Tarfeller's father, who had commanded a horse company in the Jameson brigade; the pistol had not been removed from the hook where he had hung it shortly before his death twelve years ago) she thought: Deliverance hangs in the scabbard. Suicide took up much of her thought, until she met Macready. So perhaps he played a dual role, as savior and seducer. He had played others more contradictory.

But why he had come to Ithaca, why he had come to Mississippi at all, remained a mystery even to the men with whom he sat night after night, wearing broadcloth and linen in contrast to their denim and serge. At the poker table in the rear of the Palace Saloon his face was pale and handsome among the weathered unshaven faces of the small farmers and tradesmen hunched about the circle. Apparently he took no pleasure in the game, though he generally won and it was obviously his means of livelihood. He was not hostile or even uncivil. He just sat there, white-faced and aloof, not bothering to watch his opponents, not even looking at his cards until it was his turn to bet.

He had arrived on a Sunday, the countryside serene with that dynamic idleness of rural sabbaths, so intense that even cotton and corn, the growing things, seemed to have reached a standstill. Soon people began to observe him, riding a tall quarter-bred horse in town and on lonely country roads, still in broadcloth and not even wearing boots. None of them spoke to him and he spoke to none of them. There was nothing reciprocal about it: these were just two facts which, though they existed side by side, as in an encyclopedia, bore no relation to each other. He sat his horse with the same indolence that characterized his poker, and when he passed surreys and carriages filled with local men and their wives, even though in many cases he had spent ten hours the previous day in the rear of the Palace with some of the men, his eyes were like green china, looking neither right nor left.

While riding one of these country roads, wearing the garments of a modern musketeer and wearing them with a flared and somehow arrogant ease no gentleman ever accomplished, he met Bertha Tarfeller. What occurred then and subsequently between them no one really knew because no one saw, but the affair was discussed and enlarged upon by the people of Ithaca. Versions varied but they all agreed that it must have been the girl who, seeing Macready as a sort of cloak-and-sword principal, made the overture. His face told her there would be no repulse when she rode forward and spoke.

Now it had reached the anonymous warning stage. Mrs Tarfeller folded the letter and put it into her reticule. She told her maid, "Linda, tell Miss Birdy I said to step here." She waited until her daughter came to the door. "Come in, Bertha." The girl entered and sat on the bed. "How often must I tell you not to sit on a bed?" She made a resigned gesture. "But never mind. I called you in to ask you a question: a straightforward question I have been told, that is in*struct*ed, to ask you. And mind you I want a straightforward answer."

Bertha had risen from the bed and now she stood beside it, her face sullen. She leaned against the bedpost, her hands behind her, remembering other similar scenes when she was a child and had done something wrong. "Who is Downs Macready?" she heard her mother ask. It was meant to be said in an easy, offhand tone, but Mrs Tarfeller's voice jumped during the pronunciation of the surname, so that, instead of Macrady, it came out Macreedy.

Bertha's face did not change. The sullen expression was unaltered as she replied, "He's a man, a man I know." Man! the mother thought; she called him Man! Then Bertha's expression did change. She swung away from the bedpost, arching her back. "He's a real man. He's the one I'm going to marry. I love him."

"Then why havent you asked him here for us to meet?"

"You know why!" Bertha cried. She tossed her hair. "You know well enough why."

"Here," Mrs Tarfeller said. "Dont use that tone with me, girl. Dont you dare."

Bertha was quiet then, her face resuming its morose, pouting expression. "You hate me," she said. "Youd hate anyone I thought would make me happy. I never go anywhere: I never do anything. I hate you all and I'm going away. I'm going away with Downs." She ran from the room, her mother calling after her:

"Bertha! You, Bertha!"

Ten minutes later, her husband sitting where she had sat, herself standing where her daughter had stood, Mrs Tarfeller said, "Cassendale. . . ."

When he heard his name unabbreviated (his wife was the only one who used it so, and she did so rarely; he was always called Cass) Tarfeller realized that something serious was about to be communicated. His reflexes, however, were slower than his mind. He was still smiling as he said, "Lindy said you wanted to see me." He had formed the sentence as he came upstairs.

"Yes." She smoothed her dress, watching the cloth ripple beneath her fingers. Then she started anew: "Cassendale, there is a thing you must do. I cannot tell you how to do it, because it is man's work. But I can tell you it must be done, and quickly."

He was still smiling and nodding agreement with whatever she was about to say, but now there was a puzzled look around his eyes. "Why, yes, dear," he said. "You know I'll do it."

"Well—you have to give orders to a man. You have to challenge him, maybe: call him out."

"Ah." He did not say this to signify that he understood; he said it as a sound to show that he was listening. Then, after a short and fruitless period of thinking, he said, "What am I going to call him out for?" Then came the question he should have asked at the outset: "And who am I going to do this to?" He said this last hurriedly and in a surprised tone, for it occurred to him suddenly.

"Downs Macready," Mrs Tarfeller said. "He plays cards at that saloon in Ithaca. He's a gambler and a loose man, and he has defiled your daughter."

"Bertha? Defiled her?"

"Yes. So you must make him go away. Or kill him."

"Kill him? About Bertha?"

"Yes."

"Goodness," Tarfeller said, and still it was not an exclamation of comprehension; still it was a sound made to show that he was listening.

IT WAS not until he sat down to write the letter, seeing the sheet of notepaper pale against the rosewood secretary, that Tarfeller began to realize the role his fatherhood required of him. In this he was like a boy walking into his first fist fight or a young man on the way to his first assignation, making the initial movement to destroy a negative state. With no aid to be sought or even advice, he was alone for the first time in his life.

He wrote the challenge in a sprawling schoolboy hand, and though he addressed it as his wife had told him, the note—blunt and even brutal communication such as he had never encountered, much less issued—was his own.

Briartree.
Aug 12

D. McRady
Palace Saloon
You will leave town with 24 hrs or anser to me—I will

43

shoot you on site if I see you Tuesday when I come down town & I mean it.

Cassendale Tarfeller.

He sealed it carefully and gave it to his coachman to take to Ithaca. He imagined it being delivered, the Negro removing his hat and entering the saloon, approaching the bar and asking that Macready be pointed out, then handing the envelope to the gambler with studied courtesy ("Mr Tarfeller's pleasure, Sir") and then bowing, retiring.

Probably this last was gleaned from something he remembered being read to him in childhood, the elder Dumas or Walter Scott; Tarfeller was given to such imaginings, such dreams of things as they never were. At any rate it did not come off that way. For when the coachman returned and Tarfeller asked "What did he say?" the coachman replied:

"I aint seen him, Mr Cass. You aint ax for no answer, so I left it with the tender."

"The bartender?"

"Yassir."

"At the Palace?"

"Yassir: big heavy-set man with shiny hair."

"Oh," Tarfeller said, disappointed. "All right." The coachman left and Tarfeller sat alone in the library lined with unread books.

Maybe he wont get it, he thought. Maybe when I go to town tomorrow he wont even know why Ive come. He realized that somehow his every action, apparently in direct ratio to the gravity intended, took on a ludicrousness which made him appear not only simple but even buffoonish. And how will I know him? (I'll know him, all right.) Maybe he wont even know me when I come. What do I do? Just walk down the street? . . . Thats it: just walk down the street.

At four oclock the following afternoon Tarfeller came out of the house with a parcel under his arm. As he stepped into the carriage he wondered, Does a man ride horse-drawn to shooting? But he was a poor horseman, and besides, he wanted an easy period, without discomfort, in which to think. To his surprise he hardly thought at all. The landscape sweltered in August heat, distorted by a slight shimmer; he began to feel a throbbing behind his eyes. Halfway to town, a brown thrasher watched him from a rail beside the road, the steady yellow bead of the bird's eye following, the long bill turning in profile until the carriage came abreast: whereupon it sprang away from the rail with a single quick motion, its wings and narrow tail the color of dusty cinnamon, and was gone.

On the outskirts of Ithaca he began to notice the life around him, horses and mules drowsing at hitching posts, heads down near their knees, and people moving about their everyday purposes, unaware of the challenge. It was neap tide of the Delta summer, the biding somnolent heat and dust producing a taste in the mouth like brass. At the first store-front he halted the carriage, got out, and stood on the boardwalk with the parcel under his arm. "Wait here," he told the coachman, and stepped inside the store to unwrap the parcel. It was his father's cavalry pistol, an ungainly weapon, long and heavy, still in the holster which his daughter had called a scabbard and where she had told herself deliverance hung.

When he came back onto the boardwalk he wore the pistol strapped low about his hips beneath the skirts of his coat. The holster belt was drawn to the final notch but it was so big in girth that the pistol hung very low, squarely in the center, the grip leaning outward and the barrel pressing into his groin. He wore a linen suit, a string tie badly knotted as always, a broad-brim panama which sat low and level on his head. His arms did not swing as he walked.

He stopped suddenly, halted in midstride, when he saw from under the hatbrim a man seated on a bench against the wall of the depot. Young, slim and at ease, looking quite cool in the heat, he seemed to have been there a long time, for no one paid him any special attention; he seemed willing to sit there indefinitely. Tarfeller stopped only for an instant, his head thrown slightly back to

45

watch from under the hat—a man who carried his forty years of idleness upon the flesh of his face, the physiognomy pinched and unsunned, without a line of worry, but with little whiskey-pouches under eyes whose lashes and brows were almost invisible, as well as upon his figure, belly paunched against the buttoned waistcoat, shoulders sloped and frail—then continued his walk down the heat-shimmered hundred yards of dusty street. Am I doing it right? he wondered. The hot dust of the street sifted into his shoes, each grain like a spark.

People were hurrying into the stores to clear the line of fire; they watched from windows and doorways. He walked, his stride made clumsy by the heavy, inward-leaning pistol. Then he noticed that the young man had a rifle on the bench beside him. Thirty yards from the bench he halted, standing with one foot advanced and holding his arms away from his body. As if the voice came from a long way off—he saw the motion of the face before he assimilated the words—he grew conscious of the threat spoken by the young man with the rifle now across his thighs (Tarfeller saw him as if through the wrong end of a telescope; the words took shape in his brain after the mouth stopped moving): "Reach for that pistol I'll kill you."

The words took shape, and it was as if the young man were an instructor, a prompter reminding him what to do. For almost immediately, with a motion neither slow nor hurried—as if he were reaching to lift something offered him on a tray, or to scratch a place that did not particularly itch—he moved his hand downward and inward until it touched the slick hard butt of the pistol.

At this motion Bart stepped out of the bank, where he had been for the past half hour on business and from which he had watched for the past few seconds the action in the street. The bank was diagonally opposite the depot. There was a crowd in the lobby, some of them just in off the street, all saying the same thing: "Cass aint got a prayer." From the doorway at the corner of the building Bart saw Macready sitting calm and ready on the bench where loafers and old men sat all week, whittling, and Tarfeller standing

46

ankle deep in dust, looking neither cool nor excited, looking merely foolish and doomed as he moved his hand toward his father's cavalry pistol.

Bart walked into the street toward Tarfeller, but he kept his eyes on Macready. The rifle was a big one, a Henry .44 repeater, each bullet carrying two hundred grains of lead. When he saw it go up to Macready's shoulder Bart shouted, "Wait! Wait!" and threw up one hand in hope of distracting the shooter. But the rifle bucked twice, the two explosions so close together that no one blinked between them, and Tarfeller pitched forward. His hand was just in front of his head, the unfired pistol half buried in the dust. He did not even twitch; he lay in the hot white dust, stained but not bloody, as if even the dignity of bleeding were denied him in his belated assumption of a heritage for which he had never been fit, as if to show that he could never have attained the qualities of other, better men even in his expiation of a daughter's promiscuity, even though he had attempted it under a code evolved by the honorable gun-carrying men who were his forebears. The past had brought him to death in the dust.

Bart felt something of this when he came out of the bank to halt the shooting. 'Dont fire,' he wanted to tell Macready; 'Dont fire. He couldnt hit you even if he managed to point it your way.' But now, when he saw the rifle go up, heard the two quick shots, and then saw Tarfeller pitch forward, he knew the injustice of the death.

He went to where Tarfeller lay, then stood beside the body, looking at Macready. Macready sat in the same position on the bench, the rifle again across his thighs, just as when Tarfeller had reached for the pistol; he had not even stood up to shoot. He watched Bart. "You want some of it too?" he said. And as Bart bent for the pistol, the rifle rose again with the same sudden motion. Across the thirty yards of hoof- and boot-pocked dust he saw Macready's eye above the foreshortening barrel, above the muzzle, and then above the yellow spurt of flame.

The bullet struck him just above the belt, the impact making him grunt as if he had been struck by a fist; he fell backward into a sprawled but vigilant sitting position. He already had the pistol, however; his fingers had closed on it when he bent his knees and stooped. Sitting in the dust, his knees drawn up, he held the big horse pistol with both hands and pulled the trigger steadily, thumbing the hammer until it clicked on the first cartridge again. The first shot nearly bucked it out of his hands, but then he knew it and steadied it, and put the remaining four into the man with the rifle.

Macready fired twice but the second shot just kicked dust. The pistol balls threw him against the depot wall, each impact knocking him back against it as his body tried to topple toward the shooting. He slid down the planking in a series of forward and backward jerks. Two feet above where his head had been, the mark of Bart's first shot showed on the weathered boards of the wall. Another had gone through his clothing, struck the edge of the bench, and ripped a long pale splinter which now stood upright on the plank, naked, like an admonishing finger.

When the watchers came out of doorways and out of open windows onto the street, Bart was slumped forward, his shoulders between his knees. He was bloody all down the front of his trousers and the lower part of his shirt.

"This one's alive," one said, leaning over Bart.

"Well, this one aint," another said of Tarfeller.

"Nor this one neither," a third said of Macready.

They carried Bart into the saloon and laid him on a table in the rear, in the room where Macready had played such indolent poker. When he opened his eyes he saw Murphy Lane looking down at him. Others, strangers as well as men he knew, stood in a loose, respectful circle, studying his face and bloody clothing with an air of condolence. "Hello, Murph," he said. He looked around. "Put me in something and carry me home."

There was some discussion of this—some thought it best not to move him—but finally they lifted and carried him out to John Cowan's buggy, hitched at the rail in front of the saloon. Cowan got in and took the reins, and Lane sat on the other side of Bart; they held him propped between them. A third man, a stranger who had been first to reach him after the shooting, climbed up behind. "This is fine, I thank you," Bart said. "But, John: drive those horses easy, please." He used the deliberate politeness of men who believe themselves close to death.

MRS BART came into the room soon after the three men and the doctor went out. Bart was already asleep. Billy Boy, who was sitting by the bed to fan him, stood up when she entered. She had been in Bristol since the day before, spending the night with her mother. "What did the doctor do?" she asked Billy Boy.

"Nothing, Miz Bart. Just painted him."

"Painted?"

"Yessum: where he's shot. That doctor painted it. Bullet's still in there. I reckon itll stay in there, too, if it's depending on that doctor to get it out."

They stood beside the bed, whispering. "All right," she said. "Thank you. I'll watch him now."

"Yessum," Billy Boy said, and tiptoed out. Mrs Bart took up the fan.

It was nearly an hour before Bart stirred. When he opened his eyes he saw his wife's shadow on the wall, the palmleaf fan moving with slow, deliberate strokes. For a moment he thought he had died and this was the after-life. Then he turned his head and looked at her. "Did you have a good trip?"

"Yes, Mr Bart."

He was quiet, a little sheepish. "The trouble: did they tell you?"

"I heard about it," she said. "I saw Mr Cowan and Mr Lane downstairs." The fan made smooth, full strokes. "I know you couldnt help it: I know you did what you had to do." Her expression did not change but she straightened a bit in the chair and she halted the fan as she said, "But youll have to start being more careful now, Mr Bart. Thats why I went to Bristol: to see Dr Clinton.

49

He says it's true." She settled back, beginning to fan again, the same long easy strokes, while Bart lay watching her face. "We are going to have our first child, Mr Bart."

This would make a difference: and did. To the land, the bank account, the growing prominence was added another Hugh Bart, born in March of 1891. Bart waited in the library (called so because it once had been, not because it was: there were no books on the shelves) looking out over the lawn toward the lake, white-capped now and frothed by the wind. He sat by the window all morning, rose for dinner and ate alone, taking the dishes from the solemn houseboy. When he had finished, or at least had made a show of eating, he returned to the library and took his seat by the window. This time he had been there less than an hour when the Negro came in, more solemn than ever. "Doctor say come up now. Baby's borned."

Bart took the steps two at a time and went into the bedroom. The midwife stood by the bed, her dark hands clasped at her waist. Dr Clinton, a neatly dressed young man with a wide mustache, was in the far corner with his back to the door. "Tell him about it, Florence," he said over his shoulder, smiling. She lay in the center of the bed, only her head out of the covers; her body seemed as flat as a plank beneath the sheet. Her hair had just been combed, parted precisely and still damp.

"It's a son," she said. She turned her eyes toward the doctor. "Dr Clinton says he's big."

"Over ten pounds, I guess," the doctor said. "Look." He came toward the bed, carrying a bundle. He stopped near Bart and held out the bundle. "Take him?" Bart shook his head in alarm. "Oh ho," the doctor said with his practiced joviality. "I'll bet I know who wants him whether his daddy does or not."

Mrs Bart watched him gravely. When he put the baby in the bed beside her, she turned back a flap of the swaddling cloth. Leaning forward, Bart saw a red, ugly, wizened face, eyes tight shut: the face of an old old man, with a little hand beside it unable to close into a fist because the fingers would not bend properly; each of these fingers had a tiny pink nail at the tip. Its skin did not seem to fit its neck, and its nose was hardly a nose at all. Mrs Bart watched him as he looked at the baby and then back at her, puzzled. "It's all right," she said. "Dr Clinton says they all look like this for a while."

"They do, they do," the doctor said, laughing and rubbing the palms of his hands together. "Except few of them are this handsome." Bart and Mrs Bart watched him gravely. He was like a vaudeville comedian playing to a poor house.

Mrs Bart was quiet for a time. She looked about the room, then up at Bart. "I was born in this same room," she said. She pursed her lips, thinking. "Or maybe the one across the hall. I cant remember which Mother said."

Bart nodded. It was one of the few times she alluded to her former life at Solitaire.

SHORTLY AFTER this and to everyone's surprise, because though he had been ill for some time now, they had thought he would live forever, Judge Wiltner died. It was cancer of the rectum, which had been progressing for years (that was why he sat on his spine and propped his feet on the desk) but which now began to gallop, as they said of consumption, under the surveillance of local doctors. He was in bed six months the last time. Three weeks before he died he sent for Bart and told him about the difference that had come.

Bart entered the bachelor house, a square four-room clapboard cottage on an Ithaca side street, with two ragged chinaberry trees in the yard. Judge had lived here forty years under the care of two Negroes, a man and his wife, who for the past year had organized his life into a series of meals and naps in slovenly old-man-smelling seclusion. When Bart knocked and opened the door he saw Judge lying in bed, propped on four pillows. The stutter of a lawnmower came from the yard, and looking through the window Bart saw the Negro walking behind it, back and forth across the lawn, effortless and serene.

51

Judge lay facing the door, so that when Bart came in he did not have to turn his head or even shift his eyes; all he had to do was focus, which he did: the irises seemed to spin like little wheels, then jerked to a stop. "Hello, Hugh," he said. Bart halted, hat in hand. The voice frightened him, and as soon as he heard it he thought: He's going to die. It was still a booming voice, still chest-deep in imitation of the gone Southern orators, but there was a rattle of weakness in it that had never been there before—as if the voice, disembodied, knew what was going to happen to the body it occupied. The great gray mane was unchanged, ruffled like a dusty fowl against the pillows, but the face, ungraced now by the squints and grins Judge used in conversation as much as he used the scraps of Latin, was that of an old man about to die. Beneath the sheet the body showed in outline, slack and weary, disseminating an odor of unwashed bachelor flesh.

"Good evening, Judge. I was coming past. . . ."

"Sho, son. Take a chair."

Riding home to Solitaire half an hour later, the sun going down, bloodying Lake Jordan to his left, Bart considered what Judge had told him. "Youre getting different," he had said.

"You want me to stay the same all my life, Judge?"

"Thats it," Judge said. "Thats how youre different. Youve stopped changing, or youre about to stop."

"You want me to keep changing all my life?"

"Yes, son: keep growing. I marked you for a big man from that first day we got together. I thought the plantation was going to be a step along the way." He was quiet a moment, his long, dying face lowered, watching his fingers twisting lint on the blanket. "I even thought the wife and child were going to be steps along the way. I see now I was wrong; I can see that now. Theyre not steps: theyre the edifice. Well, go on; go on. Make a good farmer."

Bart was embarrassed, like a prize pupil told by his professor that he has done well in an examination, but less well than was expected. He felt uncomfortable, sitting there with his eyes on a level with the lined, death-touched face on the bed. Judge spoke again, the face big and motionless except for the mouth, like a tragedy mask:

"Youre made another way, son. If my reasoning is right (and I know men) and if youre half what I took you to be, you cant stop like the rest of them. You cant loaf on a slope, no matter which way youre heading: youve got to keep moving. If you stop youll fret; youll lash out for action. And you wont pick an action that will carry you toward the things your life points to; youll just grab the first action that comes to hand. And if it isnt the kind that will carry you along the way you were born to travel, youll snarl up the whole business. Youll undo in a hurry all youve done. Youll bungle, son; youll bungle. Youll die with the whole thing gone crash in your lap."

— A long speech, Bart thought, riding north on the road to Solitaire, the red sun sinking.

He wore the dignity and detachment which the insecure assume to guard against intimacy and possible insult, and he had begun to put on weight, flesh building a barrier about the robust frame, incasing the still-hot blood. Waist and shoulders had thickened on security; the lines of his face were set and definite, like the face of an acquaintance once you have seen his portrait. Riding the horse on the lakeside road toward his wife-kept, heir-sheltering mansion on five square miles of land that were nearly his by now, Bart was thirty-one, young. But already when he thought of the past ten years, the way-winning years uphill, he was like a boy touching the coat his father had worn to war, and he felt the same pursy awe a man would feel after somehow managing to swallow a cannonball.

A long speech, he thought, veering from consideration of what the dying man had said, occupying his mind with awe for the number of words rather than their import. And as he veered, took sanctuary within inaction, his invulnerability left him with a rush like wind; gallantry fell from him like a garment; the open simplicity of his mind went like smoke. It required another ten years for him to realize what had happened, as if the grossness of the flesh had insulated his mind's quick, but that was the day it began. Three

53

weeks later at Judge Wiltner's funeral (Bart had not been back to see him) the face beneath the coffin lid represented all his unadmitted fear.

JUST BEFORE the birth of his second child, a girl, in August a year and a half after the first was born, Bart made his first big-business venture. It was the beginning of the antagonism he was to feel for all who made their livelihoods by the manipulation of nothing but money. Previously the element of chance, supposed to attend all such dealings, had made it less detestable—like money won at poker, say—but now he learned that this element was not always present, with the result that he became disgusted with the entire group and steered clear of its members whenever possible.

It began when Lawrence Tilden, whom Bart had known only as a nodding acquaintance, came out to Solitaire with what he called a proposition. Wearing russet side-whiskers which older men said made him resemble a Yankee commissary officer, Tilden had brought to his bachelor uncle's bank in Ithaca something of the feverish progressiveness of modern business methods. He was from Kentucky, a tall young man with well-tended nails, a precise manner of speaking, and a passion for orderliness unaccustomed in the Delta. This last even led him to propose a personal file for his uncle. The old man used a table in one corner of his office, scattered with everything from plantation mortgages to the odds and ends of Mississippi living—letters, almanacs with fishing notes for the past ten years, prescriptions for chilblains and heartburn, poker ious, invitations to veterans' gatherings, and other such documents —though he could lift from the dusty litter whatever paper he wanted, provided its seeming disarray had not been disturbed by the old Negro who swept and dusted every morning. The uncle balked at this innovation, but Tilden did succeed in installing a system of cost accounting and a sliding rate of interest, and he looked forward to other improvements.

Bart was well ahead of his mortgage notes: money from last

year's crop lay idle in the bank. That was what Tilden came to see him about. He knew a merchant in Bristol who was anxious to expand, who wanted to borrow $16,000 to enable him to lay in stock and remodel his store into something finer than anything between Memphis and New Orleans. The merchant's name was Wisten. It was a good investment, Tilden said: if Wisten defaulted there would be no trouble finding a buyer who would pay beyond the amount of the loan. Bart said all right. He did not know the merchant but he had been thinking about the money lying idle at four percent when it could be lent out at eight percent.

Tilden rode back to Ithaca. Four days later he returned with the mortgage. Upon failure to receive payment in one year's time, Bart would be owner of the largest dry goods store in Bristol. "I dont want any store," he said. "Just fix it so I get my money, I'll be satisfied."

"Of course." Tilden smiled. "But it cant go wrong, and even if it does youll find yourself even better off."

"Lets get this straight," Bart said. "I dont want any store. I never sold a thing in my life except a yelling calf I raised back east. And I was beat in the trade, by a one-eyed man at that." Tilden laughed his polite, wooden laugh and said again there was nothing to worry about.

Abraham Wisten, who took the loan believing that the realization of his dream was at hand, was an Austrian Jew; he had left Vienna in 1869 to escape conscription. After the steerage voyage he lived for six months in New York, earning three dollars a week sweeping out a Bowery poolhall. He shared an under-the-eaves room with a red-haired Scotsman who spent his nights inventing a bomb. The room smelled of sulphur and saltpeter; some nights Wisten would come awake violently, the explosion rumbling in his ears, the room swirling with smoke, and the landlord banging in protest at the door. Even now, better than twenty years later, Wisten would shudder when he remembered those months, the loneliness of the stone city, the terror of nights in the locked room with the mad Scot, the shame he felt when the poolhall clients laughed at his accent and called him sheeny.

When he had saved six dollars and bought a suit of American clothes he traveled west, first through a region where the barns were better than the houses, then through the upper Mississippi Valley, filled now with veterans still wearing parts of their blue uniforms. Sometimes he would think he had found what he was seeking and he would stop for a time, though never for longer than a week; he always moved west again. Then he struck the river, and he knew he had found at least part of the dream he was after. He got a job collecting tickets on a showboat. It went south, down the Valley, past lonesome Illinois and Missouri hamlets, past quiet green stretches flanking the wide brown river. Every morning he went on deck to watch the landscape slide past, and every morning it was closer to what he believed he wanted. He might have gone all the way to New Orleans like this, but two hundred miles south of Memphis something happened.

There was an actress, a large woman with hair that glinted like brass. At first she merely joked with him at meals, and he rather enjoyed it, though she was well past her youth. She was the soubrette, wife of the banjo player. Two nights south of Memphis Wisten woke and found her in his cabin, bending over him, breathing a reek of cheap whiskey. At first he did not realize who it was. Then, while he was trying to persuade her to leave, the cabin door came open again. It was the banjo player, with a pistol.

Wisten went out by the window. The first shot seemed to pass through his hair; the second, which came as he rounded the turn down the gangway, was not even close. He hid behind some bales in the hold until the showboat owner came down with a lantern. "Here, Abe," he said, giving him ten silver dollars. "We'll make Bristol by morning, and I'll send one of the niggers down with your clothes." He was portly, dignified; he was called Colonel, the rank he claimed to have held in the Confederate army, though everyone knew he had been a provost guard corporal with Ben Butler. "I hate to lose you," he added. "But you know yourself, Abe, I can find another ticket taker lots easier than I can scare up a banjo man." The lantern gleamed upon the gangway, rising, then passed from sight. Wisten was alone again in the dark. He expected the husband with the pistol any minute. Just before dawn the boat touched bank and the Negro came down with his clothes. He saw nothing of the banjo player as he went ashore, but he stayed out of sight until the showboat cleared for Vicksburg.

Here his search ended. This was 1870, dirt roads clattering with the drumfire thunder of night-riders, horsemen passing sheeted and hooded against the red glare of crosses burning in the night. It seemed to Wisten that he had entered another world, a region of transmuted values, where men burned the symbol of their worship as an avatar of terror.

Next day he was hired by a clothing merchant. He learned to sell to Negroes, to haggle over a price, to send them away with more than they came to buy. He took to it well. Two years later he married the daughter of the man who had hired him, and with the five hundred dollars that came as dowry, he opened his own store in competition with his father-in-law. Within ten years it was the leading store in Bristol. And now, twenty-three years after the morning he left the showboat, he was laying in stock for what he called "The finest merchandising bazaar between Memphis and New Orleans." He had wanted to say between Chicago and New Orleans but was persuaded not to. "No, no," the printer told him. "You dont want to get your tagline too flamy because then it dont mean much to the reader."

"Oh," Wisten said. He was a small man, very neat, in tight clothes. He wore a cameo and a ruby on one hand, a Masonic ring on the other. At his bosom, brilliant against the boiled shirt-front, there was a two-carat diamond stud, flat, slightly yellow, and a bit smaller in diameter than a dime. "Well: you fix it," he said. "I'll just sell them."

This was four months after he had taken the loan from the Ithaca banker, and already he had the store he had always wanted, plate-glass showcases and all. But within another four months he began to realize that it would take time for people to appreciate the stock he offered. It certainly became apparent that he would not be able to meet the mortgage. So when ten months were up, he decided to go to the banker and tell him how things stood. He rode the thirty miles in a rented buggy. "We'll make a outing of it," he told his two sons. Small and dark, they sat in the buggy in front of the bank, frightened by the Ithaca boys who grinned at their starched collars, ribbed stockings, and button-top shoes.

Tilden sat behind a desk in his narrow, tidy office at the rear of the building. He looked up and smiled when he saw Wisten in the doorway. "Good evening, Mr Tilden," Wisten said. It sounded almost gay: that was his manner, at once hesitant and effusive, anxious to please, with a quality of conscious inferiority.

"Good afternoon, Mr Wisten. Come on in." He lifted the lid of a box on his desk: "Cigar?" and Wisten took one.

"Thank you," he said, leaning toward the cupped flame. He sat facing Tilden across the desk, holding the cigar as if it were a soiled stick.

"How are things in Bristol?"

"Fine, Mr Tilden, just fine."

"Good: good."

They were quiet then, Wisten smoking nervously with short infrequent puffs. "I come to talk to you about the loan," he said at last. "I was, ah, wondering. I told Mrs Wisten yesterday: I said, 'Hannah, it dont look like I'm gonna make it quick as I figured.' And she just looked at me—you wouldnt beleaf it, Mr Tilden; she's got more good sound bissness sense than the rest of us put together—she just looked at me and said: she said, 'Then you better go see Mr Tilden down in Ithaca. Tell *him* about it,' she said. So, Mr Tilden, I come to see you right away, in the buggy, the boys and me. Here we are."

"Yes, Mr Wisten?" Tilden was watching him.

"Yes sir, here we are, and I . . ."

"Yes, Mr Wisten?"

The young banker's quizzical intentness distressed Wisten. It seemed to show that while he, Wisten, did not know what was coming next, Tilden knew it already and was therefore in the advantage. "I come to get a eggstension," Wisten said lamely.

Tilden lowered his glance and lifted a ruler from the desk, sighted along its edge at the inkwell, moved it slowly sideways like a Gatling gun raking fire. "Ethics," he said, moving the ruler from right to left. "Integrity," he said. He mowed down invisible infantry in a miniature war, then concentrated on the inkwell, pouring a steady fire there. He spoke slowly, pedagogically: "This bank conducts its activities on the same principles by which a man of honor conducts his life. We consider it in keeping with those principles, Mr Wisten, to expect you to live up to the promises you made ten months ago—on paper, Mr Wisten—to repay at the stipulated time what was lent you in good faith." He paused. "I have heard it said (and I believe it) that you are a man of integrity. We could never have granted the loan in the first place if we had not thought this was true."

He leaned back, the swivel chair creaking, and pointed to the calendar on the wall behind his head. Through the 15, each square of the month of June, 1893, had been scored with a deft red x; this was how Tilden ended each day, sort of a silent peacetime sunset gun. He tapped the last x with the ruler, then lifted the top two sheets. Wisten watched the tip of the ruler point to the 15 on the third sheet, and exactly across it, in a neat angular hand perhaps like that in the doomsday book, his name was written: *Wisten.*

"You have two months," Tilden said. "Surely that is ample time for a man in your position." He looked directly at Wisten for the first time since he had begun speaking, and now it was Wisten who lowered his glance.

"Mr Tilden."

"Yes, sir?"

"Mr Tilden, I . . ."

"Yes, sir?"

"Good day, Mr Tilden."

The banker rose and stood behind the desk as Wisten fumbled at the door. Then the older man turned, holding the door ajar, and made an awkward bow, including a slight bending of the knees.

Tilden responded with a stiff bow, from the waist only, as Wisten went out.

Tilden did not speak of the merchant's visit; the first time Bart heard Wisten's name mentioned, since the granting of the loan, was in early August, seven weeks after the request for an extension was refused. He and Peter Durfee were sitting in the dining room. The Durfees had been to Bristol and had stopped for supper at Solitaire on their way back. Their wives had retired at the end of the meal (Mrs Bart was far along in pregnancy) and now the two men sat watching the houseboy clear away the coffee things. It was just dark, the windows glaring yellow at intervals as heat-lightning flickered across the sky. Long tendrils of cigar smoke writhed among the candles.

"I didnt want to mention it in front of Mrs Bart," Durfee said, frowning and sharpening the tip of his cigar against the ashtray. "It's all the talk in Bristol today. Abe Wisten, the Jew who owns the store there: he shot himself this morning."

"Wisten?" Bart said.

"Yes. Everyone was fond of him, they say."

Then Bart remembered the name, which had meant nothing to him at first, and as Durfee told about it, Bart thought—but not out of callousness and not without feeling, though the words themselves demonstrated none—It's my first without a gun. I always used a gun before.

Durfee knew only a few of the particulars. What had happened was this:

From the time he climbed back into the buggy hitched in front of the Ithaca bank, rejoining his sons who had sat there afraid to move as they watched the country-bred people going back and forth along the dusty street, Wisten had known he was not going to be able to meet the date the loan would come due. His days were filled with remorse. More than anything, he dreaded seeing again the young banker who explained honor and integrity so that they added up to ruin and disgrace. "I'm an honorable man," he would tell himself, speaking aloud in the store. "An honorable man about to be stripped of my honor. In the eyes of everyone, all my friends and lodge brothers, I'm about to be proved dishonorable and ruined."

For six weeks he talked to himself like this, standing in the store, bemused, in neat, outlandish clothes, pinstripe trousers, patent leather shoes, and claw-hammer coat. He would be standing there, muttering, and suddenly his eyes would brim with tears. He began to note a stomach disorder, a dull ache that never seemed to leave him, though he had almost stopped eating. Now it's ulcers and cancer, he thought. "I'm losing my health with my honor," he said, watching an unspoken thought pass before his eyes like a printed streamer: *Youre going to die before long.* The ache, the neurasthenia never left him; his sleep was filled with horrors.

Clerks at the store, his wife among them, noted his nervousness. It increased until finally, in early August, he became excited and ordered a customer out of the store, a finicky country girl. "I buy and I buy," he cried. He threw up both arms. "The best quality merchandise I buy, trying to make this town a center of culture and fashing. Yes: and remodel, too, at expense you cant imagine. To help you people I do it, and here you come pinching the cloth, disranging the lay-out, and say you dont like it. My God." He stamped his foot so hard his coat tails flapped. "Ged out my store. Leaf my place of bissness. Leaf! Immeditly!"

He ran to the rear, to the washroom under the storage stairs — it was the first to be installed in a Delta store—and sat on the commode, weeping and tugging at his hair. His wife came and stood by the thin, swing-hinged door; she could hear him sobbing. "Abe, Abe," she whispered hoarsely.

Wisten was startled. He sat bolt-upright, seized the chain that hung beside him, and in his anxiety—he thought perhaps the voice had come from heaven, an angry Jehovah — pulled it. The commode flushed with a deep, throaty roar like an animal or the river. Then (this was its flaw) it sighed, flooded, and subsided as if nothing had happened; which was plainly untrue, for a little stream ran under the door and against Mrs Wisten's shoes, and Wisten himself, crying miserably with his hair in wild disorder, emerged through the swinging door, flinging it back with his hand. He stood there dripping water as the door halted on the backswing, hesitated and recovered, then swung back, gathering momentum, and smacked against his dripping coat tails with a flat, squdgy report. "Oh Hannah," he cried, "Ive lost my honor and all, all I own, and now I aint even pitiful; I'm apsurd."

That night Wisten lay flat on his back in bed, looking up toward the invisible ceiling. A faint breeze stirred; the moon rose red and full. His eyes gleaming, he turned his head and watched his wife sleeping. Just before dawn he got up. He took off the three rings, put them on the night table, and stood beside the bed, his limbs frail and knobby, his chest showing a thin mat of gray hair like smoke at the throat of his nightshirt. His wife did not stir.

From a drawer of the bureau he took a small nickleplated revolver. Holding it gingerly in one hand, he padded back to the kitchen. The swinging door creaked as he passed through. He sat in a cane-bottom chair at a table beside the cold range and in front of a window grayed with light. A clock on the wall whirred and struck five. Wisten listened with his head bent, counting the strokes, then raised his arm and put the pistol on the table. "You poor fellow," he said aloud, watching again the printed streamer of unspoken thought ripple past his eyes like a headline dummy: *I told you you were going to die before long.*

Against the tender flesh beneath his left ear (Wisten was left-handed) he felt the small cold circle of the gun muzzle. It started him trembling. "You poor poor fellow," he said again, and took the pistol in both hands. Making a little moaning sound of pure terror, he put the barrel into his mouth. His teeth chattered against it; his tongue jerked in reflex away from the slick metallic taste. Then all of a sudden the fear was gone; it was exultation, triumph, as he clamped down with his teeth, thrust his tongue against the metal, and with his thumb looped awkwardly through the guard

in reverse (*Hear, O Israel, the Lord our God, the Lord is One*)
pulled the trigger.

—And it was cleaner that way, Bart thought. With a gun it was
cleaner.

He was amazed at what money had done. Even from Durfee's
account of what had happened, he could see that it was money that
had killed the merchant, or the lack of it, or the threat of the lack
of it; and he was amazed. Without thinking the words, he realized
now what he had never understood: how desire for money — not
what it procured, not even the thought of what it could procure:
just the naked, handworn money itself — could make men go any
lengths, face any indignity, sacrifice any principle, steal, tell lies,
cut throats. His reaction resembled a desire to secede from the
human race.

Early the following morning he was in Ithaca, waiting outside
the bank when Tilden arrived. "Good morning, there," Tilden
said. "Come in, Sir." He unlocked the door and stood aside for
Bart to enter.

"Go on," Bart said gruffly. But Tilden insisted.

"I've got good news for you," he said, following.

"You *what?*"

"I have you a buyer. At a real price, too."

"Just what do you mean?"

"I mean twenty-five thousand dollars, Mr Bart. Jenks of Memphis wants it. I named the price."

Bart looked at Tilden in surprise. "When?"

"They'll take over within two weeks."

"No: I mean when did you arrange the sale."

"Oh. Two months ago, about. In June."

So now Bart knew that the arrangement had been made while
Wisten, who had come five thousand miles to find a dream, was
choosing between death and what the banker called dishonor. His
face became ruddy with the sudden rush of blood. "God damn
your soul, give me my money," he said. "I dont know how I keep
my hands off you."

Now it was Tilden's turn to be surprised. "It hasnt been paid yet," he said. "They wont buy until the title's clear. But the deal is set, Mr Bart. The entire amount, twenty-five thousand dollars, will be paid September first."

"I dont want twenty-five; I want sixteen. And I want it now, today, so we can be quits before I throttle you."

"Very well," Tilden said coldly. "Youll have the money immediately. I'll bring it to you this afternoon."

"No," Bart said. "Dont bring it. Send it. If it's not there, at Solitaire today, I'll be in Ithaca tomorrow morning." He turned and walked out of the bank.

At dinner that afternoon they heard the cattle-gap thunder. Then the houseboy came into the room. His name was Ernest. "Gempmun say it's the bank."

Carrying his napkin, Bart went onto the porch. It was the end of summer, the grass parched and yellow on the lawn sloping down to the road and beyond to where a file of lightning-scarred cypresses, holding their blasted limbs athwart their gray trunks, stood sentinel at the margin of the lake. Beyond the far shore, wavering in the shimmer of heat, the levee was like a dark thread held between the earth and the high blue sky of dog days.

Two men sat in a surrey in front of the house, the cashier from the bank, with a satchel and notebook in his lap, and the driver with the reins held limp in one hand; they watched Bart come out of the door. "Good day, Mr Bart," the cashier said. He moved to get down, a pleasant-faced man enjoying a daytime release from his high stool at the bank. The steel rims of his glasses glinted in the sunlight.

"Never mind, sir," Bart said. "Ernest, take the gentleman's satchel."

"Here's the receipt," the cashier said, holding out the notebook and a pencil.

"Just hand the satchel to the boy," Bart said. Ernest received it and came up the steps. "Now you can go."

"The receipt . . ."

"Get off this place," Bart said. He took the satchel from the Negro and stood with it hanging at his side, partly covered by the big napkin. The men in the surrey stared at him, their eyes bulged with alarm. "Git."

CHAPTER THREE

THE LAKE

Now THAT the second baby was born—the first already a growing child, learning to walk and talk, big enough anyhow to lift without fear of his coming apart, and without that terrifying heartbeat at the top of his skull—now that life was an organized flow of seasons and even years, Bart found time to examine the success he had attained. He had made this life-way the goal of his early years; yet when he first reached it he was like a man who, overcome by a desire to leap into a whirlpool, thrashes about inside it, too busy to analyze his present sensations, let alone the nature of the impulse that prompted the leap. But now, as if the whirlpool had ebbed or the thrashing become accustomed, Bart could look about and see his days following a pattern, alike within their separate seasons (one chopping day was like another: one picking day was like another) but all filled with incident and decision, the boundless activity all farmers have known since Cain soured the Lord on them.

He rose between five and five-thirty during the work season. The mules would already have been distributed by the hostler and the hands were mostly in the field, though a few of the late ones might still be harnessing, tightening girths and hames, kneeing the mules to make them let out their breaths. Bart stood at the lot gate, talking to his overseer, a short red thick-set man named Patterson; he had been on Solitaire for two seasons now, ever since the place had been clear of debt. Patterson was the son of a small farmer who had lost his land and had entered and died in share contract. With his father's example behind him, Patterson had saved his money and made down payment on two hundred acres of land. He went about this in dead earnest, not even taking time off to get married. It was a modest beginning but his hopes were real enough: he intended to multiply his holdings over not too long a stretch of years.

But the year he began, 1885, was the year of the great rains, a steady drumming on roofs and fields, and Patterson was foreclosed for his furnish. It was pure hard luck, common enough in the region. He returned to his old position, farming forty acres of another man's land with another man's mules; that was the pass he had reached when Bart hired him. Bart recognized his right to every ounce of bitterness in his soul. During the period following his failure, Patterson had acquired a real dislike for large landowners, the men with bank accounts to tide them over the torrents. In point of fact, however, the hatred was not so intense as might have been expected; he was too hard a worker to have much time for his position to rankle. And now, working for Bart, he began to know something like peace for the first time since he had lost his land.

This came out of his respect for Bart, who not only handled all the financial details of the plantation but also worked as hard as anyone on it, including the overseer himself. Also, Patterson believed that Bart's position was not much different from what his own would have been except for the torrents of '85: a belief, however, that did not take into account the likelihood that if Bart had been in Patterson's position, the disaster of the rains somehow would have been overcome. He did not take this into account because, in the first place his self-esteem would not allow him to admit that any man in his position could do better than he had done and, second, because he had neither the simplicity of Billy Boy nor the insight of Judge Wiltner, the two men who knew Bart best and admired him most, each in a different way. Patterson had ability (he showed it year after year on Solitaire) but it was not accompanied by that spark Bart carried in his breast, which made his advances possible and was the mainspring of his reaction when choice was necessary, which enabled him to reach out in the dark and touch Right when other men, lacking the spark, would not have been able to distinguish it from Wrong in broad open daylight. This inner quality, a combination of simplicity and insight—so that in a sense Bart was a sort of Billy Boy Wiltner—made him a man of action who never faltered, a man of intelligence who never erred, so long as he obeyed the spark.

There were three conferences a day between owner and overseer, the first as soon as the lot was cleared, held over coffee in a room at the rear of the commissary, the second in the afternoon, held in the field wherever work was concentrated under Patterson's eye, and the third at dusk-dark just before supper, held in the commissary again. Between times both were riding the place, observing the crop. It was still nearly all cotton; Bart planted no more feed crops than he had to. Years later, men were to say that he had had no respect for the land; "Just look at it," they said, and justifiably, for it was depleted. But they were wrong about respect: Bart's fault was that he had too much respect.

For he had come to manhood in another country, a region one hundred and fifty miles east of the Delta, where the plant was called Bumblebee cotton because it grew so low that pickers had to crouch over the knee-high, sparsely bolled stalks. He was the fourth of six sons in a family that had shared in the development of the region. His father had outlived three wives; he owned land and three slaves, a considerable number in that section of Mississippi. His name was Ephraim. Morose, narrow, Spartan, he seldom spoke to anyone save in curt, monosyllabic orders. Something had caused a break between him and his family—a dispute about property, Bart thought—and now he not only would not speak to them, he would not allow his children to speak to them, nor even to mention their names. At the outbreak of war (Bart was born in May of the year before) Ephraim called for the mules to be hitched, drove into town, parked on the square directly in front of the courthouse draped with Confederate bunting, climbed into the wagon bed, and announced over the tailgate to all the upturned jeering faces his allegiance to the Union. Back home again, he assembled the household, family and servants, and forbade mention of secession no matter who won or lost the war: whereupon all three slaves promptly ran away, going to work with the defending armies of the South.

One of Bart's earliest memories was of an afternoon in March, 1864. He was sitting on the gallery with his father and his five brothers, the oldest fourteen, the youngest still in skirts. His father's wife was in the house with his two sisters; he could hear them moving about, setting the table for supper. It was between five and six, nearer to five for the sun was still high, when a small troop of cavalry rode up to the gate. He must have seen them before this, patrolling the countryside despoiled by Sherman and marauders—Confederates, they were called: gaunt, ragged men on sorry horses, lean and hard-ridden and always hungry, with tangled hair that was rolled in back from being slept on—but these were the first he remembered. Two dozen mounted scarecrows sat beyond the fence listening while their captain spoke, a man who looked no different from the rest save that it was he who spoke and with a voice that demonstrated leadership; the stars on his collar had been weathered to the same color as the cloth. He removed his hat with a gesture which was not sweeping—the heroics were gone by now, along with the firegilt buttons and the sashes—but which appeared to be so because of the wideness of the brim. He requested corn for the horses and space in the yard for the men to sleep.

Ephraim, who sat with both hands clenched on the head of a stick planted between his knees, kept his face toward the captain, hearing him out. There was a moment of silence when the speaker had finished. The tatterdemalions, on horses that resembled discards from a carrousel factory, awaited the accustomed formal reply. Then: "No," the old man said. "And get away from that gate. It's Union."

Bart had no memory of what followed, how the soldiers made no protest, neither the captain nor his men, but moved on to the next house down the road, where later their campfire gleamed against the night: he just remembered his father as ugly and stern, sitting with both hands on the head of his stick and watching them ride away. But next morning the oldest brother, the one who was fourteen and bore his father's name, was not at breakfast, and when they went out to the barn soon afterward, one of the stalls was empty. They as good as knew already what had happened. It was confirmed when the neighbor in whose yard the soldiers had slept came over with word that the boy had joined the cavalry troop, had ridden away with them when they broke camp at daylight. That explained the missing plow horse. Old Ephraim made no reply to this, did not thank the neighbor for his trouble. And when, less than a month later, he heard that the boy had been killed in a small action east of Jackson ("Gone up," the messenger said in cavalry phraseology) he made no reply either, beyond ordering his wife and daughters to hush before they even had time to begin to keen. Apparently there was no event with which his ugliness, his sternness, could not cope.

This was the Black Prairie belt. The earth was dark and rolling, scarped with outcroppings of rock and dotted with scrub oak. It nurtured a frugal people who, in their vocational lives, resembled the Pennsylvania Dutch (there were silos and windmills; barns were neat and sturdy, with blooded cattle in them) but who otherwise were more like dons in the heat of their convictions. Immediately after the war it was the hottest section of Ku Klux activity in the state; Bart's boyhood nights were loud with the whoops and hoofs of night-riders clattering past. These were times when he heard his father go downstairs in the dark, taking the Mexican War musket down from its peg above the mantel, and sitting with it in his lap while the Kluxers rode by, thinking his house or his barn might be the next to go up in a pillar of fire because he had refused to join them.

Schoolboy fights had the same intensity as the boys' fathers' shootings, for the arguments often were identical. Tibbee Creek, which alternately watered and drained the land, would leave its bed and sprawl in the marshy bottoms; hunting and fishing were excellent there. When Bart was nine he was dropping squirrels on the jump with a smallbore rifle (ten years later he was startled to find squirrel hunters using shotguns in the Delta) and was spending the rest of his spare time fishing in the bottoms.

He did not have much spare time, however. His father was a stern taskmaster. Under his eye Bart learned to run a straight furrow unstintingly from dawn to dusk: "kin to caint," the Negroes called it. The day's work was rounded on both ends with milking and bringing in stock, work so back-breaking and tedious, coming as it did in those crepuscular hours when sleep was either cloying or achingly desired, that all the balance of his life Bart could not see a cow without a vestige of distaste and even distress.

He was fifteen when he first decided to leave home. During the past year he had grown five inches and now was about as tall as he would ever be, five feet eight, his wrists and ankles protruding from outgrown clothes. There was little here for him, he thought, third now among five sons. His father was sixty-five, an old man; he supervised the farming from a buckboard, what time he was not sitting at home in a wheelchair with arthritis; he slept very little and spent his evenings apart from the family, alone in a small back room, reading the Bible and religious tracts. When Bart went to him in this room and told him he wanted to go, the pale eyes watched him from behind thick, square-lensed spectacles. "No," his father said. "Youre needed here and you know it." The eyes behind the spectacles watched him turn and leave the room. He had never disobeyed his father; he never would.

Old Ephraim died the following year but Bart did not leave yet. He stayed with his brothers and sisters and his father's wife. This was not Bart's mother. His mother, his father's third wife, had died in childbirth before Bart was a year old. She was eighteen when she died, he knew, though there was no daguerreotype, no tombstone even, and no one had ever spoken to him of her. All he knew he learned from the back of the Bible, information entered in his father's spidery handwriting beneath two others exactly like it except for names and dates: *6 July 1859, Susan Hughes. Born October, 1842, Quincy County Missippi & died Falaya County 4 April 1861.Unnamed infant (girl) died too same day. Thy will be done.*

Sometimes when he got to thinking about her, wondering how she had looked, whether she had been tall or short, dark or fair, he considered making a trip to Quincy County just to ask, but he never did. He wondered how she had met his father and why she had married him, better than thirty years her senior. Maybe it was a Fourth of July picnic, he thought, and they got married two days later. But Ephraim was never one for picnics, at least when Bart was old enough to observe; it would be unlike him to meet and marry within three days. Finally Bart gave up wondering. It was enough that he carried her family name, even though it had been shortened to Hugh.

He stayed two years after his father died, until 1878. Then he took one horse as birthright, packed his clothes in a saddlebag, and rode the hundred and fifty miles toward the setting sun, the mile-wide fabulous river, the Delta.

Here he joined a great-uncle—or so they called him: actually there was no kinship; the man was his father's first wife's second cousin. Bart could not remember having seen him, but he had heard of him through another prairie kinsman who had a letter from him soon after his removal to the Delta. In the letter, the only one he wrote, he described the richness of the soil he had settled on. You dropped a seed and ran, he said, for fear of being impaled. Even allowing for poetic license, which they did, it sounded good to those back home in the stone-cropped prairie region.

This great-uncle, so-called, had been gone eight years when Bart rode west to join him. He had ninety dollars in five-dollar gold pieces sewed into the waistband of his trousers, accumulated over a two-year period since his father died. Most of it came in a lump from the sale of a bull he raised; this was the transaction of which he said afterward, "I was beat in the trade, by a one-eyed man at that." Four days after the morning he left, Bart reined in his horse at the gate of his uncle's house, a renovated cabin with a dog run and an added wing, and addressed the man on the porch: "Mr Chester Garret?"

"Thats the name, young man. You hunting something?"

"I'd like to talk with you, Mr Garret."

"Well, hitch and come on up. Twont cost you nothing."

Bart introduced himself, explaining their connection, and Garret was pleased to see him. He was forty, unmarried, farming two hundred acres. They talked of home, Bart telling him who was dead, who was married, who had been born. Then he told him why he had come. "I saw that letter you wrote to Mr McQueen right after you left."

"Oh," Garret said. He leaned forward and spat over the edge of the porch, then sat back, wiping his mouth and smiling behind his hand. "Well, I aint done all that well, of course. I reckon I need some help, and if youre your daddy's boy—which I aint doubting, mind you—I guess youre just the somebody I been needing."

Bart had been quite short for his age before the growing spell of his fifteenth year. He was wiry and lank without being tall; his frame had been so busy lengthening it had not had time to widen. But he was strong, as he showed in the work he did for Garret. During the four years of working as a sort of combination hoe-hand and overseer, he learned Delta farming and filled out his frame, lithed into a well-formed man. Without making any really close friends, he became widely known and admired by the men of his uncle's acquaintance, small farmers working hundred- and two-hundred-acre places, and by the other men of Issawamba County, bartenders and blacksmiths, storekeepers and politicians, as well as by a rather large group who apparently were without vocation, who thought of themselves as too smart to work and frequently said so, who waited indolently for opportunities to make quick small sums through exchanging things they did not need for things they either needed or could sell.

73

This last was strange, for there was no group with which Bart had less in common. Perhaps, as his overseer was to do fifteen years later, they believed that he embodied what they could have been if their love of leisure had been replaced by whatever it was that made them admire him, like junky horses admiring a Percheron. Or perhaps something of the bored manner which he assumed when doing work that no longer taught him anything, required no concentration, suggested to them a tie between them and him, as if the studied carelessness glorified their own inertia of mind and body which made them choose easy work, with low or intermittant pay, over hard or just regular work with high or steady pay.

Whatever it was that drew them, Bart was able to dazzle them into electing him to the highest office their vote could bestow. And whatever it was that impelled their choice, enlisted their confidence, secured their votes, they chose well. He made a good sheriff. He had integrity and devotion and bravery, and there was never cause to doubt a one of the three. When he moved forward and upward again, got Solitaire plantation and thereby left not only their county but also their company, they still watched without harshness and even without envy; they still thought *There but for this and that go I* though they never analyzed the this-and-that because they feared that analyzing the deterrent qualities would destroy them, as indeed it might have done.

And when he made a go of it, paid off the mortgage, established himself among the planters he had joined on Lake Jordan to the north, the men back in Issawamba County still watched him with admiration. It seemed to them that Bart represented them, that he showed the others, out in the crass unimaginative workaday world, what could come from their group, demonstrating what they believed was their intrinsic worth to the others, the arrived, the secure, the ensconced.

YET IT had already begun to stale.

The change was imperceptible at first, not even suspected by himself: yet now that he had the land and the bank account, the wife and progeny, now that his life was identical with the lives of fifty other planters on the lake, he began to have a vague, uneasy feeling of having accomplished what he had set out to do. This was not at all what he had expected. Success had come smoothly— or so he thought: the fact that he had worked hard and taken risks was not considered; he was born for work and risk—and now while he was still young, just approaching what should have been his prime, it was all behind him. He still worked hard: there was no let-up there: but it was the same from year to year, no mortgage to stay ahead of, not even anything needed for the house. Excepting the growth of the bank account, a year's work brought him ex-actly where he had been the year before. Now that the odds were with him, he no longer was making a reputation for successful farming: he was just substantiating the reputation he already pos-sessed. The striving was not new and strange; it brought no fatigue to the mind, displaced no fretfulness, calmed no discontent.

So he began to cast about, seeking an outlet for the energy his work no longer consumed. He began to pay attention to his clothes, for instance; now that he was a successful planter he dressed the part. He wore broadcloth in winter, duck in summer, made peri-odic visits to a Bristol tailor, and began to be particular about the hang of his coats, the height of his trousers, the way they felt in the crotch. This made him look slimmer, fitter, but it also gave him a stiffness, a formality which resembled a show of pride and satis-faction with himself. He was thirty-six that year, 1896, yet people seeing him on the street in Ithaca, with his high-stomached carriage and his careful way of planting his feet when he walked, might have taken him for a successful middle-aged small-town banker.

Ithaca itself was changing, though not in appearance. Within ten years of the day the professor of Greek had opened his tavern, it had become the trading center it was to remain for eighty years— until that final, irrevocable, garish (and still future) transformation that was to be effected by the gasoline pump and the neon sign. Now, near the end of the century, it was much the same as it had been back in the second quarter: two rows of stores and houses,

75

half of them with their backs to the lake and half with their backs to the fields. The dusty or muddy street that ran between them, flanked with hitching posts, was dangerous to walk on at night because of the dogs and hogs that slept there.

Reconstruction almost passed over its head—the Klan was more fraternal than terrifying; night-riding was more for coon hunts than for whipping-bees—and when the Memphis paper began to say the dark era was over, people were glad without knowing exactly what they were glad about. By the time Bart came to Issawamba County, in the late '70s, men were too busy getting rich to take much interest in what history had to say, and during his term as sheriff, in the early '80s, they were too busy going broke because of the depression and the torrents, defaulting to the mortgage companies and moving away, to care about anything.

The change was not outward. Looking at Ithaca, no one who had been away for years would have seen any difference beyond a few new names across the store fronts and an occasional new hitching rail displacing an old one gnawed to frailness. The change was internal, as if the town, like Bart, had finally realized that nothing was going to happen that was any different from what had happened last week or last month or last year. The frontier had caught up with and passed it; life now was no more than variations on a theme already stated. The day was coming when Ithaca was to react much as Bart had done when he began to pay attention to the cut of his clothes; the store fronts would be painted and the windows decorated: but that was still in the future. Now, unlike Bart, the town was willing to take what came and be glad there was nothing new, as if—unlike Bart in this, too—it knew the twentieth century was coming with gadgets and high pressure, and was getting rested for the shock.

PRINCIPALLY, BART'S relief came from hunting. He was a great hunter: it had been his sanctuary always; it was the one field where his supremacy was never doubted, and in some ways it was his chief activity in the world of men. At any rate it was the one that lasted longest. Years after his death, after the men who had known him best were senile or dead, after his imprint on Solitaire and the lake was gone, his name would be mentioned and men who had not even known him, some of them even too young to have seen him, would say, "Oh: the hunter. Yes, Ive heard of him. I remember my daddy used to tell about a shoot he was on with Hugh Bart over in Arkansas. That was a long time ago."

In the winter of 1896 he set the ducks-bagged record for the region. The planters had built a lodge at the upper end of the lake —"To get away from our wives," they said; it was for poker too— where they would spend three or four days, frequently as many as ten or a dozen of them staying there at once. Each had a duck boat and a paddler, and every morning, in the chill gray pre-dawn, each would set out with a hundred shells in his pockets, sitting in the bow of the boat with his gun across his lap. Risible, eager, they would call to one another across the water, making bets on the bag and joking about yesterday's luck.

Bart set his first record the year he joined the hunters at the lodge. He came in with seventy ducks, enough to break the previous record by four. It stood for five years, until Bryant Sadlier, eighteen-year-old son of one of the planters, returned one freezing January morning with seventy-nine. "Theyre all over the sky," he said, excited, flushed with pride as he helped his paddler unload the boat, laying the ducks in a long row on the wharf. "Yes, sir. And I got three more, I swear, but we couldnt find them."

Near shore there was a crust of ice on the water; the willows were bent with the weight of ice on their limbs. It was bitter, biting cold. There were not many hunters at the lodge that day. Bart was in Ithaca when he heard about it, at the barber shop with a towel over his face. "That Sadlier boy: Bryant: got seventy-nine this morning. Says theyre coming over in droves. The sky is black with them, he says. Seventy-nine. How's that for shooting?"

"Well, he can have them," another said from beneath the razor. "You been out on that lake and felt that wind?"

Bart spoke from under the towel. "Hurry it up, Jud. Once over lightly."

By nightfall he was at the lodge, riding the stallion, the boatman on a mule beside him, a talkative coffee-colored boy named Jim, an expert paddler. "We figured youd be here looking after that busted record," the hunters said.

"Are they really that thick?"

"They were today. Cant tell about tomorrow."

"Then we'll find out tomorrow."

He left the poker game early: cashed his chips, got up deliberately when the others protested, and went back to the dormitory, a long room open across the back where they slept on canvas cots, like rows of dead in a winter tomb. When Jim came to wake him next morning he was already up, dressing in the chill darkness of the central room. Last night's fire was cold gray ashes with a faintly luminous base of coals giving no more warmth than a light-globe. "Lord, Mr Bart, you scared me," Jim said. "You up early."

"Boat ready?"

"Yassir. Bailing was easy: I just broke up the ice with the oar and thew it out in chunks."

"Mm. Make us some coffee, Jim."

"I already did," the boatman said. He went back to the kitchen and returned with two tin cups of coffee and two torn hunks of hoe-cake. They sat in front of the cold hearth, sipping the coffee and eating the bread. After a while the ashes began to stir with the pre-dawn wind in the chimney. Bart stood up, took a final swallow of coffee, and flung the dregs into the fireplace. He took his shotgun out of its case, put on his canvas coat that was heavy with the hundred shells. "All right. Lets go."

That was about six-thirty. At eleven they returned, Bart sitting in the bow, the Negro paddling laboriously in the stern; the boat resembled a top-heavy feathery raft. Bart was grinning, his nose bright red with the cold. He sat hunched forward, his hands inside his coat and his gun across his knees. There were eighty-six ducks in the boat.

The others came onto the wharf to watch him arrive. Continuing their poker, they had stayed indoors because of the weather. They brought the cards and glasses they had been holding when one of them glanced up, saw the boat from a window, and said: "Lord God. He's bagged a lakeful."

That record—86—was never broken (and soon never could be broken, for the government put a limit on the bag); it stood for future generations of hunters to wonder at and never hope to equal, not only because of the limiting law, but also because before long the ducks had thinned. Bart never talked much about that morning. It was Jim who told the story, told it often all the balance of his life. Thirty and forty years later, still young-looking, still coffee-colored, and still quite talkative, he told it in almost the same words he had used that morning when he and Bart returned in the duck-swamped bateau:

He was putting on his boots when I come through on the way to rouse him. Told me to make up some coffee, and all the time I was back in the kitchen getting it poured, I heard him stomping into his boots, cussing them under his breath. And when I brung it to him he set there eating and sipping and fidgiting like he was wanting to hasten daylight. Finely he couldnt stand it no longer. Say, "Come on, Jim": say, "Less us go."

It was still so pitch black dark I couldnt see the water where the paddle was going. Up front about half a mile, where the willows was thickest, ducks was honking, setting up a ruckus. They was just waking up, waiting like us for daylight so they could feed or fly; sound like more than a jillion. Out in open water where we was, away from bank, the going was easy. But no sooner we put in for land than we begun to come up on willows and ice. Oh-oh, I thought. Mr Bart taken a pole, broke ice out front. Sometimes the whole boat would go up on the ice and we be still for a minute, setting up high and dry, waiting, and then it bust with a crack: *Whap!* and we drap back in the water with a splash like the boat was going under.

All right: so far so good. When it begun getting daylight, all the ducks step up they honking. Mr Bart was setting in the bow, kind of hunkered over with both arms wrapped round hisself. It was cold, I tell you. We wait till daylight make some more. Finely he turn his head in my direction: say, "Put her up in the willows, Jim," and I put her. Ducks was honking all round us.

Daylight was making faster and faster. We aint been up in the willows a good five minutes before Mr Bart stood up with his gun at the ready. Say, "Holler, Jim": say, "Get um up." And I hollered and the ducks went flapping, watching us over they shoulders the way they do, rising up off the water all round us, all over the sky. He swung round: ba*loom!* then round again, taking a little more time with the left-hand barrel: ba*lam!* and then it was just the ducks flapping they wings. I ax him, "Where they?" all set to paddle. I aint seen nothing fall so I aint know which way to head.

But he just stood there, looking at the gun, helt it in both hands like a book or something, looking at it the way a bull will look at a bastard calf. Then I knowed I had seen something I aint never seen before: nor nobody else, I reckon: nor never see again. He done miss with both barrels, one after the other. I thought for a minute he's ghy throw the gun in the lake: he looked it. I was shamed to be there, shamed to be setting in the same boat with him, breathing the same air he done miss with both barrels in. I felt kind of hang-dog, shamed. Lord.

He set down. I hear him fetch a deep breath but he aint say nothing, just set there. I aint say nothing either. Some ducks was still in the willows, honking. Mr Bart breathe deep again, a moanful sound, unbreech his gun and put in two more shells. I felt better then, for at first I thought he's ghy say turn round; I thought for a minute he's ghy say go back to the lodge house. When I seen him stand up again, all set, I wham on the ice with the paddle and holler, getting up ducks. Ba*loom!* Ba*lam!*: two ducks. He aint miss this time; no Sir. He aint miss this time.

And aint miss again all morning, I'm here to tell you. But what with the ice and cold and all, the way the willows was froze and stiff, we lost at least a dozen ducks: a dozen at least, for I know for a fact there was times he got two at a clip, lined up. I set there watching his pockets get flatter and flatter whilst he burnt up the shells, gun going ba*loom* ba*lam* and me pulling ducks out the water faster than mortal man could keep track. I paddle all over that end of the lake, from place to place.

Finely he turn round to me where I was watching him over the pile of ducks between us. It was middle morning by then and his pockets was flat: he didnt have a single nother shell left out the hundred. Say, "All right, Jim": say, "Less go back." I brung the boat around and paddle home, so loaded down with ducks it was a job to keep from capsizing. I had to what you call warp in.

Them other gentlemens that aint come out in the weather was on the porch, watching us warp in. Then they come out on the dock and stood there watching, cards and whiskey glasses in they hands. One of them—it was old Major Dubose, that died of a stroke in the flood of Oh Three; had playing cards in one hand and a whiskey glass in the other—say, "Lord to God, just look at yonder": say, "He done bagged a lakeful sho enough." All of them ohing and ahing, eyes bugged out, and we come on in and unload at the wharf. It was a new record. You ax down on the lake if it aint true. We sot a new mark which never is been broke to this good day.

Hunting was not Bart's only diversion at the lodge on the upper end of Lake Jordan. He learned to play poker, too, and his luck was phenomenal: a sort of extended beginner's luck that had not lagged during four years of play. For the first month he sat outside the circle, watching the progress of the game, the drawing and betting. When he believed he had learned enough to sit in without special instruction, he took a seat at the table. That first night, playing his cards well enough but betting with little ability, he won five hundred dollars.

And this original luck stayed with him. Four years later he still was able to bet not only on the cards he held but also on the cards he was going to hold. His luck was so strong that occasionally he managed to win without holding top cards, doing so by bluff, by making the others think his cards were good because they nearly always were. He played with a sort of ruthless joviality, laughing and raking in pots with both hands and gibing at the losers. Best of all, he enjoyed placing a stack of chips on the cloth and sitting back to watch the man across the table fret, especially if the man was a deliberate, calculating player. "Oh you scientific sharpers," he would say. "Youre the ones I'm after."

He had never been this way about any other form of competition—certainly not about hunting, for instance, at which he was just as good as anyone cared to claim—but poker fascinated him and he appeared to be so good at it that he was able to continue that roughshod, overweening manner which many players adopt until they learn better. He was not a good loser—not because of the money: he was well ahead of the game anyhow: but because of the pleasure it gave him to win, to outdraw and outdare the others around the table—and when he lost a hand, he was too busy nursing his chagrin to learn anything from the loss. He did not become absorbed in poker theory, as so many of them were, figuring the relative value of hands, calculating the odds against drawing certain combinations, determining what to draw to, what to discard; he played blindly, boisterously, riding his luck, incautious, erratic, a little too eager. In this he was like fortunate beginners at other things than poker: like a beginner at skating, say, who in imitation of Browning's thrush must repeat his first fine careless rapture, until the inevitable nasty spill sobers him and either makes him good or makes him quit.

That was mostly during hunting season, when the weather was raw. Other times, when the weather was fine, he enjoyed being at Solitaire with his family. He especially liked spending the period between supper and bedtime with Hugh, who was five that spring. They watched the dark come down, daylight dissolving upward, merging into the overhead darkness like pale dust. Above the lawn, which sloped gently from the house to the road and beyond to the cypresses at the lake shore, lightning bugs performed their scattered, pulsing gleams. Crickets choired, and usually there was a pair of mocking birds in the sycamore beside the steps, splitting their throats with song, while from the lake came the deep unremitting boom of bullfrogs, a heavy chorus.

Bart sat in a big rocker, his shoes on the floor, his feet on the railing, his socks making two white blobs against the outer darkness. His cigar tip glowed off and on like a signal lamp, a tumefying ruby that grew brighter as twilight waned. Hugh sat beside him, his head on his hands on the railing, barefoot as he always was except Sundays, eyes limpid, hair shining in the light that fell through the open doorway. He listened to the crickets, the birds, the frogs with that rapt, isolated expression of people at concerts. Except for his yellow hair he looked much as Bart had looked when he was five, wearing identical knee-length jeans buttoning at the waist to identical collarless blouses.

Mrs Bart and her daughter, who was three and was called Florence too, sat on a low cushioned bench at the rear. They stayed until soon after eight oclock, hearing the concert change, insects and birds getting softer and frogs getting louder, until finally it was only a bass rumble from down by the lake. Then, the girl asleep on her lap, Mrs Bart would say, "Hugh: it's time," and the boy would get up and wait while his mother handed his sister to the nurse, who had been sitting on the steps all this time. They would pass indoors and up the stairs, leaving Bart alone on the porch.

Sometimes he would stay only a short time, sometimes an hour or two; he liked it here, alone like this. But at last he would rise, moving awkwardly, cramped with long sitting, a little pursy already with the accumulation of flesh, thickened from armpits to fundament. Carrying his shoes, he would climb the stairs, turning out lamps as he went.

The children usually were asleep by then, the nurse asleep too on a pallet between their beds. Bart would turn out the lamp in the upper hall and move in darkness to the bedroom door. Mrs Bart always left a candle burning for him at the bedside. Some nights she would still be awake, her eyes glinting in the flicker of light, but more often she was asleep, her starched nightcap shining like mother-of-pearl, its fringe having that firm, lightsome, meticulous quality of carved marble and pastry icing. Bart would undress, groaning like an old man as he hunched off his suspenders, stepped out of his trousers, and lifted his shirt over his head. He always waited until his nightshirt was on before taking off his socks and the bottom half of his underwear.

He would cross to the bed and blow out the candle, getting in on the near side because he would be first to rise in the morning, though she was never far behind him. And sometimes, if she was awake, he would put out one hand in a groping motion, fumbling like a man in a strange dark room, and lay it flat against her far thigh. That was the signal. Then he would hitch up both their garments, avoiding any show of haste or urgency, and mount. It would be careful and controlled, Bart holding his weight on knees and elbows and maintaining an even breath because any display would be distasteful, until the end was accomplished and he could turn his back and sleep.

Thus the first two children had been conceived; thus two more were to be. Their third was born in June of that year, on a Monday. It was a boy. In the early hours of the following morning it died. Unlike the other two, who had been quite ugly at birth, this was a beautiful baby. When Bart came into the room after the delivery, he looked down into the baby's face and said, "Look, Florence: look. He's laughing." Nodding his head, he laughed himself. "Kitchy, kitchy," he said, bending over. "Kitchy, kitchy." He insisted on holding it; he even rocked it a bit in his arms before handing it back to the midwife. "Did you see him laughing? He was laughing." Mrs Bart watched him; it had not been a difficult birth but she was weak. "He looks like you," Bart told her. "Look at his eyes. Blue, like yours."

"I see them," she said, too tired to remind him that all babies' eyes were blue.

"But just look at him. Look at him." And Bart even insisted to Dr Clinton how beautiful the child was.

"Yes indeed, a fine one," the doctor said, somewhat taken aback by this show of feeling. However, he soon recovered his effusive bedside manner, his practiced joviality. "Youre right as rain: he looks like his mother. You werent going to let him have all the children, were you, Florence?"

Mrs Bart shook her head. "He looks like baby pictures of Father," she said.

The two men were silent, remembering the dead general. "Then maybe he'll be a soldier," the doctor said.

"Thats it," Bart said. "We'll make a soldier of him. With buttons on his coat and a pair of those things on his shoulders; you know . . ."

"Epaulets," Dr Clinton said.

"Thats it. Thats it."

Late that afternoon he stood on the porch, seeing the doctor off, watching the buggy go up the road toward Bristol, spokes twinkling in the dust. It was a fine day, brilliant with sunshine, the first really hot day of the long summer. Planting was over, leaves showing tender and green down the rows; it would be at a stand within the month, and in the churches the planters gave thanks for the punctual activity of the rain. Bart went to the stable and saddled his horse—a sign of unusually good humor, for generally he shouted out of a window for Billy Boy to saddle it while he put on his boots—mounted, and rode toward the rear of Solitaire, the jungle beyond the creek at its eastern limit.

He nodded to all the fieldhands, smiling gayly, and stopped to speak with those who had been there longest. "It's another boy, Uncle Jerry," he told an old Negro who had been on the place for forty years, since the time of Mrs Bart's grandfather.

"Well, sir, Mars Hugh. You sho dont waste no time."

"What I want to be wasting time for, Uncle Jerry?"

"It's the truth, gospel truth."

"Come up to the house tomorrow. I'll show him to you."

"And maybe a dram to drink?" Jerry leaned on his hoe, looking up.

"Might be something like that for you, Jerry."

"You aint ghy forget it?"

"Be there: I'll show you."

"You knows I will, Mars Hugh, you knows I will." He grinned and shook his head. "I bet thats one fine baby, lak his paw."

"He looks like his mother."

"Lak little miss?"

"Just like her, Jerry."

"I knows it's a fine baby, then. Efn he look lak Miss Flaunts, I be bound they aint no finer."

"Youll see for yourself. I'll show him to you when you come for that dram tomorrow. Good day, Uncle Jerry."

"Good day, captain. . . . Mars Hugh!"

Bart reined in the horse. "Yes?"

"What you done name him?"

"Name him?" Bart looking down at the toe of his boot, quiet, speculative. Then he said, "We're going to name him for his grand-daddy, Miss Florence's father."

"For the genril? For old marster?"

"Thats right, Jerry.'

"Oo-ee. It sho ghy be some shouting round this place come christening day."

BUT THAT night, sleeping in a room across the hall, Bart was awakened by a voice calling, "Marster! Marster!" Starting up, he saw that it was the midwife; for the past two weeks she had been sleeping in the room with Mrs Bart. She wore a cast-off petticoat and a shirtwaist made from flour sacking. "Come quick, Mars Hugh. Mistis say come quick." She stood in the doorway shouting at him. In her excitement her head shook so that her turban was a white blur in the dark.

"What is it?" he said, raising himself in bed, not yet awake.

86

"What is it?"

"Come quick, Mars Hugh." That was all she could say, shaking
her hands up and down. "Come quick."

When he reached the door of the room across the hall he saw his
wife on her knees in the center of the bed. She was bending over
something, and she was wailing. Then Bart reached the bed and
saw what she was bending and wailing over. It was the baby—
stiff, convulsive, and (even in the dim dawning light he could see
this) quite blue. "Lie down, Florence, lie down," he said.

She turned to him with both hands over her mouth and her eyes
stretched big. Still running—he had not stopped; he had seen the
baby and spoken as he ran—he described a rather wide curve and
ran back through the doorway, into the hall and downstairs to the
kitchen, wondering: Warm or cold? Warm or cold? He remembered hearing somewhere that a child in convulsions should be
immersed in warm or cold water, but he could not remember
which.

Perhaps because he finally had decided (if so, he had decided
exactly wrong) or perhaps because there was no hot water and it
would have taken time to shake up the stove and heat some, he
pumped a big copper boiler full of cold water and ran back upstairs with it. Water sloshed onto the carpet and onto the front of
his nightshirt, clammy against his belly and thighs. While he lifted
the baby from the bed and splashed it into the boiler, Mrs Bart
continued to moan with both hands over her mouth, her eyes still
wide.

Though he had chosen wrong as to the temperature of the water,
it made no difference, did not matter at all—as so many decisions
men make hurriedly, their hands trembling and their hearts knocking at their throats, do not matter at all—for the baby was dead,
and had been dead when Bart ran into the room the first time. So
the running, the worry, the drawing of the wrong water, all had
been quite useless, just as what he was doing now, kneeling beside
a copper boiler on the floor and slapping cold water onto a small,
contorted, apparently boneless blue body, was quite useless. At

last he realized this and sat back on his heels, looking blankly at the baby in the boiler. The moaning on the bed had stopped. Mrs Bart said, "Is? . . . Is? . . ."

"Yes, Florence," he said softly. "He's dead. Dead now."

At this the midwife threw up her hands, the palms showing pink in the early light, and began to keen. It was a high, piercing crescendo, like a siren. "Hush," Bart said. "Hush that. Hush!"

Mrs Bart did not attend the funeral held Wednesday afternoon in the cedar grove five hundred yards south of the house. This was the old Solitaire burying ground, a shady plot, carpeted brown with droppings from the cedars and fenced off with rusty barbed wire to keep out stray cows and runaway mules. People passing along the road by the lake could see across the fields to where Clive Jameson's tombstone stood big and pale against the backdrop of dark, stunted trees. On its left were the smaller stones of old Isaac, the founder, and his barmaid wife who had had such handsome arms and hair. On its right, beyond a four-foot gap awaiting the diggers who would come when Mrs Jameson died in Bristol, were the graves of two children, one without a marker because the child had died at birth, the other with a small sandstone obelisk from which the inscription had already begun to wear away.

The central stone was nearly eight feet tall, ornamented with scrolls. Beneath the great seal of the Confederacy (*Deo Vindice* it said under a man on horseback holding one arm extended, the whole surrounded by a wreath) the following time-heavy inscription had been cut deep into the marble:

CLIVE WINGFIELD JAMESON, BRIGADIER GENERAL *C.S.A.* *8 March 1833–2 Febrvary 1884: Patriot Soldier Gentleman: Fearless, ever actvated by the highest motives, ornament of his time, and hero of his nation, neither cannon's roar nor death's awfvl lance stay'd him in the service he gave ¶ Devotion to his covntry's cavse, a sense of responsibility to those who follow'd him, fearlessness in battle—these will cavse him to live forever, in the hearts of those for whom he fovght, beneath the*

*vnsvllied banner of a Nation that pass'd withovt sin, and
lives vndimm'd in the hearts of her citizen sons, 'til the
time be come to establish her anew* ❡ *"Earth, reverence
thy bvrden 'til resvrrection bring new birth."* Beneath
this, in smaller characters: (*This monument placed here
1890, Clive Jameson Chapter, U.D.C. Funds supplied in
part by veterans who served in his command.*)

Bart remembered the day they came to Solitaire for the dedica-
tion of the monument. It was in November, nearly seven years ago,
five months after his marriage. All afternoon a slow unremitting
drizzle fell. They stood in a close half-circle about the draped
stone, female progeny of defeat, wearing seamed tarlatan and taf-
feta that had been cut and stitched in the days when their young
men were still alive. They had met in the volunteered parlor
months before, submitting their rough drafts of the inscription.
After combining them in feverish collaboration, inserting a phrase
here, a comma there, striking out what seemed to lack the spark,
until the final, purple, obsequious language was ready for the stone,
they went out in groups, collecting reluctant dimes and fifty-cent
pieces from veterans. When the fund was complete they dispatched
a fair copy of the inscription by U.S. mail to the hated North to be
carved into stone from a Vermont quarry. Then, when the monument had been set up in the cedar grove at Solitaire, they gathered
in the rain, all eyes on the draped square-shouldered stone while
their leader, elected for a term after victory by cabal, jerked the
cord and the drapery fluttered damply to earth. The veterans,
shouldered slightly toward the rear by the eager and unrecon-
structed dames, managed to give an imitation of the Rebel yell, and
the ladies, stirred by the yell and pleased with their success, de-
parted to seek another project, another outlet for their omnivorous,
impervious maiden energy.

He remembered that scene now as he walked the five hundred
yards to the cedar grove, following the four men who carried the
coffin, two on each side. It was an easy burden; it seemed hardly
larger than a shoe box. The four men followed Mr Clinkscales,

the Bristol rector; he was lame in one ankle and walked with the prayer book held close to his face, looking down over it to watch his step. When he stopped near the grave, the men with the coffin came to a jumbled halt behind him. He read: *Jesus saith to his disciples, Ye now therefore have sorrow: but I will see you again, and your heart shall rejoice, and your joy no man taketh from you.* He stepped aside, motioning, and the men set the coffin on the ropes; they let it down fairly evenly. He dropped a few clods into the grave and droned: *In sure and certain hope.* Then he bowed his head. After a moment of silence he prayed again, then ceased. Bart felt a hand on his arm. "Let us go up to the house," Mr Clinkscales said. As they walked away they heard the diggers throwing in dirt. The clods made a hollow thumpthump sound, like something out of a dream.

There was a group of men on the porch; they rose when Bart and Mr Clinkscales came up the steps. Bart went into the house and climbed the staircase. Wives of the men below were in the upper hall. When he saw them he remembered he had on his hat, so he removed it and bowed to the women. They returned the bow by extending their necks, performing supple gooselike motions. There were five of them in the bedroom. Bart crossed to the bed, where Mrs Bart was lying, and stood with his hat against his knee. "Youll excuse us, ladies," he said awkwardly. They hurried out, their feet hidden beneath their skirts; except for the patter they might have been floating.

Bart stood by the bed, looking down at his wife, and she looked directly into his face, waiting for him to speak. "It's done," he said. "It's over now, Florence." Suddenly her eyes brimmed; they shone in the sunlight filtered through the curtains. This was the first time she had cried since the death of the child. The tears accumulated, slipped over the lower lids and onto her cheeks. As they began to flow quite fast, though there still was no motion in her face, Bart knelt beside the bed and held her hand. "Dont cry, Florence," he said, his mouth against her wrist. "Please; please dont cry."

But the tears continued. They continued for two more days.

Then, as if the ducts had gone dry—as if though they were still pumping, there was nothing left to pump—she lay in the same suspirant attitude of sorrow, recovering from both the birth and death of her child. At any hour of the night, Bart would waken and feel the tension of her grief, the tearducts pumping at emptiness, the dry eyes open, addressing the invisible ceiling, but not focused.

This passed too, gave way to another period in which her grief was lighter because it permitted action, but also was sharper because it let up on the dulling of her perception. Now the full force of her loss became apparent to her. This almost drove her back into her first prostrate condition. But it did not, for she busied herself with running the house; she became a driver of servants because she could neither bear to be idle herself nor to see those about her idle. All the furniture was rearranged, the carpets beaten; special dishes appeared on the table at every meal.

Bart watched with some of the amazement of a man seeing what he had thought was a spring breeze develop into a tornado. At night too, in bed, she was not the same. Now it was she who made the overture. Spurning their old signal, she would roll against him, rigorous, spasmodic, urgent, already jerking at the hem of her gown. She made little throaty sounds of passion; she writhed. Bart was aghast and did not understand.

This passed too, in its turn. Not four months after the death of the child, this second and furious period ended. It did not play out: it just stopped, gave way to her former passive manner. The frenzy was finished, gone. She became meek again, almost bovine. Bart recognized the symptoms, her careful movements, her attitude of inward listening. But still she did not tell him; she waited until she was sure. Then one night she told him. They were in bed. She said, "We are going to have our fourth child, Mr Bart."

CHAPTER FOUR

THE RIVER

MRS BART gave this child the name that had been intended for the one who died; she called him Clive for her father, General Jameson. He was like the first two, red and ugly. Bart displayed none of the enthusiasm of a year ago, did not mention epaulets or remark on the blue eyes, but he was pleased. He began to spend more time with his children. He had the plantation carpenter convert a rear bedroom into a game room, where he played Slap-Jack and Battle with Hugh and inspected Florence's doll house. He considered bringing a tutor up from New Orleans for Hugh, who was seven, but he decided against it since none of the other planters did so. Lake children attended a one-room school in Ithaca, where a small and timid old lady, with a foredefeated air of fear and palsy—she was one of those who had lost their young men in the war—unfolded by rote the elements of arithmetic and reading.

Girls later were sent to the convent in Bristol and subsequently to one of the Southern seminaries, usually in Virginia. Boys went to military preparatory schools, then either to Ole Miss or Sewanee, and if by that time they had chosen a profession, medicine or law or the army, they went to an Eastern university, Harvard preferred, or Virginia. Education was not intended to prepare them for either work or life: it was just the accepted occupation for boys and youths, something a man had behind him in after years. Their real education came when they returned to the plantation and learned from their fathers' overseers how to farm cotton. What was intended was the repetition of a cycle, maintenance of a static life-way.

Three things defeated it, when it was defeated: the easy credit that could be drawn on as long as there was an acre left to mortgage, the precariousness of a crop as subject to weather whims as a barometer, and the violence of the avocational life they inherited from and were schooled in by their fathers. Hunting and poker and drinking were their pastimes, and it was the accepted belief that the way to test a gentleman was to take him hunting, play high-stake cards with him, or get him drunk.

Usually their initial sexual experience, consummated after months of masturbation which they discussed and even performed in groups behind a barn or on the creekbank, was with either a sullen Negro girl from one of the plantations or a boisterous Negro prostitute in the Bristol red-light district: Negro because of the code which made white girls untouchable—untouchable, that is, until promiscuity had somehow been established; whereupon they engaged in wholesale coitus-bees. Something made them not want to be alone at such a time: they would ride into the woods, as many as five or six of them in the buggy with the one girl, and would alight and wait their turns like sheep at a shearing or dogs. They would stand in a slightly pimpled group, laughing nervously and smoking cigarettes with a squint, drawing straws to determine who would be next, occasionally calling: "Have you fainted in there? Come on, come on, man," while under the trembling bush that partly screened it, the adolescent two-back straining continued muffled and profound.

This phase ended when they boarded a northbound train on their way to school. They went in pairs, like bird dogs to field trials, and roomed together in barracks of crenelated stone. Here they wore brass buttons and learned the manual of arms along with a smattering of history: learned, too, to collaborate on lies about life in the Delta, to be homesick but not admit it until they became convinced that homesickness was something to brag about. Going away opened their eyes in this respect. They would tell the others, boys from other states and other sections, "It's well enough to say youre not homesick. You didnt leave what I left."

They got so they even believed it themselves, believed it so implicitly that the homecoming itself was disappointing. There would be the Negroes and the lake and the house and the Christmas fireworks, all more or less as they had described them: but the overtones of romance, the colors with which their imaginations had tinted it, were gone. With the frustrate yearning of boys wanting to be men and men wanting to be boys again, all during their school days they talked about home and all during their holidays they talked about school.

When they came home on this first Christmas holiday, everyone remarked on how much they had changed. And it was true. They spoke now in a tone unlike any they had ever used before, even at the school they had left two days ago. They spoke to their parents and the servants in a tone of condescension and looked down on their old playmates with a superior mien much like that of tapped freshmen at the first class-meeting after pledge week. This did not infuriate the parents, however, any more than it did the servants. It pleased them. "Look," they said, parents and servants alike. "Look how manly. He'll make a fine man before long."

But toward the girls, quite different creatures now after three months of separation, their manner was gallant and polite, florid and concerned. This exasperated their younger brothers, but it delighted the girls. These young men, home in their tight-fitting uniforms, danced with their heads well back, left arms stiff and high and chests thrust forward. It was really painful to the girls, the way the buttons dug into their flesh. But painful or not, undressing for bed in the late hours after the dance, the girls observed the marks the buttons left—eagles volant, latin stamped in reverse —with the tender perversity of masochists caressing their whip-scars.

Their way of life had been much the same as the boys' until, at about the age of ten, a breach was established which lay unspanned for the balance of their lives. It dated from a boy's first hunting trip, soon after the Christmas when he received his first gun. Returning from the hunt, the boy displayed a false, superior manner which, though it was not without its comical aspect, the girls some-how realized was not to be taken lightly. From this day things were different between them, and they knew it. Young men and women, later husbands and wives, were like two tribes that had mingled but not merged.

At first, immediately after the hunting trip, the girls felt hurt, like children expelled from a game without knowing the reason. But later, when they saw its relation to other peculiarities in the way life went, they accepted their role with the same willingness they had shown playing Indian. They followed their female share of the pattern, exciting at first only contempt, then indifference, then mystery, then love, and then respect.

Marriage claimed the majority before they were out of their teens. Nothing in their former lives had indicated that they would make good wives or housekeepers or mothers or even companions. They had been flighty, supercilious, inconsiderate; they had been occupied mainly with dances and gossip and clothes, unconcerned with cooking or sewing or anything that had to do with running a house. But immediately after the wedding, indeed sometimes at the ceremony itself, something stern and predatory would show in the bride's expression. In their outside dealings, once they had a house of their own to manage, they were sharp-tongued and predacious. These qualities, ugly enough in themselves, would have been de-spicable in a man, yet their presence in the character of the women was what made planter society hold together as long as it did. They bore children early and continued to bear them right into middle age, sons and daughters who followed the pattern their fathers and mothers had followed before them, and followed it with a faithful-ness that did not require teaching because it was inherited, appar-ently, along with the bone structure of their faces.

That was the life-way of young people on the lake, male and female; that was the pattern laid out and waiting for Bart's three children as they entered the new century, a boy of eight, a girl of six, and a year-old baby boy. No life-way could have been more completely unlike the one he had been raised under, back in East

Mississippi. He might have reminded himself at the outset to expect a different product.

LAKE JORDAN had once been a bend of the Mississippi. But long ago, before the time of man, the river ran off and left it, and now they were five miles apart at the closest point, separated by a jungle of barrowpits and canebrakes infested with alligators and wildcats and moccasins. Early settlers built a corduroy road that ran from the upper end of the lake, westward across the wasteland, to a steamboat landing where they loaded their cotton for sale on the New Orleans market. In the old days, and in Bart's day too, road and landing were communal property, their upkeep shared by the planters using them. From time to time the landing would be washed away (floods came roughly one every seven years) and the planters would meet to vote on replacing it.

That was what happened in early February of 1903. And it happened quite suddenly, for on a Thursday when Bart rode over to the river on a hunch inspection, the landing was intact, though foam was lapping between the planks. Saturday morning Luke Fink, a trapper, saw Bart on the street in Ithaca. He was on his biannual spree, an undersized man with long greasy hair, teeth yellow and broken, breath sour. "You fellers best get you a builder and shell out," he said. "Yer landing's plumb gone. Aint hide nor hair of it left, cep whats smack atop the levee."

"Washed clean away?"

"Yep: clean." Fink swayed in his filthy buckskins, screwing up his eyes. "But I believe I'd put off building, though, fI's you, brother. You aint ghy ship no cotton this year, brother; no Sir. Not lessn you done found a way to plow it under water."

Bart rode over that afternoon, and it was true. His hunch had been right, except for being a couple of days early, and in fact it was not so much a hunch as it was a calculated probability. Rain had continued through late fall and winter. Even back in the dog days there had been sudden downpours, which were of short dura-

tion and did nothing to relieve the heat, but which flooded yard
and field with the abrupt fury of a waterfall. Then toward the
end of October a day had dawned chill and gray; fog blew in off
the lake to be dispersed by the rising sun, which then, however,
as if it had accomplished all it came to do, hid itself behind a
high murky haze, and the rain began to fall. This was not one
of those abrupt short torrents that had come with the end of
summer: this was the slight steady drizzle of true autumnal rain.
It rained through dinner, cotton hanging in bluing skeins on dead
brown stalks, getting darker, and when people went to bed after
supper they heard it on the roofs, a faint insistent patter. "Another
year gone," men told their wives, lying in bed and hearing the
rain come down. "Thank God I bout got *mine* picked."

October, November, December: the rain did not stop. January
brought a brief let-up, yet cold weather did not come. At the close
of the month the rain returned harder, more insistent, as if to void
the respite. The Memphis *Appeal* reported that it was general all
over the Valley, and there was an editorial captioned *Another
Flood Year?* which provoked a response under *Letters from our
Subscribers*; thanks to government engineers, floods were things
of the past, the letter said. Yet stages advanced three and four feet
a week. River men said perhaps; ominous, obscure, rather vain,
they shook their heads; "It aint no telling what He'll do," they
said, meaning the river.

"But what do you think?"

"Think? I dont think, son. It aint no telling when that old
river's concerned. He'll let you know in His own good time. Just
wait: He'll let you know."

So Bart came back that afternoon and reported what he had
seen. Monday the planters met at Clyde Allard's house; they met
in the living room, about forty of them. Murphy Lane, who acted
as chairman because he had served a term in the legislature, stood
on the hearth at one end of the room. He leaned back, elbows on
the mantel, a big man wearing a wide brown beard to hide a reced-
ing chin, and outlined the plan under discussion. The question

was whether to build immediately, and if so how much money to spend. "Thats how it is," he said in conclusion, and waited for someone to speak.

"Well and good," Prentiss Kent said. "But can we build with the water up high as it is?"

"That one was done in '87," Major Henry Dubose said. He was seventy-three years old. "The one before it was done in '81. Both times we had more water than now."

"How much?" Leroy McClain asked.

"Whoa here," Allard said. "Who wants to build in the face of a flood? Some folks say theres water coming."

After a short silence Peter Durfee said, "What the devil do they know about it?"

"Or anyone else, for that matter."

"I believe it," Major Dubose said suddenly. The others were quiet, respectful, watching him. "It was just this way in '93, this same kind of weather exactly."

"That landing held all the way through it," Durfee said defensively.

"Thats it," Walker Ertle said. "Build one that will ride it if it comes."

"Youre talking more money than I like to hear talked," old Bryant Sadlier said, and young Bryant, sitting beside his father, said in a rather shrill voice:

"I think so too, I think so too."

There was a general grunt of agreement. Then Major Dubose said, "Wont no landing hold if the river really wants it. Not if He really wants it." The short respectful silence fell again.

"All right," Lane said, taking his elbows off the mantel. "All right: what about it? Whoever wants it built now, stand up." About three-quarters of the men stood up, though some of those who were standing crouched to keep from being counted among the ayes. "All right, gentlemen," Lane said. "We build now."

"Youre a bunch of damned fools," Kent said gruffly. "We're going to watch our money wash away."

This landing was to be no different from the other three they had built in the past twenty years. By the opening of March workmen were replacing lost pilings and strengthening old ones. Labor and materials were furnished by the planters, but they hired a Memphis engineer to supervise the job. He was young, enthusiastic, a hard worker, and spent much of his time up to his hips in mud. "Gentlemen," he said, "I believe I can promise you this is the last one youll build: the crest will pass in a week. And besides, itll take a damn sight more than water to wash this one away."

The planters stood beside their horses, watching him. Major Dubose was among them. "He is a damn sight more than water, son," the major said. "Listen." They heard a deep constant murmur, the current sucking at the pilings with a faint purring whisper. "You hear what He's saying? Prr. Hear what He's saying. Prr'r: 'I'm go have it, I'm go have it.' Youve dared Him now, son, and He dont take a dare. We mought as well go home and wait for the water."

Major Dubose spoke with a broad full-mouth South Carolina accent. He had come to Mississippi as a young man in 1855, and excepting the four war years with Wade Hampton, he had been in the lake district ever since. He was always neat and clean — not sectional characteristics — wearing tight-fitting lightweight black suits, even in summer, and shirts whose starched bosoms had that smooth, milky glaze seen in oyster shells. He was always cleanshaven and wore his sparse white hair clipped so short that his scalp showed through like a pink, fleshy egg.

Thin and slight, wearing no jewelry, not even a watch, he spent his afternoons writing what were said to be his war reminiscences, though no one had ever read a page of the manuscript and the major never discussed a battle — not even Five Forks, where he was in on Tom Rosser's shad bake. It was also said that General Hampton once called him the fieriest man he had ever seen in battle, but this may have been in one of the General's expansive moments, and probably was evoked by the fact that the major, a very small man, had adopted in his youth a certain game-cock jauntiness.

He lived in a square frame house with a veranda all the way

around it. He had lived alone here since the death of his wife, thirty years ago. She had died in childbirth, and the infant (it was a son; they had wanted a son) outlived her less than a week. Major Dubose wept at night, alone in the wide bed, and for five years he refused to be comforted. Then people going past on the road began to see him on the front veranda, sitting straight and severe at a large deal table, wearing his coat in even the hottest weather, making microscopic characters in an angular, cramped calligraphy. He had been doing this for better than twenty-five years; the manuscript filled a six-foot chest that sat in one corner of what had been his wife's parlor. "Major's still at it," passing people said.

Once a white tenant, stepping up unexpectedly to report an incident to the major, caught a glimpse of the manuscript. He told about it that night at the general store, sitting with a crowd of men around him. He said that as Major Dubose herded him toward the other end of the veranda, away from the table, he saw the topmost page. "Hit was a big sheet," he said. "Close-writ. Now I aint no reader and I aint shamed to say so, but I kin read figures as well as the next man, maybe better. That number was six, four, oh, three."

So now people believed that three years ago, in the spring of 1900, Major Dubose had completed his six thousand four hundred and third page. "Then I reckon he's through Shiloh," one said grinning.

"Shiloh?" another said. "Shuck: he must be taking his fiftieth whack at Appomattox by now."

By the end of March the new landing was ready. The planters came for the approval, half a hundred of them riding in a body like a cavalry troop in civilian dress. The young Memphis engineer was in higher spirits than ever, rubbing his hands together and laughing a sharp staccato laugh while he indicated strong features of the construction. He explained why he believed it would last. "Look at those stringers: cypress, every one. Look at those pilings, too: sunk twice as deep as any used before. Itll last you, mark my words. In the first place, we built it under conditions about as bad as any youll see."

"He talks like he's trying to defend something," the planters told one another. "A landing or a levee dont need defending. It's its own defense. It's either good or it aint. Talk wont make it any stronger."

The engineer was wrong about one thing at least. The crest had not passed. Two weeks later the river was still on the boom. Cotton planted in early April came up pale green, sappy, tumid; it was weedy and the choppers could not get at it. "Might as well flood," men said, watching the steady rain. "What difference which way it comes, out of the sky or overland?"

Stages continued to rise. Flood stage was twenty-five feet, and already it was past thirty. Forty feet would top the levee. But it would break before it reached forty. That was agreed.

It broke early the morning of May third, the first clear sunshiny day in more than a month. Word came first by telegraph: BACHELOR BEND OUT SIX OCLOCK STOP SPREAD WORD EVACUATE REPEAT EVACUATE and then a locomotive came from the north, the direction of the break, balancing a plume of steam on its whistle. It did not stop; it did not even carry cars. "Water's building up behind us!" His Negro fireman sweat-drenched behind him, the engineer leaned out of the cab, shouted the news to way stations off the telegraph line, and pulled the throttle open again: a short, violent screech of the whistle and, chuffing, it disappeared down the track as suddenly as it had come, dragging a dirty bank of smoke over its shoulder like a dog running with one corner of a blanket in his teeth.

Two hours later, people milling about the streets of Ithaca heard the steamboat blow for the landing. Women and children, loaded into carriages and wagons, were taken over the corduroy road to the river. The road was crowded, clotted in places by breakdowns. Women sat with babies on their laps. Older children were yelling at each other or crying because they wanted to stay with their fathers and see the water. Younger ones sat with their legs straight out before them, big-eyed, watched the teamsters crack their whips: "Hum up, Dolly! You, Smoke: hum up hyar, sir!"

As they arrived they passed over the stageplank, joining other refugees aboard the steamboat and on the barges lashed alongside. High in the cupola, his hands on the big wheel like the master at a lottery, the pilot blew a blast on the whistle and the sternwheeler, panting stertorously, backed from bank, came about in a wide, listing swing, and hung churning at the crest of a wave. The pilot pulled the whistle cord again, this time for a short goodbye screech like a hurt animal's, and rang full speed ahead. As the boat recovered, gathering momentum, the men on the levee watched the refugees gazing back in mute acceptance. Soon the boys were running about the deck, playing Steamboat.

Before it passed from sight around the bend, Bart shouted for the mules to be headed back. At a hurried meeting that morning he had been appointed to be in charge of the wagon train to and from the landing. While others were going about the countryside collecting women and children, he had commandeered mules and wagons and teamsters from the nearest plantations, and had them ready to transport the refugees, dispatching each wagon as fast as it was filled. Now he led the clanking column back to the east shore of the lake, where he dismissed it.

By nine oclock he was back at Solitaire. With Billy Boy as foreman, Bart went to work saving his property in a battle against time. They were not fighting water, the flood itself: that would be like trying to box a snowstorm. They were fighting the diminishing period of time that remained until the water arrived. Hitching mules to ropes run through pulleys, they hoisted gin machinery to overhead beams and lashed it there. Commissary goods were stacked on boards that had been laid along the rafters. House furnishings, rugs and pictures and drapes, were carried upstairs. The servants worked with feverish efficiency, running up and down the staircase, bearing their burdens and grinning at each other like amateur actors at a dress rehearsal. By noon the work was finished; they could sit down and await the water.

It came like an immense plate being slid over the ground, shallow, opaque, innocent-looking, flecked with foam and littered with chicken coops and fence rails. Bart was in the kitchen, eating. Three hundred yards in front of the house the lake was rising swiftly.

"Dar hit," a voice called from an upstairs window, but Bart continued eating. It may be my last hot meal for some time, he thought. I wont spoil it, not just to look at water. I'll get my fill of looking at water soon enough.

When he had finished eating he went upstairs. From a second story window he could see it: an apparently motionless, limitless, level sheet like rusty cast iron. It was very quiet, violence reduced to its simplest terms. Then, above the wide brown expanse and above the near rim with its reaching tatters of water, he saw buzzards wheeling rigidly in slow, tight spirals.

When the flood reached the upper end of Lake Jordan it halted, flowed down the shallow bank with a constant sucking sound, murmuring deep but not loud, a smooth curve of dark water running downhill without foam. The lake, already high because of the fall and winter rains, began to fill swiftly. Water climbed the wharf pilings inch by inch until it had submerged them, then began to mount the slope toward the lakeside road and the houses beyond. But when it reached the road it was on a level with the sheet at the head of the lake, and it stopped. As if this were its cue, the sun came out again and the flat, perfectly joined expanse continued its forward motion, again like a sliding plate but shining now in the brilliant May sunshine, as if it had sloughed its tarnished surface into the lake basin and been burnished.

Somebody is going to get a chance to make that old joke at the major, Bart thought as he watched the water ripple up the lawn from the road. This joke dated from 1857, two years after young Dubose had arrived from Carolina. He was a young man then, a bachelor, and he changed the name of his plantation, calling it Ararat as a sort of boast because his house site was the highest in the district. This angered a neighbor, for when water lapped the eaves of his house, Dubose's would be sitting high and dry. Naming it after Noah's mountain was the crowning insult.

So when the great flood of '57 came, though the neighbor's house showed only its ridgepole, there was consolation in seeing water swirl two feet deep inside the house called Ararat. The neighbor had himself rowed to a point above Dubose's front yard, from which he could look through the doorway and see the owner wading among ruined furniture. Halting his boatman, the neighbor sat solemnly in the stern and addressed Dubose: "Aryrat, hey? Look to me like you ought to named it Nary Rat." Then he had himself rowed away, not even glancing back at the young man standing kneedeep in the doorway and shaking his fist at the skiff.

Bart remembered this as he put on hip boots. When he came onto the porch there was already half an inch of muddy, flecked water washing about, slippery, treacherous as oil, viscid with old river-bottom slime. While he stood there watching it, booted like a musketeer and wearing a full-skirted coat, water began to ripple over the door sill and onto the polished hardwood floor in little reaching rivulets, blunt fingers of brown water creeping toward the staircase as if it knew that was the way upstairs.

Sitting on the first landing with Billy Boy, Bart watched the water submerge step after step. It was strange. As long as he watched it, the water did not seem to rise a fraction: but if he turned his head, even for an instant it seemed, he could see a difference as soon as he looked back. There was an illusion of being able to control the flood by looking at it intently, the way a cat can do with a pack of dogs.

Just before supper-time, when water ran five feet deep in the lower story, it stopped rising. A current dimpled by eddies and humped by boils ran the length of the downstairs hall. There was nearly a foot of silt on the floor. In one corner of the parlor, where the current ran full tilt into converging walls, shattering itself against the plaster, sand and silt were built above the water line, black, shifty, as soft and slick as grease.

"I bet that stuff will grow cotton," Billy Boy said.

"Um hm," Bart said, nodding positively. "We're evermore going to make us some cotton, next year."

After watching the water a while longer, they went upstairs and sat in Mrs Bart's sewing room. Soon after dark, sitting among a jumble of downstairs finery—paintings in carved gilt frames leaning against the baseboards, showing landscapes with the unearthly trees and colonnades of Victorian Rome, wooly sad-eyed animals saving children from the rims of cliffs and the surf, nineteenth century ladies and gentlemen posing in fatuous attitudes as if they had swallowed ramrods except that they also gave the impression of not being able to swallow anything, and in one corner a massive Duncan Phyfe table upside-down with its legs in the air like a dead mule—they heard a voice calling, "Hello, hello! Hello, hello!"

Bart went to the window. Looking down he saw two men in a skiff, their shadows flung gigantic and shaky on the whorled night water by a lantern. One was amidships, flicking the oars to hold the boat in position. The other, holding the lantern, stood in the bow. Both were Negroes.

"Mr Bart?"

"Yes?"

"Mr Bart, Major sick."

"Major Dubose?"

"Yassir. Say he dying. I spec he is, too. He look lak he dying."

"Hold the boat: I'll be right down."

He turned from the window and stomped into his boots again, then put on his coat and took a snub, two-barreled derringer from a desk drawer. "Look out for things while I'm gone," he told Billy Boy.

"Sho," Billy Boy said, watching him go. Then, alone in the overfurnished sewing room, he pursed his mouth and said aloud, apparently addressing the figures looking blankly at him out of their gilded frames: "I aint apt to walk off."

ROWING BACK to Ararat, the Negroes told Bart what had happened. It was not very clear, but from what he could piece together out of their incoherent mumbling, Bart gathered that Major Dubose had had a stroke. He had been getting his gear into the loft of the barn, shouting at the workers and even carrying things himself. He did not fear for the house—there had been no flood water in it since '57 —but barn and gin were on lower ground. Then his seventy-three years began to tell on him. In all this excitement he became over-heated ("raid in the face," the Negro said) and went toward the house to rest. But he did not make it into the house. He just made it as far as the steps, where he fell.

The Negroes picked him up, carried him in and put him on his bed, then stood around frightened, not knowing what to do next, while water crept up the slope toward the one-story house. It rose in the yard; then it came onto the porch and into the house itself, rapacious, implacable, fore-victorious. When water purled a foot deep in the bedroom where the major lay, two of the Negroes finally did what they should have done before. They came after Bart, the nearest white man.

And now, rowing back toward Ararat—which they had left three hours ago, though it was only just over two miles away—they could not tell Bart what had delayed them. As far as they were concerned, words had not yet been coined that could describe it. "Us run into some trouble getting hyar," the Negro said, holding the bug-swarmed lantern.

Crossing the ordinarily sluggish creek which was the boundary between Solitaire and Ararat, they had been seized by a purring, undeniable force that seemed to grip the very grain of the planks of the skiff, hurling them—for a moment in outrage, and then in pure terror—spinning and sideways in the opposite direction. Trees fringing the creekbed fled past with the jerked swiftness of the old stage sets that moved behind galloping horses. The creek had backed up: it was flowing in reverse.

So at length, when it flung them aside with the same abrupt and disinterested fury with which it had seized them, they found them-selves in calm water, as if nothing had happened—except that the sun was half gone behind the water line and they were in the center

of what had been a cotton field, five miles off on a tangent from
the direction in which they had been traveling when they were
made off with. It was outside all their experience; all the Negro
with the lantern could call it was trouble; "Us run into some
trouble."

Returning, however, they crossed the creek without mishap;
they rowed beyond it into the yard at Ararat and up to the house.
Bart stepped onto the porch and waded through the hall to where
a golden rectangle of light was cast on the water through the door
of the major's bedroom. There were six Negroes in the room, four
men and two women. They sat on tables and chairs, their feet
drawn up, their eyes bulging white against their faces.

Major Dubose lay on the bed, which had been chocked clear of
the water by books placed under its legs. His coat and shoes had
been removed, his waistcoat unbuttoned. His shirt front was
crumpled and soiled by his fall in front of the steps four hours ago.
His eyes were wide open, straining, but he was paralyzed and could
not turn his head; he did not see Bart until he walked into his line
of vision. Then his eyes strained more and he began to make gut-
tural sounds far back in his throat, the tendons of his neck standing
out like cords.

Bart went to the bed and leaned over him, trying to make out
what he was saying. "He done been talking lak that ever since he
come to," a Negro said. Major Dubose was quiet for a moment,
gathering strength. Then, his mouth close to Bart's ear, he said:

"Scp. Scp."

Bart shook his head. "I cant understand," he said. "Is there something you want me to get you?" Major Dubose blinked, meaning
Yes.

"Mm. Mm. Scp."

"Dont try," Bart said. "Just lie quiet. You can tell me about it
tomorrow."

"Scp!" the major said, furious.

"It's all right," Bart said. "You can tell me later."

"Man. Man you. Scp." He seemed to gather all his energy for

the effort; Bart sensed the tension, the strain in the aphasic brain. "Man," Major Dubose said. "Man you."

"What man?"

"Man you. Scp."

"Man I what?"

"Man." The major strained. "Skip," he said, and Bart saw his lips form the final t although no sound got through.

"He talking bout his papers," a Negro said, the one who had come in the skiff with the lantern.

"Manuscript," Bart said, and the major blinked. Bart turned to the Negro. "Where does he keep it?"

"In the parlor," the Negro said. "In the chess. He dont 'low it to be dusted, even. It's on the flow, in the corner."

"On the . . ." Bart ran to the door, calling over his shoulder: "Bring the lantern."

By the faint yellow gleam of lantern light Bart saw water washing over the top of an iron-bound chest in the far corner of the parlor. It was six feet long and less than two feet high. There was already a thin deposit of silt on the lid.

Bart and the Negro crouched in the water and caught hold of it, lifting. It did not budge. "Try again," Bart said. It did not budge. "All right: get the others."

The other four took position around the chest, two on each side, Bart and the lantern Negro at the ends. He could smell them, the combined sweat of fear and exertion. "Get your back into it," he said, panting, and they heaved it onto a couch at that end of the room. It was heavy and water streamed from it.

"Major got the key," the Negro said. "In his vess."

Bart went back to the bedroom and took the brass key from a waistcoat pocket of the man on the bed, then returned to the parlor where the Negroes were standing in front of the couch. Bullet-headed, long-armed, simian in the lantern glare, they resembled performing apes misplaced in the seal act, knee-deep in water and watching the streaming chest. Bart turned the key and took the lock from the hasp. The lid made a wet, sucking sound as he lifted it. What he saw inside was not immediately recognizable. Looking at the sodden pulpy mass, which did not even float, Bart thought: What am I going to tell him? What will I say when he asks to see it?

But he did not have to tell the major anything, could not tell him anything: because as he and the five Negroes stood looking into the shipwrecked chest, shaking their heads at the ruined manuscript, they heard a sudden excited murmur from the bedroom, and when Bart reached the door he saw that Major Dubose had died. And almost immediately, almost soon enough to make it irreverent—but it was reflex; for the past fifteen hours his brain had been running in combat with the threat of water and then the water itself; it did not stop now—Bart thought: How in God's name are we going to bury him?

First he considered using a sheet for a shroud, weighted with rocks, sewed tight about the body, and let down into the lake from a boat. But he rejected the idea. It would split and rise, he thought. Besides, there ought to be something to point to afterwards, after the water was gone: a place to point to and say, There. Then he remembered the big iron-bound chest in the parlor. Six men had had to strain to lift it. "Bring the lantern," he said. "And come on, all of you."

They surrounded the chest again, the six of them, panting and straining, taking short mincing steps as they carried it across the parlor, down the hall, and into the bedroom. Bart felt his bootsoles slipping on the silt-settled floor. "Pick up," he said, panting. "Pick up." They set it beside the bed, using four straight-back dining room chairs, one at each corner, to keep it clear of the water.

Major Dubose's body appeared even smaller than it had in life, as if in death he had somehow drawn into himself. "Has he got a uniform?" Bart asked.

"No sir," the Negro said sadly. "He give it to Purdum; Purdum was buried in it." This was the major's body servant, who had served him through the war and afterward; dying, he had requested that he be buried in uniform, and he went into the ground a Confederate major. The Negro looked mournfully at the body on the bed. Suddenly he brightened; "Got a sword and a paper," he said.

Carrying the lantern, he led Bart into the parlor. "Dar," he said, holding the lantern close to the wall. A Confederate saber hung above a framed sheet of paper, a valor citation, signed *Wade Hampton Lt Gnl CSA.*

"Fine," Bart said, taking them down from the wall. "This is enough." Yes: enough, he thought, wading back to the bedroom. Not only the sword that won the bravery, but even a document to validate it. Yes: more than enough.

He smoothed the shirt-front as best he could, put the light black coat back on the body, and straightened the arms at the sides. He closed the eyes, and they remained shut, which surprised him; he had thought he would have to use coins. Then he took some of the ruined manuscript out of the chest, pressing an indentation, roughly the shape of the body, into the pulpy mass. Here, lying on the indecipherable foolscap which had consumed his afternoons for the past twenty-five years, Major Dubose lay as in a casket, a candle at his head, the saber at his right hand, and the framed citation at his left.

Bart sat in a chair, taking cat naps. After a while the room was filled with snores. When at length dawn paled the flame of the second candle, he stood up, closed the lid of the chest, and snapped the lock. "Wake them up," he told a woman who lay on a table watching him with her head on the crook of her arm. They got up, stiff from cramped sleeping, gathered around the chest again, and carried it to the back porch where the skiff was moored.

"Easy," Bart said. "It's got to ride on a balance." But when they set it on the skiff and tested it, the boat careened, one gunwale going under. "Catch it!" They shifted the chest and tested it again. It yawed in the opposite direction. "Catch it!"

Then one of the Negroes began to back away, wading slowly backward through the water, his hands behind him. "Here," Bart said. "Whats the matter with you?"

The Negro shook his head. "Major rolling," he said, walking backward.

"Come back here!"

But he was gone through the doorway. The others looked ready to go, their faces gray in the growing light of dawn. Bart took the derringer out of his pocket. It was blunt, an over-and-under. "All right," he said. "Catch hold."

When they finally got it balanced Bart said, "Get in." One of them got in testily, then another. Both sat quite still, balancing with their hands on the gunwales. When a third got in, the keel touched the floor of the porch. "All right," Bart said. "You get back out." The skiff cleared the floor planks again. "Get the other boat," he told the Negro who had come for him with the lantern. He was the only one of the five Bart felt he could trust, but there was nothing certain even about him. It's a chance Ive got to take, Bart thought. "Bring some rope," he said.

From the kitchen wall he took a board used for kneading dough and on it carved BODY OF MAJ H DUBOSE with his clasp knife. This took some time, for the yellowed wood was very hard. At one end of the board there was a hole for hanging it on a nail. Through this Bart ran one end of a light clothes-line, knotted it, and tied the other end to the hasp of the chest. He put the board on top of the chest, the rope coiled neatly beneath it.

As the approaching sunrise tinted the sky behind him, the man Bart had sent for the other boat paddled to a point directly above the back steps. It was a bateau, and he held it in position by hooking one of his arms around a pillar. In the skiff with the chest, still floating over the porch, the two Negroes balanced gingerly. Their eyes shifted right and left but their heads did not move; their shoulders were hunched and tense. They probably cant swim any more than I can, Bart thought, standing alongside them, kneedeep in water.

"Throw me the painter," he told the man in the bateau. He caught it and made it fast to the bow of the skiff. Then he got into the bateau. "Give me your oars," he said to the men in the skiff.

The Negro in the bow turned loose with one hand, still balancing, and handed the oars forward to Bart. "Head for the cedar grove," Bart told the Negro in the bateau with him, nodding toward the dark green tops of the trees on Ararat's burying ground. "You better balance careful back there," he said to the men in the skiff.

They were at opposite ends, the chest ponderous between them. They sat with their knees drawn up, hands gripping the gunwales, their arms quite stiff, faces set grim, teeth showing a bit in what looked like a leer but really was fright, eyes rushing hot and white against their dark faces.

"Captain, for lordsake," one said. "I caint swim."

"Neither can I," Bart said harshly. "Balance, and you wont have to." He turned to the Negro in the bateau with him. "All right: lets go."

So THEY put out, the two boats one behind another like freight cars, the painter rigid like an iron bar between them. Bart sat in the stern of the bateau, facing the skiff. At his back, amidships, the lantern Negro pulled at the oars, grunting softly with each rhythmic reach and recover. The other two, panting and wild-eyed at opposite ends of the skiff, watched the water slide past, two inches below their gunwales. Thus the two boats, the bateau a tug, the skiff a catafalque, moved toward the cedars five hundred yards away, downhill beneath an expanse of rosy, dimpled water on which trees squatted as if they had been jerked from below in a joke by an underground god. The sun was up now, no cloud in the sky, as they glided perilously and in mortal fear over ten feet of smooth, chocolate water.

There was a strange new countryside all around them. Roads, fences, shrubbery, the old landmarks, the lake itself, all were gone. Now there was only the limitless stretch of water, littered with flotsam and dotted at random with barns, houses, tree tops, and a line of telegraph poles marching in even progression beside the submerged railway.

They were halfway to the cedars. "Want me to spell you?"

Bart asked. The oarsman just wagged his head, pulling steadily, reach and recover. "All right, back there?" The men in the skiff made no answer at all, still gripping tight and balancing. Then all of a sudden a gar broke water just to the right of the bow of the skiff. The forward man lurched left, the port gunwale shipping water until the man in the stern leaned hard to starboard, bringing the boat back onto an even keel.

"Hold still, nigger," the man in the stern cried out. "God damn!"

"Hush up that cussing," the other said. "Dont you member what we caring?"

Theyre all right now, Bart thought. But wait till they see what we have to do. "All right," he said. "Hold what you got."

The lantern Negro lifted the oars clear of the water, then took little choppy strokes, halting the boat in the center of the ring of cedars. In the skiff the two men looked worried. They know already, Bart thought. Then he told them, explaining it carefully. "We cant do it any other way," he said in conclusion.

"Captain . . ." The forward Negro licked his lips nervously. "Captain, I aint lying: I caint swim a lick."

"We'll be right there," Bart said, untying the painter. "You cant miss."

"Spose I dont never come up?"

"Youll come up. If you stay clear of that chest."

The man in the stern had his head down, looking stubbornly into the bottom of the skiff. "I aint ghy do it," he said. "And never would a come out here in the fust place if I knowed you was planning any such of a thing as this here." He kept his head down, and Bart saw for the first time that his hair was quite gray.

"I'm sorry, uncle," he said. "But youre going to do it, all right. Youre going to do it, even if it means I have to capsize you myself."

They had to get the chest overboard. The skiff would not float all four of them, even if the four of them could have managed to lift the chest. If the two men were careful to keep clear of the chest as they went over, Bart told them again, they could be lifted into the bateau almost as soon as they struck the water.

"Captain..." the forward man said.

This isnt getting us anywhere, Bart thought. "I'm tired of talking," he said, taking the derringer out of his pocket again. It was snub and ugly; when he cocked it there were two dry, thick, deadly sounds. "Now stand up, both of you." The forward man stood up quickly, looking anxious but persuaded. The old man in the stern raised his head, blinking his bloodshot eyes. "Get up on your feet, uncle."

"Boss," he said, rising slowly, his legs bent slightly at the knees. He blinked, watching the pistol. "Boss, you can shoot me if you want, but God be my witness, this aint no way for a man to have to die."

"Pull up longside," Bart told the lantern Negro. "Not too close. Thats right." He put the derringer back into his pocket. "Now remember," he told the men in the skiff. "Jump this way and stomp hard on the side as you come over. We'll be right here to catch you soon as you hit the water." If we dont get swamped, he thought. I should have learned to swim.

He was watching the old man in the stern while out of the tails of his eyes he saw the forward Negro put one foot on the gunwale and come over the side, lunging as he came. The chest loomed huge, shifting its weight, and fell toward him. It threw a wave against the bateau, which rode it sideways, retreating like a skittish horse, as Bart leaned outward, his arms stretched toward the old man. He had remained in his half-crouched position, blinking his eyes as if the light hurt them. When the skiff went over, it threw him clear, but he went under as soon as he struck the water. And just as Bart reached for him, the wave hit the bateau and it fled away with a coquettish scamper. Bart missed him. "Get back close!" he shouted. Then he saw the gray head underwater, rising, and reaching down he gripped the old man by the scruff of the neck, pulled him over the side and into the bateau.

"Lord God, Lord Jesus! Aint I seen the Hosts!" The old man wailed soprano, sanctified by baptism. "Grace on the Lamb! Grace on the Lamb!"

As Bart turned, seeking the younger man, the biscuit board
lurched up, the weight of rope holding it upright, half submerged
in the dark water: BODY OF. It seemed to veer past, stiffly vertical
like a shark's fin, and Bart realized the bateau was moving: the
lantern Negro was rowing hard away from the capsized skiff. Bart
called, "Wait, the other . . ." Then he saw him.

His head wet and slick like a swimming seal's or a floating cannonball, the Negro who had jumped from the bow was fifteen
yards away, performing a furious dog paddle. His feet threw up
geysers and his hands moved rapidly; the water seemed to be boiling all around him. When the bateau came alongside, Bart got hold
of him with both hands and lifted him into the boat. His clothes
plastered to him, the Negro sat amazed, surveying a widening
puddle of his own dripping in the bottom of the bateau.

"Thought you couldnt swim," Bart said.

"I never knowed I could," he said mournfully, panting.

After leaving the two wet men on the porch at Ararat, Bart and
the lantern Negro headed back for Solitaire in the bateau. All
around them the flood gleamed with a rich copper tint. Far to the
west, beyond where the lake had been, they could discern the faint
line of the levee like a dark thread afloat. There were other boats
abroad now, boatmen exchanging salutes with almost a holiday air.

They drifted through the front door at Solitaire, crouching as
they passsed beneath the lintel, then on to the landing of the staircase, where Billy Boy waited. Bart got out. "Goodbye," he said.
"We'll finish that job when the time comes."

"Goodbye, captain," the Negro said. "Hope yawl be all right
hyar." He backed water, sculling, then turned on the seat, facing
the other way—the bow of the bateau now became the stern—and
passed through the low rectangle of light onto the bosom of the
flood.

Bart watched him pass from sight. "How were things?" he asked
Billy Boy.

"Got nothing to do but sit and wait on it going down," Billy
Boy said. "How long you reckon itll take?"

"*I* dont know."

They went upstairs, where Bart began going from room to room, looking under stacked furniture, into closets and bureau drawers. Billy Boy followed, his face blank with a biding acceptance of all Bart's vagaries

"Tell me, Billy," Bart said. "Do you remember where I put my fishing tackle?

By July the water was almost gone, just ponds of it left stagnant in the low spots; the lake was reestablished and people were raking silt from their houses with hoes and shovels. The planters met to vote on a new landing—that was one more thing the Memphis engineer was wrong about: it went out, deep pilings, cypress stringers, and all. While the water was falling (it fell far more imperceptibly than it had risen; there were graduations of brown stain on walls and tree trunks, fractional bands paling in ratio to their distance from the surface of the water) Bart fished and visited. All the lake wives were gone; there was nothing to do but wait, as Billy Boy had said, and perform such occasional services as transporting the sick. Much of the time was passed at poker, and Bart made nearly as much money that year as he would have made if he had planted a crop. As soon as the ground began to show on Ararat they held Major Dubose's funeral, a sloppy affair, for the grave filled with water as soon as it was dug.

In midsummer Bart joined Mrs Bart in Vicksburg, where she and the children had been living in a hotel. The children liked it there and wanted to stay, but she was anxious to go back to Solitaire. Bart laughed and said, "Oh no. Weve got all winter to clean house and worry about next year. Besides, the mosquitoes would eat you alive back there. We're going to have a vacation, you and I and the children."

They went to the Mississippi coast, near Biloxi, rented a house, and stayed through August. It was a small white house with a breezy veranda overlooking the Sound across a strip of beach. Bart sat in the sand with the children, building castles with moats and towers; he learned to swim and went out on the gulf with oyster men. Families were here from all over the lower South, wealthy people grouped for pleasure, filling restaurants and bars with their laughter and shouts. They rode in carriages fit for royalty, attended by Negroes in white duck. The men dressed with the fine excess of Europeans, and the women smiled and emitted little screams of mock delight or terror—Like whores, Bart thought. But soon he grew accustomed to them and even learned to enjoy the spectacle.

Just before he left, set out for Solitaire with Mrs Bart and the children, he thought: Ten years ago, or five, or maybe even one, I couldnt have stood being near all this; I couldnt have stayed a week. Now Ive been here more than a month, and I kind of dont want to go back. Something is happening. Something is happening to me.

All the way home on the train, watching the landscape flick past the Pullman window, the conviction continued: Something is happening to me. And now for the first time he tried to examine, to analyze the elements that composed this advancing self. He remembered Judge's admonition a dozen years ago: "Youll bungle; youll bungle," and he wondered if it had already come to pass.

"Is something bothering you, Mr Bart?" He did not hear her; she had to ask again. "Is something bothering you, Mr Bart? Have you got a pain or something?"

"What? No. No, Florence. Just watching the country go by. Thats a nice cut of land over there, aint it?"

If something were to happen to the train, if it were derailed or held up, he would be the one who would take the initiative, be the leader in righting the mix-up. He told himself this and it gave him reassurance. But then he remembered that Judge had not said he would become inactive: Judge had said that the ache for action, the desire for strain, would never leave him; he had even said that this ache, this desire would be the force that would drive him to his fall. It would be when there was no object on which to expend the energy, allay the ache, that the sightless lashing-out would come, and after that the fall.

"Papa: tell us a story."

"Yes, papa, a story!"

"No. No story now. Finish your nap."

My life is no different, he tried to tell himself: I do all the things I did before; I still farm. But he shied from considering that he was not moving upward now but outward. Like the actual physical change in his body, once he had got his growth, his mind was not growing taller or deeper; it was expanding on the same plane. He knew well enough that he was a different man, no matter how much he tried to tell himself otherwise: six weeks on the Coast had taught him that. It all boiled down to the initial disturbance: Something is happening. Something is happening to me.

Back at Solitaire there was work to be done. Patterson and Billy Boy had organized a squad of fieldhands; working with shovels and brooms, they had cleared the house and moved the furniture back downstairs. But their notion of clean was a long way short of Mrs Bart's: it was all done over again. Creeks resumed their placable, tortuous ways; their banks reestablished among scrub oak and willow, they wound through the region in loops and turns, doubling back on themselves like a snake fighting lice. Weeds took everything, field and creekbank alike; even the yard was overgrown with creepers. Bart had every Negro and every mule working every day, breaking the land. The flood left wide, deep cracks in the fields, and now they turned powdery white under the August sun. By late September they were whipped back into shape, ditches cleared and all the plowland harrowed.

"Come spring we're going to put down our best crop," Bart said. "Mind what I'm telling you."

All through that winter he laid his plans with Patterson. In mid-March, when the moon was full, he planted. He planted all of Solitaire in cotton. The price was up and Bart was up every morning before the sun. He drove the hands hard, demanding that Patterson match his energy, at the same time raising his salary to one hundred dollars a month. "Youre earning it," he said. Patterson knew very well he was earning it. His life was all work; sleep was a short black blot between hot hard days.

By May they had a stand. Observers called it the best ever. Bart thought so too: there was hardly a weed on the place. They were picking in late July, and by the end of October the last bales were ginned.

"We got a long winter coming," Bart said.

"Not me," Patterson said. "I'm going to sleep right through."

"Why dont you take yourself a trip?"

"Not me. I done enough tripping to last me a while."

Bart laughed. "You ought to been here with us in the 'eighties. Ask Billy. We really drove it, then."

CHAPTER FIVE

THE HUNT

GAME WAS scarce in the Delta that first year after the flood. What was more, it was the earliest season the planters could remember: usually they were not through picking before Christmas, but this year the gins closed down in mid-November and the planters were left with time on their hands. Or they would have been, rather, if they had not organized and built the Ithaca Gun Club. Through November and well into December, as long as the weather held fair, they spent most of the daylight hours shooting over a trap. To many of them, Bart included, this was a new experience. They stood at shelved posts in relays of five, holding their guns at the ready and facing an open field, while sixteen yards in front of them, in a low hut built over a pit for his legs to hang in, a man sat loading the machine that threw the targets out over the field whenever the shooters, one after another, yelled their signals. The targets were called pigeons or birds, little black saucers of clay that sailed fast in alternate, unguessable directions. To score, a shooter must break off a visible piece before his bird hit the ground.

It looked easy after a lifetime of firing at zigzagging dove and thundering quail, but for a time Bart could not hit them. Then he discovered why. Partridges came out slow, speeding up; targets came out fast, slowing down. He had been waiting until they were far out over the field, sailing lazy, and he had been missing them. It was too slow, too deliberate for his eye. So he altered his style; he began breaking them as soon as they came into sight, frequently knocking splinters from the forward edge of the pit-hut roof, shooting quick and low, blasting the saucers into puffs of black powder: "Dead!" The scorer—usually one of the planters' sons, hoping strong for his father—would call *Dett!* whenever a hit was made, and when a target was missed he would drawl *Laws!* in a mournful voice.

Each shooter had his distinctive way of signaling for a target. Many cried "Pull!" speaking with their lungs full of breath, clearly anxious under pressure. Some made other sounds, for any kind of noise would serve to inform the man in the pit that they were ready. Peter Durfee, for instance, grunted "Agh!" and waited long before he shot, following the targets all the way out until they began to come down, then leaning far back, shot with a quick nervous flinch; he was a poor marksman, so he treated the sport as a joke to hide his shame. Others yelled "Whee!" and shot laughing. Prentiss Kent cried "Howee!" and shot quick, leaning forward over his post as if he wanted to hit the pigeon with his gun barrel —"Getting close as I can," he would say, neck stretched; "Howee!" Whenever the loader in the pit heard a signal he pulled the trip: the bird went sailing against the sky, right or left or center, and the explosion would come, flat and dull like a single hand-clap, and the target either would be broken to fast-falling bits (dead) or would float on serene and whole (loss) until it came to rest with a bounce on the grass, by which time the man in the pit would have the trap loaded and ready for the next signal: "Pull!"

Shoots were frequent that first year, almost daily. Contestants and spectators came from all over the county, from Farset and Bannard and Troy, all the way from Indemnity to the north and Sligo to the east. There was always a group from Bristol; cosmopolitan, they clustered behind the trap to watch, buzzing with comment, betting on their favorites, talking guns and dogs and horses (one always followed the other) and exchanging drinks from their flasks. Their women came with them, fluttery in gay dresses, spots of brightness against the drab background of broadcloth. Talk was a steady hum, punctuated with the abrupt, shrill laughter of the women and the shots of the contestants.

Bart was a favorite with the crowd; it was so exciting to watch him shoot. His style was spectacular and sudden; the act of firing was quick, almost savage in contrast with his manner and the tone of his voice when calling for targets. He was the special favorite of the Bristol people; coming from the metropolis of the district, they were inclined to be somewhat clannish, to champion a common preference. This pleased Bart, flattered him. He began to stand and talk with them between turns at the trap. The women were frankly admiring; they cooed their praises, looking up into his face. "Oh my, Mr Bart," they said. "Oh my goodness, you shoot so quick!" They were entranced, they said: that was the word they used. One nudged another (there was more smoke than fire here, but already an openness of speech had come to Bristol, filtered south from Memphis, where the breakdown of the old life-way began): "You reckon he's that sudden in bed?" and went off in peals of laughter while her companion passed it down the line to the others.

They did not speak this way to Bart to his face, but some of it was transmitted. It was new to him; it scandalized him, though not unpleasantly once he had become accustomed to it. Despite the success, the wealth, he was country-bred; he was cut off from those who had been born to all he had gained. The trips to Memphis and New Orleans were commonplace by now (he went in both directions twice a year; that was the custom on the lake) but it was not as a Memphian that he picked his way down Union Avenue and spent heavily in the stores, and it was not as a New Orleans blade that he walked the dim narrow sidewalks of the Vieux Carré and heard voices, mellow and soft with sin, waft down from the lace-work wrought iron balconies over his head. Wherever he went, he went as a countryman; whatever he saw, he saw with the eyes of a planter who did his own farming. He was indeed ingenuous, even naive, but his bearing lent such dignity, his bank account lent such prestige, that his innocence was never under fire. The money men kept away from him with their wild-cat schemes, and even the Bristol women, who by now were far from backward, went no further than to coo at him.

He still enjoyed spending evenings at home with his family, sitting on the porch after supper as always, watching the daylight fade and the stars burn through the roof of night, like sparks on a blanket, and hearing the mocking birds trilling and fluting in the sycamore beside the steps. The scene was much the same as it had been from the start: these might have been the identical mocking birds. His three children, however, were leaving childhood fast. Hugh was fourteen; next year he would be going to school in Tennessee. He had turned out handsome, a pale reproduction of his father, blond, with more delicate features and a shyer manner. He also had inherited his father's love of hunting; he was easily the best wing shot among the boys on the lake. Bart gave him a Parker double, a twenty-gauge with a cut-down stock, and often took him shooting.

Florence was a mystery to everyone, especially to her father. He tried but he could never understand her. She was twelve now. Usually she seemed older, almost grown, though there were times when she acted like a child. She had hoyden ways; she rode horses that fell on her jumping fences; she climbed into the loft of the barn and swung from rafter to rafter, whooping like an Indian. Other times she kept to her room, dressing and undressing her dolls, nursing them through imaginary ailments. She was calculatingly disobedient and would go into tantrums if she was denied her way in the smallest matter. Even as a baby, barely walking, if she was crossed she would hold her breath, puffing her cheeks and growing red and redder in the face, until she frightened her nurse into letting her have her way. Later she abandoned this method for one more drastic, more satisfactory to her love of excitement: she would fall on the ground, preferably mud and preferably when she had just been bathed and dressed; she would kick her heels and squall. Whipping only made her show more effective, for then she would hold her breath until she was blue in the face, making her eyes bug out. Bart was puzzled; he could not understand. Why should a child deliberately want to be bad?

If Bart had a favorite among the three children, the favorite was Clive. He entered the Ithaca school that year, 1905, and was the special delight of his teacher, Miss Bertha Tarfeller; she had taken the place of the palsied old lady, who had died since Hugh and Florence started to school. Clive was the handsomest of the three, dark, a little fat, precocious, always laughing and talking. Hugh avoided him and Florence plainly detested him; they would leave the room when he went into one of his acts. But this gave him small concern: what he wanted was the admiration of adults, especially his father, and he got it.

Bart was forty-five that spring. "Look how the years mount up," he said, shaking his head slowly from side to side. "I'm getting old, Billy: old." But he did not believe it any more than Billy Boy did.

That winter they began to attend dances at the Elysian Club in Bristol. These were the prime social events of the Delta year: invitation lists were a roll call of the elite. Nominally they were intended for young people in their teens, but everyone went; dancing was only a part of these affairs. Mothers and grandmothers sat against the wall around the dance floor; loaded with jewelry and waving feathered fans, they formed what was called the Rocking Chair Brigade, watching with satisfaction or dismay how many or how few of the stags cut in on their daughters and granddaughters. It was an important step in a woman's life — a step toward death — when she moved from among the dancers and took a place among the chaperones. Fathers and grandfathers collected in the adjoining club rooms; men of all ages from thirty to seventy, uncomfortable in stiff-bosomed shirts and dinner jackets, they talked cotton and politics and flood control while the young people wheeled and pranced in the noisy ballroom. That was an important development in a man's life, too, when he found himself spending more time in the outer rooms, preferring conversation to dancing.

There were only two of these balls a year, one at Easter and another at Christmas, but the members made up for this by the extensiveness of their preparations. They gave dinners beforehand and breakfasts afterwards, and they tried to make every ball better than the one that had been held at the same season the year before.

Visitors came from what was called out-of-town, which meant that they came from anywhere in the world beyond Bristol, from Bannard ten miles to the east or from another continent.

Here Bart found something else he had never known before, and here again he liked it. He enjoyed being part of all the groomed elegance, lounging in one of the club rooms, smoking cigars and listening to the talk. He also liked to stand at the rim of the ballroom, watching the young people dance to the jerky foxtrots brought up the river from Storyville, to marches such as *Maryland My Maryland* played in jig time, to waltzes by Strauss which made him feel slightly seasick, thumped and puffed the way they were by Negroes in button shoes, peg-top trousers, and high boiled collars. The grand march was especially colorful; Bart looked forward to the time when his sons or daughter would lead it. He watched all this with a show of reserve, but inwardly he was like a boy at the circus. Grand, he thought. That was a word he had never used before.

So in contrast to the glitter of these new experiences—chatter and flattery at trap shoots, music and decorum at the Elysian Club—the Lake Jordan life paled. It had been solid and estimable; it had been worth the labor spent. But now he saw things beyond it. There was a region where his accomplishments on the lake were nothing in comparison with what people native to this land received on the day they were born. Now that this was open to him, he told himself, there need be no bogging of his faculties, because here was a new field for endeavor. He did not have to lash out for action, he told himself in the words of the dead prophet; the action was here; it was ready at hand.

Next spring in Memphis, accompanied by a group from the lake and competing against a field of two hundred marksmen from Tennessee and Arkansas and Mississippi, Bart won the tri-state trap shoot championship. He broke one hundred straight in the qualifying round and ninety-seven in the semi-finals. This last was not very good; however, since most of the shooters were off form that round, it was good enough to pass him into the finals with nine other men. One of them was Dr Jacob T. Tidings, a Memphis surgeon, present champion and three times winner of the shoot; he was a soft-spoken elderly man, a favorite in Southern sporting circles.

The finalists stood at two traps, five at each, with a crowd of three thousand murmurous behind them. Bart wondered how much this would bother him once the pressure was really on; he had never shot in front of a large crowd before. What was worse, this crowd was partial: whenever Dr Tidings missed, which was seldom, they groaned a collective Ahhh. The slim gray doctor and a short fat young man from Little Rock broke a hundred each in the first round. Bart and two others broke ninety-nine. Then they stopped for lunch.

Dr Tidings came to the table in one of the tents where Bart was sitting with John Cowan and Peter Durfee, eating. He clapped Bart on the shoulder, looking down at him. "Ive been wanting to talk to you," he said. Bart got up, fumbling for the napkin in his lap.

"Join us, doctor?"

"Thank you, I just finished. I'm due for my beauty nap now." He smiled, his hand still on Bart's shoulder, and Bart saw the network of tiny wrinkles around his eyes, the big square yellow teeth, the stiff white hair. "I just wanted to tell you," the doctor said, his face suddenly serious. "Youve got the most spectacular style Ive ever seen. I'd enjoy talking to you about it when we can find time after all this hubbub is over."

"Well . . . thank you, doctor."

"Youre going to win this shoot, you mark my words. I saw that bird you lost. You didnt miss it: I saw dust fly. It was just a tough one."

"Maybe I didnt hit it square."

"Nonsense. I saw it jump."

"Thank you," Bart said awkwardly; he also thought the scorer had called it wrong. There was a pause.

"Well: good shooting."

"The same to you, doctor. Good day."

"Good day," Dr Tidings said. They shook hands, and Bart watched the shallow wrinkles deepen around the gray eyes as the doctor smiled.

They would shoot the final hundred that afternoon. "How you feel?" Cowan asked.

"Fine," Bart said. "I feel fine. I'm going to break them to smithereens."

"Lord God, you better: Durf's got a cool five hundred on your nose, at three to one. These Memphis folks think a lot of their doctor."

"I do too," Bart said.

Durfee turned on him, frowning. "You bust those pigeons: thats what you do," he said. "For the sake of old Mississippi the magnolia state, for the sake of our unbounded confidence in your marksmanship, for the sake of my cool five hundred: dont you miss."

Bart missed. It was his third target, a low straight swift one, the kind he liked best. "Loss!" the scorer cried.

"That does it," Bart said, breaking his gun and watching the disk sail on until finally it came to earth with an exasperating bounce. A polite sigh went up from the crowd: this was the first miss of the afternoon. Soon, however, there were others. Dr Tidings missed his eighty-fifth bird. When the round was over, three of the shooters had scored ninety-nine: the doctor, the fat young man from Arkansas, whose name was Trimble, and Bart.

He had quite a following by now among the spectators grouped behind the trap. "That quick-shooting fellow from the Delta," they called him, buzzing with excitement as the three men took their posts for the run-off. There would be twenty-five targets. Bart saw Durfee and Cowan in the front ranks of the crowd; they were laughing and joking with the people around them, but Durfee had an uneasy look on his face. Bart was at the first post.

"Pull," he said.

"Dead!"

I'd like to see Durfee's face, he thought, watching his eighth target sail on unhit and hearing the scorer cry "Loss!" Trimble missed three in succession. Dr Tidings shot steadily, calling for targets with a level voice. He stood straight and slim, breaking bird after bird, until the twenty-first one, which he missed. Bart had not seen the shot, but he heard the scorer's mournful, apologetic cry and he heard a collective groan go up from the crowd. Durfee's face, he thought. He kept his eyes down, ashamed to look toward the doctor's post at his right.

"Pull," he said.

"Dead!"

In the dual run-off Bart and Dr Tidings stood at their posts, firing methodically at the soaring disks. The doctor missed his twelfth, his nineteenth birds; Bart did not miss at all. When the last shot had been fired, Dr Tidings crossed to Bart's post, grasped his hand, and shook it firmly. "You see?" he said. "I know a winner when I see one."

"It was your shoot, doctor, all the way through."

"Well . . ." Dr Tidings glanced down, eyelids lowered for a moment, then looked up again, smiling. "We'll see next year, hey?"

All the time Bart was receiving the cup—a large urn with staghorn handles, engraved down one side with a space left blank for his name—Durfee's face was crimson with pleasure. He had won fifteen hundred dollars. "Just think," he kept saying. "Three-to-one odds. What a time, what a time we're going to have tonight!"

PEOPLE WERE in and out of the hotel room all through the early part of the night, other shooters and their wives, two newspaper reporters, and a succession of drummers for shell manufacturers. The reporters brought a photographer with them, a small man with pale eyes and a smell of hyposulphite. "Do you have your gun here with you?" he asked. He seemed anxious, loaded down with equipment.

"Here," Durfee said, patting the scuffed leather guncase. "Here's the boomstick that did it, that won us the tri-state cup."

"Ah, good," the photographer said in a high voice, and he began to explain what he wanted—something properly posed, he said, something with action in it. He looked about the room, overlapping his thumbnails to make a frame with his hands.

"I dont know," Bart said doubtfully, watching the photographer and wondering what he was up to. "I never was in action in a hotel room before."

"I'll take out the background," the photographer said encouragingly, setting up his tripod.

Bart said he was not so sure, but the reporters persuaded him ("Just think," they said; "It's going all over the world") and he struck an uncharacteristic pose, standing stiff and self-conscious in one corner of the room, holding the shotgun slantwise in front of his chest like a recruit at inspection arms. He tottered a bit while the photographer was bringing him into focus, upside-down on the ground-glass plate.

"Now," the photographer said, sprinkling flash powder. He went under the black cloth and his voice sounded far away. Then he emerged, holding the flash-pan high. "Hold it . . . Hold it . . ." !! There was a yellow glare, an angry swirl of smoke. "A beaut," he said. He beamed. "Now. How's about something artistic, Mr Bart?" He wanted to take a picture with the camera pointed down the gun barrel at Bart's eye. He would call it *The Marksman*, he said, and enter it in a magazine contest.

"Sounds kind of silly to me," Durfee said.

This offended the photographer; he looked hurt. One of the reporters nudged Durfee. "You shouldnt have said that, doc. He's touchy about his art."

"Oh," Durfee said. "Well—I'm sorry."

"Thats all right," the other reporter said. "He's used to it by now."

"Pose it for him, Hugh," Durfee said, by way of apology. "Strike something artistic."

"How's this?" Bart said. He aimed at the camera, squinting heavily, and froze in position with the muzzle about eight inches from the lens, his finger on the trigger. He tottered and steadied, tottered and steadied.

"Hold it!" the photographer cried, and he dived back under the hood, then reappeared, one arm holding the flash-pan high. "Hold it ... Hold it." ! ! "Fine," he said. "Oh my, thats fine."

"Look," Bart said. "Look what I forgot." He had broken the gun at the breech, and now he showed them what he had forgotten. In their twin chambers, neat, round, precise, as deadly as science, lay two unfired shells.

"Dear God," the photographer said, big-eyed.

"Who wants a drink?" Durfee asked abruptly.

"Me," Bart said. "I'll have one with you."

"Wont we all?" the two reporters said.

That night, for the first time in his adult life, Bart had to be helped into bed. There had been a constant influx of visitors; they came to congratulate him and stayed to talk of their experiences at trap shoots all over America. They spoke admiringly of Bart's performance that afternoon, and he was obliged to take a drink with almost every one of them. Durfee, ebullient over winning his long-odds bet, kept handing him drinks. "Drink it down," he kept saying. "Your shooting won the whiskey. Drink it down."

Bart's first realization of his condition came when he observed a step-up in his speech. He began to talk fast and at length and, it seemed to him, with considerable acumen. He had never found it so easy to express himself. "Mr Carter, I'm happy to hear you say that. Happy, sir. What we've been needing for quite a long time now is a really national organization for the gunners of this country. Mississippi, I can promise you, will furnish her share of the members, her contingent. Yes, sir: I'm happy to hear you—ah—broach the subject." I sound like Judge, he thought, and was quiet for a while.

Soon there was a new collection of callers, and it all began again. About two oclock he looked around and saw that there were only five men left in the room, including himself and Durfee and Cowan. It had been this way for the past hour: every time he opened his eyes the scene had changed, which was something like living in a kaleidoscope. The other two men were strangers; he could not focus his eyes to see their faces. I ought to go to bed, he thought. I wish I could get up. The two men were explaining or relating something about goose hunting in Canada; or was it moose? Whatever it was, it was highly complex.

Then, as if from a long way off, he heard someone mumbling. "Of course," he said. "Is it very important?" There was the mumbling again, but the words did not come through. It was dark in the room. "I'm sure youre right," he said. "Tell them I said yes. Say I said yes to everything proposed." Then one of the voices got clearer, filtering through the fog. Bart opened his eyes, and the room was not dark at all; the lights were blazing. Cowan and Durfee stood in front of his chair, and they were grinning. "Hello, you two," he said. "I aint seen you all in a long time."

"Lets go to bed," Cowan said.

"Time all good boys were abed," Durfee said.

"Who?" Bart said, resenting the levity. "Durfee, you been drinking."

Finally they helped him out of the chair and guided him across the room to his bed. He sat there and they took off his shoes, his coat and trousers. While they were undoing his tie and peeling his shirt down his arms, his head rolled on his shoulders, and as soon as they took their hands away, he fell sideways onto the pillow. Durfee swung his legs up, grunting, and he lay calm and suspirant in socks and underwear. "Gen, gen, gentlemen," he muttered while Cowan raised the window and Durfee fumbled at the sheet, tucking it clumsily under his chin. "Gentlemen, you have no idea how this bed is spinning."

"Put one foot on the floor," Cowan said. He seemed genuinely concerned. "Thats what I always do."

"Ah," Bart said, flat on his back in spinning malaise, already beginning to snore a little.

"Look at the champion," Durfee said.

FROM THEN on his mail was heavy with invitations to trap shoots all over the country, especially the lower South, from Louisiana, Arkansas, Tennessee, Mississippi, Alabama, and Georgia. He went to so many and shot with such success that the library, a small bookless octagonal room directly behind the entrance hall, was converted into a trophy room. Cups and ribbons gleamed on the glass-fronted shelves.

Christmas of 1907 Solitaire was crowded with guests, sportsmen from all over the South. They filled the bedrooms, and all the extra leaves were put in the dining room table. They were a good-time group; every night after supper they gathered in the parlor, talking and drinking and strumming the new piano Bart had bought with his winnings at a Georgia shoot that fall. When it arrived, a big crate carefully packed—the heaviest, Billy Boy thought, since the stone tub twenty years ago—Bart said, "Look what I won you." Mrs Bart, watching it being assembled, laid the tip of one finger at the corner of her mouth.

"Who's going to play it?" she asked.

"Florence, I reckon. She can take lessons. Aint that what most of the girls around here do?"

Mrs Bart tried for a moment to imagine Florence confronted with a music teacher. She shook her head; You dont know your own daughter, she thought. And it was true: Bart had been away from home so much this past year, he hardly knew any of his children.

Florence was fourteen. Next year she would be making her debut with other lake girls of her age. But she was unlike the others; there was nothing willowy in her nature. She spent a good part of her time on horseback, riding astride like a man and with a flaunting recklessness that resulted in some bad spills. To her mother's despair—superficially it delighted Bart—she preferred flat-heel boots, serge riding skirts, and her older brother's shirts. She had no use for boys, however, and was more at ease fighting them behind the barn than she was receiving them as callers in the parlor. She spent more time with Negro families on Solitaire and adjoining plantations than she did at home. She would ride up to their cabins, dismount, and sit on their porches all through the afternoon, propping her boots man-fashion on an upright, eating cornbread and greens in their kitchens, and even taking midday naps in their beds. Damn was her favorite word.

Her father would have liked to transfer some of her rough-and-tumble hoyden ways to Hugh. He was sixteen; next year he was due to complete his training at the Tennessee academy. It was already doubtful if he would make it by then, however; his report cards were invariably poor. They came once a month by mail, accompanied by a note from the commandant, who complained of Hugh's failure to apply himself; his indolence, the commandant said, was a sort of tactical inertia by which he avoided exertion in all its forms. With the ladies, however, he had a different manner. They admired him; they praised his politeness and often remarked on the sweetness of his face.

In this he was completely unlike his younger brother. Clive was in his second year at the Ithaca school, a great favorite with Miss Tarfeller; she was flattered by his attentions and rewarded him with high marks and kind looks. This increased his unpopularity with the other pupils, but that gave him small concern. He preferred the admiration of grown-ups: they were the ones who ran the world, who handed out favors and laid down restrictions; they were the ones to cultivate. Clive discovered early that more could be gained by being attractive than by just being diligent, and as long as the former achieved by itself what seemed to be the object of education—high marks on a report card—he saw no need for the latter. He was intelligent, and it was here in the one-room Ithaca schoolhouse that the intelligence was channeled.

Yet whatever their shortcomings, however conscious Bart was that they did not measure up to what he had hoped for, he was quite proud as he introduced them to his guests this Christmas season: Hugh in uniform, his blond hair dampened and neatly brushed, Florence with her high pale forehead and dark eyes, just short of becoming a woman, and Clive in high button shoes and a

big bow tie, plump and cheerful, always ready to recite humorous
verses for the guests:

Ladies and gentlemen, bear in mind
The jaybird's tail sticks out behind.

Two men and a woman to bear my name, Bart thought. Three of
them to beget children who in turn will beget more children and
carry my name on down.

At the end of the holidays, when Bart stood at the steps and told
the last of the guests goodbye, then turned and entered the house,
he could count twenty-one years on Solitaire and $100,000 in the
bank. He owned other property, too—was half owner of a steamboat, for instance, as a result of calling a Missouri banker's bluff in
a Memphis poker game: it was stud; Bart had a pair of eights showing; the banker had four high cards up and had bet on them heavily
all along; Bart called the final raise; "I'll see that," he said, and the
banker sighed and flipped his cards together, including the case
eight he had held in the hole: "Youve got half a steamboat; a good
one, too. Run them." Though he had never been able to figure it
exactly, his holdings and cash totaled close to a quarter of a million
dollars, and like anyone in Mississippi who owned above a hundred
thousand dollars, he was called a millionaire.

He was five feet nine inches tall when he stood up straight. Deep-
chested and rather wide across the shoulders, he had the flat legs,
the slightly rolling, straddling gait of a horseman. He weighed a
hundred and seventy pounds, most of it bone and muscle, and he
had never been really sick a day in his life. His eyes were gray-
green, with thick dark lashes and brows; a network of shallow
wrinkles had come into the skin beneath and beside them, as if from
too much squinting into the sun. His hair, which was dark brown,
had receded above the temples and now was beginning to grizzle;
he wore it clipped short. A thick mustache, cut to the width of his
mouth, arched over his lips, hiding them except when he threw his
head back to laugh. His jaw had never been strong and now he had
developed a dewlap which showed when his head hung forward.

His teeth were yellow and regular, strong; he had never been inside a dentist's office or used a toothbrush in his life.

He dressed invariably in black or gray, wore white shirts with plain gold studs and cuff links, a soft collar and a loosely knotted short bow tie. His shoes were snub and black, fitted with hooks instead of eyes on the uppers, and a loop of webbing was stitched to the heel of each for pulling them on. Cotton socks flashed white when he sat down. His clothes were neatly brushed but seldom pressed; he changed his shirt and socks daily, but wore the same underwear, tie and suit through Saturday. Sunday morning he bathed in his bedroom and put on his good suit, the coat longer and looser in the skirt, the trousers fuller at thighs and knees, tighter at the ankles (choke-bore, he called them) and a bit higher in the waist because with them he wore suspenders. Every four years he bought a new good suit, cut from the same pattern by the same tailor, and gave the old one to his coachman.

Except for the trap shooting jaunts, the two-a-year business trips to Memphis and New Orleans, life followed the old pattern. Once a month he went to church in Bristol with Mrs Bart and whatever children were at home and available (Florence usually hid in the loft of the barn, where she had a hiding place behind some bales of hay); the other three or four Sundays they gathered at ten oclock in the downstairs parlor, the house servants ranged along the rearward wall, to hear Mrs Bart read the assigned portion of the Psalter. Her mother, she remembered, had done the same in her time.

EARLY THAT spring, during the first warm spell, Bart went to Bristol for a cattle show, and while he was there he experienced something that frightened him beyond anything he had ever known before. For the past month he had felt cramps in his arms, little shooting twinges of pain, not in the biceps but at the backs, along the radial extensors. Rheumatism, he thought: at my age. This began after a three-day shoot at Corinth, so he blamed it on the kick of the gun—strangely, though, the pains were worse on the left, and he was a right-handed shooter. Two weeks later the ache was gone. He put it out of his mind. Then it returned, much sharper now, and he renamed it: he called it his sciatica, his lumbago. I'm old before my time, he thought.

That afternoon, at the stock show just outside Bristol, he was leaning against the fence, one of a group watching cattle being led past before the auction. As he listened to a Bannard planter talking about the future of cattle breeding in the Delta, the muscles along the backs of his arms began to twitch. Whats this? he wondered. Suddenly there were stabs of pain moving down his arms and back. They were unlike anything he had ever felt before.

"Excuse me," he said. He turned from the fence and began to walk toward the rear. "Excuse me," he said quietly, frowning to keep from wincing as he passed among the men who crowded forward to take his place at the fence. Then, clear of them, he saw his surrey, the horses standing stiff-kneed among buggies and carriages and two or three sharp-nosed, incomplete-looking automobiles. Lord, those things are ugly, he thought, turning his mind from the pain. Both sides of his back felt as if they were being pricked with needles, and the rearward muscles of his arms twitched with little shoots of pain; he could not clench his fists.

A gray-haired Negro named Doll Baby—he had been Bart's houseboy in the bachelor years; now he was coachman—stood at the horses' heads, talking to a tall ginger-colored man, one of the hostlers. "I told him straight out: say, 'What surrance you ghy give me?' Looked him right square in the eye and laid it on the line: 'How I'm ghy know you telling me the truth?' That stopped him, you hear me? Stopped him before he got started." Then he saw Bart coming out of the crowd, walking stiffly toward the surrey. "Scuse me," he said to the hostler, and went to meet Bart. When he saw Bart's face he said, "Whats the matter, Mars Hugh?" Bart did not answer; he went on toward the surrey. Then he stopped beside it and reached for one of the arm-rests to pull himself up.

"Dont touch me!" he said quickly as Doll Baby moved to help

him. "Go tell Mr Lane and the others I had to go back to town for something. Tell them I'll send you back as soon as I get there."

When Murphy Lane returned with the coachman, Bart was standing where he had stood when Doll Baby left him, unable even to try to mount. "What is it?" Lane asked.

"I dont know," Bart said. He faced the side of the surrey, his arms held slightly away from his body. He turned his head cautiously, looking at Lane, whose full square beard was like a doormat covering the lower two-thirds of his face, ungrizzled, strong, as stiff as if it had been currycombed. "I just hurt."

It was a little more than a mile into town. Doll Baby drove slowly, holding the middle of the road to avoid the ruts. Bart and Lane sat in the rear, Bart not saying anything after he said "I hurt," and Lane uneasy, embarrassed. Seeing Bart sick, he thought, was something like seeing a gentleman rider unhorsed on the flat.

They were better than twenty minutes reaching the doctor's office. An attendant met them. "You gentlemen go right back," she told them. "I'll send for the doctor." She was a thin-faced Negress, the color of *café au lait*; she wore a freshly laundered, starched white uniform and spoke with a clipped, exact pronunciation.

The consulting room was furnished with chairs and stools enameled dead-white. The examining table in the center, with its cranks and worm-gears, made Bart think of a torture machine. A sterilizer bubbled in one corner. Soon Dr Clinton came in, walking jauntily and whistling *Sunbonnet Sue*. He wore a gray sports coat with button-down pockets and a belt all the way around; he had been at a croquet party two blocks away. Facing Lane, he pressed his palms together and kneaded them briskly.

"Murphy Lane, in the flesh. Whats ailing you? It had better be something serious: you broke up my game. I was three wickets ahead of the whole shebang." With the shame-faced air of a man allowing someone else to accept a challenge intended for himself, Lane jerked his thumb in Bart's direction. "Oh," the doctor said, facing Bart. "Hello. Yes?"

"Pains," Bart said. "In my back, my arms."

"Pains?"

"Yes. Shooting."

"Hm. Well: take off your coat, please. Warm today," he said, turning on a light above the washstand. He twisted the tap, waiting for the water to run hot. "Elnora." The Negress appeared in the doorway. "Get me a bar of soap. But wait. First help Mr Bart off with his coat."

When she stepped toward him, Bart recoiled slightly. "I can do it," he said. "Give me a hand here, Murph." Her face inscrutable, the attendant went down the hall, silent on rubber soles. By the time she came back with the soap, Lane had the coat off Bart's shoulders and was sliding it down his arms. "Eee," Bart said. Dr Clinton received the soap; tearing off its wrapper, he looked around at the two men.

"Shirt too," he said. "Let Elnora help you, Mr Bart. What in God's name does Murphy Lane know about undressing another man?"

Skillfully, impersonally, the limber yellow hands slipped the studs, undid the tie and collar, and shucked the shirt back, then lifted it with an easy jerk so that it came from under the belt without snagging. "Now sit back down," Dr Clinton said. He watched his face in the mirror over the washstand, his lathered hands going frictionless and swift, enveloping each other. "My God," he said as he turned and looked at Bart. "Dont you know warm weather is here?"

Bart was still standing, his long underwear tightly incasing his trunk and arms, buttoned tight at the throat and ribbed snug at the wrists. "Peel him, Elnora," the doctor said. But Bart would not permit this. He unfastened the buttons himself and had the garment half off his shoulders when Lane came forward and jerked it awkwardly down Bart's arms.

Dr Clinton held his hands under the tap, shaking and rubbing them again (He washes them like they dont belong on his arms, Bart thought: like theyre part of the office equipment, instruments) until they were free of soap, shining flesh-colored again, the nails clipped close and very clean. "Sit down, sit down," he said. Bart sat on a stool and the doctor pulled another stool behind him and sat there, surveying Bart's back. It was very white, back and arms, sharply separated from the sun- and wind-tanned skin where collar and cuffs left off. Bart sat looking directly ahead, like a man submitting to an indignity. The top of his underwear drooped from his belt, the ribbed wrists touching the floor.

"When I hurt you, say so." Dr Clinton placed his hand on Bart's upper arm, squeezed gently. His hands were surprisingly strong, not at all the way Bart had expected them to be. "Hurt?"

"Yes."

"Hm." He moved his hand, pressed. "Now?"

"Yes."

"More?"

"About the same."

This continued: "Now?"

"Yes."

"Hm. Now?"

"No: yes. Yes."

"Hm"—until at last the doctor rose, went back to the washstand and began to scrub his hands again, as carefully as before. I feel kind of insulted, Bart thought, watching him.

As he worked the soap into a lather Dr Clinton made faces at himself in the mirror. Still washing and without turning his head he said, "You can put your things back on now." He began to whistle *Sunbonnet Sue* again and dried his hands, paying particular attention to his nails. Then, tossing the towel into an enameled bucket, he faced Bart—who by then, with Lane's help, was putting on his coat; the pain was letting up—and said brightly, as if he were making an announcement of checkmate, "Rheumatism." He held up a clean forefinger, wagging it. "Youve got an old man's ailment: shame on you." Bart looked puzzled. "What did you think you had? Colic? Like a mule?"

"What must I do?" Bart asked. This was all quite new to him, and strange.

"Ah," Dr Clinton said, and added decisively: "Liniment. Not just ordinary liniment, though: none of that fancy stuff for you. Horse liniment, full strength. Treat you like a mule even if you havent got the colic." The doctor laughed, a quick hard bark: "Ha!"

So every night, two hours after supper and just before bedtime, Billy Boy had the job of applying the liniment. Bart sat in a reversed chair, hands gripping its back, while Billy Boy crouched or stood behind him and rubbed the fiery yellow liquid into his shoulders and arms. There was a standard procedure for these occasions: Bart would whistle an approximation of *Dixie* while Billy Boy worked, the notes getting shriller as the burning increased, until finally they reached a climax: "Fan it, Billy; fan it!" and Billy Boy would put the bottle down and pick up the palm-leaf fan, making short rapid strokes to cool the bright red flesh. When the whistling began again, low and even, he would take up the liniment and continue the massage, the whistling mounting the scale, getting shriller and shriller.

Then one morning a week after the cattle show, a blustery March day of exploding spring, Bart woke up and found the discomfort gone. It left as mysteriously as it had come, and though he never stopped fearing its return, he could not even remember exactly how it had felt. He gave the liniment credit for the cure and felt a little guilty about his dislike for Dr Clinton.

When Bart told him the liniment treatments were over, Billy Boy was disappointed. He had enjoyed those half-hours spent with Bart: they were more or less like the faraway days when they were two bachelors, living alone at Solitaire. "Cracky," he said. "You heal quick."

"I'm tough, Billy: tough. I'm like the elephant, old and tough."

THAT WAS a fine spring. Like all the seasons in the Delta latitudes, it came quickly; it seemed to arrive overnight: people woke up one morning and found it waiting for them, just outside their windows. Trees put out their tender green. The air was soft. High in the sky, strung out in long, almost invisible vees, clotting and attenuating with urgency and fatigue, ducks and geese came over, flying north again; they cried like lost things, almost out of earshot. Lizards flicked and scampered in the flowerbeds and ventured onto the sun-warmed boards of the porch, where they were captured by children and dressed in harness of thread. Twilight returned, the atmosphere of suspension and peace which winter, whose night came down abruptly like a curtain, had destroyed and even blotted from memory.

Bart quickened his interest in running the plantation; he was at home more that spring and summer than he had been at any time for the past five years. His rheumatism reappeared only once, and though it was only for a day, he resented even that time off his horse. He rode over Solitaire constantly and spent more time with the Negroes, not only watching them at their work, but also sitting with them in the shade during rest periods. Gradually he began to see beyond his white man's attitude, though he never lost his belief that they were surely the worst labor in the world, and began to show an interest in their private lives. They were always having woman trouble, and Bart set himself up as an expert on the subject: "Let her ramble if she wants. Dont make a move in her direction. She'll be back." This amused them: "Listen at him! Hear what he say!" and though they never went so far as to take his advice, they delighted in hearing it; they applauded his suggestions and hinted that he must have been a terror among the ladies in his youth, an observation which was utterly unfounded but which pleased him none the less.

Hugh finished at the academy in June: the commandant had squeezed him through. Bart went up for the graduation exercises. After the uniforms and the glitter of the final dress parade, which made him feel a little inferior to his son but which seemed to have meant nothing at all to the boy, they came home on the train together, spending a night in a Memphis hotel. This was the first time Bart had been really alone with one of his children.

They talked, and Bart was pleased. I should have done this long ago, he thought. We like each other.

When they got home, however, stepped down onto the Ithaca platform and were met by their friends, young and old, the breach reappeared and widened, and Bart saw that the intimacy had not been a true one, as he had believed, but had been occasioned by the train ride, the relief at having graduated after all, and the elegant hotel suite. More, he realized that the link between old and young, between father and son, was never real, was shadowy at best, and was unable to withstand the pressure of outward claims. He saw now that any man claiming to be a friend to his son was either a father deceived by a sly progeny or a liar, for though one might lay down his life for the other in the press of circumstance, it would not be and never could be out of friendship.

"How would you like to be a lawyer?" Bart asked him. They had been home a week and were sitting on the porch. Hugh looked around; seeing his father's gaze fixed on him, he shifted his eyes toward the lake, which sparkled in the sunlight.

"I never thought," he said cautiously.

"I mean, how do you like the idea?"

"All right, I reckon, papa. I just never thought."

"Do you think youd make a good lawyer?"

"Yes Sir, I guess I could make one, all right. But . . ."

"Well: dont worry about it. I just wondered." Then Bart said what he had meant to say all along: "Because you dont care much about farming, do you?"

"No Sir." Hugh said it quickly, in a positive tone, without having to think. Bart saw that he had been thinking this for a long time, even awaiting a chance to say it. But Hugh was embarrassed at having answered so suddenly: the reply had come before the question was well out of his father's mouth.

Bart looked down at his boots. "Well, you be thinking about it. Theres lots of time yet. Whatever you decide will be what I want, I guess. You must have done some thinking already." Bart, who had worked so hard all his life, always with his goal set plain before him, whose every move had been shaped by what was ahead and tempered by what was behind, could not imagine a life without its aim in full view, could not conceive of a dormitory filled with boys who were not spending all their time planning their future. A person who had time to plan and yet was planless was like a loaded rifle without a firing-pin. But whether Bart could realize it or not, that was how Hugh was. He had no plan beyond a determination not to be a farmer, and even this—it constituted the vestige of a plan, even if it was negative—he was ashamed of, for it placed him outside the life in which he was raised, outside his heritage. And now he was brought face to face with his indecision. "How would you like to be a lawyer?"

So next morning when Hugh told him that what he wanted was the law, Bart said: "Fine, son; fine," and asked him then the second question for which he was unprepared: "What school do you want to go to?" There was no answer. "Harvard?"

"Well . . ."

"Or maybe one closer to home. Virginia?"

"It dont matter, papa."

"I guess not. But you have to decide and put in for it before it's filled up, dont you?"

"Yes sir."

"Havent you thought about it, about what school you want to go to?"

"Well . . ." Hugh paused, then said suddenly: "Papa, I thought I wouldnt go to school."

Bart watched him. "Do you think you can be a lawyer without any schooling? Those days are over and gone." Hugh looked away. "Then what *are* you going to do?"

"I dont know, papa. If . . ."

"Yes?"

"I dont know, sir."

"Nonsense," Bart said. "Pick your school and let me know." He rose, went down the steps, around the side of the house, and back toward the stables.

I been to school four years already, Hugh thought. Now he's making me start all over again.

In September he entered the University of Mississippi. He had been refused admission by two Eastern schools because of his scholastic record at the Tennessee academy and his failure to secure recommendations from his instructors there. He was accepted, however, by the state university and matriculated with a small class of farm-bred youths, cautious and amazed in clothes they had outgrown since the previous fall, and dressy representatives from the larger towns, wearing imitation tweeds and bulldog pipes. Soon they would pin to their vests the cryptic enameled badges of fraternity, and already they were equipped with a spate of glittery, meaningless phrases such as Twenty-three Skiddoo and Does your Mother know youre Out?

As for his daughter, Bart knew in his heart that he was afraid of her—actually afraid: because though not even Florence went so far as to show him any levity or disobey him openly, she wore her independence in a way that seemed to welcome interference for the sake of the hullabaloo that would follow. He left her to her mother, himself adopting a joking manner toward the girl to cover his fear.

Clive was ten, handsome and plump, still leading his classes at the Ithaca school, one of those pupils of whom teachers say that their profession is bearable so long as every hundred has one like him. He said he was going to be a doctor

"Thatll be fine," Bart said. "I'll probably be needing one by the time you get grown."

"I'll be glad to oblige you, papa. And look at all the money we'll save."

"Wont you charge me anything?"

"Oh no, papa. Doctors never charge their families. They dont even charge each other."

"I guess they take it out on other people." Bart had received Dr Clinton's bill for prescribing horse liniment.

"Thats it," Clive said. "I'll soak them plenty."

"Son, youll go far."

"I plan to, papa."

Bart took his feet off the porch railing and turned sideways in his chair, looking out over the flat fields beyond the lawn to his left. The sun was almost down; its rays came level across the lake, struck the cypresses fringing the shore, and pierced them with continuous sword thrusts, long pencilings drawn golden above the fields where cotton was beginning to burst its bolls, white dots against the greenery. The plants seemed to bow under the press of July heat. Soon now the pickers, hands nimble, backs bent, would begin to move down the rows in straggling lines, stripping the stalks and trailing nine-foot sacks.

But who is going to farm it when I'm gone?

WINTER CAME early that year. Fall was cramped to a miniature of itself, and Indian summer went past with a rush; leaves flared hectic for a week and then, like flames blown out by the wind, were gone before they had a chance to wilt; the bare limbs clacked and groaned in the bitter cold. Great floats of ice came down the river, frothed with pale brown frozen foam like dingy lace. Steamboats put in for bank and stayed there: navigation stopped. On Lake Jordan the ducks honked frantically, for the mud wore crystal armor. In late January the thermometer dropped to four degrees below zero, a record for the region.

Bart stayed indoors, miserably idle because hunting was impossible in the driving sleet. It fell every day: houses, fences, roads, the fields themselves were white with its crumbly, treacherous accumulation. Despite the outrage to Mrs Bart and the cook, and though he knew they would get fat and lazy, Bart brought his dogs into the kitchen, two setters and a pointer, and gave orders that they were not to be driven out. He was far unhappier than the dogs: they dropped heavily under the stove or moiled under-foot, making scrabbling sounds with their claws against the planks and thumping the legs of the furniture with their tails: but he was indeed an animal caged. He would stand at a window an hour at a time, hands deep in his pockets, frowning, head thrust forward, watching the dead-white landscape as it grew deader, whiter.

Then—at the very moment, it seemed to Bart, when he could not have endured another hour—the sleet stopped. After a week of static cold, the sky lowering gray, a day broke much as the others had broken, bleak and chill, until the sun came out: the sun! The blanket of sleet was tinted rosy in the hollows and sparkled like diamond dust on the ridges. By mid-morning there was a steady glassy tinkling of subsurface water; the break-up had begun. Awkwardly, then with confidence, a bird sang from the sycamore, liquid, piercing notes. Soon others joined and it became a diapason, spring's prelude. All along the lake the sky was peppered with kites made of bright-colored tissue pasted on lengths of cane; they dipped crazily in the wind, jouncing their long rag tails, and martins and kingfishers flew up to fight them. Below, boys ran shouting and cheering.

Bart turned the dogs out-of-doors and saddled his horse. He rode at a trot, splashing through puddles of melted ice and sleet, the fat lazy dogs panting behind, running with their heads down, yapping. He stopped at one of the cabins for the midday meal. When it was over, he and the man of the house sat by the fireplace. He said, "This coming year we're going to make cotton where we couldnt make conversation up to now."

"If you say we is, we is," the man said. "Just give us the high-sign, we gone to the field."

"You talk a good crop, Jerry."

"And picks one, too. And picks one, too. Aint nobody know that bettern you. Give me the high-sign, I show you."

When he got back to the house he was coughing and sneezing; his breath wheezed and his eyes were red; they brimmed with tears. Mrs Bart took one look at him and ordered him to bed. He was meek, obedient; he had never had a cold before. Teeth chattering, he got under the covers. Then, gripping the edge of the blanket with both hands, his body rigid and tense, he began to shake all over. Mrs Bart mixed him a hot toddy, a strong one made with rock candy. He sipped it with one hand out from under the covers. "Ah," he said. "This is worth getting sick for, almost," and went to sleep with the glass in his hand.

He woke up hearing his breath coming out of his chest with a rattling rasp like the sound of a chain drawn across the edge of a plank. It's me! he thought. He tried to sit up but the covers were too heavy. He thought he saw a glimmer across the room, and when he turned toward it a voice came at him out of the darkness: "No, Mr Bart; lie down." A hand was on his shoulder; something had come between him and the glimmer. He rolled his head and the whirling darkness cleared. Mrs Bart sat by the bed; she leaned forward holding the blankets on him, pressing him back against the pillow. Instead of the chill there was a burning. "Florence," he said. "Florence, I was dreaming. I thought . . ." Then in sudden panic he realized that he could not remember his dream; there was only confusion, the sound of the chain being drawn across the plank. The whirling resumed.

His body was a pilgrim in a new land: he might even have been on a different planet, with a rarefied atmosphere and altered laws of gravity and pressure, where breathing was a conscious act, audible, where blood was hot in the veins, surging as if clotted, where there was heat but no sweat, weariness but no peace, where the brain discerned a ringing the ears did not hear and was troubled by strange dreams and uncalled thoughts. Yet in all this confusion there was one thing safe and sure: the hand, the voice beside him. "Go to sleep, Mr Bart. Go back to sleep." He wanted to ask the time, but the glimmer whirled in vortex and became a band of orange light; the voice quailed and thinned and ceased, and the darkness, the dream-shapes returned.

A new voice said, "Pneumonia." Where? Bart thought. What was that? The voice again, as if from a long way off: "Pneumonia." Doctor. But what did he say? What did he say? "Pneumonia," the voice said. The word became printed on his brain, branded there for him to carry back into unconsciousness, each of the nine letters burned clear and gleaming. "Pneumonia," the medical voice said.

From time to time, between great blocks of night, he felt daylight sift like dust between his eyelids. He tried to speak but he could not shape the words; he could make the sounds but he could not make the sounds into words. Then one morning he woke and it was over, or almost over. He was calm. The room was filled with sunlight filtered golden through the shades; the air seemed thin, antiseptic, sterile. Moving his head slightly, he saw Mrs Bart sitting beside the bed. The window to her left was open, the curtain lifted a bit by a faint stir of breeze.

"It's warm again," he said.

"Thats because it's almost April," she told him. "It's April Fool tomorrow." She smiled, her hands clasped loosely in her lap. "How do you feel today?"

"I feel good. I feel right good." Then he said suddenly: "*A*pril!"

"Yes. Tomorrow will be your ninth day in bed and it's April Fool. Dont that surprise you?" Bart nodded gravely, and she went on, still smiling: "And I'll tell you something else that might surprise you. Youve got a beard, Mr Bart: a thick brown beard, like General Grant. Thats the worst part about the whole thing. We put you to bed and nurse you through pneumonia, more than a week of it, and here you turn out to look like a Yankee general."

"I'll shave tomorrow, when I get up. How do I look in the face?"

She touched one corner of her mouth with a forefinger, the gesture she always made when she was considering something. "You look right good, Mr Bart," she said. "Beard and all, considering."

He was wrong about getting up next day, though. Three days later, when he sat up in bed to shave, he looked into a mirror for the first time in almost two weeks. The beard was dark brown and thick, as Mrs Bart had said, but it was also shot with gray, which she had not mentioned. So was his hair. His eyes were far back in their sockets, and there were new scorings in his face. I need feeding, he thought. Then he said, "Aint that awful, Billy?"

148

"You wouldnt take no loving cup," Billy Boy said. He was clipping at Bart's beard with a big pair of scissors.

"Never mind being so careful," Bart told him, propped on three pillows with a towel spread over his shoulders and under his chin. "I'm going to shave off what you leave."

"How bout the musstache?"

"Dont touch that musstache. Thats my crowning joy."

When the clipping was over, Bart lathered his face and Billy Boy honed and stropped the razor, one of seven in a sharkskin case, each with a day of the week engraved on its handle. "Is that Tuesday youre stropping?" Bart asked. Billy Boy held it out for him to see. "Thats right, by jingo. How did you get it?"

"Counted three from the left."

"Why not from the right? And how'd you know Sunday was first?"

"I aint so dumb as some folks seem to think."

"Youre some kid, Billy. Billy the kid. Give me that, before you turn the edge."

He had a hard time shaving because of the trembling in his hands. When he had finished, he wiped his face with the towel and stared into the mirror. The unruly brown mustache bushed out beneath his nose, dividing sunken cheeks the color of wet cement an hour or two before it dries.

Billy Boy watched him looking into the mirror. "What did you expect? Youre spose to look like that after two weeks in bed of chills and fever, flat on your back. It aint nothing wrong with you a week of feeding wont fix."

Bart turned from the mirror. He put it aside and watched Billy Boy clean the razor and put it back into the case. For a while he did not speak: then he said, "Billy, I'm old. I'll be fifty years old next month."

"Great balls of fire: fifty aint old. I'm sixty-three, I think, and look at me. Do I look old?"

"Yes. Yes, you do."

"Well, I aint. I'm good for another sixty-three or however many the Lord will spare me."

"Well, I'm not," Bart said. "Pull down the shades for me, please, and let the door to easy on your way out. I want to get some sleep."

The following day he sat in a chair by the window, sunlight streaming around him. Billy Boy and Mrs Bart were with him. After an hour Mrs Bart told him the time was up; he should get back into bed. "Soon," he said. "I like it here."

"You look tired, Mr Bart."

"I'm all right: I feel fine." He thought for a minute and said, "Have I got any mail downstairs?"

"Yes, a big bundle. It's been coming all along. But why dont you wait?"

"I feel fine."

"Then I'll bring it to you when youre back in bed. You can read it there before your nap."

"I'd rather have it now," he said quietly, using the special tone that showed he meant it. Mrs Bart left. As soon as she was out of earshot Bart said, "Billy, help me back to bed. I cant . . ."

"Sho," Billy Boy said. "Here: lean on me." He expected Bart's weight to bear him down (I lied when I said I wasnt old, he thought) but when Bart leaned on him there was hardly any strain at all. Billy Boy's reaction was outrage; he was like the thief who lifted the display-window turkey and found it was papier mâché.

When Mrs Bart came back with an armload of letters and newspapers, she found Billy Boy smoothing the sheet across Bart's chest and she realized that Bart had sent her out of the room because he had not wanted her to see his inability to stand alone. An hour ago, he had got out of bed boldly, straight-backed, and walked to the chair by the window; "I like sunlight," he had said, like a man from underground. She looked down at him as he lay too tired to lift his arms from his sides.

He's ashamed of being sick, she thought. Ashamed of what being sick has done to him, flat on his back. Men!

THE SALE

IN JUNE when Hugh came home from the university—which he called by the same name plantation tenants used in addressing the planter's wife: Ole Miss—Bart was mending fast. Sunlight had restored his tan, and though there were plenty of signs of his pilgrimage into asthenia, they had the combined effect of making him look slimmer and fitter. The new gray hair, mingled in almost equal parts with the brown, emphasized his dignity, gave his bearing the riper mien his fifty years warranted. He was aware of this, and had assumed a formality, a stiffness beyond any he had shown before. With his high-stomached, nearly sway-backed way of walking, planting his feet firmly, heel and toe, he resembled more than ever a successful small-town banker crowding sixty.

"Good day, barrister," he said when Hugh came off the train at the Ithaca station. They did not shake hands. "Or is it freshman?"

"It's freshman, papa," Hugh said, not adding that it would still be freshman next year. He had squeezed through enough courses to permit his return in the fall, but he had failed to advance with his class.

"Boy, I declare you look almost grown to me. I could take you into the Palace and buy you a drink."

"Well . . ."

Bart went off in a burst of laughter, clapping one hand on Hugh's shoulder. "Come on. We'll go home and see your mother. She'll skin us alive for keeping her waiting like this. You got all your baggage?"

"This is it." Hugh hefted a big cowhide suitcase that was

plastered with gay pennant-shaped stickers. Leaning far to one side to balance its weight, he staggered across the platform toward the surrey. He wore white flannel trousers, tight in the legs and seat, the cuffs rolled above his ankles, and a blue-and-orange blazer that was belted across the back. His shoes were needle-tip, light tan, turned up at the toes. A wide-brimmed boater, worn slantwise, glinted in the sunlight; it had a candy-striped band and a length of string that drooped to the buttonhole in one lapel to keep it from blowing away. Bart followed, looking at the blazer, the hat, the narrow shoes, the orange-clocked violet socks. People all along the station platform were turning, rubbing their eyes.

"You look like a dude in that rig," Bart said.

"It's what theyre wearing, papa."

"Hm."

That was a pleasant summer. The crop was good, and except for an occasional twinge of his rheumatism—not really enough, however, to call for taking the liniment off the shelf—Bart was in excellent health. He spent much of his time on horseback and looked forward to a round of trap shoots in the fall.

Nine months at the university had done things for Hugh; he was beginning to come out of his shell. Most nights he was gone soon after supper, off with a crowd of boys in a buggy, saying vaguely that they were on their way to a dance, and coming in long after everyone else was asleep. Mrs Bart said she was worried, but Bart said, "Did you think he was going to stay a child forever? Let him have his fling. I'm glad to see it."

Then one night in late August he woke up and Mrs Bart was nudging him in the ribs. "Sst! Sst!" she said. He sat up in bed. "Somebody's downstairs," she told him. "I heard a racket."

He listened and heard nothing. "Nonsense," he said, and as soon as he had said it there was a clatter, the sound of a chair being overturned. He got out of bed and went to the head of the stairs. Looking over the banister, he saw a group of people in the living room. They were striking matches to find their way about, whispering like stage comedians:

"Shh."

"If this spook would just tell us where his room is."

"Lets leave him on the couch."

"Yair, lets do that."

"Shh. You want to wake up the fambly?"

There were five of them. By the light of the matches Bart saw that they were quite young. They wore white linen suits, which meant they had been to a dance. Just then the big grandfather clock at the foot of the staircase cleared its throat and struck three. This was followed by silence, and then the whispering resumed:

"There. You hear? Pretty soon itll be daylight."

"Wheres your room, spook?"

"Shh: youll wake up his old man."

"Ah, put him on the couch, like I said."

"Shh!"

Bart came down the stairs. "What can I do for you young gentlemen?" He said it in a normal tone of voice but it sounded booming after all the whispering. There was abrupt silence. Then there was darkness as the matches went out one by one. They were not blown out, nor even dropped; they just failed, one after another. Bart recognized the young men. They were between sixteen and nineteen years old, sons of planters and Ithaca tradesmen.

They did not answer his question, but when they moved aside Bart saw Hugh. Two of the young men held his arms across their shoulders; his knees were bent and his body sagged; his head hung forward, his chin on his chest, and the front of his suit was stained with vomit.

"I'll take him," Bart said. "Thank you." He reached forward and put his hands beneath Hugh's armpits. "What was the matter? Couldnt he keep up?"

"Yes sir. He just tried to stay ahead."

"Ah. And did he?"

"He did till this happened." Someone sniggered. At first they had been abashed, but now it had become a joke.

"Ah," Bart said, holding Hugh upright. It was like trying to balance two sacks of meal, one on top of another. "Well, thank you, gentlemen, and good night."

"Good night, Mr Bart."

"Good night, sir."

He stood and watched them go, holding Hugh against his hip, both arms around his chest. The young men clotted at the door, elbowing each other and milling a bit. They laughed going down the steps, two and two and the fifth at the rear. "Lets go to Adah's," Bart heard one of them say as they climbed into the buggy. A whip lashed: "Hum up, there!" and wheels creaked on the gravel of the drive. Bart was fifty but this was the first time he had heard himself called old. They called him spook, he thought. They called me old man.

Upstairs again, he placed Hugh carefully on the bed, undressed him, put the nightshirt over his head, and pulled it down beneath the weight of his body. Moonlight streamed through the open windows. He lifted the sheet to the boy's shoulders, smoothed and tucked it neatly. In the doorway he turned and looked back: Hugh might have been a corpse, laid out for a wake. Bart said aloud, "If youd taken it a little easier you might have made the party at Adah's. Let that be a lesson to you next time the bottle comes round." There was no reply from the bed.

Mrs Bart was awake, sitting bolt upright in bed, her nightcap pearly in the moonlight. "Yes?" she said.

"Yes indeed," Bart said, climbing in. "Nine months in a Mississippi school—where they really learn such things, I hear—and he still cant hold his liquor."

Hugh did not come down for breakfast. "What did he say?" Bart asked the houseboy who had been into Hugh's room earlier that morning to waken him.

"Say he dying, he spec."

"I guess he just about is. Or wishes it, anyhow. Take him some ice water, Ernest, and tell him I said to stay up there till he's able to come down in some sort of decent condition."

When Bart got back from Ithaca that afternoon Hugh was sitting on the porch. His face was gray except for the sockets of his eyes, which were dark, almost sooty, and in them his eyes had a feverish glitter, like agates. "Afternoon, papa," he said.

"Afternoon," Bart said gruffly, halting halfway up the steps. "If you cant handle that corn you ought to let it alone. You hear me?"

"I'm sorry, papa."

"Sorry, hey? I reckon you are. I reckon if I had the head you had this morning I'd be sorry too." He sat in a chair beside Hugh, turned sideways, facing him. "Look, son. You do all the drinking you want. Theres a minimum of whiskey every man has to run through his system, they tell me, and you might as well get it done while youre young. Besides, a drink is a mighty fine thing, on occasion. But listen: listen carefully. If you cant come home standing alone, moving on your own two legs and holding your head up ... dont drink." He had intended to say 'Dont come home at all,' but he changed it, and Hugh knew that he had changed it. "Learn how to hold it before you try leading the pack. It's the fool young dogs, yapping and prancing, trying to stay out in front, that the bear gets."

As he spoke he grew more and more aware of the emptiness of words. He had tried to make it sound convincing, but he knew it was not much good; it was mostly a piecing together of things he had heard other men say that they had told their sons. He was not even sure Hugh had heard him. "Why dont you go back to bed?" he said quietly. "You look like you died and were buried and then got dug up. You look awful."

Then it was September again, the year beginning to draw to an end, supercharged, potentially terrible, gathering itself like an animal, tawny and tense, for the leap into Indian summer. There was a shimmer of heat over all the fields; the stubble appeared to be burning. Hugh returned to the university, and though he had not presumed to ask not to have to go back, he told himself one thing was sure: this was the last time; this was the very last time. He wore the coat of many colors that he had worn home on the train in June, and more or less like biblical Joseph, he was ready for the pit.

The crop was gathered and the Ithaca Gun Club reopened. Bart's scores were as good as ever, his style as spectacular. Once bird season opened, he was out every day, often alone with his dogs, sometimes with friends. He had always bagged the lion's share of the game and now he did so more than ever, for he had developed, by drill during the summer, a new fast-loading action that gave him four shots at every covey, even when the quail all rose together. The breaching appeared to coincide with the trigger snap, and two shells, held parallel between the fingers of the left hand, slid into their chambers. It was instant, deft: bang bang, snap, bang bang: "Fetch, boy, fetch! Fetch here!"

CHRISTMAS WAS quiet at Solitaire in 1910: there were no guests, and Hugh and Florence were mostly in Bristol at dances. Once the presents had been distributed, unpackaged, and admired, the holiday itself was uneventful. There was turkey for dinner, baked golden brown with all the trimmings, and fireworks on the lawn at dusk—sparklers, roman candles, rockets, and pinwheels: all down the eastern shore of the lake the night was hung with streamers and trickles of red and blue and yellow fire. It was much like any other Christmas spent by any other family on Lake Jordan.

After supper, however, Clive was sneaking up on the coachman, planning to surprise and frighten him with a fire-cracker he had saved (Doll Baby was asleep on the back porch, tipped back in a split-bottom chair, digesting his turkey) but something went wrong; Clive held it too long or fumbled it or something: the fire-cracker went off in his hand. Doll Baby said afterward that the yell that followed had frightened him more than the bang.

Mrs Bart soothed the burn with a soda poultice and wrapped it in gauze; the bandage resembled a big white mitten. Clive was always hurting himself. Not that he was clumsy: he just did such foolish things. There was the time he had a loose tooth and decided to pull it himself. As usual, it had to be done in a special way. So he took ten feet of string and a large rock, climbed onto the roof of the stable, tied one end of the string to his tooth, the other end to the rock, and standing on the eaves at the peak of the roof, dropped the rock toward the ground. For a single terrible instant he watched it fall, already feeling in his imagination the pain of the yank on the tooth. No! No! he thought: with the result that, before the slack in the string was taken up, his nerve gave out; he jumped. He landed on the rock and sprained his ankle (that was painful too, but at least it was not the awful pain of anticipation) and as he hobbled away something whirled him around; there was a tiny sound of breaking, almost a twang. The tooth came out so easily that he hardly knew what had happened until he saw it lying on the ground, still fastened to the string running back to the rock.

He went to his mother, as always, and she comforted him, just as she was to do later when the firecracker went off in his hand. These were only two incidents out of many; he was always hurting himself as a result of his inventiveness and curiosity. Bart looked at him now, at the big white mitten bandage. "Look at him," he said to Mrs Bart. "Banged up again. He's going to keep on till it's something serious, you mark my words. Why cant he stay out of devilment? He sprains his ankle, cuts his foot, breaks two ribs, comes close to putting out both eyes, and now he burns his hand trying to blow up Doll Baby with a firecracker: all because he cant stay out of devilment. Why is that?"

"He certainly didnt get it from me," she said.

Florence, on the other hand, had quieted, though she was still far from demure. She was seventeen. She still spent much of her time on horseback, but she rode less recklessly and she stayed at home more often. Generally she kept to her room, reading the English poets, Byron and Shelley and Keats and lately Browning. She was collecting their works, a book a month; Bart was glad to give her the money to order them with; "Well, well," he said; "Maybe we're going to have a scholar in the family after all."

In the year just past she had bloomed without softening. She had begun going to dances, for one thing, but this was mainly because there was nothing else to do: it was more from boredom than for pleasure. She saved no dance cards, made no scrap book, kept no romantic diary. Bart continued his joking manner in speaking to her; he was still somewhat afraid of what she might do if pushed, and now that she had begun to spend much of her time reading books, awe was added to fear. She was more a puzzle than ever.

As for Hugh, however, all the problems of his life and character were resolved—at least in the sense of being brought to a point—by something that happened two nights after New Year's. Bart and Mrs Bart were sitting in the downstairs parlor with Clive (Florence was spending the week end with a friend at Indemnity, north of Bristol) when they heard the sudden clash of the cattle-gap, the sound of gravel on the driveway being slued and crunched by rubber tires; a motor coughed, sputtered, coughed again, and died; there was a pause. They looked at one another, wondering: it was already past bedtime, no hour for visitors. A car door slammed, then another. There were footsteps on the porch, another pause. They heard someone whispering just beyond the door, then a soft nervous laugh that was more like a whimper. As Bart crossed the room toward the door, it opened and Hugh and a girl, a young lady, walked in.

"Hello, papa; hello, mamma," he said, talking rapidly, standing in evening clothes beside the girl. Satin dance slippers peeped from beneath the hem of her bright blue dress. Drunk, Bart thought; He's drunk again. But Hugh went on talking. "This is Kate," he said. "Kate, this is mamma; this is papa. —We got married tonight and we've come home." He spoke rapidly to ward off interruption. When he had finished he grinned nervously as Bart came past him and closed the door against the January weather.

"Whats that?" Bart asked. "Whats that you said?"

"You havent met Kate: Kate Bateman."

Bart recognized the name but he was uncertain about what to do. I cant just say howdy to her, he thought. So he made a shallow bow and said, "I think I know your father, Lester Bateman?"

"Yes sir," she said, and her voice was almost shrill.

Bart looked at her. Her mouth was small, held in a coquettish pout above the short, round chin. Her hair, which was thick and dark, was combed low onto her forehead, and her brows were straight, narrow lines above violet eyes. Beneath the powder, obviously put on while the car crunched gravel on the driveway, he could descry a faint saddle of freckles across the bridge of her nose. She's really scared, he thought; I can see her heart pulse in her throat. He remembered a wounded quail he had reached under a log to get that morning: both wings were shattered and one leg was gone; a bright eye watched him sideways, unwinking, and as he held its feathered warmth against the palm of his hand he felt the tiny furious heartbeat ticking faster than a watch in the moment before he broke its skull on the gun barrel.

SHE WAS nineteen that fall, six months younger than Hugh, and an only child. Her father, a Bristol cotton factor whose wife notoriously domineered him, was scraping bottom on a fortune that went back four generations to one of the three original men whose riverside plantation downtown Bristol was built on. During the past four years her only concern had been young men (but she never called them that; she called them boys) and such functions as involved them, mainly dances. She had acquired a reputation. Watching her, people spoke out of the corners of their mouths; they called her a wild one, using the same tone of voice they would use a dozen years later when they said flapper; they looked at her and shook their heads; "A wild one," they said.

It had begun at school, at the convent where all the 'nicer' children went. Boys discovered that they could pass notes to her—*I think your real pretty. How about meeting somewheres after school? Tear this up*—and she not only would accept them, she would read them while the sender watched, not even blushing, and sometimes she would even answer them. They got a disproportionate pleasure out of this, for she was high-born, or at least what they called high-born: her great-grandfather had been one of the founders.

That was the year she was twelve, a very strange year. Everyday functions were corrupted from the normal until they were no longer organic, and though everything was somehow connected, a confusion of history and self, she could not find the thread. Her simplest actions were filled with ambiguity; they were at once eloquent and crass, distorted beyond all present perception. She had grown so fast this past year, legs like bean stalks and something crazy happening to her waist and hips so that her skirt refused to hang right any more; the suddenly pointed nipples on her chest were as red as drops of blood, so raw and tender to the touch that she had to hold her middy blouse away from contact with them; her nose no longer fitted her face, and her mouth seemed as ugly as a wound. There were always eyes, everywhere eyes, watching her, shaping the curve of her rump, the swing of her thighs. She began to have mysterious dreams that made her feel guilty.

Then she was fifteen, going to dances. Life was less strange and infinitely more exciting. It revolved around boys. You got them to dance with you, to form a ring around your portion of the dance floor, to ask you out. You tricked them in various ways, and everyone rated you by the number you tricked. She learned all this; she did well at it. She was thin and dark, with a prominent collar bone and a wealth of hair. Her breasts were small and acute; they stood out smartly on her narrow chest. Her voice was always shrill, always as if she were raising it against a background of dance music.

All this time people were watching, seeing her pass in front of the barber shop and poolhall windows, wobbly on high heels, usually with girls older than herself and without her heritage. They saw her sitting at the marble-topped tables in the Kandy Kitchen with high school hobbledehoys and riding in bright-spoked buggies with young men home from college. And always, wherever she went, she seemed to flaunt her pleasures in their faces ('Look at the fun I'm having,' she seemed to say; 'Look at the fun youre too hide-bound or too old to have') and they responded with the talk she seemed to invite; they gossiped for four years.

They never would have kept it up this long—unadorned frivolity was tame and common enough, and doubtless even the talkers knew there was more smoke than fire here—if she had not represented one of the leading families. It had been a good one in its day; had included, besides the founder, statesmen and soldiers and at least one reputable governor. Thus once when she passed before the plate-glass window a barber looked up from his work and said, "If thats blueblood I'm glad I didnt have none to pass on to my daughters."

"You cant tell," the man beneath the razor said. "Maybe one of them governors' wives got mixed up with a flag salesman or something."

"Ah no," another said from down the line. "Thats blueblood, all right. I can spot it every time."

That was the way it went. She led this kind of life, postponing tears that were bound to come, staving off retribution with the sentient negation an invalid uses to put off an operation because of his fear of the knife. Life continued to be a series of young men variously skilled at getting from under the eye of the chaperone, a series of nights in the side-porch swing where they spoke in whispers because her mother's bedroom was directly overhead.

It was like war, with a skirmish every night. At ten-thirty her mother would rap on the floor with the heel of a bedroom slipper. That meant for the young man to leave, for Kate to come upstairs, and she shaped her tactics accordingly. Her kisses grew more intense, her breathing more spasmodic, but always at the apparent height of her passion, the nadir of her resistance, there would come the sharp tattoo from overhead—like the bugle that clangs in light fiction when the cavalry comes over the crest of a convenient hill —and she would sit up abruptly, would straighten her clothes and smooth her hair, demure again, all signs of passion gone; her voice would be level, matter-of-fact, and barely tender: "I have to go up. Good night," and the young man would be left below to pick his way home through the moon-dappled streets, cursing her and her mother too and swearing never to try again, though even as he made the oath he knew he would break it.

This continued, and likely if it had gone on long enough she would have been outgeneraled, would have come up against an adversary skillful enough, or perhaps just patient enough, to break through her defenses, defeat her stratagems, make her ignore or perhaps not even hear the slipper signal. But it did not. Before that happened she stopped. She stopped quite suddenly, in the fall of 1910.

The watchers, the men who had discussed her in the barber shop and the poolhall, were at a loss to explain it. They had been too busy condemning the wildness to consider that it could have an end. They wondered, though. Perhaps the comet had something to do with the change. Dragging a long, broad, hazy tail, it had flared in the northwest sky above the river, a warning sign hung out by God to signify impending judgment. Newspapers carried features predicting the end of the world; preachers thundered in the pulpits. It was coming soon, and sinners had better get right: on the night when the earth was scheduled to pass through its flaming wake, they would all be burnt to cinders in their beds or choked by the poisonous gases. That night came and passed, however, and people emerged into a dawn that was much like the one of the day before. Mostly they were elated at having been spared the fire from heaven, but they were a little disappointed too; there was not even any stardust in the streets. Whatever else it was, it was certainly anticlimax.

Others among the watchers, seeking a cause for Kate's volte-face, said that her mother must have brought pressure to bear. But even those who said this did not believe it. They knew that Mrs Bateman, having married somewhat above her station—and what was worse, having been sadly failed by her husband—took refuge in a sense of caste that abrogated any notion of error, let alone sin, within her ranks. Everyone knew that it was not she who accomplished her daughter's sudden and tearful transformation. Others (they came closest to the truth) said that Kate had drunk so deeply from the cup of pleasure that the dregs had begun to taste.

Whatever caused it, it was certainly sudden. In late October she came home from a dance and told a surprised young man good night at the front steps. She went upstairs, undressed, put on her gown, and sat at the dresser, quite removed from a world she believed not only alien but embattled. As she sat watching her reflection in the mirror, there swirled around her, as if in vortex, the odor of cosmetics and silk and faintly yellowed dance cards. Photographs of a dozen suitors watched her from their frames; their eyes, which formerly were tender with love, seemed hateful. She addressed them one by one as enemies. You! she thought, nodding at each in turn. And you! And you! And you!

It was quite late when she came downstairs in the moonlight. Her face appeared lipless, for she had stopped by the bathroom and scrubbed hard at her mouth with a soapy washcloth. She came across the living room, her gown billowing behind her, and as she entered the dining room she heard a sigh. Turning, she saw her father at the sideboard. As always, the decanter chattered a bit at the rim of the glass as he poured.

His father before him had lost most of the family money and land, mismanaging and gambling them away, and now Bateman operated a cotton office. Whiskey, taken from hour to hour, had made him a vapid but congenial observer of a world that had done nothing for fifty years but deprive him of the things he was born to. He was not resentful, however, nor even bitter; he merely watched from within a sort of alcoholic lambency. When Kate came across the living room and entered the dining room, he was startled (in the gown that flowed behind her, thin as gauze, she resembled something celestial, or maybe infernal) and when he recognized his daughter he was startled again, but differently.

He put down the glass and decanter, held out one arm. Kate put her head on his shoulder, her face against the side of his neck. She began to weep, not loudly but with many tears and short, quick sobs, her breasts jiggling against his ribs. He was uncomfortable in position and uneasy in his mind: he felt that something was expected of him but he did not know what. So he pulled up a chair with his free hand and sat down slowly, lowering his daughter onto his lap. Her head was still on his shoulder and she dampened his neck with her tears; the tickling in his ribs continued, like little fingers at work. He was surprised to discover how small she was.

For what seemed a very long time he sat there saying Shh Shh with one arm over her shoulders, his breath scented with whiskey and cloves. His hair was mostly gray, tufted at the back around a neat tonsure the size of a silver dollar. "There, there," he said. "There, there." This made her cry more loudly, which was not at all what he had intended. "Sh, honey," he said, "Youll wake up your mother."

"Daddy, daddy," she whimpered. "I'm so tired of their mouths and their hands and their talk . . ." Bateman was somewhat horrified. Her chin and nose were wet against his neck; he wanted to shift her head, but it occurred to him that this might seem unpaternal. He just sat there. "Nobody hates me," she began to say. "Nobody hates me, daddy; they dont even hate me. It's all a game they play."

"Of course nobody hates you, honey . . ."

"Thats just it, just it," she said, punctuating her words with sobs. "If they would even just do that."

"Who would, honey?"

"*They* would," she said. "All of them." He patted her arm, trying to soothe her, saying Shh . . . Shh over and over again, and suddenly she sat bolt upright in his lap, eyes glistening. "I: am: stopping: right: now," she said evenly, looking out into the long room flooded with moonlight. The big mahogany table gleamed like a moonlit pond.

"Of course, honey." He did not understand. He was thinking, I reckon these things are awful but I reckon these things pass. At least I can be glad I'm not young again.

"I'm so tired," she said. "So tired of coming in night after night with my mouth all slick and weak from kissing."

Ive got to stop being shocked, he thought as his eyebrows jerked up. He said, "All right, honey, all right."

"And then theyll hate me, maybe. Maybe they will." Her mouth was drawn in a line.

"Come on and go to bed," he told her. "Get your sleep and youll feel fresh and fine tomorrow."

Bateman was glad to find a way to end the scene. He lifted her off his lap and they crossed the living room together, his arm still about her shoulders. At the foot of the stairs he stopped and watched her mount. She did not look back. From the side and below, he could see her face lifted into the moonlight. She passed from sight. He shook his head, then turned and picked his way back to the sideboard. The decanter chattered against the rim of the glass.

That was in late October, and that was still her frame of mind six weeks later when Hugh came home for the university holidays. Whatever else she gave up, she did not give up dancing. Hugh saw her at the first Bristol dance before Christmas, and though he had known her before, more or less from a distance—he was younger than the admirers she encouraged—now they found that they had thoughts in common. Melancholia was fashionable that year, along with the Rubaiyat. Before the night was over, they sat out several dances and Hugh was in love. He realized it with a suddenness that knocked all other thoughts from his head. Afterwards he lay in bed and thought about it. "I'm in love," he said, breathing the words.

He saw her five nights running. The sixth night he asked her to marry him. "All right," she said, and then she let him kiss her, the first since October. She shuddered and put her fingers in his hair. "Ooo," she said.

"We'll have to elope."

"All right. Whatever you say." She turned her face up to him, jaws apart; her breath was warm and moist. The heel of the slipper beat its fast tattoo.

He arranged it for the night before the day he was to return to school. There was a dance in Bristol. He rented an automobile, practiced all afternoon learning to drive it, and called for Kate that evening with another couple and a chaperone in the tonneau. They went straight across the ballroom, down the fire escape, got back into the car, and drove to the home of the old clerk and j.p. who issued the license and married them, using his wife and his oldest daughter as witnesses; they stood by in bathrobes and curlpapers, smiling. Within twenty minutes of the time they left the dance, Hugh and Kate were back in the car again, as man and wife.

"I dont want to go home," she said when he headed in that direction. "Please. Please." She clung to him, leaning across the steering wheel, suppliant, urgent, voluptuous. Overhead the stars were bright and cold: this was one night no slipper would beat a curfew. He turned south toward the lake, toward Solitaire.

Maybe she got married to get away from home, he thought. And then it came to him, swift and sharp, in a whisper: Like maybe I married to get away from school. But I love her, he told himself. I love her: I love her.

THEY SLEPT apart, however. Bart spent the night in Hugh's room with him, and Kate stayed with Mrs Bart in the master bedroom. "We'll talk this over tomorrow," Bart said. "Besides, I want to have a few words with Mr Bateman."

Next morning when Hugh woke up, the other bed was rumpled and empty. He got up. Conscious that Kate was in the adjoining room, he knelt and used the chamber silently, then dressed and went into the hall, which was dim, almost dark, as it always was in early morning with the sun behind the house. As he started down the staircase he heard a door creak, and looking around he saw his mother come out of her room. Hugh stepped back onto the landing. "Good morning, mamma," he said. "Is she . . . ? Is my . . . ?"

"No, son: not yet. Lets go to breakfast. She's a town girl. Let her sleep."

Hugh wondered if his mother's calling Kate a town girl meant disapproval. They went downstairs. "Wheres papa?" he asked.

"Gone to Bristol."

"Oh. Did he . . . ?"

"He caught the five-fifty before I was up."

"Oh." She dont act mad, he thought. But what was she doing back upstairs? Why was she back in the room?

After breakfast he went out and sat on the porch. When he had been there about an hour he heard someone coming down the stairs. Turning, he saw that it was Kate. "Good morning," he said. He rose and opened the door.

"Good morning. Look." She smoothed her skirt with both hands. It's Florence's, Hugh thought. Thats what mamma was doing back upstairs. Kate said, "I found it on a chair by the bed."

"Mamma laid it out, I guess. It just about fits you, and thats funny: I thought Florence was lots bigger than you." He remembered her only in evening dresses. "How did you sleep?"

"Wonderful!" She added without pause, in her rather shrill voice: "I just love your mother."

"She must like you too: she laid that dress out. Want some breakfast?"

"I dont know. Oh yes I do, I'm *fam*ished. Lets eat together."

"This way," Hugh said. He led her into the dining room, where they sat at one end of the table. He did not tell her that he had already had breakfast an hour before she was awake.

Bart returned in the early afternoon. To his family's surprise— always before he had refused to get inside one—he was riding in an automobile, sitting stiffly upright on the rear seat, watching the back of the driver's neck mistrustfully, outraged at the noise and the fumes of the engine. The man beside him had slumped forward, asleep.

"It's daddy," Kate said as they pulled up in front of the steps. "He's rented that old automobile again."

Bart got out and stood looking down at the sleeper, feeling

awkward about disturbing him. "Mr Bateman," he said hesitantly.

Kate came past him giggling. "Daddy! Daddy, for goodness sake!" She shook his arm.

Bateman opened his eyes, and a little shudder passed over his body, the way it always did when he first came awake. "Oh-oh," he said. "You got married and your mother's mad at you." He sat up, smiling and shaking his head.

"I dont care what she is," Kate said. She pouted, then giggled again. "Daddy, you remember Hugh."

Hugh made a short bow. "How do, sir."

"I'm fine," Bateman said decorously. "How are you, my boy?" Hugh bowed again, even shorter. Bateman said, "Mr Bart, Ive been asleep. I believe I have."

"Some of the way," Bart said. "Come in, sir."

After an early supper, Hugh and Kate went back to Bristol with her father. "Look here," he told her. "If you think I'm going to spend another night like last night, alone in that house with your mother as mad as she is, youve got another think coming. This was your doing, young lady—and you too, young man— and youve got to take your share of what comes."

Hugh followed in the automobile he had rented the day before; Kate rode with her father in the battered touring car. It belonged to the driver, an old bachelor who had never been able to hold a job until he bought this automobile and set himself up in business as Bristol's first public chauffeur. Whenever Bateman had had too much to drink, or enough at least to make him feel what he called kittenish, he rented the car and made the rounds, picking up whoever would join him on the spree; he had an understanding with the driver that he was never to be taken home until he was too far gone to face his wife or hear her reproaches. This was one time he would have to face her, however, along with the bride and the groom.

Bristol was two hours away. Following the other car up the greasy buckshot road with a rush of air coming cold around the windshield, Hugh thought: This seems like a lot of trouble, just to be getting married. I wonder how long theyll keep this up?

It was a premonition of unfulfillment, for this made the second night they slept apart. Mrs Bateman sent Kate upstairs as soon as they arrived; "Go to your room," she cried, and Kate went. Usually she was defiant; often she was rude: but tonight she was frightened. Hugh looked blank and then scowled. "Now, Mr Bart," Mrs Bateman said, a large broad-shouldered woman with fierce eyes, and then it was Hugh's turn to be frightened. "What do you propose to do?" And that was what frightened him most, this question which he had known was bound to come and which he could not answer because he did not know.

There was no honeymoon, no week or even week end in New Orleans. They returned to the lake by train the following day. Then finally, the third night after their marriage, they were left to themselves. Even then, however, Kate was tense, expecting to hear the slipper.

After five days of idleness (Hugh and Kate walked in the yard a good deal, but never far from the house) Bart said to his son, "I guess youre through with school, with your plans for a law degree?" Hugh nodded and Bart said, "Do you want to work here for me, then?" He watched Hugh's face. "Because youve got to work somewhere, you know. Youve got a wife."

"Yes sir."

Bart smiled. "It looks like you got trapped into being a farmer anyhow, dont it?" Then, watching Hugh's face, he wished he had not smiled as he said this; it gave an impression of gloating.

"It's what I want," Hugh said.

"Fine, then. We'll ride the place tomorrow morning. I'll show you the ropes." Bart looked away, remembering the honeymoon that was not quite over yet. "After breakfast," he said. He went down the steps and around the house toward the stables.

Alone on the porch Hugh thought, but without conviction: Maybe I'll make a good farmer, after all. Maybe all Ive been needing is to have to.

THAT SUMMER, leaving Hugh to ride the plantation in his place—
He'll do better if I'm away, he thought—Bart began to devote more
time to what an observer once called the extracurricular activities
of Delta agronomy. Two or three days out of every week he went
to Bristol and lounged in the cotton exchange. He even played the
market a bit, but he did so in a rather desultory way, like a sophomore writing poetry—for what sort of gambling was that, he wondered, in which your opponent sat in Washington or New York
and studied the cards an hour before they were dealt to you? The
figures being chalked up by a man in a green eyeshade meant no
more to him than the Morse code clatter that brought them over
the wire. He went for entertainment, the atmosphere of bantering
comradeship. There was always a crowd in the smoky room, the
in-town farmers, the idle well-to-do, the speculators, and the old
men who, white-haired and patriarchal, carrying canes and wearing sober broadcloth, no longer farmed the land themselves because (Like me, Bart thought) they had sons to succeed them.
That was perhaps the chief pleasure he got from being in town:
the knowledge that his presence announced, without need of elab-
oration, his son's transformation from wastrel to worker, sustainer.

Soon Bart was a familiar figure in Bristol, known by officials and
businessmen as well as by the hunters and the poker players who
had met him on the lake. And if toward the end of a day the telephone rang at Solitaire (he had had it installed that spring, along
with electric lighting) and the dispassionate, inflectionless voice
said, "Bristol calling reverse will you accept the charges please,"
Mrs Bart knew that it would be her husband:

"I'll see you all tomorrow afternoon. I ran into something up
here," which meant poker and another spell of seeing his chair
vacant at the head of the table.

That was in the summer. In the fall there were longer absences,
announced in advance; one night the big Gladstone would be
packed and next morning he would be gone to Tennessee or Alabama or Georgia for deer hunts or trap shoots or horse shows. It
was as if he were running from something, keeping his mind oc-

cupied every minute because otherwise he might come face to face with himself.

Kate was pregnant by then, swollen and frightened, stalemated by a biological trick which she had been afraid to ward off. When Mrs Bart had tried in a halting flustered manner to explain a device called a womb veil, a stop-gap of sponge, Kate had been embarrassed, had wanted to giggle; she was afraid it might get lost up there, she said, and Mrs Bart had been so shocked by this remark that she had stopped trying to tell her. So now she was pregnant (which she probably would have been anyhow, since the older woman's method seemed not to have been very effective in her own case) and Hugh was always busy in the fields, morning and afternoon, too weary once the sun went down even to sit up and talk to her. They were left alone in the parlor after supper, two neglected wives, the older one harried and dreamy, like an odalisk worn by time and afraid of losing her status, the younger one sullen and torpid, germed and eared by the old male trickery, bulwarked behind the swollen evidence.

Her mother had never told her anything: all she knew she had learned from older girls, a spate of misinformation. Her dreams were nightmares, and they were filled with fury. Galloping wild-maned stallions were about to run her down; grotesque bird-shapes wheeled in rigid volute before diving at her, looming silent and deadly with beaked human faces, out of the overhead darkness; Mrs Bart sat in a rocking chair and held up one hand, thumb and forefinger a quarter-inch apart, saying "Sponge. A tiny piece will turn the trick," and then rocked primly, self-satisfied, while her face dissolved like a sugardoll's left in the rain; Bart laughed with gold teeth and bright blue upright hair, breaking saucers with a mallet; a goat with eyes as big as billiard balls chewed its protruding tongue, then lowered its horns and charged. She dreamed all this and more, and always the dream progressed toward a scene in which her baby, grinning big-headed and still fetus, like a picture a girl had once shown her in a book, peered at her out of a cave with the steady beady eyes of a homunculus; "Wake up, wake up," this voice kept insisting; "Wake up, Kate, wake up," and she would come out of the dream to find Hugh gripping her shoulder, the room reverberant with the sound of her screaming.

He would get out of bed, go to the washstand and splash cold water on his face. "Youve got to stop that," he would say. "Youre scaring me half to death the way you scream."

And Kate would lie there in the darkness, feeling the child kicking, afraid to go back to sleep because she knew the dream terrors would return, and she would tell herself that she hated her husband. *He* did this to me, she would tell herself. He planned it every step. I was all right: Lord I was lovely, wasnt I? I want to be thin again; I want to dance and dance. I want to be with Neal and Albert and George and Pete and Snooky and Joe again. And she would recite their names, seeing the adolescent, somewhat pimpled galaxy of faces she had known before marriage lifted her from among them, transported her thirty miles overland into a world so different, even apart from the condition of her body, that her former life was like something out of a pleasant and faraway dream, a previous incarnation. Sometimes she would say it aloud, full-voiced and yearning: "I want to go back; I want to go back. I want to be like I was when I was holding off Neal and Albert and George and Pete and Snooky and Joe."

MRS BART helped him pack the bag, as always, including a stiff-bosom shirt for the victory banquet, a new one still in its original tissue wrappings, one of the best in case he should be guest of honor and have his picture taken for the newspapers. This time he was going farther afield than ever: this time he was going to Kentucky, to Louisville for the National. "You know I always meant to go," he said. "I'd have been there long ago if I'd had anybody here to run the place while I was gone."

Three friends went with him, Peter Durfee and two men from Bristol. Their pockets were stuffed with money given them by sportsmen from all over Jordan County, along with instructions to bet it on his nose in case the odds were right. They left on a sum-mery morning in early November, the four of them laughing and joking like boys on the way to school, Bart with his guncase under his arm, waving goodbye to the crowd that came to the station to see him off.

Durfee and one of the Bristol men came back eight days later, full of talk about the shoot. They carried armloads of Louisville papers with cuts on the sports pages showing Bart in action at his post, hunched forward over the breech of his gun, the barrel a blurred gray line like a prolonged eye-beam, or in front of barbecue stands with a collection of dandified men in canvas jackets and slim cat-looking women whose mouths and brows and pupils came out black on the newsprint, the group a little compressed, crowding together like cold sheep and craning to get into the frame, Bart in the center wearing the wooden, stern-lipped expres-sion he always assumed when he knew there was a camera within range. Durfee and the Bristol man were a bit late with the news, however; it had been in the Memphis paper two days ago: DELTAN WINS U.S. TRAPSHOOT CROWN *Hugh G. Bart, Lake Jordan Planter, Triumphs over Field of* 300 *at National Meet.*

Mrs Bart read it at Solitaire, the *Hugh G. Bart,* and thought: G. Bart? G. for what? Gone away?

The story beneath was date-lined Louisville: "Shooting with a style so spectacular that half the 2500 spectators were gathered behind his post here at Blaketon Park, Hugh G. Bart, Mississippi planter and sportsman today nosed out a field of three hundred top marksmen from all over the United States to carry the coveted National Trapshoot Championship trophy home to the Delta country whence he came.

"Asa Perceran Gold, Louisville tobacco magnate, was runner-up with"—and it went on to list the other contestants according to how many of their allotted clay saucers they had chipped or pulverized, finally returning to Bart: "The writing on the wall was as clear as a bell from the time the modest, hard shooting Mississippian reeled off his first fifty disks. Veteran sportsman and novice alike had picked him as their favorite at the outset, though he dropped both his lost targets in the initial hundred"—and so on for two columns more.

Reporters clustered about the finalists before the last round. Bart was favored to win, though the man named Gold was only a target behind. There was no time for statements then: the reporters fell back. But as soon as the last shot was fired they surged forward, surrounding Bart, shouldering each other amiably. Their faces were anxious; their pencils moved across their pads. "How does it feel to be number one U.S. trapshot, Mr Bart?"

"My shoulder's a little sore, if thats what you mean."

They laughed, scribbling feverishly. "Say, Mr Bart: how do you spell your middle name?"

Not 'Have you got one?' Bart thought. Not even 'What is it?' Just 'How do you spell it?' But all right: thats the way they make a living. He looked at them for a moment, blinking, and then said: "G." The reporters hesitated, pencils poised.

"Gee double-ee?"

"No, just G. The initial."

"Oh: G." They wrote it on the pads but they seemed dissatisfied. Seeing this, Bart thought: Maybe they get docked for not getting it all. But at least I saved them something. If I'd told them the truth, maybe theyd have to go hungry all next week.

When he had told them whatever else they wanted, his age, his plans for the rest of the season, his opinions on matters that had nothing to do with trapshooting but which served to touch up their stories, he went to receive the cup. It was presented with ceremony; a member of the governor's staff made a speech about how much the governor regretted not being able to come and how much he himself, acting for the governor, was honored at this chance to thank the contenders and congratulate the winner. The governor took a lively interest in sport, he said, and hoped they would all come back next year for a bigger, a better shoot; Kentucky was glad to play host to so fine a body of men. In conclusion he was reminded of a poem the governor frequently quoted. If

memory served him right it went like this: "When that one great
scorer comes To score against your name, He writes not that you
won or lost But how you *played* the game."

The cup was a big one, almost three feet tall, highly polished,
urn-shaped, obviously representing money. Yet when Bart posed
for the photographers, holding the cup by both handles in front of
his chest, he discovered that it was not very heavy. The engravings
printed in the evening papers showed Bart with a scowl on his face—
but the governor's representative, standing beside him, wore a
smile that ran from ear to ear, full of gleaming teeth.

Asa Gold, who finished second, invited the four Mississippians
to go on a deer hunt he was organizing; Theodore Roosevelt would
be going. Bart accepted, as did one of the Bristol men—his name
was Ireland—but Durfee and the other Bristol man declined. They
had to get back with the winnings.

"Say hello to my grandson for me, if he's come," Bart told
Durfee.

GOLD WAS a rounder. After the deer hunt, Bart and Ireland went
with him up into Canada shooting geese, then back down to Virginia for a horse show. There was always something to look forward to; that was the way Gold lived. They spent Christmas Week
in Washington with a group of the Kentuckian's political friends
and stood in line at a White House reception to shake hands with
President Taft. I thought he was always laughing, but I reckon
thats just for parades and such, Bart thought. In mid-January
when they came home to Mississippi, Bart found his grandson being
wheeled about the yard in a perambulator, looking up with an air
that Bart considered intelligent, though the baby burst into tears
and howled the first time Bart approached him. "Well, he's got
spirit," Bart said, his enthusiasm dampened.

"He hardly ever cries," Kate said. "I dont know whats gotten
into him."

"Let him holler. It's good for his lungs."

When he told Mrs Bart about meeting the President—he said it casually, between two other off-hand statements: "I shook hands with Mr Taft"—she offered no comment, asked no questions. Bart was a little sheepish after this. She dont care about Mr Taft, he thought. Mr Taft is a long way out of her mind.

So next day he went to Bristol, where there were people who did care about conditions in the East and the worried expression on the President's face. Bart was there more often than ever. The old plaster at Solitaire was coming loose from its lathes: at any hour of day or night, unannounced by a creak or a tremble, square yards of it tore down from the ceiling, came tumbling sixteen feet to the floor, abrupt, Damoclean, filling the air with white dust. Bart was outraged; "The damn house is coming apart on us," he said. Early in March he told Mrs Bart his decision (they were in bed; it was late: he lay flat on his back, arms straight at his sides; he did not look at her as he spoke); "I'm selling the place," he said. Faintly, from behind closed doors across the hall, they heard their grand-child wailing.

It came that suddenly. She had had no intimation. He had become jolly of late to hide his despair; he had held her off. She had watched the gathering of the forces that led to this, had felt it in the plexus of her love—the continued absences, the increased concern with outside matters, the forced jollity—so that her realization of mounting tragedy was like the seepage of pain felt by a soldier who knows he is dying of a wound which he can see but which shock has rendered almost analgesic. She had watched and waited, and then it was brought home to her by the sentence spoken in bed that night: "I'm selling the place." She thought: I knew something was going to happen. I even knew it was going to be bad. But not this bad. Not this bad.

This was brought home to her over a period of time coincident with her daughter-in-law's gestation. Bart's break followed Hugh's marriage, as if his son's assumption of responsibiity had abolished the ullage of his life-way: once it was complete he was through with it, like a painter and his picture or a knitter and her sock. Mrs Bart had watched this through what share of the nine-month period he was at home, attaching significance to every remark he made, seeing in his smallest actions a reason for subsequent events. A thing would occur and she would look back into the preceding time in search of a sign: He stood up after dinner and said he was going to look at his horse. Yes; I remember; he said, 'I'll be at the lot if you want me.' Why is he so considerate all of a sudden? Does he know something awful is going to happen? Is it because he wants to make the days that led up to it pleasant when I look back? Or is he ashamed? Or is he scared?

She wondered. But when the final announcement came, when he told her they would move to Bristol, to town where his new friends were—those others who had claimed him, had taken him from her with the same irresistible pull as if it had been another woman he loved or desired past cure—all wondering stopped: she was going back. It was a cycle of more than twenty years.

For Bart, too, it had been almost that long. It had begun on an afternoon twenty years ago, when he had looked into the face of the dying man who told him he would bungle and come to heart-break at the end of all his labor. From then on, while wealth ac-cumulated and experience broadened (honors came too; he was a national figure, with his picture in the newspapers, and he had shaken hands with Taft) he had watched his children grow: Clive who was still a boy but who even Bart now knew, in the phrase of the time and place, was not worth the powder it would take to blow him up, because he had no interest in means but in results, because he lacked what educators call application and what sports-men call heart; Florence who was foreign to this land because she cared nothing for a living soul she had ever known, least of all for herself, who was running hard even now toward no one knew what catastrophe: and Hugh, who had failed.

This last had become certain a week ago, in the downstairs trophy room that had once been the library. Bart was sitting at his desk, going through the mail, when Hugh came in with his hat in his hands, looking grave. "Hello," Bart said, glancing up. "I thought you and Patterson were going down to Talleyrand."

"We just got back."

Bart opened another envelope. "Things all right there?" he asked, not looking up.

"Yes sir."

"Fine . . . Just listen to this. Here's a man wants me to set him up in farming, sight unseen. Says he's—"

"Papa." Bart looked up. He looks tired, he thought. He looks scared, too. Here it comes! "It's something Ive got to tell you," Hugh said, and cleared his throat.

While he heard him out—it was halting and hangdog, but it was no less definite for all that—Bart kept his hands clenched on the desk, his eyes on the letter between them, his head slightly lowered. Only occasionally he glanced up at his son. When he did this, the young man shifted his eyes, not so much in shame, however, as in fear of return argument. "I cant," Hugh said. "It's not so much not wanting to as it is I cant. I cant. Ive been here more than a year now, farming, and I know I cant—unless you say I have to. If you say I have to, I'll stay anyhow. It's just that I cant."

"You dont have to," Bart said quietly. "But what do you want?" Hugh did not answer. "I see. You dont know what you want: you just know what you dont want. Is that how it is?" Hugh watched the rug. "All right. If you dont want Solitaire, I reckon Solitaire dont want you."

And now, a week later, upstairs in bed with his wife, whom he had just told "I'm selling the place," Bart thought, as he had been thinking ever since he said "Solitaire dont want you": I shouldnt have said that; he didnt see what I meant. Because Bart had not meant the house, the home; he meant Solitaire, the land, the five square miles of cotton rows and the random cuts of corn and hay —as if the growing things were sentient, as if they would renege, bloom and boll clamp shut with indignation, and stalks jerk back into the ground.

BRISTOL

THE PITKIN house, on Lamar Street just off Marshall Avenue, had
been vacant for almost a year now, held in escrow though the
owner was not dead or even bankrupt: far from it; he had run
away, absconded. A pretentious two-story white mansion with
fluted columns and a carved pediment, it was the sort of house a
man would put up as a brag. In April of the year before, Chester
Pitkin, the banker who had built it, suddenly disappeared—without
reason, people thought (that was a Sunday) until Monday morning
when they went to the bank and found the door still locked. Leaving his wife and four children, he had taken the town's savings with
him. Six weeks later one of his closest friends, superintendent of
the Sunday school in which Pitkin taught young people the moral
precepts, received a postcard from him, counterstamped at an un-
pronounceable Mexican hamlet: *Dear Alvin, Tell my many friends
and business associates I regret my departure had to be so sudden
that I did not get to say fare well. It was urgent, as you know by
now. Climate lovely here but I'll be moving on in a day or so for
parts unknown. Ta Ta.* There was no signature, no mention of the
wife and the four children (the same friend, who also had been one
of the bank's largest depositors, took them into his house until the
wife's parents sent for her) and Bristol never heard of Pitkin again,
except in rumors that reported him living in Texas or California,
broke or rich. The postcard passed from hand to hand, worn limp,
the penciled scrawl no longer legible. People laughed or brooded
over it, depending on how hard they had been hit, and there was

some discussion as to whether Ta Ta meant goodbye or thank you; finally they decided it meant both.

Bart did not buy the house: he took a five-year lease, beginning in March of 1912. "How do you like that?" he said when the carriage drew up at the curb in front. Mrs Bart just sat there, looking, but Clive, who was sitting between them, began to bounce up and down on the seat, crowing with pleasure at the magnificence of his new home: "Gee willikers, gee willikers, lets go in!" Hugh and Kate and Florence sat in back, Kate with the child on her lap. Like Mrs Bart, they said nothing.

These were days of unfolding spring, light hurried rains, blue skies, bright sulphur suns. The grass on the neatly barbered lawns was greener than the grass had been in the country. The streets were paved; every morning a crew of Negroes from the city jail moved down them, busy with brooms behind the sprinkling cart, wearing the same Sunday finery they had been wearing the previous Saturday night when the police broke into the barrel-houses and caught them with the cards and dice in their hands. Towards evening there was a period of quiet broken only by the cries of children, shrill and birdlike as they romped in front of the houses and under the streetlamps before being called in to supper and tub and bed. Twilight lingered longer here than it had at Solitaire, as if light consisted of particles that adhered to house-fronts and sidewalks and carriage blocks, giving them a luminous, ghostly, faintly saturnine air of unreality like stage properties in a deserted theater. They darkened to pale and then deep blue, though for a time yet, overhead, dim against the carmine band that striped the western cloud bank, there was still a plane of light in which the oaks' higher leaves showed transparent and fragile above the dark nether limbs and made a diminutive tinkling, like fairy bells, if there was a stir of breeze. Then night came down.

Marshall Avenue, Bristol's main street, was less than half a block south of the house. The Elks Club was one block west, and the river was four blocks beyond it. In spring, when the river was on the boom, townspeople could look up and see above the rim of the levee—above the grassy wall of dirt into which the east-west streets ran with the same faith as if it had been made of stainless steel a hundred feet thick, inviolable, and beyond which the Mississippi purred with the gentle, undeniable insistence of a tamed and not particularly hungry lion—the fancy stacks and pilot houses of steamboats moving against a backdrop of sky and lazy clouds with the frictionless decorum of a scene drawn meticulously but not well by a student just beginning to work in oils. All afternoon the levee's shade, with the shadows of the steamboat cupolas gliding along its edge, moved eastward down the shallow, brick- and glass-walled canyon of Marshall Avenue. The buildings included banks and saloons, law offices and markets, but mostly they were clothing stores whose façades were slashed with banners flaunting ruin and opportunity in foot-high letters: FIRE SALE! BANKRUPT! FORCED TO SELL! BUY NOW! One among them was the Wisten Brothers Emporium, founded by the two sons of the merchant, using their father's insurance money as soon as they came of age. It was a small store now, but within another ten years it would be the style center of the Delta, all that Wisten himself had ever hoped for: "The finest merchandising bazaar between Memphis and New Orleans."

This four-block business section, an intricate and highly effective snare baited mainly for Negroes, ended at the Elks Club, at which point the first of the town's three residential sections began. Here the leading merchants, the bankers and lawyers, doctors and cotton men lived, the two hundred families whose names were listed in the newspaper—two columns of them, plus a column of guests—for attending the Elysian balls. The second residential area, not quite so large as the first but with better than twice the population, lay north of the business section, near the river. Here the white day laborers, the policemen and firemen, clerks and bookkeepers, bartenders and small tradesmen lived, fiercely Anglo-Saxon and predominantly Baptist. The third residential area, called Lick Skillet, bisected by Ram Cat Alley, lay south of the business section, beyond a block of one-story office buildings known as Cotton Row.

Lick Skillet was as large as the other two residential sections combined: two-thirds of the population of Bristol lived here. They were Negroes, all of them. Their houses were flimsy two-room shotgun cabins, lighted with coal-oil lamps and papered inside with newsprint, each about four feet from its next-door twin, three steps giving down from a low porch to a grassless plot of polished earth decorated with up-ended bricks and shards of colored glass set in geometric patterns. The air was thick with a mingled odor of frying catfish and pork and hair oil, privies and boiling soap, the sound of gibberish and laughter.

Bristol's population was eight thousand, to be doubled and re-doubled within a generation. They worked at their jobs, prayed in their churches, took their pleasures as they could, and though they were segregated thus, flung out to three points of the compass, they were all the people of Bristol.

Industry surrounded the town with tin buildings that glinted like silver in the sunlight and kept up a shrill whine from August through December, ginning the cotton, and with long, low, dead-white concrete warehouses for storing it once it was baled. Cotton was Bristol's wealth, its reason for being; the market price was a perfect barometer of spirit and condition. Yet the gins and ware-houses were a barricade against the sweat and vagaries of the farm-ing life that produced and nurtured their well-being. People here —'town' people, Bart had called them when he was on Lake Jordan —were unlike those he had lived among up to now. The farming activity, which absorbed the lives of the men he had known on the lake, had been replaced by a zeal for other things; they said Money with a tone of reverence, and when they used the impersonal pro-noun they gave it a capital I.

This was a period of historical unrest. So much was changing, the people were bewildered. The railroads had out-done the river packets; the motion picture and the automobile had altered all con-ceptions of leisure and love; the electric light and the telephone no longer were gadgets—all these, and more, were part of a new and different life, unlike the life this generation had been born to. Something called civic pride was being born: local merchants, who soon were to set up a chamber of commerce, called Bristol "The Queen City of the Delta," just as other towns scattered at fifteen- and twenty-mile intervals about the broad flat Yazoo basin had adopted sub-names which they considered descriptive and attractive—"Golden Buckle on the Cotton Belt," "Biggest Little Town in all the Southland," "Dimple of the Delta"—naive self-assertions which (they were not aimed at tourists; that voracious and ubiquitous American had not been spawned yet; and even if he had, the bottomless buckshot roads would not have allowed him to infiltrate) did not express belief so much as hope, nor hope so much as vigilance of a particular new urban form.

Bart and his family, with three of the Solitaire servants and Billy Boy, found all this waiting for them when they moved into the absconded banker's house on Lamar Street. Bart had liquidated his holdings, had sloughed his responsibilities with the decisiveness of a snake when it casts its skin; he had taken the cash and let the worry go. In the Commercial National Bank at Memphis, under the name of Hugh Bart, retired planter and number one U.S. trap shot, was a sum that totaled roughly two hundred and fifty thousand dollars.

"It's a deal of money to have in cash," Mrs Bart said when he showed her the bank statement.

"Aint it," Bart said. He smiled. "What do you want for your birthday?"

—Solitaire, she almost said. But she just sat there, looking at the glossy sheet with the column of figures down the right-hand margin. Bart folded it, put it back into his pocket, and patted it flat. They sat together for nearly a full minute, neither of them speaking.

"Well, you be thinking about it," he said at last. He rose, looked around the unfamiliar living room until he located his hat, then stood in the doorway, holding the brim in both hands. "Whatever you want," he said. He turned and spoke over his shoulder: "I'm going down to the club for a while. Good night."

"Good night," she said.

HUGH STAYED on his first job almost two months. Bart had gotten it for him from Percy Ireland, soon after they moved to Bristol. Ireland was Bart's closest friend now; they had gone together to the Kentucky trap shoot and the deer hunt that followed, and they had stood side by side to shake hands with Taft. He was in the lumber business, one of the wealthiest men in town. They were in the cotton exchange and Bart said, "I wish youd let me know if you hear of a job being open for a young man, something with a chance to get ahead in."

"I thought youd retired," Ireland said, smiling. He was a small, dandified man; he wore candy-striped shirts and high hard collars with rounded points. The fine gold chain of his pince-nez dropped to a spring-button at his lapel.

Bart laughed. "I said young man, Perce. It's for my boy."

"The oldest one?"

"Yes: Hugh." Bart turned and stared at the cryptic market board. "He wasnt much for farming."

That dont mean he's anything for lumber, Ireland thought. But he said, "All right. Sure thing. Send him down to the office Monday morning. I'll tell Mr Critz to sign him on."

"Put him doing anything you want to, for a starter. Carrying lumber, anything. He's a good boy, Perce, if I do say so myself. He's married and has a child. Maybe he'll make you a good man."

Meaning maybe I'll make *him* one, Ireland thought. But: "All right," he said. "Tell him to come on down and start to work."

It was a small, dingy office, not much more than a shed, set in one corner of the lumber yard. Hugh's job was checking and filing invoices; the pay was twelve-fifty a week. Two other men worked here: Mr Critz who was nearly eighty, who wore steel rim spectacles, a straggly gray mustache that overhung his mouth, bombazine sleeve protectors, and an isinglass eyeshade that cast a green parabola down the upper half of his face; he had kept the same set of books for Ireland's father thirty years ago, sitting on the same high stool with his feet hooked into the rungs; and Sparky Russell, Ireland's nephew, who was two years younger than Hugh and

whose jowls were spattered with pimples, each tipped with a pale
thin ichor because he was always squeezing them and treating them
with mail-order unguents; he was a baseball enthusiast, but mainly
he liked to talk about girls: he had them listed in a notebook, with
a complicated system of stars, crosses, and circles by their names.

Hugh did not like Mr Critz, who was always peering over the
rims of his spectacles, sniffling. Sparky was even worse, with his
praise for Christy Mathewson and recountals of his date the night
before: "Another half hour and I'd a had it sure; I swear I would."
Ireland was almost never there. Like Bart, he had given up work,
though he had not dissolved his connection with it.

During his last three weeks on the job, Hugh let it slide. It was
not that the work was hard, for an intelligent child could have
handled it easily, nor that the pay was low, for low as it was, Hugh
knew that the money was more than the job was worth. He just
lost interest, stopped caring. Invoices collected faster than he
checked and filed them. When Mr Critz spoke to him about this,
Hugh said "Yes sir, yes sir," but he kept on letting the work ac-
cumulate. Then Mr Critz told Ireland; "That boy's no good," he
said, and Ireland let him go.

"I'm sorry, Hugh. But you see I have to, dont you?"

"Yes sir, I see."

"Then why . . . ?" Watching Hugh, Ireland thought: It wont do
any good. This is just the way he is and nothing's going to change
him, nothing at all. "All right, son: I'm sorry. I hope your daddy—"

"Yes sir," Hugh said; "Thank you," and took his hat down off
the shelf and left.

It was June; the streets were bright with sunlight. Unaccustomed
to being free while the shadows fell west, he spent the rest of the
morning strolling around town. Every now and then he wondered
how he would go about telling his father that he had lost his job.
He tried to think of some way of leading up to it. He remembered
Solitaire, the lake. This was the chopping season; the hands had been
in the field since daybreak. He saw them in his mind, hoes rising
and falling in glittering cadence, backs bent, heads lowered, him-

self on horseback riding down the rows, and he thought: We ought to be there, ought never to have left. Yes. But I couldnt; I couldnt, and cant.

When he got home that afternoon, turned in at the gate, he saw his father coming out of the front door. This was the moment he had feared. I'll wait till tonight to tell him, he thought. He stopped at the foot of the steps, looking up. Telling it would be easy enough, once he had led up to it properly. But how could he do that?

"Mr Ireland was here a while ago," Bart said. "He told me what happened. Why didnt you quit sooner if you didnt like it down there?"

Hugh looked at his father quizzically. "I didnt quit, papa. Mr Ireland let me go."

"You mean he fired you? Why?" They stood in the slanting sunlight, like two actors, Bart's head lowered, Hugh's tilted back, the fluted columns soaring on both sides.

"I just wasnt doing any good."

"Wait a minute..." Ireland had told him Hugh had given notice and quit. Now that Bart knew differently, he wondered how much else there was that Ireland had not told him. It suddenly occurred to him that Hugh might have had his fingers in the till. "Did you do something you didnt have any business doing?"

"No sir. I just didnt do any good."

Bart came down the steps. "Well, all right, Hugh, I'm sorry." He passed down the walk, then through the gate, and turned toward Marshall Avenue, a solid figure in broadcloth and linen. Still at the foot of the steps, Hugh watched his father walking on the opposite side of the wrought iron fence, the spearhead pickets flicking past like cracks in a defective film.

He left home every afternoon about this time, walking the block and a half to the Elks Club, a gray three-storied stucco building with wide concrete steps leading up to a high porch. The top floor was a ballroom, cutglass chandeliers reflected on the polished hardwood, flanked by leather-cushioned window seats and a dais in one corner for the orchestra. A balcony overlooked the avenue, and there were several small adjoining rooms for cloaks and smoking. The second floor included the main lounge, which was dark and cool in even the hottest weather; here men drowsed in overstuffed chairs and sofas, newspapers over their heads. Opposite the lounge was the billiard room, its walls racked with cues like weapons; the pool cloths were bright green under garish cones of light, and the air was thick with talcum motes, the dry, clicking staccato of balls, and the cries of players.

The bottom floor, entered at ground level through a U-shaped tunnel opening on each side of the concrete steps, was honeycombed with card rooms. Here Bart spent most of his waking hours, one segment in a circle of hunch-shouldered men with chips stacked on the table and gay-backed oblongs of pasteboard spread fanwise like bouquets above their fists. Their faces were profoundly immobile; they wore their hats for luck. They were like denizens of some unvisited quarter of hell, victims of a nightless punishment. Neglected cigars and cigarettes, dangling from the corners of mouths or smoldering in ashtrays, lifted slender columns all the way to the ceiling. The light here had a greenish undersea tint, so that the players resembled corpses propped in their chairs or tipped forward with their chests against the table. There were sighs and humorless laughs; otherwise there was silence, punctuated at intervals after the cards went round:

"Raise."

"Call."

"See you."

"Pass."

"I'm out."

Every afternoon Bart walked into this. Acknowledging nods and greetings, he went first to the rack where a hunchback Negro, his upper teeth a line of solid gold, relieved him of his coat and hat and faced the other way, grinning, while Bart lightly touched his hump for luck. At the table where the game was under way, Bart stood for a moment to give the players good-day ("Gentlemen"—nod—

"Gentlemen") and took a chair while someone pushed a stack of chips in his direction and entered the amount against his name.

He had taken to it well. A stranger, entering this sterile, clicking atmosphere, would not have been able to tell him from the old-timers. If he sat a little straighter in his chair than most of them did, if his manner of holding his cards and anteing his chips was stiffer and more studied, that was only because he had been like this about everything all his life; he had even wooed his wife and farmed that way.

In September Florence left for school in Virginia. She stayed a little longer than Hugh had held his job at the lumber yard. In late November an express van delivered her trunk at the house. The family had had no warning; they had heard from her once, a post-card mailed from Washington in early October: *Seeing the sights here. School is all right so far.* "Ten words," Clive said when they showed it to him. "I bet you if it was a telegram she'd have used eleven or twelve." He always noticed things like that.

Florence arrived next day, the screen door slamming behind her with that vicious slap Mrs Bart could never get used to, though it followed Florence's every entrance and exit. She had walked from the railroad station, carrying the suitcase that was scarred white in patches where the school stickers had been pasted; her money had given out somewhere east of Memphis and she had had nothing to eat since the day before. The family was at dinner. When the screen door slapped, Mrs Bart looked up and saw Florence go past the dining room door on her way upstairs.

"What was that?" Bart asked. He sat with his back to the door.

"It was Florence," Mrs Bart said.

Hugh and Kate looked up. "Jimminy," Clive said—he had seen her too—"I bet they shipped her."

"Excuse me," Mrs Bart said. She put her napkin on the table and left the room.

"Jimminy," Clive said. "You reckon they did?"

"Eat your dinner," Bart said.

Later, when Mrs Bart came back downstairs and they were alone, Bart asked: "What did she say?"

"She said she just got tired of it."

He frowned. "Did she say why?"

"She said she didnt want to talk about it."

"Hm. Well: she's your daughter."

He had intended to return to Louisville at the end of the month to defend his trap shoot crown. Ireland planned to go with him again; Gold had invited them both to another goose hunt up in Canada. But two days after Florence came home, Bart told Ireland the trip was off. "I wired them this morning," he said.

"Forfeit?"

"Yes."

Ireland screwed up his eyes and wagged his head, his pince-nez glinting. "Well, Kentucky is a far piece to go anyhow, just to bag a cup you cant even drink from." Then he changed the subject casually.

Bart never explained this sudden change of plans; he never told anyone what prompted it, not even his wife. But Ireland could see that something had happened. Everyone could: it was written on his face. He had received a letter from the headmistress of the Virginia school; a check refunding the tuition was inclosed. Florence had been expelled, and the letter told why. Bart burned them on the hearth of his room, letter and check and envelope; he stood watching the lick, soar, flicker of flame, smelling the thin, acrid odor of burning paper that might have been the odor of sin itself, then ground the char with his heel and kicked the powder into the fireplace.

So now they were all together again in the rented mansion on Lamar Street, seven of them including Kate and her child, eight including Billy Boy. But there was a difference. From the day he burned the letter, Bart was away from home even more than he had been during the last months at Solitaire. Poker was everything now: what time he was not playing it he was thinking it; poker replaced the old steady endeavor, the uphill trudge. He was always ready to join any game being formed, and generally he was the last to agree to a break-up. Though he exaggerated his outward calm to hide an inward jangle, he was betrayed by the little twitches that had appeared at the outer corners of his eyes. As he sat at the rim of the circle, elbows in his lap and cuffs pulled back showing the dark hair on his wrists, the expression on his face, intended to be arcane and careless, was in truth merely bleak. His careless days were over; he had become entranced with Number— 4, 13, 52—and made a cult of the law of averages, following what he learned to call runs and fevers.

Mrs Bart watched this with a dismay similar to that of a second watching his boxer reel in the ring under the fists of a stronger opponent, except that there was no bell-flanked interval in which to say 'Get your guard up,' or 'Keep away from him,' or even 'We are whipped: lie down.' Nothing in her past experience had prepared her for what was happening now; she watched and waited.

Hugh watched it with some understanding, or at least with some sympathy, for he too had known disappointment and flailing unrest. If poker would have eased his mind, he would have turned to poker. But it would not: nothing would, and he knew it. He was awaiting his turn, his destiny: it was coming across three thousand miles of ocean. He seemed to know it. He awaited it like a sparrow on a wire, looking down the reversed sights of an air rifle at a small boy's hot unwinking eye.

Florence did not watch at all. She seldom spoke to her father after a night in late November, soon after she came home from the Virginia school. She told him, "I want to go to Europe."

"Why?" he said. "Why there?"

"To see it, all those things Ive read about. Will you let me?"

"No. Stay here and look at Bristol," and she turned away and never mentioned it again. But she told herself: I thought he was just stupid but thats not all. He's brutal too, the brute.

A week before Christmas (it was still warm; they were saying there would be no 1913 winter) Bart came into Billy Boy's room, downstairs at the rear of the house, and found him sitting sideways on his cot, his elbows propped on his knees, his chin on his fists. "What are you thinking about?" Bart asked him. This had been the banker's study, a small square room unfurnished now except for the cot and a packing case which Billy Boy used for a wardrobe; that was all he wanted. Bleached rectangles on the wallpaper showed where pictures had hung in the days when the banker had sat here making his plans for abscondence.

"I wasnt thinking. I was just sitting here."

"Wish I could do that," Bart said.

"It aint hard."

From the exact center of the ceiling a naked light bulb hung by its cord like a hard white pulpless fruit on the end of a vine. Bart sat beside Billy Boy on the cot. "How are you liking Bristol?" Billy Boy did not answer. "You dont much like it, do you?" Bart rose and switched on the light. It burned with a sudden white glare, and when he snapped it off again the room seemed darker than before. The dead bulb swung in a decreasing arc. "*Do* you?" Bart said insistently.

"I like it all right. What I want that I aint got?"

"I dont know. You looked mighty lonesome just now when I came in."

"Holy smoke, I aint lonesome. I never been lonesome a day in my life, hardly." He turned sideways, facing Bart. "Have you?"

Bart sat on the cot again. "I dont know," he said. "Maybe I have. I never thought about it much."

"If youd been lonesome youd have thought about it."

"Then I reckon I havent," Bart said. He was quiet for a while. They could hear the cook moving about the kitchen, lifting pot lids and laying out silver; it was getting close to supper time. Bart said, "You should have gotten married, Billy. It's a —"

"I did," Billy Boy said. "Once I did. It didnt last long, though."

Bart was surprised into silence. Billy Boy married was something he had never imagined. Then he said, "Death is a terrible thing when it comes like that."

"It sho is. Like what?"

"Like that: between man and wife."

"It sho is," Billy Boy said sagely, nodding his head. Then he said in sudden negation, "She didnt die. Far as I know she mought be living yet. She run off."

"Left you?"

"Sho she left me. Thats what I said: run off."

"You must have made her mad or something."

"I didnt do nothing," Billy Boy said quietly. He kept his head down while he spoke, watching the tips of his shoes. "She took up with a man that played the trom bone. Reilly his name was, a black-face in a minstrel. I guess the trom bone was what done it, or maybe them tight silk pants they said he wore. She never even told me she was leaving. We'd been together two years, going on three; I thought she was happy.

"She was twelve when we married up, not out of hair ribbons yet. She lived down the road with her folks; they had a whole passel of young ones. First time I seen her—to notice, I mean—she was swinging on the mail box, making eyes. I said to myself, Just look at there, a child like that; whats this world coming to? So then I begun to notice her, the way she was bulging her clothes in all the right places. I bought her things, candy and stuff—you know."

Bart nodded, but Billy Boy was not looking at him; he still had his head down, talking to the floor.

"I was making a crop on my own, a bachelor man, so I went to her folks and made my offer for her hand. They said they didnt mind, they had so many. We married up and she moved in with me. Looked like I couldnt do too much to please her; she was always laughing, clapping her hands, and even brung her dolls along and kept them in a box right by the bed. It was all a kind of game to her, playing House—you know. We never had no chaps, though. Maybe I aint able; I dont know.

"It went on like that for two years, going on three, and then this minstrel come to town. I had to go down the road on a matter. That night I come back and she wasnt there: kitchen empty, stove cold, no supper on the table. I said to myself, Whats this? Whats this? And I waited and she didnt come. Whats this? I said to myself, wondering. All night I waited, thinking every minute I'd hear the gate squeak and her feet coming up the steps.

"Next morning I struck out looking. I went from person to person. 'You seen a girl about so high, that wears her hair like this and a ribbon here?' Nobody had, until finally a town fellow told me he had seen her drinking lemonade and eating barber-pole candy with a man from the minstrel show, the one they called Reilly, Reilly the trom bone king. He went prancing round the stage with his face blacked up, except for a space left plain around his mouth: wore tight silk pants, they said, and a stand-up collar, blaring a tune on that slide-action silver piping. I never seen him you understand, but folks told me what he looked like. They said you could tell he was handsome, even under the burnt cork. He must have looked like all her dreams to Minnie.

"After that, for a good long number of years, ever time I seen a trom bone I wanted to cry. I'd see one in a store window and it would knock the wind clean out of my chest; I'd go blocks out of my way to keep from passing a music store where there might be one on show. But that was a long while back," Billy Boy said, looking up for the first time since he had begun speaking. "It dont bother me now, not none to speak of."

The light bulb had stopped swinging and darkness was almost complete in the room. Bart said quietly, "Theres a world of misery nobody hears about." When he rose and switched on the light, shadows leaped black and distinct against walls and floor. "Must be time for supper," he said.

As he went out he looked back. Billy Boy sat sideways on the cot, eyelids lowered against the glare, and for the first time Bart saw the deep twin furrows that ran from the wings of Billy Boy's nose to the corners of his mouth, like the lines on a tragedy mask. That nobody ever hears about, Bart thought. Yes: worlds of it.

A MONTH before his fourteenth birthday, Clive took a notion to examine the roof of the house. Idleness as much as curiosity drove him there: it was a Saturday and there was no school. He went up through a trapdoor from the attic and walked the ridge, arms held sideways like a tightrope artist he had seen at a circus the year before. Turning to come back, he lost his balance, tottered, slipped; the slope was steep and he began to slide, his face paling as his backbone numbered the slates. From the eaves he dropped thirty feet to the ground. All this time he was too frightened to cry out; the only sounds were the scraping against the tiles and the thump when he landed.

The cook, moving about the kitchen, heard neither of these. Immediately afterward, however, she glanced out of the window and saw him lying in the flower bed. She looked at him for a moment with a puzzled expression—"Lord God, Lord God," she said later, "I thought it was a bundle of old clothes"—then loosed a quavery soprano.

Mrs Bart was in her upstairs sewing room, directly above the kitchen. Clive had fallen past her window too, but her back was toward it: the instant flick of shadow across her needlework might have been almost anything, the swoop of a pigeon or the bat of an eyelash. When she heard the scream she ran downstairs.

"Clive done ruint hisself," the cook said, pointing. "Look at yonder."

The Bristol Sanatorium was two blocks away. Bart and Mrs Bart waited in the hall while Dr Clinton made an examination; Clive was still unconscious. Every five minutes Bart said, "You ought to lie down for a while," but she shook her head each time. Otherwise they did not talk.

Finally the doctor came out of the room. He was buttoning his vest, eyes lowered, face grave. When he saw Mrs Bart he brightened his expression. "It's going to be all right, Florence," he said. "He broke his legs and shook himself up pretty bad, but we'll pull him through."

"Can I go in?"

"Certainly. But he's still asleep; the shock . . ."

"Thank you." She moved past him, entered the room.

Dr Clinton looked at Bart, his expression grave again. "Mr Bart," he said. They went downstairs together. On the porch he stopped and looked out into the street. Watching him in profile, Bart damned the doctor for his love of drama. "The boy may never walk again," Dr Clinton said. "One hip is crushed, perhaps the spine, both legs and the left arm. It's all I can tell you, so far. To-morrow, next week, next month perhaps, I'll be able to tell you more. Bone's stubborn."

"Thank you," Bart said.

"Good day." The doctor went down the steps. When he reached the sidewalk Bart called after him:

"Doctor!" The doctor halted, faced about. "When will he be . . . awake?"

"Cant tell." Dr Clinton wagged his head and frowned; he dis-approved of questions he could not answer. "Perhaps tomorrow. I dont say for sure." He turned again and went on down the side-walk. The street was busy with traffic, horses and automobiles, the clopping of hoofs and the backfires of engines. Bart watched this for a while, then went back into the building, up the stairs.

Clive regained consciousness late that afternoon. His eyes flut-tered open, blinked, and closed again. Then they opened wide with fright. "Mamma," he said.

"Yes, son, mamma's here." She caught his hand, leaned toward him, face to face.

"Oh mamma."

"Sh, baby, youre hurt."

"I thought I was falling, falling."

"Thats all over now, son," Bart told him.

Then a strange thing happened. When Clive turned his head and saw his father standing beside the bed, he pulled his mother closer to him and whispered, "Dont let him hurt me, mamma. Please dont let him." Terror and urgency were in his voice.

"It's papa, Clive," Mrs Bart said. "Papa wouldnt hurt you. You know that."

Clive said gravely, no longer whispering: "He was chasing me

195

and I fell. I fell off the roof and he laughed. He pushed me! I saw him do it, mamma, and all the the time I was falling I heard him laughing." He pulled her closer, hiding behind her shoulder.

"Hush now," she said. "Be quiet. Youll hurt yourself."

The nurse was watching Bart. It seemed to him that she believed what Clive was saying; he saw wonder and accusation in her eyes. He looked at Mrs Bart, leaning between him and their son in an attitude of comfort and protection. Then he moved his shoulders in something like a shrug and left the room. As he closed the door behind him he heard Clive saying, "No, no, no, no, no."

He walked home. Turning in at the gate, he saw a man going up the steps. Bart quickened his stride and overtook him. "Yes?" he said, and when the man looked over his shoulder Bart recognized Warren Parker, the lawyer who had been handling his financial affairs ever since the move to Bristol. *Now* what? he wondered. "Hello, Warren. I almost missed you."

"I'd have waited," Parker said. Bart had never seen his face so grim. "Lets go inside."

It was nearly dark; the air was getting colder. They turned from the hall into the living room, where a fire had been laid but not lighted. Bart struck a match, leaned down and held it to the newspapers crumpled beneath the kindling, then switched on a lamp beside the hearth. "Have a seat," he said. "You want a drink?"

Parker made a gesture of impatience, then moved to the fireplace and stood with his back to the flaming paper. "Ive come to give you some bad news, Hugh," he said, holding his hands behind him. "These damned little towns." He brought his hands to the front and rubbed the palms together, kneading warmth. "We never hear of a thing till it's over and done with. Commercial National went under today." He paused, fixing his eyes on Bart's face. Then, seeing no change of expression, he said: "Commercial National Bank. In Memphis, Hugh. The one with your money in it."

"What happened?"

"Happened? Jesus. They folded, went under, went bust. Some mix-up in the executive, a run or something: I dont know. It got me too. But not to the tune of any two hundred thousand."

Bart was quiet, thinking: I should have known something like this was bound to happen; I should have known a man cant live on printed paper that he never even sees except the little he draws at a time to keep the creases out of his wallet and a bulge on his hip. "My boy fell off the roof," he said.

"I heard about that: excuse me for not asking. Ive been busy as a cat on a red-hot stove. How is he?"

"He thinks I pushed him."

"Pushed him? Off the roof?"

It seemed to Bart that Parker believed it too. "Yes. He says I did: keeps telling his mother not to let me near him. I didnt push him."

"Jesus." Parker looked puzzled, then sighed and returned to the original subject: "We'd better go up together. I dont know how much good we can do, if any, but at least we can see for ourselves how bad it is. It sounded pretty hopeless over the phone."

"I cant leave," Bart said. "You go for me. Save whatever you can."

"It dont look so promising to me, not by a long shot."

"Just do what you can. . . . How am I going to explain to my boy that I didnt push him?"

"Hell, Hugh, I dont know. Just tell him you didnt, I reckon. . . . You better come on. Theres a train at seven-forty." He took out his watch. "Thats an hour from now."

"Just save what you can," Bart said. The logs in the fireplace had begun to snap and crackle; the chimney roared. Bart leaned forward, both hands on the mantel, looking down into the flames.

Next morning when Bart came into the room, Clive did not speak of his fear, but he looked at his father with an uneasy expression. Bart decided not to mention yesterday's scene. He knows by now he dreamed it, he thought. And besides, what could I say?

Parker telephoned from the depot immediately after the Memphis train pulled in. "I just wanted to find if you were home. I'll be right over." Five minutes later there was a knock at the door, and when Bart swung it open Parker was standing there, dripping rain from the brim of his hat and shaking his head. "It's no go, Hugh. I didnt do us any good at all."

"Come on out of the weather."

They passed through the hall and into the living room, Parker shaking his head and talking steadily. "That Luddiger crowd: God damn their very souls. Theyve been expecting this for more than a month. They told me so themselves."

"Have a seat," Bart said. They sat on the sofa. "All right, now: tell me. How much do I save?"

"Save? Jesus: I just told you, Hugh. You save zero. The whole kit and caboodle went bango. Like this: *fft!*" He extended one fist in the lamplight, the skin stretched white at the knuckles, and exploded it open, wriggling the fingers and thumb.

"I see: fft and bango. You mean I'm back where I started."

"If you started at zero, thats where youre back to; yair."

Then I'm back where I started, Bart thought. Rain drummed on the roof: occasional gusts of it rattled against the window panes like tossed handfuls of gravel. They sat listening to it, both of them silent, glum. Then Bart said, "You want a drink?"

"A drink?" Parker had this habit of repeating the last words of whatever was said to him. "Why, yes, Hugh; I was just going to suggest it." He sighed. "Aint living a bother?"

IT WAS not altogether what Parker called fft. Not that Bart had held back when he liquidated Solitaire: he owned no property now except the furniture in the rented house, and all the Memphis money was as clean gone as powder after an explosion: but he had eight thousand dollars in the Bristol bank, kept conveniently near for incidental expenses. He did not think of this, however, until after Parker had left; the big loss overshadowed it. Then, sitting alone in the room, looking at the two empty glasses on the table beside the couch, he remembered it. Eight thousand, he thought. I'll run it up again. I'll play them close to my vest.

Now that what he wanted was money—just that alone, for the

first time in his life—his thoughts turned to poker, the field of his latest activity, much as a startled swordsman's hand will jerk in reflex toward his hip. He considered his previous, slipshod, boisterous style an apprenticeship to the poker he was about to play. He would weigh the odds on every hand, stake his chips on certainties, and hold off when the chances ran against him; he would open his eyes wider when other men grew lax, would press advantages he formerly had ignored because of the lack of need or concern. Close to my vest, he told himself; I'm out for blood.

Two nights later he came out four hundred dollars ahead at the end of an eight-hour game. He followed his decision, playing every hand in accordance with the book, pressing advantages but not being stubborn about staying without the cards to back his chips. He froze his face, said nothing; he let pots go and raked them in with the same expression, like Charon watching the damned. This presaged success, he told himself: it was a natural result of the change in style, the infusion of necessity and craft.

He was wrong. If that night he had played his old reckless overweening game, seeing every hand and riding the wave of fortune, he would have won far more. The cards had merely fallen his way. This was borne out the following night, when luck moved on to another player's elbow. Though he played his cards with the coolness and precision of the night before, he dropped two hundred dollars.

This should have taught him something but it did not. He looked for other reasons, and finally found one. He had gotten tired: it was that simple. Fatigue had dulled his brain, caused him to pass up advantages a nimbler perception would have pressed. Well, that was what whiskey was for, he told himself, and he began to drink to keep alert. Every fifth or sixth hand he took a jigger of bourbon, one and a half ounces of weariness-killer. And it worked, or at least it seemed to. Thought leaped like a spark across a gap, remained electric and undulled through hours of watching the cards flick back and forth, around and around, under the hard bright glitter of the arc light.

Yet once the game was over, while the other players rose and donned their collars and ties and the banker totted their losses and gains, Bart remained in his chair, his brain not clicking along a straight line now, leaping the gaps, but reeling in idleness, its work already done and only waiting to hear the result. After paying his losses or pocketing his winnings, he lunged out of his chair and put on his coat, struggling into the sleeves with the tentative, clumsy jabs of an over-aged boxer. As he made for the door, the floor tilted first one way and then another; the walls spun round. Finally there were nights like this:

Billy Boy sat outside in the buggy, the mare drooped in the shafts, posed in the immemorial attitude of waiting horseflesh, knees locked, head down, whether awake or asleep no man could tell. As soon as the other players came out of the club, stodgy from long contest, stiff in the joints and coughing stale cigar smoke, Billy Boy climbed down and took his post at one of the ground-level entrances. When Bart emerged—not staggering, but moving with terrific deliberation, an exertion out of all proportion to the gain involved—Billy Boy did not touch him, though he followed close beside him to the buggy. When Bart stood looking speculatively at the iron step, Billy Boy ran around and sprang into the driver's seat. If Bart mounted unassisted, Billy Boy registered pride and nodded approval: but if he just stood there, looking at the step, Billy Boy gripped his wrist and hoisted him up, then clucked the mare and gave her her head, disconsolately shaking his own. Bart lurched from side to side. Billy Boy watched him; he had learned to judge the danger in this, and sometimes he linked their inside arms to keep him from toppling off. The mare walked home, turned into the driveway, and halted under the porte-cochère, resuming the drooped pose of the hours outside the club.

Here again Billy Boy watched to see if Bart could manage for himself. Often he could not: Billy Boy had to come around and help him down. One arm about his waist, he guided him into the house and up the stairs, into the spare room where Bart slept these nights. Then he came back downstairs, unharnessed and baited the mare, and went to his room for three or four hours of sleep. That was enough; he already had catnapped two or three in the buggy. Besides, he never could sleep very well in Bristol anyhow: there were too many whistles and bells, he said, too much coming and going right under your window, and too many loud-mouthed people.

For Bart this was a process of months, but that was what it came to. Before it reached that stage, however, Clive was brought home from the sanatorium. It was April, the week of his fourteenth birthday. One arm and both legs were suspended in traction devices; he lay in a maze of ropes and pulleys and sandbags, splints and gauze, so that he resembled a crashed working-model of a mad inventor's airship, his face pale and saturnine among broken spars and twisted fabric. His mother sat in his room all day and half the night, reading boys' adventure stories to him. Her voice droned through volume after volume on the doings of young men in dirigibles and speedboats or just on picnics (*"Drop those rocks, Dan Baxter!" It was Tom, the fun-loving Rover boy*) while Clive lay motionless, his face so grimly set that she could not tell whether he was listening attentively or not at all.

In the afternoon, when Bart stopped by the room on his way to the club, Mrs Bart would halt in the middle of a sentence. He would stand in the doorway, falsely jovial: "How goes it today? You bout ready to come out of those wrappings?" and then pass on without waiting for an answer. She would resume her reading, her eyes dropping to the word they had glanced up from, her voice without change of tone or tempo, as if Bart had been a familiar ghost blown past by a spirit wind.

The year moved into summer, long heat-laden days of dust and no rain, early light and late dark. Hugh Bart, fifty-four—not sheriff now, not planter, not even trap shot—began to be known as ruined. Though they did not think of him as a professional gambler, people knew that he was out to mend his fortune over the card table. This was generally discussed, both in Bristol and back on the lake. Not that there was anything unusual about the situation: they had seen the same thing happen to plenty of other men, for money came fast and went quick in the Delta. But still, despite the broken hopes, the whiskey taken to counteract fatigue, they were like railbirds watching Man o War crop clover. They remembered what he had been.

Kate was repeating a pattern set by Mrs Bart a generation back: just as twenty-four years ago the older woman had returned to Solitaire, the place of her birth, so now Kate had returned to Bristol. And just as Mrs Bart had assumed management of the house on the lake, so now the younger woman had taken charge of the mansion on Lamar Street: for ever since Clive had slithered off the roof, Mrs Bart had left the household affairs to Kate and spent all her waking hours in the room with him.

Hugh was working as a weigher in a gin. He came home late one afternoon in August, and as he climbed the stairs he heard the drone of his mother's voice coming from Clive's room. He stopped on the staircase, listening. *"Bless my suspenders!" cried Professor Nestor.* Tom Swift, he thought; submarines and electric rifles. I believe she reads them more for herself than for Clive.

He went up the stairs and into his room, sat down, unlaced his shoes, and shucked off his shirt, using it to wipe under his arms and down his ribs where perspiration trickled. Dear God, he thought. He lay back on the bed, arms thrown sideways, crucified. Flies buzzed on the ceiling. He closed his eyes. One after the other, his shoes fell off. He did not even hear them strike the floor.

When he woke up, dusk had fallen. It was as if the overhead fly-buzzed ceiling had come down; that was part of the dream he was having. I'm still asleep, he thought. He sat up. Blond, rather thin, wearing rumpled cotton trousers and white socks, he began to hunt for the shirt he had taken off. When finally he found it, behind the slopjar under the edge of the bed, he took a sack of tobacco out of the pocket. The sack was almost empty. Crouched with his elbows on his knees, he rolled a cigarette, licked it shut, then snapped a match alight with his thumbnail and, holding his face cautiously to one side, brought the match toward the end of the tube of tobacco. Flame ran swiftly up the side of the paper toward his mouth. He jerked his head back, coughing a thick blue jet of smoke. Dear God, he thought; I aint getting anywhere. This was recurrent, and it was not so much a protest, or even a reproach; it was a statement of fact.

He crossed to the window and stood looking down at the darkling street. Lightning bugs glimmered and glinted, a hundred tiny beacons over the lawn. Smoke from his cigarette drifted through the screen, an attenuated cloud of paler blue than the blue of the gathering dusk. Turning, Hugh flipped the half-inch butt across the room; it landed in the slopjar with a small protesting hiss, disintegrated. He entered the hall, moved down the door-flanked distance toward the window at its far end. Highlight on the panels of doors that were ajar flickered off as he came abreast. At the door of the room where Bart had slept most nights since he had begun to come in late from poker, a spare one near the back, Hugh halted.

Bart sat in a low rocking-chair beside the window. What little daylight was left fell directly onto his face, making his eyes glitter as if with tears. His shirt-front was a narrow triangle between the dark lapels and the snub bow tie. His hands were relaxed in his lap; his knees were close together, his feet planted side by side. Like in church, Hugh thought until he saw his father's face. Then he stopped thinking. He just stood there, looking.

The face was a study in chiaroscuro. Light gathered on its flatter surfaces, cheeks and forehead, line of nose and point of chin. The rest was in shadow, the mustache dark above the slack-lipped mouth, the eye sockets touched with soot around the gleam of what resembled tears. At first it seemed to Hugh to be a representation of death, a prevision of the undertaker's meticulous handiwork. Then he saw it for what it was: the face of doom. So he must be broke at last, Hugh thought. Usually by this time of day, Bart was at the club, watching the cards go around and balancing a diminishing stack of chips against the remaining hours of play.

Hugh turned from the door. Coming back down the hall he walked deliberately slow to keep from running; it was not easy. In his room again, he made another cigarette, using the last of the tobacco in the sack, and once more snapped his face away from the running lick of flame. He lay across the bed with his head on the crook of his arm. Dear God, he thought. Beyond the footboard the window was a pale rectangle holding a wash of twilight like a mirror on the wall of a darkened room. He was sweating profusely and breathing shallowly, an aftermath of having looked for thirty full seconds into the face of ruin.

Now it's come, he thought.

HUGH WAS wrong, or at least he was premature in what he thought. This was not the final clap-to of the door that led from his father's reserve of undefeat; there was even some of the money left, the original eight thousand dollars; even Bart won some of the time. What was more, he came out farther ahead on a winning night than he trailed behind on a losing one, for he followed a rule by which he must quit when he had dropped two hundred dollars in a game. These were the nights when he left early—so early, some nights, that he would still be sober when he emerged from the stucco tunnel and shook Billy Boy awake on the buggy seat: "Hey! Hey!"

"Mm?"

"Wake up. Lets cut for home."

"Oh. Well, that was quick."

"Three queens against three kings. I dont mind the bad hands: it's the good ones cost me money. Lets go home."

What had happened on the evening when Hugh saw him sitting in the rocker by the window, motionless and alone as daylight faded, was that he had reached a stage on the downhill run. Seeing plainly the ruin that lay in his way, he was like a man in a runaway brakeless vehicle in those two terrible seconds before the crash, the wall or chasm looming or yawning directly ahead. He felt dismay and urgency, but that he could see what was coming did not mean that he could stave it off. There were no wild plans for a return to the old life with borrowed money: that had soured on him once and for all; he had left it behind, just as he had left everything behind him all his life. As he was to say at the end, he was like a blind man alone in an unfamiliar room.

That evening was only an interlude. The next he was back at the club, watching the cards flick around and back and forth, hearing accustomed voices, clicking chips. I wasnt built for sitting in chairs, he thought. What he called his sciatica was bothering him again. He blamed it on lack of exercise; he was just telling himself he was going to take a long walk every morning, when all of a sudden he felt a peculiar choking sensation down low in his throat, a stiffness in his shoulders. If I move them it will hurt, he thought. He moved them and there was an instant stab of pain. There, he thought; I knew it. For a moment he sat rigid, gripping the arms of the chair, his legs out stiff before him, toes curled back. There was an iron hoop around his chest; he could not speak; the hoop was drawing tighter. He collapsed, slid clattering under the table.

Most of the players were too surprised to do anything but sit there, faces blank, with perfectly round eyes. Others, however, leaped to their feet, dropping their poker hands to the floor among the scattered discards and skittering chips. Bart lay half under the table, partly covered by the tablecloth which he had grabbed on the way down. Terror had constricted his bowels, and some of the men turned their heads away from the odor.

Mrs Bart, in the upstairs bedroom, heard an automobile enter the driveway and stop beneath the porte-cochère; there were voices, metal doors opening and slamming. Immediately afterwards she heard the buggy turn in, hoofs clopping, the whip on the mare's back. She did not get out of bed, for by now she had watched her husband being brought in too often to go downstairs tonight just because Billy Boy had recruited some help for the job. Then she remembered the sound of the whip; Billy Boy almost never used it. She got up, put on her dressing robe, and went to the head of the stairs. A voice said, "Bring him in through here."

She came downstairs. Peeping around the curtain that hung across the archway at the foot, she saw three men carrying Bart through the side entrance, two at his shoulders and one at his feet. Billy Boy was showing them the way, and he looked worried. Still with only her head around the curtain, her face framed by the stiff frills of her nightcap and the hand that clutched the dressing robe high at her throat, Mrs Bart displayed the wronged, immured, the wryly soured expression of wives with drunkard husbands. Then for the first time it occurred to her that Bart might have had an accident; her expression changed. "What is it?" she asked.

"I'll look after them," Billy Boy said, coming toward her. "This way," he told the men.

Mrs Bart retreated up the stairs, not wanting the men to see her in her night clothes. At the landing she turned, looking back, and as the men came past the light on the lower newel post she saw Bart's face. One cheek was soiled with ashes and grime from beneath the poker table, and there was a large red bruise above one eye, where his forehead had hit the floor. He's been fighting, she thought: drunk and brawling, like any poolroom tout. She went on up the steps and into her bedroom, closing the door behind her.

Billy Boy led them down the hall, then stood at the door of the spare room, holding it ajar as the three men carrying Bart went in. They put him on the bed. "I guess the doctor will be here any minute," one said. "Murray told me he would call him from the club." Bart's breathing was stertorous, a series of labored groans. "Maybe he wants to throw up or something," the same man said.

The others did not speak; they stood in a loose half circle, looking down at the bed. Bart's clothes were caked with spit and ashes from under the table. His tie had come undone; one point of his

collar had slipped the stud and rode under his ear. Billy Boy unlaced his shoes and took them off. While he and one of the others
were trying to get Bart's coat off, they heard a car turn into the
drive. "Thats the doctor," the first man said. "I'll show him up."
He went out.

The other two soon followed. "If theres anything he needs, just
let us know," one said. Billy Boy nodded. At the head of the stairs
they met the doctor and the man who had gone to guide him. 'Hi,
doc," they said.

"Hello, you rams," the doctor said. He was a young man, about
thirty, and though he was a little below average height, he weighed
two hundred pounds. He came past them, and the three men went
downstairs together, talking.

"You really think he needs a doctor now?"

"Maybe he hurt his head when he hit the floor."

"Funny the way he tumbled all the sudden. I didnt notice he was
drinking more than usual."

"You cant tell. Maybe he's been nipping the bottle since sunup."

"Thats true; yair. But I thought he could carry it better than
that."

As they came onto the porch the first man took his watch from
his pocket and held it close to his face, turning it this way and that
in the moonlight until he could read the dial. "Ten-thirty!" he
cried. "Jesus, we just got started good. Come on." They climbed
into the car, backed out of the drive, gears whining in fast reverse,
and headed back toward the club.

"Took a tumble?" the doctor said, looking at Bart.

Billy Boy nodded. "What they told me. I wasnt there."

"Hm. Get me some water, a basin, a towel. Reckon you can do
that for me, sport?"

The doctor had played football at Sewanee, the first of a long
line of athlete heroes from Bristol. Four years of medical school, a
year of internship, and four years of practice, however, had cased
the fleet, lean quarterback in layers of fat. His cheeks were plump
and ruddy; they bulged upward so that his eyes peered out of

creases. The backs of his hands were curiously rounded. His talk was racy, a mingling of sports idiom and medical jargon, neither of which Billy Boy could understand any more than he could understand the stethoscope the doctor was using, moving it in sudden jumps and pauses across Bart's chest, when Billy Boy came back into the room carrying the basin and towel with the flustered, somewhat feverish air of a newly employed attendant in a brothel.

"Well, well," the doctor said. "Good work. Lets clean this up." He dampened the towel and wiped Bart's face. The bruise showed clean, already beginning to purple, the skin unbroken. "Bopped his head, all right, didnt he?" Bart's chest rose and fell, his breathing as harsh as ever.

"Yes sir," Billy Boy said. "But he never fell before."

"You mean from drinking?" Billy Boy nodded. The doctor wagged his head. "Listen," he said. The sound of the labored breathing filled the room. "You think it's whiskey makes him sound like that? Oh no: he's had an attack, what you call a stroke."

Billy Boy shifted his weight uneasily from leg to leg. "What stroked him?"

"Ha," the doctor said, imitating a laugh. "You want my prognosis? It's a little ailment called angina pectoris. Ever heard of it?" Billy Boy gave no sign of comprehension; considering the doctor's jolly manner, he thought perhaps the talk was all in fun. The doctor frowned. "Lots of folks have had it, sport. The woods are full of them." He frowned again and cocked his head. "You seen a pipe?"

"Pipe?"

"Yes: a water pipe. It's been in the ground for twenty years or so and they dig it up. Youve seen one?" He paused but Billy Boy just looked at him. "Say it's a four- or five-inch pipe, a really big one, but something goes wrong with the flow. So they dig it up and what do you think? Some parts of it are so caked inside with lime salts and suchlike, you can't get your little finger in it." He pointed to Bart. "Thats the way it is with him. He's got pipes that carry the blood to his heart and away again. All right. For quite a while theyve been getting crusty, caking up inside like the pipe we dug up a minute ago. But that was all right; enough was getting through to keep him going. He had a little discomfort, a few twinges, maybe even a sure enough attack or two?"

"Rheumatism," Billy Boy said.

"Ha!" The doctor smiled but there was no humor in it. He cocked his head to the other side and continued. "All right. Rheumatism or whatever, he got along. Then something happened. He was playing poker and all of a sudden: boom: a chunk of the stuff that was caking inside the pipe breaks loose, swings around sideways, and what do you think?"

"What?"

"That," the doctor said, pointing. "A pipe gets clogged, or almost clogged; not enough blood gets through with oxygen. It's like breathing air with the good gone out of it." He smiled. "It could happen to anybody, and frequently does. It could happen to you, believe me."

"Is he going to die?"

"We're all going to die. But as for right now—could be: could easily be. If that chunk of stuff dissolves, gets washed away, he'll be all right till another chunk busts loose. Thats how simple it is."

"How long before we'll know?"

"Ah," the doctor said. "Now thats a question."

Bart was a week recovering from the attack. He lay in bed for two days while the clot was canalizing; the rest of the time he sat in a chair by the window, uncommunicative, sullen. "Youll have to take it easy," the doctor told him. Hugh was in the room. "Whiskey is out, tobacco too."

"I stopped smoking some time back."

"Good. But remember what I'm telling you. No excitement, or I dont take the responsibility."

"You dont need to take any responsibility about me," Bart said gruffly. He had never had anyone younger than himself speak to him like this, and he resented it.

"O.K. then, I wont. Good day."

The doctor took Hugh's arm and walked out with him. On the

way downstairs he said, "I wasnt just blowing off. It's true what I told him just now. He might check out any time he gets excited or overexerts himself in any way. His high-rolling days are over and done. He's dropped his last bird."

This did not mean that Bart had played his last game of poker. A week from the day the doctor said these words, Bart was in his accustomed place at the club, watching the cards run, staking his chips with a new wisdom, and losing. Whiskey was part of it too. He did not take a drink for the first two hours of play, but by the end of that time he felt so great a weariness, both of body and mind and also of what he called his risking-spirit, that he said casually over his shoulder to the attendant with the golden smile, "Bring me a snifter, Terry," and when the hunchback brought it Bart tossed it off and relaxed in his chair; the mellow warmth of alcohol flowed through his veins, revivifying the brain cells, linking the ganglia like running fire. *Now,* he thought, and picked up his cards. Two queens. He opened for five dollars; three of the players called him. He caught three little ones on the draw, tossed out ten dollars, and raked in the pot when the others folded. *Now,* he thought.

Two hands later he called for another drink. A pair of aces fell to him on the following deal. He raised the opener, who called. He drew two cards, holding a jack, and one of the two was a third ace. "Check," the opener said. Bart had been so interested in his own hand that he had paid no attention to what the other players were doing.

"How many did you draw, Lyle?"

"I stood pat." Lyle said it casually but his face was a little smirked.

"Ah," Bart said. He flicked out chips with a sowing motion of his wrist. "Ten," he said. Lyle watched him for a moment, then put his cards down and began counting chips.

"*And* ten," he said.

He hasnt got a thing, Bart thought. Then suddenly: A flush! He's got a flush. "I call that," he said, pushing the chips toward the center of the table. The other players sat back, watching.

"Five in a row," Lyle said, and he spread his hand. "Seven eight nine ten jack. Theyre straight as Hiawatha's arrow."

Bart looked at the hand. "Thats a pretty thing," he said. He closed his cards, rapping them edgeways on the table like a woman closing a fan, and tossed them in front of the man whose turn it was to deal. "Another snifter, Terry."

This was one more night for Billy Boy to guide him into the house and put him to bed.

FALL

SOME DAYS Bart did not go to the club. As if he had renounced gambling, and with the cheerful earnest air of an alcoholic pledging reform between drinks, he would get up for breakfast—a thing he never did on other days—sit talking pleasantly to whomever he ate with (if anyone, for breakfast was not a family meal; they ate it one by one as they came downstairs) and wander aimlessly about the house before taking his hat and going out to walk. In the bright morning hours when other men were downtown working, he covered the north and east, woman-, infant-, servant-populated sections of Bristol, looking at the new, tight, practical twentieth century five-room bungalows where the young married learned marital bliss, patterned their lives on the dimensions of the dollar, built their dreams on expected promotions made possible by the deaths or misdeeds of their seniors, took revenge on the denying, embattled world by nagging each other or vilifying their neighbors, and sought occasional gratification and exhaustion by reviolating one another in clumsy repetition of their wedding nights. In his mind these days Bart saw them approximately thus; he saw life as a snarl of causation.

Moving along the sidewalks that ran straight and pale beside the neatly barbered lawns of the bungalows, he reconstructed the years that were gone, those in East Mississippi, those in Issawamba County, and those on the lake. Looking back, he began to think in the abstract, something he had seldom done before. It seemed to him, looking back, that each year had prepared for the next, had held the seeds of what followed; that was the way life went, an ugly snarl; you sowed and you reaped. Every instant, every idle action had a significance that could only be perceived when it was past. That was the trouble: that was the dead end. And that was as far as he got with abstract thinking.

In reviewing the swift gone years he did not analyze them. He did not need to: he was reconstructing them for himself, and he understood. It would be when he tried to describe them to someone else, a stranger, say, that explanation and analysis would be necessary. Perhaps someday he would tell someone, he thought, but he did not rehearse. It was clear in his mind, if not shaped for his tongue, because that was the way he had lived it, clearly, openly, Spartanly, somewhat blindly.

Coming home, alienor of the life that was gone, he entered an atmosphere of estranged regard. He moved cautiously, like a hostage among enemies, into and out of Mrs Bart's stolid contemplation, Clive's accusing stare, Florence's disinterest or sometimes glaring hate. This last was strangest, the relationship between father and daughter—he thinking: A being outside my life and thought, one of the family, blood of my blood? and she: Does he know? Did they tell him? And if he knows why won't he say he knows? and he: Did I sire it? and she: Brute! Brute! Offsetting these, there was Billy Boy with his grim and patient ministration, and there was Kate; she tried—ineffectively—to be his daughter as well as his housekeeper, for she knew he stood alone, somewhat as her father before her had stood.

At meals the tenseness was most evident. They sat in uneasy conjunction, the six of them, Bart at the head of the table, Mrs Bart at the foot, Clive in a wheelchair placed sideways, his legs in plaster casts like fallen pillars. Kate did most of the talking, trying to draw the others into conversation, but even her direct questions were answered abruptly or just with nods. They ate fast and got up one by one, Hugh first because he had to get back to his job at the gin or the compress; "Excuse me," they said, "Excuse me," "Excuse me," one after another, sliding their napkins into their napkin rings, until finally Bart and Kate had the table to themselves. Mrs Bart's voice droned in the parlor, reading to Clive; he could have held the book himself by now, but she never suggested it and he seemed to prefer it this way. Florence was in her bedroom with her books and manuscripts; she wrote poetry, bitter monologs done in the Browning manner, but though she submitted them to the magazines, averaging one a week, they were always rejected; every morning she waited for the mailman and frequently he had a self-addressed envelope for her.

Summer came on. In late June, on the high porch of the club, Bart heard two men talking; one had a newspaper spread in his lap. "Look here. One of those dukes in Europe got blown up by a Serb."

"A Serb? Whats that?"

"*I* dont know. Thats what the paper calls him." In August there was war. September arrived, summer's climax; cotton wagons rumbled in the streets, on the way to gins and steamboats, and young people were making the rounds in a last-minute flurry before returning to school. There was unseasonal thunder and rain: that was because of the war, people said; the big guns caused it. Frenchmen rode in taxis to the Marne. At first it was a diversion, but later people complained that it was crowding all the interesting news out of the paper.

One of these mornings Bart got up early and went downstairs for breakfast; it had been three weeks since his last day off from cards. He ate alone, then took his hat and cane and went onto the porch. The day was sultry, the sky pale blue and tinged with yellow, the color of a flame in sunlight: A scorcher, he thought. As he came down the steps and walked toward the gate he saw a man in baggy clothes turn in. When the man saw Bart he halted, shifted the satchel he carried, and took off his hat. "Ahem," he said, like a bad actor.

His sandy, gray-shot hair was irregularly parted, as if with a gap-toothed comb and in poor light. He looked old, but on second glance Bart saw that he was probably not so old as he looked; adversity had added to his years. His shirt was frayed at the cuffs and streaked with dirt, the collar bunched in front by a greasy tie. His neck had that loose, puckered appearance of a molting chicken's.

"Lady of the house at home?" he asked as Bart approached him. His jaws worked strangely with a sidewise thrust; he had lost most of his teeth.

"You selling something?"

"I—yes. Maybe you . . ."

"Go right on up and knock. Maybe youve got just the article theyve been needing."

"Well, thanky."

Bart went through the gate. As he turned to the right, toward Marshall Avenue, he looked back across the iron fence and saw the peddler tapping at the door. Stooped, his baggy clothes looking as if they had been handed down or salvaged, he held his satchel expectantly, waiting for the door to open, his hat already in his hand. What some men come to, Bart thought. He flicked his cane, watching the glint of sunlight on it.

THREE HOURS later, where the road to Bannard left the city limits (he had walked all morning; he had covered this end of the town, the hot converging sidewalks, the shimmering streets) Bart saw the peddler sitting under a tree at the side of the road. His hat and satchel were on the grass beside him and he was eating something out of a paper bag. Bart looked at him for a moment, then crossed the street and did a thing he had never done before. He began talking to a stranger, for no reason.

"How did it go?"

The man looked up, surprised. "Hello." He held two big slices of bread with an anonymous mass of meat and greenery folded between them. "It didnt go so good. It went all right, though." He looked puzzled.

"Did you do any good at my house?"

The puzzled look went off the man's face. "I remember you,"

he said solemnly. He shook his head. "No: they didnt buy any-thing."

"What you selling?"

"Soap and stuff. Toothbrushes too. You thinking of needing something in that line?"

"I dont need anything," Bart said.

"Some nice articles here."

"No thanks."

The peddler, apparently satisfied that he had done his best to make a sale, bit into his sandwich, then looked up with his mouth full of unchewed food. "On some teat?"

"What?"

He grinned, chewed fast, and swallowed as if the incompletely masticated food were a jagged rock or at best a handful of gravel. "I said: You want something to eat?"

"Oh. No thanks: I'm just fixing to go home to dinner. But thanks."

"Thats all right," the man said. "Have a seat. I'm waiting on a ride." He returned to his sandwich and was a long time eating it. Then, the sack crumpled and discarded, his legs stretched out, he said: "What would you think, just looking at me?"

Thats quite a question, Bart thought. "I dont know, just looking at you."

"I reckon not. You couldnt guess the truth anyhow. I'm sixty years old." This was volunteered with pride. "Ive seen better days. Not so long ago, either." Hair sprouted from his ears; his nose was as thin as a knife blade, the nostrils narrow, as if the wings were being pinched by an invisible hand. "My name is Sunday, like the day of rest. Do you think thats funny?" Bart cocked his head without answering. "Some folks think it's funny. Arthur Sunday. Ever heard of me?" Bart shook his head apologetically. "I'm from Hattiesburg. I had me a business there not long ago. Carriages, buggies, anything in the horse-drawn line."

"I never was in Hattiesburg," Bart said.

"Then thats why. If youd been there seven years ago youd a

seen my name on a signboard over the door. It said ARTHUR SUNDAY: CARRIAGES AND BUGGIES. I usually stood on the sidewalk, under the sign."

He told about it. He had been a successful merchant, he said, respected as one of the tradesmen of the town, until misfortune overtook him. "I was froze out," he said. The automobile and progress in general had beaten him. For three years he lived in debt, creditors goading him. Then he had been dispossessed. "I couldnt even get a job," he said. "Owed everybody: didnt know a trade." Now he was peddling soap and toothbrushes.

"Wheres your family?"

"There aint any. Just my wife and me. She's over in Bannard. We were coming to Bristol—thats what I'm doing here: looking over the prospects—but now I dont figure we'll come. This fellow was coming over this morning to market some things, so I came with him. I'm waiting on him now, to ride back to Bannard."

"I'm having a hard time too," Bart told the man. As soon as he had spoken he thought: Why did I say that? He continued, however, and all the time he was speaking it was as if he were standing outside himself, listening to the words. "I lost my money too, but not the same way you did. I lost it all at once."

"Cant you get a job?"

"Cant I. . .? No. No, I cant get one." A job, Bart thought; a job. "I'm fifty-four."

"I'm sixty," Sunday said. He nodded earnestly. "If I had a suit of fine clothes like the one youre wearing, I bet I could get a job. A good one, too."

"You dont understand. I'll tell you how it was. I came here thirty years ago from across the state. I worked on a farm and served a term as sheriff. Then I bought myself a plantation and—"

"You what?"

"I bought it on time. Nothing down."

"Oh."

"Yes—and more than half paid for it within half a dozen crops and—"

"You sho must have rolled."

"I did—and went to Memphis and bought things for my house and even tried to grow a beard, I remember. I was proud. Then I gave up the beard and got married and had a son. Then I had three more children (one died) and then—"

"I know; you dont even have to say it. They foreclosed you."

"No," Bart said, thinking: Why wont he let me tell it? I didnt keep breaking in on him like this. "I sold it. I moved to town." He paused, conscious that he was telling it badly, leaving out too much.

"Whyd you do that?" Sunday asked.

"I dont know." Yes I do, he thought; I know. "Maybe because of my children."

"What ailed them?"

"They didnt want to farm. One of them tried it, my oldest boy. He did all right for a while but he didnt like it. It wasnt his fault so much: it was my fault too. Maybe I was getting tired of it. No, thats not right. I just wanted to do other things. You know."

"Sho."

"Yes. And I sold Solitaire and came to Bristol."

"Whats that?"

"Whats what?"

"Solitaire."

"Thats the plantation: I sold it."

"Oh. I thought for a minute you were talking about a card game."

Bart went on: "And I put the money in a Memphis bank, for safe keeping, and then the bank went under. Bango, they call it: fft."

"Went broke?"

"Yes."

"Gee," Sunday said. "They froze you out and now youre broke."

"Thats right."

"You ought not to sold your land."

"I know that now." Bart paused. "But I'm not sure: I might do the same if I had it all to do over again."

"A man cant tell what he'll do."

"Thats true."

"Sho it's true. Just look at me. Would you ever think I was well-off once?"

This was the second time the peddler had asked the question, and this time Bart answered him: "No."

"Well, I was. I might not been as rich as you say you were, but I was well-off; I was comfortably fixed. I was respected, too."

Bart looked at him, the wizened face with grime worked into the creases, the scrawny neck, gnarled hands with broken nails, the hairy ears and knife-blade nose. We're in the same boat, he thought. But theres a difference. What is it? Then, looking at Sunday, Bart believed he knew: Seven years! It's just that he got a seven-year head start.

"Here he comes," Sunday said, getting up. A man in sky-blue overalls approached them along the road, driving a wagon whose ungreased wheels turned with popping reports. "We bargained for round-trip: twenty cents. Thats about all I cleared for the day." He turned to say goodbye.

"Wait," Bart said. "I do need some of that stuff, some shaving soap. Is that what you said you had?"

"Right. Pretty good stuff, too." Sunday opened the satchel, his manner becoming professional, alert. Bart saw a conglomeration of toothbrushes and gay-wrapped disks, all more or less shopworn. An odor of cheap perfume rose from the bag.

"About two dollars' worth," Bart said.

"Well, lets see." The peddler thrust his hand into the satchel and brought out a flowered disk, holding it up for Bart to see. It was about the size of a hockey puck. "This one's called Lavender Flowers; it's twenty cents. And here's one called Blue Waltz; it's a nickel cheaper but it's just as good. Same stuff, different wrapper. Thats a secret I usually dont tell."

"Give me ten of the Lavenders."

Sunday fumbled in the satchel, counting, then paused. "I only got six."

"Make up the difference with the other, then."

"Blue Waltz?"

"Thats it."

"All right: lets see. Six Lavenders is a dollar twenty, leaves eighty divided by fifteen, wont go. Wait. I'll make you a bargain offer."

"No, I—"

"I really will. I wouldnt skin you, mister: not after we spent all this time telling each other our troubles. Look. I'll give you six Blue Waltzes for eighty cents. You make a dime on the deal."

"No. If—"

"I wouldnt skin you." Sunday said this with a gentle insistence.

"All right: thatll be fine. You better hurry, though. Here's your ride."

The wagon stopped beside them, and the man in faded overalls leaned forward on the seat, holding the reins in limp hands. Sunday said, "I'm sorry I got nothing to wrap them in. Usually I sell them right at the door and there aint no need."

"Thats all right. You better catch your ride."

"Sho. Here." He loaded the disks into Bart's arms. They made a difficult burden.

"Wait," Bart said. "I havent paid you." He balanced the shaving soap pucks in the crook of one arm and took his wallet from his pocket, holding it toward the peddler; it sagged open. "Two dollars. Get it for me."

Sunday bent forward, looking into the wallet. He whistled, a single drawn-out note. "Gee. You got no cause to worry, mister. You can live out your days on whats in there." Bart always carried three or four hundred dollars in cash; it was a custom he had begun on the lake, where all the planters did so. Sunday took out two dollar bills. He closed his satchel: "Goodbye," and turned to the wagon.

"Goodbye," Bart said, watching the peddler climb over the wheel. The axles sounded their complaint, like a stick being raked along a picket fence, and Bart stood watching the wagon as it diminished down the road. This was dry, fagged September, high noon of a hot still day. He stood there, his arms filled with the bright-wrapped disks whose perfume rose in the shimmering heat, a surging effluence. The wagon was far down the road by now, the sound of the ungreased hubs like distant musketry, the two men on the seat reduced to miniatures of themselves. He is telling him about me, Bart thought: about how I was poor-mouthing with a pocket full of money.

When he was sure the peddler no longer could see him, he turned and dropped the dozen soap disks into the high weeds of the ditch beside the road. But as he moved away he thought: I shouldnt have done that; I should have saved them. If I operate on his schedule, I'll be needing them in about three years to peddle.

THOSE EARLY summer rains, which people said were caused by the guns across the water in Europe, gave way to drouth. Through August and September the land lay parched and dusty: cotton weather. Mid-October brought a cold snap, still without rain. This lasted a week and the heat returned as before; the earth seemed to be in labor, to tremble and heave in the shimmer of sunlight and moonlight. Thus Indian summer was born, a dry, hard birth. There was no wind and still no rain, but now the trees flared red and yellow and brown, and the dusk was ringed with sterile, thunderless lightning like running fire, the horizon fretted with flame like the outer zone of hell itself, sentinel and fatal, circumscribing the damned. November opened alternately hot and cool: at last the rains came, first a slow and heartless drizzle, then an insistent patter, seemingly endless. The memory of summer fled away; the Delta was wrapped in mist and curtained with rain.

When Bart came out of the club these nights Billy Boy would be sitting in the buggy, wearing a rain-slick black poncho Bart had bought him—"Because if youre bound to sit here, you might as well sit warm and dry"—nodding asleep with his feet on the dashboard, the reins wrapped round the whip-socket, the mare steaming wet in the shafts, head down. Bart had tried to persuade him there was no need to wait in such weather; it was only a short walk to the house, and he had rationed himself on whiskey now; he could make it alone. But Billy Boy would be there, rain or no, raw weather or fine, the buggy looking pristine and villatic among the adjacent, blunt, metal-gleaming automobiles. He would look up suddenly when Bart emerged—as if when Bart crossed a twenty-yard periphery a spark exploded in Billy Boy's brain—would watch carefully while Bart climbed onto the seat beside him, then jerk the mare out of sleep or oblivion, and drive the short way home. After halting under the porte-cochère for Bart to dismount, he would stable the mare, return to the house, and sleep.

Upstairs, Bart would undress in the dark and climb gingerly into bed beside his wife. As he lay there, far to one side so as not to touch her even accidentally, the poker-and-whiskey tension would ease off; he would relax, his body becoming aware of the body beside him, uxoriously remembering the old signal of palms and thighs, the period following the death of their third child when the signals had been disregarded and she had turned to him of her own accord, panting, and he would think: She's awake and she knows that I know she's awake, but she dont want me to show that I know, and I wont. Feeling the awareness, the revulsion, the tenseness communicated by the sheets and mattress and bedsprings —a taut, almost imperceptible trembling: *Dont touch me! Dont touch me!*—he would wait for sleep to come down like a cloud, and would wake in brilliant sunlight, alone on the wide bed.

So there was no one: No one I can tell it to, he thought.

But that was all right, as far as telling it went: he knew he would never be able to tell it anyhow. Ever since the day when he had tried to tell it to the peddler, Arthur Sunday, he had known that the truth amounted to more than a recountal of events. All the time he was talking that day in September beside the Bannard road, fending off interruptions and needless questions—Why wont he let me tell it? he had thought; I didnt keep breaking in on him like this—he had been increasingly aware that his attempt to present the story of his life was like trying to describe a man's appearance by displaying his skeleton. The truth lay in implications, not in facts. Facts were only individual beads; the hidden string was what made them into a necklace. But what kind of thinking was this, in which one minute the skeleton was not enough and the next the string in a row of beads was everything? The abstract was a trap: his brain was not meant for such work.

And what was worse, he believed now that to tell it properly would require as much time as had been required to live it. There was no end to what it would have to contain. All the lives that had touched his own, some of them only slightly, had a share in the telling. Cass Tarfeller, Abe Wisten, Major Dubose: all these were a part of his life; the barricaded tenant whose head he had blown off, the Negro fugitive up the hound-circled tree, Judge Wiltner in his office and on his deathbed: these were as much a part of his story as the bank crash or the letter from the Virginia headmistress or the sale of Solitaire. Yet these were only a few: there were so many others—his father seceding from the Confederacy, his brother killed in a cavalry scrape, his mother whose story he had never learned, the trip across the state to join his so-called uncle, the Christmas night when he lay in bed and watched the snow come down, the duck hunt that set the record on the lake, Hugh brought home drunk and missing the party at Adah's, the White House reception where he and Ireland shook hands with Taft, the removal to Bristol: these and so many others; how could he tell all that? Every one omitted, however, would be a space left blank on a canvas larger than life.

So finally there was no question of trying to tell it. All he could do was what he had done in the past: continue to live it, cut off and alone.

THEN, UNEXPECTEDLY, he found a link.

Mid-morning of a clear sunshiny day three weeks before Christmas—it had faired off for the holidays, as usual; skies were high and intense and summer-blue—when he came downstairs, out of the front door and onto the porch, he saw a small figure seated on the top step, chin in hand, facing the street. This was Asa, his grandson. Bart seldom noticed children until they were old enough to speak to, and even then he unbent only far enough to say hello to them. Asa, who was three, was little more than a reminder of the Kentucky trip, bearing the name of Bart's host and drinking companion for six weeks after he won the trap shoot crown; Bart would see him and think, I wonder how things are in Louisville; I wonder how Gold is getting along these days. But now, seeing the boy alone for the first time, he stopped at the top of the steps beside him. "What are you watching?" he asked.

Asa looked up. His eyes were gray-green, the same as his grandfather's. When Bart leaned toward him, his face looming larger, he cringed. It was not so much a motion of fear as it was of vigilance: Bart was a stranger to him, for though the child recognized him as the head of the house which was his world, their waking hours seldom coincided. The grandfather was to the grandson an all-powerful and, for all the grandson knew, a vengeful god who lived in an upstairs room and caused the rest of the household to move on tiptoe and speak in whispers while he slept. Still, it was not fear; the eyes did not wince.

Bart said, "Are you scared of me, Sir?" He leaned down, caught the child beneath the arms, and lifted him so that they looked directly into each other's face. As he held him, looking into eyes that were so much like his own, Bart's mind leaped the generation gap; he frowned at the naked dangling legs, the feet hanging, ankles relaxed, with that soft, blunt, boneless look of children's feet. "Are you? Hey?"

"No," Asa said.

Bart laughed. "You aint too young to say Sir to your elders, boy." When he laughed he threw back his head and dropped his jaw.

"I saw your tongue," the child said, pointing.

"Didnt you think I had one?"

Asa did not answer. He really had not known whether Bart had a tongue or not, for the mustache hid his mouth except when he drew his head well back, and during the past two years he had not carried his head very high in the rented Bristol house.

"I reckon not," Bart said. "Maybe we ought to get acquainted by having a talk. Have we ever had one?" Asa watched him. "Have we ever talked?"

"Let me see your tongue again."

Bart frowned. "Youve got a case of the smart-jacks, boy, and youve got them young." Asa laughed, his face brightening. "You think thats funny?" Asa laughed again. "You laugh too much at nothing," Bart said, beginning to laugh himself. "Talk to your grandaddy, Sir. Sit down here and talk to me for a while. Tell me: what are you doing out here all by yourself?"

Soon afterward Kate came to the door. Looking out, she saw Bart sitting on the top step with Asa in his lap, laughing, nodding his head rapidly, and speaking with that mock-serious verbose cajolery grown-ups adopt when trying to talk with children.

"Good morning," he said over his shoulder when she came onto the porch. He held Asa on his knee, smiling back over his shoulder. "I didnt even know he could talk, and now just look at him."

"Has he been bad?"

"No badder than usual, I reckon. Looks like he's got a touch of the smart-jacks, though."

Kate smiled: she saw that Bart was pleased. "He's pretty bad sometimes," she said, still smiling.

Bart lifted the boy from his knee, stood him on the step below, so that their faces were once more on a line, and then put out one hand and scoured his hair. "Youre some bucko," he said, rising.

Kate took Asa, holding him high on her hip. Their cheeks touched, two pairs of eyes watching Bart. His face was pale, puffy under the eye sockets, and a paunch of fat drooped from his chin to the knot of his tie. His mustache looked false, dark brown in contrast to the gray-shot hair and pallid skin. He's changed, Kate thought. Or maybe I never really looked at him before. Still holding the boy against her shoulder, his knees on opposite sides of her waist, she watched Bart take his cane from the pillar where he had leaned it when he stopped to talk with Asa. He tapped the floor of the porch with the ferrule. "Good day, you two."

"Good day," Kate said.

He went down the steps, then down the path and through the gate. As Hugh had done a year ago, Kate watched him move along the sidewalk toward Marshall Avenue, wrought iron pickets flicking past. He walked with that curious flat-footed stride, guarding his dignity. The gold head of his cane was a dancing gleam of sunlight, flashing on and off and on and off until he passed from sight.

Asa said, "Whats his name?"

"Why, thats grandaddy, Asa. You knew that."

"Yessum, but whats his name?"

"Mr Hugh Bart," she said. "Like your father."

"Like daddy?" How could that be? His nurse had told him everyone had a different name.

"Yes, but he's *grand*daddy."

"Yessum," Asa said.

DOWNTOWN WORKMEN were busy on ladders, decking the whiteway for Christmas, stringing lamp posts with holly whose bright red waxy berries looked incongruous in weather that was more like fall than mid-December. There was a wreath on the glass front door of the Club, and clothing store show-windows were paved with cotton for snow, each with a team of miniature reindeer and Santa Claus cracking a whip. Everyone was preparing for the round of dances and parties, draining off kegs of whiskey bought months ago for holiday drinking. Mothers shopped and sewed for teen-age daughters, sent sons' and husbands' formal wear to the cleaners, and hid younger children's presents out of reach. Two fireworks stands already were driving a trade on the curb of Marshall Avenue; "Fire*works! Fire*works!" the vendors cried in iambic-trochaic. Women who had not spoken to one another in months stopped on the sidewalk to exchange civilities. It was a time of so much bustle and anticipation that even the birds appeared to have caught the fever. On telegraph wires and in the dusty gutters, sparrows cheeped and fluttered; mockingbirds fluted and bluejays veered in raucous folly; slate-blue kingfishers whirled and flashed in the sunlight over the levee, and ducks and geese scudded across the cobalt sky in ragged vees, their cries coming faint and sad, venatic. To Bart they sounded doomed; I killed so many, he thought.

On the Saturday before Christmas, which came on a Friday that year, Bart went out after dinner with Billy Boy in the buggy. They were gone two hours. When they came back Billy Boy was driving with his arms held high; he was smiling, greatly pleased, nodding his head and shooting frequent sidelong glances at Bart, who sat with one arm around the bole of a twelve-foot cedar whose pointed peak drooped from the rear of the buggy. Three flat cardboard boxes were stacked one above another on the seat between the two men. As they turned into the driveway Bart called to the housemaid sweeping the porch: "Tell Miss Kate to come on out here."

Kate was watching from an upstairs window. She came downstairs and out of the side porch door just as the buggy stopped under the porte-cochère. Bart sat holding the tree while Billy Boy wrapped the reins around the whip-socket, climbed down over the wheel, and came around the mare. When Bart saw Kate he made a gesture of caution with one hand and said, "Wheres Asa?"

"He's taking his nap."

"Thats good. Dont let him see us. Catch hold, Billy." Billy Boy held the tree while Bart got down with the cardboard boxes in his arms. Standing at the bottom of the steps and grinning over the three-tiered burden, Bart tilted his head back, looking up at Kate. "It's a Christmas tree," he said. "A beauty, too."

"It's lovely," she said.

They hid it in the long narrow storage closet under the back porch stairs, and it stayed there until Christmas Eve, the following Thursday, when they carried it into the living room and set it up beside the fireplace. Fixed on the base which Billy Boy had carpentered the day before, it reached almost to the ceiling. "As fine a tree as I ever saw," Bart said, standing back to admire it. Billy Boy nodded agreement.

"It's a beautiful tree," Mrs Bart said, surprised at seeing him so enthusiastic. Clive sat in a chair with his crutches across the arms; he made no comment. Kate helped spread the branches. Hugh sat on the couch. Florence was the only member of the family not there; she had gone upstairs immediately after supper, which meant there would be another poem for the magazines to reject.

Bart left the room and returned with the three cardboard boxes. "Get the ladder," he told Billy Boy. He set the boxes on the floor beside the tree. The first held ornaments, colored glass balls with loops of wire for tying them to the branches, candle sockets with clips, tinfoil festoons, a box of small green and red candles, and a big five-pointed star. The second box was filled with cotton samples; Bart showed Kate how to spread it under the tree to resemble snow. He did not open the third box yet.

Billy Boy came in with the stepladder, carrying it carefully so as not to scar the furniture or sweep the lamps and vases off the tables. "Here we go," Bart said, and he guided Billy Boy toward the tree. "All right: up with your end." He anchored the foot of the ladder while Billy Boy raised and spread it. "Fine," Bart said; "Thats fine." He went up the ladder rapidly, not glancing back.

"Be careful there," he heard Mrs Bart say. Looking down through the rungs, he was surprised to discover how far away the floor seemed.

"This is high," he said.

"Be careful, now," Mrs Bart said.

"I'm all right. Hand me something, Billy."

The big tinsel star lay on top of the other ornaments in the first box. Billy Boy started up the ladder with it. "No, no," Bart said. "Thats the crowning glory. Thats for last." So Billy Boy went back down and began handing up the glass balls one by one and sheafs of ribboned tinfoil while Bart tied or hung them on the limbs.

Kate sat on the floor at the foot of the ladder, fitting the candles into the socket-clips; she handed them to Billy Boy, who passed them up to Bart. All this time Hugh walked around the room, viewing the tree from all angles and advising his father where to place the ornaments. "How bout here?" Bart would ask, and Hugh would look where Bart was pointing and say:

"Yes, sir, right in there," or: "No, sir; thats enough in there. Theres a gap just to the right."

"Here?"

"N-no: a bit more to the left. A bit more—Ho! Right there."

"Here?"

"Yes, sir."

"Thats easy," Bart would say, clipping the candle socket to a branch. "How's that?"

"Fine: thats fine. Now how about one right underneath it?"

This continued for more than an hour, until finally there were no more ornaments left in the box. Then, with a little shifting of candles and glass balls, a little bending and straightening of branches, the tree was ready to be lighted for the final inspection. Before that was done, however, Bart opened the third box and took out a pair of baggy red trousers with oilcloth leggings attached and a coat with buttons as big as silver dollars and a collar trimmed with cotton for ermine.

"Look who's going to play Santa Claus," Bart said. He held the suit in front of Billy Boy's body. "We'll put a pillow in here," he said, pointing to Billy Boy's midriff. There was also a cotton beard with hooks for the ears like spectacles. Billy Boy stood like a recruit at his first dress parade, erect but flustered. "How's that?" Bart said.

Kate giggled; Hugh laughed. Mrs Bart did not say anything; she had never seen Bart like this before, except perhaps at the birth of the child that had died. Clive was no longer in the room: he had left soon after the decking began, clumsy, hunch-shouldered on crutches, moving with a deliberate slow exertion up the stairs while his mother called after him all the way up, much as she had spoken to Bart on the ladder: "Be careful, now; be careful, now."

She had been saying these same words to Bart ever since he first went up the ladder; they had punctuated the conversation at regular intervals: "Be careful, Mr Bart; be careful, now." Standing back from the tree, she watched him. He had removed his coat, a thing she could not remember him doing except when going to bed; his shirt was wet in patches with perspiration; his collar had wilted and the loose knot of his tie was almost undone. She saw plainly now how much the past few years had changed him. The thickness of his lower trunk held him back from the ladder, and whenever he leaned forward to attach an ornament she could hear his breath rasp high in his throat and see his face and neck go crimson, his nostrils pinched and ringed with white from the strain. He got old in a hurry, she thought, and then was ashamed of having thought it.

"Who's got a match?" Kate asked.

"Here," Hugh said.

"Whoa: wait a minute." Bart put the Santa suit back into its box, unhooked the beard from Billy Boy's ears and laid it on top, suit and beard making a snow-capped red mound. Puffing, he leaned and lifted the big tinsel star from the ornament box. "First I want to attach the crowning glory." His voice was oratorical, pompous. "This is what we need to set it off."

"Let me," Billy Boy said, seeing that Bart was breathing hard and his face was flushed.

"Oh no. Who trimmed this tree? Me: I did. And I'm the one who's going to crown the glory." Bart went to the ladder and began to mount, climbing one-handed, carrying the five-pointed star overhead like a torch. At the top he halted and held the star toward the peak of the tree. "This is going to be a sight to see," he told them.

Then he stopped, frozen in the pose, one arm extended. His face had winced into something like a frown, that set and vacant expression of dismay which comes on children's faces in the instant before they burst into sobs and tears. "Mr Bart!" Mrs Bart cried. Kate's hands clenched suddenly, the nails biting into her palms.

"Papa," Hugh said hoarsely. Billy Boy's mouth dropped open.

Bart's face was a deep red; then, as the star descended, the arm that held it coming down with a slow and constant movement like a gesture in a dream, the deep red shaded toward the purple of suffocation. The star fell, twinkling silver among the dark green cedar limbs, and struck the cotton snow without a sound. At that same moment, without any previous sway or totter—the whole scene was acted with a sort of circumspect rigidity—Bart toppled from the ladder. Kate wailed but Mrs Bart and Hugh and Billy Boy just stood there with amazement on their faces, watching him fall.

He fell toward the tree and in his descent tore off all the ornaments and branches on that side. There was a tinkling of shattered glass and a snapping of boughs, their torn stumps showing yellow scars. Bart lay against the base of the tree, partly covered by the wreckage of cedar limbs, candles still in their sockets, and shards of colored glass. The tinsel star lay by his face.

"THATS ALL right," the doctor said. "Christmas and Christmas Eve are generally our busiest days, what with the overdrinking and the fireworks. We take it as part of being in the profession." This was the jovial robust young man who had attended Bart after his poker stroke four months ago. He and Hugh stood at the front end of the upper hall, looking down at the darkling street. The weather had turned cold during the night; all day the sky had been dull gray with an overcast, like the whorled surface of molten lead when it cools. "The worst thing about it is I'm not doing any good, no good at all. All I can do is hang around and watch, the same as you."

They turned from the window and came back down the hall, entering the sick room. Bart had not changed position since Hugh and Billy Boy had put him on the bed the night before. Mrs Bart, who sat by the bed, did not look around when Hugh and the doctor came in. There was a faint rose acronical glow high in the room, the beginning of twilight. Hugh stood beside his mother's chair. And thats that, he thought, watching Bart's face, the bulge of his body beneath the counterpane, the rising, falling chest. After twenty hours of hearing it, the uproar of his breathing had begun to seem almost normal; it was as if he had always breathed that way, as if the house had trembled with it for years. Bart lay in his underwear, though only his head showed from under the covers. He had been a heavy load the night before; they had almost dropped him at the turn of the stairs. Hugh remembered the fury in Billy Boy's face at the time: "Cant you do *noth*ing right?"

Yair: and I deserved it, Hugh thought. But I never heard him talk that way before.

Now that the room was darker Bart's breathing had grown louder, as if sound were in inverse ratio to illumination: it filled the house, wave after surging wave, pain and doom become audible, mensural. He breathed through his mouth, saliva rattling against the back of his teeth; this had continued for more than twenty hours, at times faster and more insistent, at times sinking to an almost normal rhythm, but never quiet. There were times when he tried to talk, not consciously but out of a wandering mind. He mentioned the names of persons and places they had never heard him speak of: he was a boy again, in East Mississippi, or he was off on hunting trips with strangers. Mostly the talk was just raving.

Mrs Bart sat with her hands in her lap, her face lowered. Grave, brooding, calm, intent, she might have been counting the breaths. Triangles of lace at her throat and wrists caught the waning light. She had sat here like this since the night before. If anyone spoke to her she gave no sign that she heard.

The doctor turned from the window at the right of the bed and came to where Hugh stood beside his mother's chair. He nudged him with his elbow. "Look," he said in a low voice but not whispering. "It's started snowing." Powdery flakes made minute scratching sounds against the panes in the silences between inhale and exhale. There was no wind.

"It's my first white Christmas," Hugh said.

Snow fell steadily for an hour before it began to stick, collecting on sidewalks and roofs and the fenders of automobiles. The flakes grew; finally they held their shape on the lawn—the grass was still green in patches; the fall had been mild once the spell of dirty weather was past—sifting down and building upon each other until only the tips of grass blades showed, like Lilliputian bayonets thrust upward through the thin, precarious coverlet. Outside the room the world turned white and was muffled in silence, hygienic. Blue dusk came down.

This was not only Hugh's first white Christmas: it was the Delta's first December snowfall since the morning twenty-five years ago when Bart lay in bed at Solitaire and told himself he wanted a family, a household like those others on the lake. Snow was falling there now, the flakes dropping soundlessly into the same watering trough beneath the same window, covering the broad flat fields in lower Jordan County where he had farmed and the rutted street of Eddypool in Issawamba County where he had been the law. It fell in the small county-line cemetery south of Ithaca upon two graves of his making, one the alien gambler's, unmarked, set apart, sunken and unkempt, the other marked with a leaning wooden headboard whose letters, *Luther Tate* 1885, had been nearly effaced by alternate summer suns and winter rains. In the Tarfeller plot two marble angels, both with the bland expressionless faces of deaf mutes, stood on opposite sides of a scroll headed *Cassendale;* one of the angels held a sword, and he seemed to have used it, too, for the other had lost his nose. A big granite tombstone twenty yards away, dwarfing all the others in its vicinity, had *Lauderdale Wiltner* carved across it in square-limbed letters, just as Judge had directed when, two weeks before his death, he called in the stone mason for instructions; beneath the snow the granite was maculate with the droppings of generations of birds, and the grave itself was as weed-rankled as Macready's. Eight miles north of here, in the Ararat burying ground, Henry Dubose lay in the ironbound chest with his manuscript, his valor citation and saber; the cedars stood in a ring, bowed inward by the weight of snow on their branches. In Bristol, less than a mile from the room which Bart filled with the uproar of his breathing, in the old cemetery occupied mainly by yellow fever victims of 1878, Gentile and Jew and an occasional lonely Chinese, it snowed too on the squat, round, Hebrew-inscribed marker of Abraham Wisten, whose grave had been of Bart's making too, in a sense. In life they had hardly known one another; for most of them Bart had been the one connection, the nexus where the threads crossed. Now the silent boundless sifting of snow included all their remains; they lay beneath one blanket.

All day there had been an influx of visitors, most of whom came to inquire about Bart's condition. Others, however, had been so busy celebrating the holiday that they had not heard of the stroke and had come to wish the family a merry Christmas. Some believed, and told each other, that Bart was in delirium tremens at last; it had been town talk for more than a year now that he was a night-drinker. When they called at the house and were told that Bart was suffering, probably dying, from a heart attack, they manifested that sympathetic embarrassment people always display when they want to show that they know they are being lied to about family matters but that they condone the lie because it is decorous. "We understand," they seemed to say, lowering their eyelids as they said it; "There is no need to explain."

Some of them were in the living room when Hugh came downstairs on his way to the kitchen for coffee. He had left Kate in the room with his father: she had promised to let him know if anything happened while he was gone. In the kitchen he sat at an oilcloth-covered table, sipping coffee from a cup held in both hands, and watched the snow fall past the window. Billy Boy was there; he sat in a far corner beside the stove, mouth pouted, eyes swollen, sullen.

"Why dont you go upstairs?" Hugh asked him.

"I cant do no good up there," Billy Boy said. His voice was high, off key, and when Hugh heard the break in Billy Boy's voice he saw that what he had thought was a sullen pout was in fact bereavement, grief. Sorrow had bulged his features.

"Youve known him longest. You belong up there, if anyone does." Billy Boy did not even answer. Maybe he's still mad because

234

I almost dropped papa on the stairs, Hugh thought. Then he said, "Billy." Billy Boy raised his head. "The doctor says it will be any minute now. He told me that an hour ago."

"He dont know," Billy Boy said angrily. "Whats he know about it? You think he's God Amighty just because he's got a head full of words out of books and a smart-alec way of using them? He's been wrong a many a time before now." He lowered his head, mumbling: "I'll know for myself when the time comes."

Behind the living room there was a small narrow room which the absconded banker had called the den, thus distinguishing it from the room that had been given to Billy Boy to sleep in. Bart called this his office, though he never used it; he had even stopped answering the invitations to hunts and trap shoots. It was furnished with a roll-top desk, two straight-back chairs, and a horsehide sofa, musty, springy, button-studded, high at the head and resting on short ball-and-claw legs. Hugh took sanctuary here from inquiring callers. The light was off and there was no fire in the grate. I'll catch me a nap, he thought. Kate knew where to find him; he often lay down here after supper. The springs complained as they took his weight, and about him, faintly ammoniac, the fusty odor of leather rose like dust.

He was tired, having slept only in snatches for the past thirty-six hours. As he lay between waking and sleeping he heard a pattering as of water poured in a small stream from a height, dull and slushy against the snow, and two voices, both of which he knew he had heard before but could not place. He raised himself on one elbow and looked out of the window beside the sofa. Two men were silhouetted against the snow. Standing on opposite sides of a pillar on the porch and avoiding each other's eyes, as men always seem to do at such a time, they shot golden sparkling parabolas into the brilliant moonlight. That was the pattering he had heard: there was no downstairs bathroom, and they had come onto the porch, which extended in an L around this side of the house. Hugh recognized them but he could not recall their names. One was a merchant or a real-estate man, Hugh could not remember which, and the other was a cotton factor—Martin, Hugh thought; Aaron Martin: thats his name. Both had played poker with Bart at the club.

Martin was doing most of the talking. Stooping to button, he was saying: "The poor man's last pleasure; yair. They cant take this away." The merchant laughed, one note, mirthless and harsh. Then he too hunched forward, performing the buttoning process. Hugh lay back on the sofa. Now maybe theyll go, he thought.

But the voices continued, coming low and clear through the closed window. Hugh imagined them standing in the crisp, clear, empty air (it had stopped snowing) looking out over the white lawn at the house beyond with the full moon balanced on its chimney like a globe on the nose of a seal. "I heard he aint got a chance," the merchant said. "Charley Hill told me Doc Haynes said he'll check out tonight for sure."

"It dont matter," Martin said. He paused for emphasis. "Not that he wasnt a fine man and a big one, in his day. We all know what he did on his own, how he come up from nothing to what he was two-three years ago when he lived on the lake. He got the breaks and he had the luck, but thats all right: he knew how to ride it. Thats what counts."

"Youre right," the merchant said.

"So when I say it dont matter, I dont mean I dont think well of him. Hell fire, I think the world and all of him; I respect him, even." He paused again. "I say it dont matter because I mean it dont matter if it's now or next week or next year. His life is through; it's finished. His time is up."

Hugh lay in the small dark room, thinking: He talks like he knows, like even if you were to prove he was wrong he wouldnt back up. Martin continued:

"I reckon you know why."

"Why?"

"It's a lot of things all rolled in one, but theres a main reason that counts for more than all the rest. Dont you know about the girl?"

"Girl?" the merchant said. "What girl? Was he—"

"No: not as I know of, he wasnt. I mean his daughter, the high-

and-mighty dark-complected one. You know: Florence—thats her name."

"Ive seen her couple a times."

"Sure you have,"Martin said. He pitched his voice in a lower key, which made it even more distinct on the other side of the window. "Thats what killed him, really. Didnt you hear? It wasnt that worthless gin-hand son marrying old Bateman the boozer's girl, the one with her bloomers always off the latch and Welcome on the doormat. You might think that was enough but that wasnt it. And it wasnt the youngest boy, the cripple, the one they named Clive for the general, that accused him of pushing him off the roof and busting him up like that. It wasnt neither one of them, though you might think either one would be enough. It was the girl, the daughter, the one with the airs; you know."

"Sure. But—"

"Listen: I'll tell you how it was. It was a letter he got from the teachers after they booted her out of that female school in Virginia. That was what told him, see. In the dark, at night, in what they call the dormitory—you know how they sleep at those schools, in one big room with the beds all shoved together—she was going after the other girls under the sheets."

"A—"

"Yair: thats what I'm saying. A gobbler. And he found out; they told him, see."

"Lord God," the merchant said.

"Sure. And thats what broke him up so bad. I'm surprised you havent heard. Everybody knows it."

"You mean he told? He told it around?"

"Hell no: Jesus. It was a girl from Bannard was in school there. She told about how all the girls were scared and went to the head madam and told her how it was, what this Bart girl was doing, and the madam says 'Oh-oh, this wont do' and gave her her walking papers and wrote a letter here to Bart explaining why. The Bannard girl told about it when she come home for the holidays. She had even seen a copy of the letter; one of the girls had snuck it out of the files."

"Lord God."

"Aint it the truth," Martin said. They were quiet for a moment. Then Martin said, "Lets get back in and see if he's checked out yet."

Hugh heard them move toward the front of the porch, still talking. I ought to shoot him, he thought. Then, remembering what Martin had said—"Everybody knows it"—he thought: That means everybody tells it. His brain was confused but he cleared it. Shoot them all! he thought, panting, seeing himself, gun in hand, running from man to man and snapping the trigger: "Take that! And that! And that! And that!" until he had covered Jordan County, the Delta: they lay in windrows all about him, dead. Then his brain sloughed its vengeance dream; he felt empty, sick, dismayed. I'm not going to kill anybody, he thought.

"Hugh!"

Perhaps he had been asleep; he started up, seeing Kate in the doorway with the light behind her. Her hands fluttered, lifted almost to her shoulders, limp at the wrists. "Hugh!" He jumped off the sofa and hurried toward her, brushed her aside and ran into the living room. As he reached the foot of the stairs he saw Billy Boy disappear around the newel post of the landing and heard his feet thudding fast on the carpeted steps.

Then this is it, he thought. He had not been sure before, but when he saw Billy Boy running up the stairs he knew the time had come; "I'll know for myself when the time comes," Billy Boy had said. Jesus God, Hugh thought, breathing shallowly; Jesus God, Jesus God. He was undecided whether to hurry or go slow; it would be all the same in the end.

ASA

I was too young to go to the funeral; they left me upstairs with Beulah, my nurse. I had been told that Bart was dead and I wanted to talk about death, but Beulah would not. "Whynt we just play something?" she said. "Fetch me yo blocks."

"Will the worms get him?"

"Ghy get us all, bless Jesus," Beulah said. "Fetch me yo blocks. Less build us a castle like we done the other day."

But I did not want to play: I wanted to know about death. It was not that Bart was near and dear to me; there were others nearer and dearer in my life: Beulah, my lead soldiers, even the neighbor's Airedale. Because I never knew him. He lifted me in his arms one morning and spoke with his face close to mine; he died fixing a star to a tree for me; perhaps at the time of his death he had plans for making me all he had failed to make his children. But I never knew him: I never even had a family name for him. I had been told he had a name, Hugh Bart, but it seemed to me that he had stolen it from my father (though I never really knew him either: he was killed soon after our entry into the 1917 war, not in battle but in an Oklahoma training camp; he stood in the path of a flare-back when a howitzer misfired and a green lieutenant opened the breech too soon; they said he went up like a strip of celluloid—a useless death, I thought until I was old enough to realize how fitting it was, how well it matched his life: ever since he was twelve years old he had lived as if he had known this was going to happen, or something like it. Thus sometimes a man's death will make all the confusion of his life come clear; you cannot understand the motivations, the whys and wherefores; it is all a senseless ineffectual snarl until you see the manner in which he leaves it: death can be like a catalytic agent dropped into a cloudy liquid) and I never learned to say Grandfather. So all my life I called him Bart and called my father Hugh: because I had not watched them through boyhood and youth across a dining room table, as others did their kin, nor even remembered the shape of their faces. They were like the old dead, the kings and traitors and heroes whose names I learned at school: with the result that in my mind, looking back on that time when he was alive, I came to think of them all by their given names, called my mother Kate and my grandmother Florence. They were each of them two persons, the person I saw when I looked at them in the present and the person I saw when I looked back to the time when Bart was alive. Bart's catabasis, enigmatic and baffled, dragged them all into that too-vivid unreality of books and dreams.

And though I know now there is no call for reproach or even regret, there was a time when I cursed him for a ruthless man; I thought that, like others of his improvident generation, Bart had thrown away the land and money which would have made my life so different and, I thought, better. By the time I was old enough to begin to learn what really had happened, however, I was too overwhelmed, too much like a man looking down into an abyss, for there to be room for anything but terror: I was heartsick. This is expiation. Men stand alone; they earn their fates. Bart had four children to build his hopes on, three sons and a daughter: Hugh and Clive and Clive and Florence. The first son turned out dreamy and ineffectual; the second son was dead before he was one day old; the third son broke his body and filled his soul with hate; the daughter turned out perverted.

Except for the one hymn, Beulah and I could not hear the service. At its conclusion, however, some of the sighing, the glad release from concentration on their common end, was borne upstairs to us. "Does that mean they are through?" I asked. Beulah did not answer. Her dark face was foreshortened and her hands were wrapped in her apron; she was praying.

The nursery was at the front of the house; two of its windows gave onto the lawn and street. Presently we heard them on the porch, the feet of the pallbearers heavy and careful as they emerged with their burden. Most of the snow had melted by then, though there were streaks of it under the fence and random patches stark against the pale grass and the dark wet trunks of trees. People in sober black filed out behind the coffin. Bareheaded, awed, they stood waiting while it was loaded into the hack (this was at Mrs Bart's direction; "It has to be horse-drawn," she told them) and then moved down the line, getting into their automobiles and whining off in low gear behind the dead-black plateglass-windowed hearse and the fat old funeral mares in sable trappings.

I still did not get my blocks. I wanted to know what it was that changed men into what Bart had become when they took me into the room to see him that Christmas morning. He was quieter then and they chose that time. I had hold of someone's hand, my mother's I suppose, and when we came into the room the air was antiseptic, sterile, and the bed-clothes were dazzling white. The doctor stood at the foot of the bed, my father beside him. They lifted me (that was the custom) and I saw that he looked cleaner too, like wax. This was a period of quiet between others of harsher breathing and raving. He had raved all morning. That afternoon he began again, and he raved into the night until just before he died.

Sometimes his words were almost logical: he was back on the plantation, working Negroes, shouting encouragement while the hoes lifted and fell in glittering cadence, or he was in the field with his gun and dogs, listening for the whip-lash cries of quail, or he was at trap shoots, calling Pull! and laughing between shots, the crowd murmurous behind him, the scorer crying *Dett* and *Laws*, or he was back at Solitaire ten and fifteen years ago, sitting on the porch as night came down and the frogs and insects chorused, or he was at the poker table in the Elks Club basement, staking his chips in the smoke-swirled radiance. Other times no one could tell what he was talking about. The words were clear, the sentences were all right for the most part, but they were disconnected—like this:

"And this man came and stood at the door, and I said 'Hiram. Do you, Hiram?' and he said 'Yes, Bart. Yes, I do,' and I said 'Then we can all right?' and he said 'Sho we can. I always said we could,' and we did. —Florence. Aint you Florence? Help me. . . . It was the man. He came and stood over me and I said . . . Florence!"

"Yes, Mr Bart. I'm here."

"Tell them for me. Say I said I hurt. My chest."

"Yes, Mr Bart. Lie quiet, now."

"Say I said. If you. But say I said bad. . . . For there they were, a covey, a big one, twenty or more. And the gun went up and off, and I reloaded and it went up and off, and I said 'Jonas, how many? How many, Jonas?' and he said 'Four. You got four, Mr Hugh,' and I said 'Put them in the bag and lets get gone. This is going to be a record day.' Then I saw the water, green, and an arrow in it. I cant mull; I cant mull. Give me something to show I cant mull. . . . He said I never saw my mother or knew her from Adam's off ox, and I said No, I never knew her, No, but her name was Susan and thats a mighty pretty name for a girl. . . . Tell them to take it off my chest, this hoop. No rule, no ruff, no roll, no rander. Tell them I hurt. (Pick up those, if you please, will you? Will you, please?) My chest, Florence; tell them to take it away away. Tell them to take it away to drain because I'm looking for a home."

Those were his last words, a surging flood the night he died. But while I was in the room he only spoke once. It was clear, full-voiced and unblurred, an unadorned statement of fact spoken after silence and followed by silence, my one stark memory of him. The rest is hearsay. He lay there motionless, calm, his hands outside the covers, his head on a pillow, the mustache dark brown and exact, his lips moving beneath it: "The four walls are gone from around me, the roof from over my head. I'm in the dark, alone."